Praise for Crystal Z. Lee's

Love and Other Moods

"This entertaining novel of Shanghai, a city with many faces, resonates with its depiction of relationships in the romantic, familial, and business spheres. The story moves between the opulence of high-fashion and the struggle of the working class effortlessly, telling of the beauty, cultural conflicts and constant pressure of living and working in such a city."

> —LINDA ULLESEIT, award-winning author of *The Aloha Spirit* and *Under the Almond Trees*

"*Love and Other Moods* is a boisterous novel where Shanghai is a character in and of itself, and where the city's cornucopia of contradictions come to life. This moving story is about the choices we make, and the journeys we undertake to find love."

> —GRACE CHON, award-winning photographer and author of *Waggish* and *Puppy Styled*

"This heartfelt, transporting story sparkles with a constellation of characters who call this city home while pursuing their China dream. As multifaceted as Shanghai itself, this novel follows overlapping narratives about the complexities of adulting, of parenting, of the urban quest for love and finding one's place in the world."

> —EMILY TING, film director of *Go Back to China* and *Already Tomorrow in Hong Kong*

"An engaging snapshot of the lives of modern Chinese transnationals, of which there is now a constituency too large to ignore in English-language fiction."

> —WENA POON, award-winning author of *Lions in Winter*

"Awash with cosmopolitan expats and jet-setting locals, *Love and Other Moods* shimmers like the diamonds adorning China's glitterati, while exposing haunting personal histories and intergenerational strife. With dazzling twirls around Shanghai's World Expo, glitzy fashion shows, art deco architecture, jazz clubs, gourmet restaurants, and disappearing food stalls, this novel compellingly pulls the reader into the pleasures and pains of becoming an adult in a city soaring to global status."

 —JENNY LIN, Ph.D., Associate Professor of Critical Studies at the University of Southern California and author of *Above sea: Contemporary art, urban culture, and the fashioning of global Shanghai*

"Crystal Z. Lee takes the reader on a dazzling tour of hyper-cosmopolitan Shanghai. Here, the city is not romanticized in the typical manner, but portrayed the way it really is: exciting, loud, dizzying, sexy, sometimes risqué but always authentic. *Love and Other Moods* expresses the truthful energy of Rising China over the past decade, which those who've been would instantly recognize, and those who haven't will find fascinating. It's one of the most international places in the world, where everyone has a story, and some of those stories are told right here in this novel."

 —RAY HECHT, author of *South China Morning Blues* and *Always Goodbye*

"An intimate look at contemporary Shanghai and its glittering array of inhabitants as they search for love, fulfill their dreams, and reinvent themselves. This novel explores cultural dissonance, identity crisis, and the question of home. Third-culture kids especially, will find resonance with this story."

 —LAURA RAHME, author of *The Ming Storytellers, Julien's Terror,* and *The Mascherari*

"*Love and Other Moods* is about the various kinds of love we experience in life. Lee's poetic words jump off the page and right into your heart. We witness love stories between a woman and a city, sweeping down to those types of familial love like that from a single parent to an adoptive family. Crystal Z. Lee also thrusts you into the anatomy of the colorful, chaotic city and explores all the senses."

 —*Reader's Favorites Book Reviews*

Love
and
Other
Moods

情旅霓城

CRYSTAL Z. LEE

BALESTIER PRESS
LONDON · SINGAPORE

Balestier Press
Centurion House, London TW18 4AX
www.balestier.com

Love and Other Moods
Copyright © Crystal Z. Lee, 2020

A CIP catalogue record for this book
is available from the British Library.

ISBN 978 1 913891 01 5 (pbk.)
ISBN 978 1 913891 02 2 (ebook)

Photographs by Peter Zheng

CONTENTS

For immigrants, expatriates, sojourners, third-culture kids,
and all those whose home drifts between nowhere and everywhere

"Yesterday we obeyed kings and bent our necks before emperors.
But today we kneel only to truth, follow only beauty, obey only love."

—KHALIL GIBRAN,

THE VISION: REFLECTIONS ON THE WAY OF THE SOUL
(TRAN. JUAN R. I. COLE)

PROLOGUE

WHY SHANGHAI

Why Shanghai? We're asked. Why not Paris, New York, Dubai?

It's because we believe in certain ideas about this city—that it has the potential to be invincible, that it could be ours.

That's what lured us away from our jobs in Manhattan, from our families in Philly, from our future in London, from the boredom of Brisbane, from the idyll of Chengdu, from our affair in L.A., from our friends in Kuala Lumpur, from the responsibilities, the expectations, the dignity, the indignities, from the failures and phantoms we left behind.

We're bright young things, fresh off of our flights from mega cities that rival Shanghai, or plucked from obscure rural towns on our first foray to the city, or disembarked from far-flung countries like Ghana, Malta, Panama. We hail from all over the world, all corners of China. We are twenty-and-thirty-somethings. Some of us are single, some of us are married, most of us are looking.

Some of us know Chinese, most of us are clueless, and not just ignorant about the language, but about most things. We're willing to fall, to learn, to become insomniacs, to put in the hours, to put up a fight, to put in every last drop of sweat and blood. We're an insatiable lot, we're hungry—for success, for respect, for healing, for wanderlust, for lust, for transformation, for ambition, for adventure, for an awakening.

Many of us know the basic outline of the city's tumultuous history: foreign colonialism, the opium trade, world wars, Mao's Cultural Revolution, the One Child Policy, Deng Xiao Ping's Open Door reforms, the Chinese economic miracle. Yes, we're enthralled with the city's stories, but we've come here to make our own history. We fancied ourselves as all kinds of experts: capitalists, socialists, feminists, chauvinists, communists, hedonists, sadists, artists, optimists.

Some of us came here prepared. We're sent by our companies back home on a mission to China, to grab whatever we can of the expanding economic pie. The firm equipped us with a promotion, a corner office, a chauffeur, a maid, an apartment overlooking the Bund. Of course, we're expected to work non-stop 'round the global clock, logging in the regular China work hours, as well as taking marathon conference calls from the western hemisphere when everybody else in Shanghai is already in bed, in bars, in clubs. Then after the calls are over, in the middle of the forsaken night, we'd join them. In this city, the nights aren't for sleeping.

Nights like these, full grown adults—executives, salesmen, entrepreneurs, dreamers, travelers, bachelors, philanderers, flaneurs, the broken-hearted, the heartbreakers, the loveless, the lawless, the hopeless—morph into hapless adolescents. Too drunk and too full of ourselves, we rave and revel into the dark oblivion. We mistakenly believe this is a land of no repercussions. We cling to the nights possessively, fanatically, feverishly. Then in daybreak, we manage to don a different mask as we drag our overworked bodies into offices.

In other cities, the same work might be spirit-crushing, soul-deadening. But because countless industries are new to the China market, there is scant research and sparsely a precedent or a model we can subscribe to. We indulge in the city's fluidity, there are no hard rules here—we make it up as we go along. We're fresh and determined to impress, so we buck up and soldier on, we suck it up and swallow our insecurities, our tears, our fears, our frustrations. We're blinded by the ever-increasing paycheck, blindsided by the never-ending parties.

Even if we live far from the Bund, we're there all the time, for the parties, the people, but most of all, for the view. It's where Shanghai flaunts her full glory, where she becomes a bejeweled femme fatale, beguiling all to her corners and crevices. This city is a doubled-edged sword, she makes us frayed and anxious, bestows bravado and renders us indomitable. She'd save us, but when she wants to, can also devastate us.

Some of us flew by the seat of our pants, landing in this city on a whim. We had watched the Beijing Olympics with awe, had heard from the economists, the professors, the media—they all said this century belonged to China! Here, the opportunities are ripe, and are ours for the seizing. We're eager to fill the abundance of jobs in this city: English teachers, tech managers, film directors, doctors, bankers, lawyers, analysts, chefs, architects, engineers, designers, editors, marketers, restaurateurs. We feel like intrepid explorers in a new frontier. We're never content. *More* is our mantra. We roam the city in search of more money, more goals, more time, more ruin, more love, more luck, more fame, more friends, more faith.

Some of us paid a high price to be here: we'd left girlfriends, boyfriends, families, familiarity, security. We had traded that life in—we'd rather be out here, in the wild, in the unknown, in the uncomfortable, with strangers, with friends, with soon-to-be-lovers, with soon-to-be-exes. We're professional flirters, we thrive on the flirtations of unchartered adventures, of perilous trysts, of our ever-changing adaptations. We alternately laud and loathe ourselves. We're urban, we're suburban, we're dazzling, we're grotesque, we're noncommittal, we're tenacious, we're creative, we're cliché, we're entitled, we're scared, we're shameless, we're socialites, we're influencers, we're easily influenced, and more often than not—under the influence of some substance. We are walking episodes of shapeshifting irony. We torment ourselves and everybody else because we can't decide which versions of ourselves we like better.

Some of us came here to find pieces of ourselves left behind by previous generations. Once upon a time, our parents or grandparents or ancestors had traveled to, lived in, loved in, left their hearts in Shanghai. They had made their mark here, had called this place home. We're third-culture kids—we may look like we're from China, yet this country is foreign to us. We have heritage here, yet we were born and raised in somewhere else entirely: Singapore, Santiago, Taipei, Penang, Honolulu, Melbourne, Milan, Manila. Then we had left home and received our education on another continent, in cities like Vancouver, Vienna, Boston, Sao Paulo, Tokyo, Cape Town. In our adulthood we grew weary of the glass ceiling, of being the minority, so some of us decided to try our luck back east. Some of us have always had questions about our history, and now we came to Shanghai for the answers, for the search, for our roots, our reason, our identity. We came to see if we too, could claim this city as our own.

Some of us have grown up here, yet the place of our childhood barely resembles the megalopolis of our adulthood. Buildings have been razed, whole villages relocated, tragic wartime stories forgotten. The skyline is ever-shifting. Every day the city and its inhabitants transmute and metamorph. Some of us have amassed more wealth in the last five years than others have in their entire lifetime. Sometimes we feel like we're visitors in our own city. On occasion, our grandparents feel like they've landed on a foreign planet.

Then there are those of us who live an itinerant existence. We've become addicted to traversing time zones, to floating across borders, to the freedom and anonymity of permanent impermanence. We live trans-continentally, we've long given up repatriation. We arrive here looking for a reinvention, a new purpose, a new temporary residence.

Some of us came to Shanghai not knowing what to expect. The only thing we're certain about, is that this maddening metropolis, this magnificent city—is *it*. It would take us on a journey, would test our limits, would kick us in the ass, would renew our convictions, would fling us out of our comfort zones, would break or make our fantasies, would seduce us to fall in love, would feel like home.

At least, that's the hope.

PART *1*

NEW YORK TO SHANGHAI

AUTUMN 2009 – SPRING 2010

"...for love is a vagabond, who can make his flowers bloom in the wayside dust, better than in the crystal jars kept in the drawing-room."

—RABINDRANATH TAGORE,
THE HOME AND THE WORLD

"Wherever you go, go with all your heart."

—CONFUCIUS,
THE ANALECTS

1

SHANGHAI SOCIALITES

It was September ninth, 2009, a Wednesday wedding. In Chinese, the number nine, *jiu*, was considered an auspicious number since it was a homonym for "longevity." *Tian chang di jiu, bai nian hao he* was a popular greeting guests would shower on a couple at their nuptials. It meant "as long as the heavens and earth, may your marriage prosper a hundred years on." It was the reason this "triple nine" date was a coveted wedding date in China.

It was also the reason Naomi Kita-Fan found herself at the Paradise Ballroom of the Xijiao State Hotel in Shanghai, in a heather gray tulle bridesmaid dress that reminded her of a humpback whale, while she fidgeted awkwardly next to Seth Ray, her ex-fiancé.

Seth looked equally uncomfortable. He kept adjusting his lavender necktie while attempting cordial small talk with her. Naomi zoned him out as much as possible, silently commanding herself to keep her composure. The lilac peony bouquets Naomi and the other bridesmaids clutched, matched the gargantuan artificial peonies that hung low from the ceilings hovering over the banquet tables, each with vivid centerpieces of indigo snapdragons and tiger lily orchids. Naomi had heard that peonies were traditionally the flowers of Chinese nobility. It was said that Madame Qing herself so loved peonies that she ordered the royal gardens to be filled with them. Naomi felt like they were at a Chinese royal wedding.

As the orchestra drummed up the ceremony music, Seth extended his elbow toward Naomi, gesturing for her to take his arm and get into position. They had not touched each other since yesterday, when it had all imploded and they had called off the engagement. It was terrible timing, since they were supposed to be the glowing couple in Joss Kong and Tay Kai Tang's wedding party.

Naomi knew she had to put on an appearance for the cameras today, for Joss's sake. She begrudgingly linked her arms with Seth's and faked a smile as they walked down the aisle. Joss had no idea what had transpired yesterday, and Naomi wasn't about to let her broken engagement rain on her best friend's parade.

Baccarat chandeliers graced the high ceilings, and the windows gave a clear view of the hotel's manicured Victorian gardens. On each banquet table, a towering croquembouche stood embellished with fine spun sugar. Naomi scanned the room and estimated there were nearly fifty banquet tables, half of which were probably connected with the Chinese government in some capacity. In fact, the Xijiao State Hotel was known to be a favorite among government officials, with a storied history of hosting the Emperor of Japan, Queen Elizabeth the Second, and Chairman Mao himself.

Naomi stopped shifting in her itchy gown and tried to focus on Joss. She was in a voluminous Zuhair Murad couture wedding gown, comprised of thirty meters of Chantilly lace, silk chiffon and organza silk. Naomi had accompanied her to the dress fittings, but she was still utterly astounded at this very moment. It wasn't the couture gown, or the luxurious venue, or the high-fashioned guests that made the moment extraordinary, although indeed, it was all extraordinary. No, it was something else, something so perfect in its simplicity—it was the way Joss and Tay had looked at each other, as Joss came waltzing down that aisle. He beamed, she glowed. They were wholly fixated on each other, as if they were in on some secret, in a world of their own. Despite five hundred pairs of eyes looking on and an unending sequence of blinding camera flashes, the couple held steady to each other's gaze, as if nothing else mattered and nobody else existed. And it's true, it was plain for all to see. That magical moment, belonged to them and them alone.

Naomi had forcefully swallowed her tears before the ceremony, but they fell like torrential rainfall as soon as Joss and Tay began their vows.

"Dan yuan ren chang jiu…" On stage, Joss and Tay were performing a duet to a Chinese ballad the emcee had introduced to the audience— the classic Teresa Teng's "May We Be Together Forever," famous for its lyrics featuring excerpts of a popular Song dynasty poem. Joss glistened in an intricate body-hugging crimson qipao and a golden headdress that looked like it weighed more than she did. Earlier, she had made her grand entrance onto the stage sitting in a traditional curtained Chinese bridal sedan held up by some of the groomsmen.

Naomi poked at her dessert. Almost everybody at her table had finished off their own chrysanthemum buttercream slice from the couple's seven-tiered cake.

"Do you live here? Or are you visiting for the wedding? Great maid-of-honor speech by the way," one of the groomsmen asked.

"Thanks. Um…I guess I'm visiting…" He seemed confused with her hesitation. Naomi was confounded herself. Was she a visitor? As of yesterday she'd been regarded as a resident, a former New Yorker who had called Shanghai home for a month now, who had planned a future here, who had a fiancé and an apartment in this city. *Had.*

Naomi checked her watch. By now Joss and Tay had finished their ballad duet and were onto the fourth attire of the night, executing a Ginger Rogers and Fred Astaire-style tap dance.

Seth met Naomi's eyes. Her cheeks flushed and she took a gulp from her Riesling. She hoped he hadn't caught her staring. Her thoughts drifted to her first day in China, when she had arrived at Seth's company-sponsored sprawling apartment, riveted. They had his employer to thank, a venture capital fund based in New York which was launching an arm in Shanghai. It was hard to believe that less than two decades ago wide swaths of this metropolis were still stretches of swampland and farms. Were there really more than eleven thousand skyscrapers in this city? She was awestruck at the sheer number and scale of Chinese progress.

It was now past eight in the evening. The heels had come off, ties were now knotted on men's foreheads as the wedding guests danced to a

Chinese rap song. Naomi felt her energy depleted. Just as she was about to kick off her strappy heels, the emcee burst onto the stage and announced that it was time for the bouquet toss. Naomi found herself being pulled to the center of a mob of unmarried women, as Joss turned around and made a conspicuous show of winking and pointing at her. Before Naomi could shake her head and telepath a message to her giddy friend on stage, she had aimed the offending bouquet straight into Naomi's arms, her ears bombarded with clapping and whooping of "you're next!"

Then the guests were up on their feet, the emcee billowing their gratitude, and people started gathering their items and vacating their seats.

"See you at the afterparty," a groomsman reminded her. The afterparty was a private affair for the couple's closest friends. Naomi drained her champagne glass before heading out the hotel.

Naomi sipped on her smoke-emitting nitrogenized cocktail then took a bite of the rose petal nectar popsicle. Across from her seat, the windows gave a sparkling vista of Lujiazui's illuminations reflecting off the Huangpu River, a steep contrast to the view on the other side of the lounge, which looked out to a serene century-old Roman-style church. The interiors of the lounge offered an Old Shanghai fused with Belle Époque Moulin Rouge kind of vibe: rococo chandeliers, bird cage motifs, scarlet leather sofas, exposed brickwork, rose murals. At the entrance, a windmill was affixed to one side of the wall, and a Warhol rendition of Mao on the other. It was a multi-concept space, with a dance floor on the first level, a cabaret stage on the second, and a rooftop jacuzzi overlooking Pudong's panoramic skyline on the third.

An assortment of Asian languages filled the venue: Shanghainese, Cantonese, Japanese, Korean, Taiwanese-accented Mandarin, and every variety of English—Singaporean, South African, Canadian, British, American, Australian. The air smelled of perfume, nicotine, marijuana, perspiration, cologne. Most of the group was congregated on the first floor, imbibing and dancing.

Naomi had participated in the first round of shots with the other bridesmaids and groomsmen before excusing herself to the restrooms. In the stall next door, it sounded like a miserable woman was throwing up bile, or maybe the last three rounds of Bourbon. Naomi suddenly felt sick herself. She slipped out onto the terrace into the breezy night air. She gazed out as the lights scythed off the murky thick of the river, reflecting flashes of the shimmering skyline—a collection of jagged geometric angles and a giant jigsaw of steel and metal, each edifice more ludicrous and wondrous than the other, collectively forming a mighty concrete wild, an enigma of smoke and mirrors.

"You can't keep ignoring me." Naomi inhaled sharply and turned around. Her ex-fiancé was inches away.

She threw him a look that said *I can and I will*.

He shook his head, throwing his hands up. "Well what about all your stuff? It's still lying around my place."

She kept her tone even. "I'll pick them up."

"Fine."

Just as she turned her head and was about to walk away, his voice rose an octave. "You know you're being ridiculous. I already told you it was only one night, and it meant nothing. I don't even talk to her anymore." The image Naomi had found on Seth's phone yesterday invaded her mind again. There she was, legs sprawled out in a diaphanous number, her head thrown back as if enjoying the longest climax in the world. Only half of his face was visible, the other half was buried in the silhouette of her lingerie. The photograph was blurry in the dim lighting, but Naomi could've recognized that man's lips anywhere. It was the raciest selfie she'd ever seen.

"And it was a work trip!" He was sounding more exasperated now. "Someone's gotta pay for our bills."

Every ounce of control she had held onto all night came crashing in that instant. She charged at him with fists and legs kicking, tears streaming down her cheeks as she pounded into his hard flesh. He was quick to grab her arms and pin them behind her back, hurting her wrists, as he tried to force his mouth onto hers. She hurled a string of obscenities, then fell silent and looked up.

He was a full head taller. She stared hard at his brows, those eyes she melted in, those irises that now broke her. For a second he softened too, letting go of his grip on her arms. He lifted her chin, wiped away a tear with his thumb, and tried to kiss her again. But her right arm was flying now, her right hand curled into a fist, striking his nose with all the rage she could muster.

2

THIRD-CULTURE KIDS

NAOMI AWOKE FROM THE BRUTAL CONSTRUCTION NOISE. SHE groaned as she eyed the clock hanging on the wall. 7:03 a.m. She opened the window and glanced at the men milling about, some were in hard hats, most were not. She buried herself back under the violet duvet, re-adjusting to fetal position on the sofa bed. Its faded chartreuse green upholstery had been torn in some parts and it wasn't very comfortable.

She had found the place online. It belonged to a Shanghainese couple who rented out the studio on a week by week basis to foreigners. Tapestries with clashing patterns hung on every wall. The hardwood floors creaked and groaned. The third-floor walk-up was so close to the next building that she could hear the slamming of doors, the clanging of dishes, the white noise emitting from the streets: sirens wailing, trucks barreling, cars revving and honking.

Joss and Tay had helped her move in, even as they insisted that Naomi stay at their villa in Pudong. Although Naomi was grateful for the offer, the truth was she couldn't stand to be around the newlyweds and their bliss at the moment.

Naomi had packed four suitcases from New York, and right now they were stacked unevenly on top of one another in the hallway, forcing the front door to open only halfway, just tight enough for her to slide in sideways. She couldn't remember the last time she had lived by herself. The lonely apartment was mildly depressing.

Going back to sleep now was a lost cause. She freshened up, haphazardly pulled on jeans and a tee, threw on a coat and left sans makeup. She trudged downstairs, pausing in front of the woman sitting on the pavement in front her apartment, and deposited all her spare change in the paper cup in front of her.

Naomi felt like walking aimlessly. She passed by wrinkled men playing a game of Chinese chess, teenage girls in designer sunglasses taking photographs of each other, a woman gesticulating wildly as she yelled into her cell phone, tourists examining a guide book, a cloud of second-hand smoke drifting from outside a cafe, Uighur men selling kebabs, well-heeled shoppers clinging to their purchases, two men in yarmulkes talking heatedly, shrieking children competing with the racket from honking vehicles, and the sea of commuters gushing out of the Huangpi Nan Lu metro stop. Naomi let herself be swept up into the human river, bodies crushing against each other, arms brushing and shoving, no apologies no offense taken. Being in this city meant your senses were constantly accosted.

A sudden wave of fatigue washed over. Naomi felt weightless, like she was wandering in a wide expanse of sea. It was only weeks ago when she had discussed a destination wedding with her then-fiancé. Maybe Okinawa, maybe Kaohsiung. But Seth had insisted on delaying the nuptials until his schedule permitted. Lately, she had been plagued with a recurring dream: she'd run as fast as she could, but as much as she tried, her muscles wouldn't cooperate. It was as if she were running underwater and her limbs weren't able to move fast enough, as if she were being slowed down by some current greater than herself.

A man approached her with a flier featuring images of iPhones, Rolexes, LV handbags, and said that their shop was just ahead, hidden behind an alley. She declined and quickened her pace. She spotted an empty bench by a bus stop and flopped down. Barely noticing as the traffic whizzed by, the lewd selfie on Seth's phone resurfaced in her head. A steady stream of downpour coaxed pedestrians to open a colorful array of umbrellas, or duck into convenience stores, boutique shops, mall entrances. Naomi felt wholly unequipped and unprepared, again, by this city.

Her hair was stuck to her face and her forehead was damp. She was relieved that the inclement weather matched her mood, for tears had started forming and slithering beneath her eyes, blending with the droplets of rain running down her face. She wiped it away with her sleeve. She just wanted to throw up all the fury and regrets that were lodged in her stomach, she wished it could all be flushed out of her head.

It was starting to hit her, the reality of having no boyfriend, no job, and nowhere to live.

She wondered if the sprawling metropolis of Shanghai was too small to co-exist with her ex-fiancé.

Joss requested to be seated among the quartet of gilt-wood armchairs next to the windows at Brasserie on the Bund. The Pudong skyscrapers disappeared amidst the polluted fog. Inside, the lounge reeked of second-hand smoke. The surrounding booths were stuffed with coltish women dressed to the nines. The neighboring booth erupted in shrieks of laughter. They were playing a drinking game, some form of rock paper scissors she had never seen before.

"Bye, love you too." Joss hung up with her sister and glanced at her husband, who was texting somebody.

She peeked over at Tay's phone. "Hey! What does he want?" she asked accusatorily.

Tay put his phone away. "Chill out. He asked what I was up to tonight, and I said now's not a good time." He took a sip of his drink. "This lychee gimlet is a bit too tart. Your review?" He passed the glass to Joss.

"Don't change the subject." She took a quick sip. "It's never going to be a good time with him, not anymore. Not after what he did to Naomi. Why are you even talking to him? He's blacklisted."

"We go way back."

"Me and Naomi go back longer," she reminded him. Naomi had been her roommate in college, at the Fashion Institute of Technology in Manhattan. They shared much in common—both loved omakase, Wong Kar-wai, Comme des Garcons. Both had been raised by single parents. They were both third-culture kids who spoke multiple languages, growing up in Asia in their formative years before immigrating to the

States: Naomi in Taipei and Tokyo before moving to California with her mom, Joss in Shanghai and Hong Kong before her family settled in New York.

"You only met Seth in grad school. And you're right, this drink is drowning in too much lime juice," Joss said. She set the glass back on the table. "Listen, you cannot mention him in front of Naomi."

"Yes ma'am." Tay gave Joss a reassuring peck on the cheek. "And how's Jamie?"

"She just went to senior formals last night." Joss scrolled to her sister's dance photo at Chelsea Piers and held up her phone.

"Wow. This is what kids are wearing in high school? You bought that for her, didn't you?"

"That's what big sisters are for." Joss was twelve years older than Jamie, a whole Chinese zodiac cycle. It was only recently Joss felt they had finally entered that coveted friend zone, where their conversations made sense to each other, where Joss felt less like her mom and more like her sister.

Tay's phone buzzed and he picked it up at the first ring. Joss could tell from his solemn expression that it was Tang Zhaoyi, her father-in-law, President of Tao International Auctions, the most prestigious auction house in the country.

"Everything okay?" she asked, after he hung up.

Tay flicked his lighter six times before tossing it and asking a waiter to light him up. The thing Joss loathed, but somehow came to tolerate, was Tay's smoking. She despised smokers in general, but Shanghai was full of them. After a night at the bars or clubbing, she would come out smelling like she had smoked a whole pack. Before the summer he had been cutting down, but the stress of working for Tang Zhaoyi made him regress considerably.

"Things will get really busy after we're back from the honeymoon. We have an exhibition at Taikang Lu."

"I'll be preoccupied too. You know, with the magazine."

"Right. When does that start?"

"Mid-November." The editor-in-chief had called Joss this morning, raving about her "Why Shanghai" writing sample, summarily offering her a job. Joss was now the new food editor at *Shanghai Scene*, considered the best English language publication in the city.

Joss didn't need a job. Tay said she should sit back and enjoy being a *tai tai*, a trophy wife, a lady of leisure. But she thought she would find the work fulfilling, although her in-laws didn't look amused when she said so. As a *Shanghaining* who grew up in both Chinese and U.S. cultures, she thought she could inject a balance of local and western perspective in the magazine. Most of the other staff on the magazine were foreigners, some were completely ABC—American born Chinese—who either spoke stilted or no Mandarin at all, and didn't know the difference between an authentic Shanghainese *xiaolongbao* and the variety which were Nanjing *tangbao* imports. Most thought the soup dumplings served in Ding Tai Feng were the real deal, but strictly speaking, those were tangbao because the broth often caused their dumplings to sag between one's chopsticks. Inside an authentic Shanghainese xiaolongbao, the filling should be meatier, bouncier, tasting of rice wine and soy sauce.

Naomi arrived. Joss embraced her, making a mental note that it seemed like she hadn't brushed her hair in days. Naomi's usual ponytailed hair was in a tangled mutiny, her under eye circles which were typically dabbed over with a concealer, seemed darker than usual. Normally she looked stunning. She had those puppy dog eyes, gazelle-like legs (inherited from her Taiwanese father), wavy raven hair that revealed a widow's peak (gifted from her Japanese mother). The Chinese called the widow's peak *mei ren jian*, beauty's peak, and that was exactly what it looked like on her.

Tonight, Naomi was dressed in a baggy t-shirt and leggings, a far cry from her customary bohemian chic. Compared with her avant-garde flair, Joss liked to think of her own fashion sense as sophisticated luxe. Even though Joss wasn't as fit as she would've liked and her teeth were just a tad crooked, at least she had a supple complexion and sculpted limbs like a Roman goddess. Joss knew she turned heads too. She also knew it was often due to her luxurious outfits. Tonight, she was in a Proenza Schouler fringe leather jacket over a shiny Givenchy sheath dress; her Alexander Wang ankle boots and crocodile Bottega Veneta clutch completed the ensemble.

"...and he had the nerve to post a picture of her..." Joss tried to focus as Naomi droned on. It looked like Naomi had been cyber stalking her ex. Again. For once, Joss was glad that Facebook was blocked in China.

Truth be told, Joss wasn't all that surprised at this outcome. Seth Ray was textbook. Even when Joss first met him years ago, she could already tell he was an utter narcissist. He talked too much about himself, about Yale, about how important he was at work, and his eyes darted everywhere when he was talking to you, like he had somewhere else better to be. He was one of those guys who had been the nerdy overachiever in his youth; now that he had found confidence through his Ivy League degree and no longer had the pimpled face, he suddenly had an over-inflated self-esteem. And Shanghai probably just shot his ego through the roof. This place was a man's playground. Joss had heard enough gossip among Tay's friends that she was rarely shocked by unhappy endings.

"Vincent! Over here." Tay motioned to his friend, Vincent Tu, who just arrived. Joss was secretly relieved at the interruption—Naomi desperately needed a distraction.

Vincent came with a friend, who he introduced as Logan Hayden, his business partner. Together they had opened three dining establishments in Shanghai: a British gastropub, a Californian-Asian fusion restaurant, a Sichuan-style restaurant lounge, and next year they would be opening a dessert bar. Vincent also mentioned that Logan was single, giving Naomi a meaningful look.

Over glasses of Japanese whisky, the group fell into various topics. Somebody brought up the conspiracy theory about the Chinese government staging military drills in the Gobi with makeshift structures mimicking the grids of D.C. Then they veered into China's gold mining industry, and how the Chinese being the largest importer of gold meant that one day the government could launch a new global monetary system based on the renminbi. Afterwards they argued over the significance of government censorship in the works of contemporary Chinese journalists, writers and artists. They went on to theorize the fate of a Chinese starlet who had disappeared from the public eye since she was charged with tax evasion allegations.

Soon Logan launched into a discussion about the government campaign to clean up the city in preparation for next year's Shanghai world's fair, or Expo, as everybody took to calling it. "The construction is annoying as hell," Logan quipped, "but just like the Beijing Olympics, Shanghai Expo will catapult China to the global stage. And it's great for business! New jobs and tourism opportunities is a win for everybody."

Vincent agreed whole-heartedly. The Shanghai World Expo has been likened to the 1893 Chicago world's fair when the U.S. was presenting itself as a major world power, and the 1889 world's fair takes credit for the creation of the Eiffel Tower. Who knew what sort of legacy the Shanghai World Expo would leave for China?

Tay had a different perspective. He had heard stories of locals who'd been forcefully resettled out of their homes by the government to make way for Expo.

"So, what are your plans?" Joss let the guys continue their deliberation about Expo and turned her attention to Naomi. "Are you going to be okay next week when we leave for St. Tropez? Do you need somebody to take care of your visa?"

"It's your honeymoon! Don't worry about me. Oh you're right, my tourist visa is running out."

"Those visas are such a hassle to renew here. You should really get a work visa."

"That would entail getting a job."

"So get one."

"What am I going to do here? Work in the mall?" Naomi sighed.

"Don't sell yourself short. You're trilingual and you were a manager for an up-and-coming fashion label. And I remember you were a fantastic designer!" It wasn't too much of a stretch. M. Joie Couture indeed had at one point been trending. Naomi had worked there for as long as Joss could remember. It signified commitment at best, indolence at worst.

"Please, that was in art school. You know I don't design anymore. Plus, I'm only bilingual," Naomi corrected her. "My Japanese is fine but my Chinese is not." Her Chinese verbiage was limited to small talk. Very, very small talk. "And I was an assistant store supervisor. But thanks for the vote of confidence. That's why I love you."

"Manager. Supervisor. Semantics. Get your resume ready and let me introduce you to some people. In this city, all you need is *guanxi*."

"Meaning?"

"Meaning it's all about who you know. Trust me, you'll do just fine here."

Tay Kai Tang was part of a curious breed people in China called *fuerdai*, the equivalent of trust fund kids in the west. Tay's father, Tang Zhaoyi, wore several hats: he was a former army official who founded Tao International Auctions, and had a reputation for keeping the best private collection of ceramics once owned by the Qing emperor Daoguang.

But Tay was not the typical fuerdai who in recent years had grossed a notoriously foul reputation in China. There were the endless antics of fuerdai's tasteless wealth-flaunting that flooded *Weibo*, China's answer to Twitter. Photos of China's one percent buying Bvlgari jewelry for their pets went viral. Stories of fuerdai spending two hundred thousand renminbi in one night at a club circulated the web. Tay's usual crowd consisted of the much more entrepreneurial fuerdai from a mix of regions: Mainland, Hong Kong, Taiwan and Singapore. Tay's friends were using their capital to develop start-ups, restaurants, fashion labels, foundations, earning the moniker *chuangerdai*, or "second-generation entrepreneurs." He also had friends who were *guanerdai*, the privileged sons and daughters of government officials. Tay's family was not on the *Hurun* China Rich List, but they knew many who were.

Tay came into Joss's life three years ago. At the time, she was a freelance writer for *International Palate*, a food culture magazine based in New York. She was active in the Manhattan restaurant scene and counted many as friends: the owner of Nakazawa, the sommelier at Charlie Bird, the manager at Masa, the head chef at La Grenouille. In order to write an article about the Jiang Nan Group—an upscale food and beverage operation who was then in negotiations to cater for the olympics—she accepted a research assignment in Beijing.

Two days before she was due back in New York, she met him. At a Halloween party in Lan Club, Tay was dressed as a Qing dynasty emperor, complete with a golden robe. Joss was draped in a makeshift Aphrodite costume formed from bed sheets that she somehow managed to turn into a high-slit dress. That fateful night, the Chinese emperor and the Greek goddess were inseparable. While their friends shared more than five bottles of Dom Perignon, Joss and Tay talked until dawn.

Joss ended up staying in Beijing past Thanksgiving, Christmas, and New Year's. In Joss, Tay found somebody to be vulnerable with, a trait that was seldom accepted in his circles. In Tay, Joss discovered a loyal friend and her biggest fan.

After Joss returned to Manhattan, Tay applied to Columbia's Executive MBA program and was enrolled there within the year. The day Tay presented her with the key to his Upper East Side apartment, was the moment Joss knew that she would one day, eventually, marry him.

After Tay proposed, Joss had no qualms about moving back to Shanghai, the city of her birthplace. Her family had immigrated to Hong Kong when she turned three, then to Flushing, New York, when she entered the fifth grade. After that, she rarely visited her home country, until she decided to take the research trip to China for the magazine. Looking back, Joss is thankful she had chosen that assignment over another one which would've taken her to Lisbon, instead of to Beijing.

That's what *yuan fen* is. Fate.

One split decision could alter the course of your entire life.

3

HOME OF THE FREE

A PERSISTENT OCTOBER RAIN LAID SIEGE ON THE CITY. THE
pre-dawn feathery drizzle in the morning gave way to a hard, thick pour
by noon. The winds howled and the rain drummed against the windows.
Pedestrians shivered under their umbrellas while taxis sped by, making
waves out of puddles.

The rain didn't deter Naomi. She donned her rainboots, texted Logan
Hayden that she was on her way, and quickly flagged down a taxi. During
that first meeting at Brasserie on the Bund, he had asked her out. She had
declined straight away; she hadn't felt ready to break her self-imposed
isolation at the time. Then several weeks ago, after Joss and Tay had left
for their honeymoon, after hibernating in her sweats and binge-watching
pirated DVDs for days, she finally decided that she was ready—ready for
change, for something. *Anything*. So she signed up for city tours: she had
tea at Yu Garden, saw a show at the Shanghai Opera House, went to the
history museum inside the Pearl Tower. She polished her resume and
registered for Mandarin classes.

She also called Logan back, who on one night had invited her to Club
Attica. Sometime in the course of that night somebody had vomited on
Naomi's shirt in the club. Logan had tried to clean it off, but the smell
was still overpowering. Then a guy approached, took off his shirt and
offered it to her, on the condition that she discard her tee right there
in the club. She was unabashed, she had on a sports bra and it was dark
anyway. Later, she had climbed onto a mechanical bull, riding it as if her

34

life depended on it.

It had all seemed very thrilling—roving this foreign city in a stranger's shirt, riding a bull with a gang of random revelers.

She felt alive again.

Naomi gave the taxi driver the Xujiahui address now. She leaned back and closed her eyes, only momentarily. The lights outside the windows were hypnotic. Parts of Shanghai were utterly monochromatic by day: the charcoals and drab grays of steel, concrete, construction cranes, even the polluted skies. But by night the metropolis morphed into a polychromatic wonderland. Lights of all saturated hues blinked and flashed, illuminating the city well unto dawn.

She thought of Xujiahui district as the Technicolor Land of Shanghai, with its maze of malls, endless riot of neon signs and explosion of garish colors, exhibiting that Capitalism was alive and thriving in China. She exited the taxi on Zhaojiabang Lu and was confronted with a rainbow of shop signs, building windows, glass edifices towering over pedestrians power walking on the pavement to their post-work revelry: restaurants, cafes, clubs, bars, boutiques, stores, hotels, lounges.

There was no signage to the speakeasy, which was situated in between a pharmacy and a flower shop. The view to the front door was obscured by a clothesline of laundry. It had an unassuming entrance, save the metallic Bentley parked outside, and the burly Chinese bouncer with a buzz cut guarding the venue.

Inside, it was so dark that Naomi nearly tripped herself trying to make out the languorous figures draped over various velvet cushions, illuminated by subdued amber bulbs. Various sections were cordoned off by brocade curtains while waitstaff meandered with trays of drinks. She found Logan in a corner, sipping on cognac.

"You're here alone?" She asked, surprised. He had mentioned meeting a group of friends.

"I'm here for work. Scouting out the competition. We're entertaining the idea of opening a bar across the street." He looked at his watch. "More people will trickle in a bit later."

Naomi listened as Logan described a work situation, something about managing contractors and bribing government officials for building permits. She tried to focus, but after half an hour of him talking, she excused herself to the restroom.

When she came back Logan was on his third drink of the night. "So, what are you in the mood for?" he asked.

The night was young and the endless possibilities seemed to stretch before her; she felt momentarily speechless.

"C'mon Naomi. Literally everything is still open in this city. Or just about to open," he winked.

"Not so fast, playboy. It's a school night."

"Okay, okay. Nothing crazy. No dancing on bars and singing on tabletops?" he smiled.

"Is that what people do in Shanghai?"

"Always. Anytime, anywhere in this city." His eyes lit up. "I've got it. There's something you've got to see. Something you can only do right here in Shanghai."

"Put me down! Put me down!" Naomi shrieked. Her feet dangled in the air, her curls fluttered over her shoulders. She didn't dare look out or down at the staggering stratospheric skyscrapers looming below, at the ant-like automobiles whizzing by. She felt dizzy and light-headed, as if she was about to be overcome by vertigo.

She swiped Logan in the face, and he tightened his grip underneath her knees, his right arm holding the weight of her back while she clung for dear life onto his neck. He grinned lasciviously.

They peered down the glass floors beneath his feet, beguiled with the verticality of towers, with the kaleidoscopic skyline that resembled Tomorrow Land, everything gleaming and shiny and new, promising a future that was limitless. Logan looked exhilarated from poring over the aerial view of the city. For a moment it seemed as if they were suspended in the skies.

Naomi yelped again and burrowed her face in his shirt. She had an intense fear of heights, and her reaction was producing chuckles around them. They were surrounded by locals and tourists milling about, taking selfies by the floor-to-ceiling glass windows, or daring each other to lie face down on the transparent floor panels. They were on the eighty-ninth floor of the Shanghai World Financial Center observatory, inside the current tallest building in the world. The view was spectacular, but not for the faint of heart.

He lowered her to her feet. "Just wanted to give you a prime view."

"You do that again and you'll be enjoying the view alone."

"Okay okay. So, where to next?"

Naomi checked her watch. "How about something we can finish in an hour?"

"I know something we can finish in an hour," he smiled and arched his eyebrows.

"Dream on, prince charming."

"The dream shall live."

After they exited the building, they headed toward the Bund Sightseeing Tunnel and boarded a windowed cable car. The car meandered through a tunnel with psychedelic, flashing liquid crystal display lights. A Mandarin-speaking narrator filled the background noise interspersed with English phases such as "meteor shower." Naomi felt like she was on the set of an outer space slash seventies themed movie.

Naomi chuckled. This had to be the most garish, tacky, bizarre tourist trap. Fifty renminbi for a five-minute ride to cross the river, it was hardly a good deal. It would have made more sense to taxi it over. But she had to laugh. There were endless amusements in Shanghai. It was so entertaining she almost didn't notice Logan taking her hand inside the cable car.

Afterwards, Logan insisted on Naomi checking out his loft. She initially refused, but then agreed to *just one drink* after considering her lonely apartment. Once they were on the road, he waited no time before he casually pushed his tongue in her mouth. She resisted for a minute before surrendering. His Davidoff cologne had been wafting in her face all evening, and he looked particularly dashing in his dapper suit. The taxi drove into the circular driveway of Infinity Towers, and Naomi almost got out with him. But it was in that moment, the way he stretched out his hand, his expectant eyes, that crude grin reeking of Scotch, that reminded her of Seth and Rex all rolled into one.

The thought sent her reeling back into the car and slamming the car door shut, leaving a bewildered Logan standing there alone.

Logan Hayden took a seat in his usual spot at Citadel, a lounge bar on Fumin Lu—a brisk eight-minute walk from his apartment. It wasn't the most popular bar on the street, which he liked, because it meant it wouldn't be swarmed with foreigners who usually took to the newer establishments. Still, Citadel attracted well-heeled locals and discerning expats.

He was flying solo tonight. His male friends were working late or too busy jacking off. He didn't mind. These days he was a walking boner and sometimes his friends cock-blocked him.

Logan checked his phone. No text from Naomi today. He'll check in with her tomorrow. They had hung out four times in the last three weeks. He had put the moves on her but was met with a bizarre rejection. After the incident, she had texted that she only wanted to be friends. Maybe he had been too forward, but it usually worked for him, in this city. Yesterday they met up for a group lunch and she had acted as if nothing was amiss.

Sometimes he still fantasized about her, especially after he had one too many drinks. Everything about her sparked desire, every part was luscious—her clavicles, her knees, those curves, that ass, her voice that was naturally raspy. He tried not to entertain lewd ideas about her. She was stunning to look at, but he knew he wouldn't get anywhere with her, at least, not right now. They were much too deep in the friend zone. Although he didn't rule out the future. This city was ever-changing, and so were its inhabitants.

The calendar that hung next to the wall-mounted television at Citadel's bar caught Logan's attention. Was it really the twelfth of November? Holy crap, today marked his third anniversary in Shanghai. His thoughts drifted back to his previous life in a backwater town in Pennsylvania. He remembered being bored out of his mind there, how challenging it had been to meet women. Well, partly because he'd been such a pussy back then, although he'd never admit that to anybody. Even after he had moved to Philly the situation didn't get much better. He had landed in Shanghai impulsively, almost recklessly, at the recommendation of an Asian girl he had met through OkCupid, who told him stories about Shanghai.

He had visited home only once in the last three years. There wasn't much to go back to. His dad was a drunk in perpetual debt, his twin brother was going through an ugly divorce. It wasn't exactly festive at home during the holidays. Two years ago, he had spent Christmas with a beautiful Balinese girl at Rawa, the private island owned by the family of the Sultanate of Johor, and last Christmas he had rented a villa in Boracay with friends. Yep, he was living *the life*. Life, he thought, had begun only *after* landing in Shanghai. He felt at home here, he jived with the rhythm of this city. Logan was always one to satisfy his compulsions. He was in tune with all his senses, and believed in treating them, in satiating them, whether it was with gourmet meals, luscious wine, lustrous women, all of which this city ran amok with.

He assessed the layout at Citadel now. There was a smattering of couples on dates dotted throughout the room. Near the bar sat two Chinese couples and a white guy wooing a local, plying her with drinks. In another corner sat a rowdy co-ed group of English-speaking Asians. Off to his left, a smaller group of Europeans were celebrating a birthday. And in the sitting area behind the bar, a handful of suits and short hemlines were cavorting in the shadows.

Logan himself seldom needed help with picking up women in this city, but he knew guys who resorted to desperate measures to get a girl, such as using GBL, a common date rape drug. His friend Tom Konan got his GBL stash from a Lithuanian who had profited handsomely in this city. Logan resisted drugs, most of the time. He was a traditionalist in that sense. He much preferred getting intoxicated with a solid drink his mixologist concocted at the bars of his restaurants, than becoming delirious off of something with ingredients you couldn't name.

But Logan could see where Tom Konan was coming from. Tom had told him his sob story before…something about his wife leaving him or something like that—Logan had only been half listening. Rejection could change your psyche, mess you up like that. Tom was not as charismatic as Logan was, he didn't make nearly as much as an expat should, he had a lazy eye and was balding. At least he was getting some in Shanghai. If Tom was back in the States, he'd still be un-laid, rotting, wasting away in suburban Portland.

Logan finished his beer. There was a hottie with a ponytail and low-rise jeans in the co-ed group that was looking his way. But Logan usually tried to steer clear of girls where a guy was already lurking nearby; you never knew if he was a boyfriend with anger management issues. He had learned that the hard way before. Logan scrolled through his phone to appear preoccupied. He hoped it wouldn't be a slow night.

The front door swung open and more people walked in. Some headed toward the sofas, some went straight to the bartender. Logan eyed the Chinese girl in the slinky fuchsia skirt leaning over the bar. She had a slight double chin and was fleshier than the other girls congregating nearby. She would've been considered of average weight in the U.S., but in this city, she was positively Rubenesque. Her shiny skirt complimented her racehorse legs, clung to her ass in a way that left little to the imagination. Although she was wearing a cardigan, her sequined top was low-cut enough to imply she wasn't exactly a prude.

Logan swaggered up to the bar and flashed his hundred-watt smile. "Ni hao mei nu." *Hello beautiful.* His Chinese repertoire was limited to pick-up lines and taxi basics. He hoped her English was better than his Chinese.

"Can I buy you a drink?" He placed his hand at the small of her back. She didn't flinch. Many of the local women gave off the impression of the freshly plucked, or of the guile, but would surprise you behind closed doors.

The girl giggled and nodded. He engaged her in small talk. *What's your name? Do you live or work nearby? Are you here alone?* She seemed to comprehend his English perfectly, but he could only understand half of hers. Logan guessed that her English comprehensions skills were superior than her vocabulary, similar to many of the locals he had met here. Logan kept his arm around her waist and pulled her closer as he downed his

Jägermeister and ordered another one for her. She went on and on about her work as a sales supervisor at some Danish furniture brand in her halting English. Keeping the smile plastered on his face, Logan feigned interest as his thoughts drifted.

For a communist country, the sexual marketplace here seemed much more deregulated than the U.S. What Logan appreciated about China was that it readily recognized that there was a yin to a yang. Logan learned through his language lessons that *yang* was the light, the surface, and *yin* denoted the shadows underneath. Back home in the U.S., transparency was extolled as the superior way. But the Chinese understood the tension, the necessity even, of the world that existed in the shadows, hidden from view, unspoken of and undisturbed. Yes, some parts of Shanghai were utterly dirty and uncouth and unacceptable in western standards, but that's what Logan liked about this city.

From the way this girl was responding, he was confident they would be back in his apartment within the hour, two hours tops. *Happy anniversary to me*, he smiled inwardly. People could complain about the communists all they wanted, but to Logan, China was truly the land of liberty, home of the free.

4

YEAR OF THE TIGER

THE FIRST THING NAOMI NOTICED ABOUT SHANGHAI: IT WAS A LOUD place. People talked loudly here, drivers honked all the time, diners argued in restaurants with waitstaff, and the clubs and bars blared music like rock concerts. People here laughed bombastically, they hollered into their cell phones on subways, at the movies, in restaurants, basically anywhere, unaware or unruffled by who was in their immediate vicinity. The residents of this city were garrulous, bellicose, enthused. The Chinese did none of that hand over mouth thing so many of the Japanese did. Sure, cities anywhere were noisy. But compared with Tokyo or Taipei or Manhattan, Naomi felt Shanghai was at a whole other decibel.

You learned certain things in China—that prolonged gazing was not improper, that encroaching on another's personal space was not impolite, that cutting in line, although offensive to some, was not abnormal here. Naomi welcomed the disarray, the disturbance. She relished exploring her environs on her own, forsaking her dependence on Joss. That was the thing about learning a foreign language, you had to start somewhere. It was as simple as getting into a cab by yourself, or ordering in restaurants without the crutch of your friends. Eating out had been the least of her concerns, since there was a plethora of restaurants with English menus. Other American aspects she had grown accustomed to took some time to adjust to. In China, temperatures were in Celsius, not Fahrenheit, weight in kilos, not pounds, distances described in kilometers, not miles.

Naomi had been taking intensive language courses. She recognized certain Chinese characters from learning Kanji in her youth, but most were as foreign to her as Egyptian hieroglyphics. Currently, her taxi Chinese was mildly coherent, her Starbucks Chinese was passable, her restaurant Chinese was laughable, and the rest was unintelligible.

While some in Naomi's situation might have considered moving back home, she just couldn't imagine returning to New York right now, coping with all those people judging, prying into why her engagement had been called off. Going home now felt like admitting defeat.

Armed with a newfound determination, Naomi segued into subtle self-promotion to Frida Du, a striking Shanghainese woman who worked at Jun Cleo, an integrated marketing agency catered to multinational fashion and beauty brands in China.

They were at Yin Par Le Garcon Chinois on Hengshan Lu. The chinoiserie wallpaper in shades of peach and mint, coated with intricate details of peacocks and blossoms, plastered the Old Shanghai themed restaurant and lounge. Faux songbirds in gilded cages hung low from the ceilings. Naomi felt full from the wine and delicious dishes: soy sauce braised pork belly, tiny wontons suspended in broth, lion head meatballs, fried lotus dumplings, truffle *xiaolongbao*.

Although Naomi hadn't originally planned on dressing up—she was practically living in her sweats every day—Joss had convinced her to glam up a little, knowing the fashionable Frida Du from Jun Cleo would be there. Frida said she had named herself after her favorite Mexican artist. Naomi thought Frida looked like a work of art herself; she had strawberry blonde highlights, bangled arms, pink-rimmed glasses without lenses, and was in a floral taffeta dress adorned with jewel-toned embellishments. Joss and Tay were a chic throwback to Old Shanghai, his hair slicked back, her qipao glistening. Naomi was glad she took Joss's advice and came in an off-the-shoulder sheath dress with a sleek smoking jacket.

Naomi had heard all about Frida Du's interesting family history: her great-grandfather was Du Yuesheng, the notorious Chinese mafia boss of Shanghai in the 1930s. Supposedly he had quite a number of great-grandchildren dispersed all over the world, since many of his mistresses and liaisons had since left China. Another one of Du Yuesheng's great-grandchildren, Drew Seyer, also lived in Shanghai. He was half-white half-Chinese and the Managing Director of a competing agency, Frida had told the group with disdain. "He's only twenty-seven years old and was promoted to MD of Hetchman! Isn't that unbelievable? If he was in New York or London he would *at most* be at the director level. Work titles are so inflated in this city. The fact that he's male, and looks white, certainly helps."

The bar was getting crowded as the night turned into a revolving door of co-workers, acquaintances, and friends of friends. There were people from at least seven different countries, some from places that were utterly exotic to Naomi, such as Kazakhstan, Belarus, Guam.

Ari Peng arrived at the adjoining bar after dinner. She was a friend of Frida's and a former colleague at Jun Cleo, but had quit after her wedding so she could "pay attention to getting pregnant." Her in-laws were exerting pressure to produce a grandchild.

Naomi made it a point to sit with Frida and Ari, and it paid off. By the end of the night, it was agreed that Frida would pass on Naomi's resume to HR at Jun Cleo. The company was looking for new staff to replace Ari in the Experiential Marketing team. Naomi wasn't familiar with the industry term, so Ari put it in layman's terms. "We curate the consumer's experience with the brands. Essentially we're in charge of events—fashion shows, road shows, salons, galas, press previews, pop-up shops, installations, exhibits, you name it." It all sounded exhilarating to Naomi. It was one of the rare moments she felt this city was finally working for her.

Ari did her best to warn Naomi about the horrendous hours, the demanding boss, the manual labor required, but Naomi seemed resolute. Ari smirked internally. Working at Jun Cleo, one of the most sought-after marketing agencies in fashion and beauty, was a dream job for many women. But the ritzy image of the agency was just a façade. Working there was far from glamorous. She had hated working with Cher and Pearla and the whole lot. She was doubtful this doe-eyed Japanese-Taiwanese girl would last long there.

*

Naomi was appreciative of Frida, who pulled some strings to get her resume to the top of the pile. Frida provided Naomi with tips on resume building, adding that an attractive headshot was a *must* for job seekers in China.

It was the most nerve-wracking and grueling interview process Naomi ever experienced. She came in four separate times, meeting with the HR Director, the Experiential Marketing Director, the VP of Marketing, as well as the President of Jun Cleo.

Naomi was almost certain her prospects were botched when they asked for her events portfolio, which caught her off guard. She had nothing to show. She had organized seminars and holiday parties at M. Joie Couture, but nothing like the thousand-person gala Ari and Frida had described. The Experiential Marketing Director seemed pleased with the fact that she had worked at her last company for five consecutive years though. Apparently staying in a company that long was not common in Shanghai, where an exuberant economy and abundant job opportunities did no favors for the retention rates at multinationals.

"So, tell me. Why are you here, in Shanghai?" the President, Auguste Reynaud asked. He was a stout Frenchman with a doughy face, thoughtful gray eyes and a bespoke suit, his silk tie in a firm Windsor knot.

Of course Naomi wouldn't mention Seth, it wasn't the appropriate interview response. But the truth was, she landed in this city because she had been the dutiful girlfriend following her soon-to-be-husband and his ambitions.

Now Naomi wanted to make this her city, her destiny. It no longer belonged only to Seth.

Naomi took her time replying to Mr. Reynaud's question, stating all the remarkable statistics she had read in *Forbes* about Shanghai's economy, its rising middle-class consumption, its robust luxury market.

Mr. Reynaud said the company was not actively hiring foreigners. Naomi was aware that hiring staff with foreign passports was more expensive for the company, since housing allowance and health insurance designated for foreigners were equated into the package. She knew she had to excel in this interview and stand out among the stack of eager local candidates who were cheaper to hire.

His final question was, "Tell me about your most impactful event."

Naomi thought about it for a minute. She didn't have any fancy galas or benefits or fashion shows on her resume. But she wanted to talk about Terry Ralstein and her failing liver. Terry had been an ex-colleague, a soft-spoken, blink-and-you-miss-it kind of girl. She had collapsed during work. Two days later, her doctors had revealed she was in dire need of a liver transplant. Naomi had taken the initiative to organize the search effort, which included canvassing at Jewish centers, working with the New York Organ Donor Network, and spearheading a "Help Terry" website. Terry's doctors at the NYU Langone Medical Center had listed Terry as a "status one" on the national transplant waiting list, which meant she had about one month to live.

Three agonizing weeks into the search campaign, Terry had been successfully matched with a donor. At her wedding a year later, Terry had cried tears of joy, as she introduced Naomi as her guest of honor.

Auguste listened intently as she took her time explaining the ordeal. Although many other candidates possessed a stand-out events portfolio, seldom did he hear about charitable campaigns undertaken by the applicants. After Naomi Kita-Fan completed the interview, he googled "Terry Ralstein" and "New York liver transplant." Scores of articles from the *New York Daily News*, the *New York Post*, and some Jewish newsletters chronicled Terry's story, some even quoting Naomi. For the next half hour, Auguste became engrossed in the articles, and his conversation with Naomi reverberated for days after. His own sister died from liver failure a decade ago, and hearing stories such as Terry's, still brought back acute memories.

*

Naomi stirred the contents in the hot pot. She inhaled the aroma of garlic, chili, coriander, and poppy seeds. After a few minutes, she helped herself to a generous serving of noodles and dipped it in a bowl of sesame oil and peanut sauce, savoring it.

The tyranny of Shanghai's lacerating winter had crept up on them. The sniping wind assaulted her ears, the air was bone-penetrating freezing and damp. It wasn't easy locating a building in Shanghai with central heating. Each room in Naomi's apartment was insulated with a growling, rumbling, antiquated air conditioner mounted high on the wall, and rarely did the hot air circulate to ground level. She had purchased a portable heater which could be rolled from room to room. It hadn't worked very well, and suffice it to say, Naomi felt relieved to flee the chill to Taipei at the invitation of her aunt, where it would be at least ten degrees warmer.

For the past week, Aunt Sylvie had planned a busy itinerary for them—hot springs in Beitou, boat ride at Sun Moon Lake, night markets at Keelung Harbor, historic Dutch colonial building tours in Tamsui. Today they had hiked the mountains near Shifen Waterfall, then painted lanterns in Shifen Old Town.

Sylvie tossed some dry goji berries into Naomi's tea now. She threw into the boiling pot squares of tofu, slices of beef, lettuce, okra, quail eggs, and flat noodles. "Let's go visit Nai Nai's grave at Taichung tomorrow. You know she loved you so much. She was so happy when you came to see her three years ago."

Naomi nodded earnestly. "I miss her so much."

"I'm glad you were able to come to her funeral. Although we were shocked when your mother didn't make it. How is she? Is she still doing that direct selling clothing business? What was it called…Stella?"

"Stellar," Naomi corrected her. She sighed internally. She had tried all week to avoid the landmine topic that was her mother. "Mom works with Stellar on the side. Her main job now is at the travel agency." Reina Kita was a tour guide based in Southern California who catered primarily to the Japanese demographic. She traveled seventy percent of the year, taking her Japanese-speaking customers all over the U.S. and Europe.

"I don't know how she can stand flying so frequently like that," Sylvie shuddered. Naomi understood her adverse reaction. Her only brother—Wesley Fan, Naomi's father—had died in a plane crash.

"So you don't see her much?" Sylvie asked, as she dunked the mushrooms into the pot.

"No. Her travel schedule is busy."

"Not too busy for her daughter I hope." Sylvie didn't hide her contempt. The feud between Sylvie and Reina could be traced back decades ago, when Sylvie's brother married a woman she didn't approve of.

"It's a good thing we renewed your Taiwan passport last time you were here. You are always welcome to visit and stay with me. For as long as you like." It was a more than generous offer, considering Sylvie had seen her niece less than a handful of times ever since Naomi left Taipei at two years old.

"Thanks Aunt Sylvie. You too."

Sylvie shook her head. "You know how I feel about flying. And I'm not very interested in China."

Naomi nodded but didn't look at her aunt. She quickly shoved a spoonful of soup in her mouth. All week long she had held her tongue as Sylvie grumbled about a city she had never been to—Shanghai's smog was toxic, food was unclean, censorship was senseless. She didn't want to encourage Sylvie on the subject. The people of this island were impassioned about politics. She already knew her aunt was in the "deep green" camp, believing Taiwanese independence was the superior solution to the island's tenuous relationship with mainland China.

"You know," Sylvie continued, "if you don't get that job in Shanghai, I can always help with getting you one here, in Taipei. You went to design school, right? I know people in the fashion industry."

"Thanks Aunt Sylvie, but I haven't designed anything in awhile. And I wouldn't want to trouble you," Naomi quickly replied. "I have a good feeling about the position I just interviewed for." As she compared Taipei with Shanghai, Naomi was acutely aware of the velocity of her newly adopted city. In Shanghai, you could feel the unyielding buzz of traffic, the continuous waves of people, the rush of adrenaline. In Taipei, people went about in a much more leisurely pace; they took the time to greet each other, to give strangers directions, to queue in line. Naomi appreciated these qualities about this island, and even missed them. But for now, in this season of her life, she knew she belonged across the strait in Shanghai, where her unfinished story still laid.

"Well okay. I'm glad you are at least learning Chinese. Chinese is the language of the twenty-first century. It's a shame you're only learning simplified characters though. The traditional characters carry over four thousand years of history. For example, the character for 'love' is written this way." Sylvie took out a pen from her purse and started scrawling on a napkin. "But the simplified system used in China takes out this key part of the character. And you know what this part means? It means 'heart.' The simplified version of 'love' takes out 'heart' from the character, and what is love without heart?" Sylvie shook her head. She scooped up asparagus tips from the pot into Naomi's bowl.

"If only your mother would've listened to me and had sent you here for Mandarin camp in the summers," Sylvie prattled on as she cut a piece of *oh-a-jian*, Taiwanese oyster omelet, and set it on Naomi's plate. "You remember how many times I called and wrote to her, but she always refused. She's a difficult woman, your mother..."

Naomi stayed quiet, even if she mostly agreed. It was one thing to gripe about your own mother, and quite another to hear somebody else disparage her.

"...she is so stubborn. You know I objected immediately when your mother and father said they wanted to move to Japan. If only he had stayed..."

Naomi's thoughts drifted. She had heard this story a thousand times. In 1981, Reina Kita was a twenty-one-year-old student at Joshibi University in Tokyo. She went on a study abroad program to National Chengchi University in Taipei, and met Wesley Hsiang-Shuo Fan, an Assistant Professor in Art History ten years her senior. Seven months later, Reina became pregnant. They married, and in the summer of 1982, Naomi Kita-Fan was born at the Taiwan Adventist Hospital. Despite his family's protests, Wesley and Reina moved to Japan when Naomi turned two. Reina missed her home and Wesley had secured a position at Kyoto Art University.

One rainy morning in November 1984, Reina went to see Wesley off at Tokyo Haneda Airport as he boarded a Japan Airlines flight to Osaka.

He kissed his wife and daughter goodbye, promising to be home by the end of the week. That would be Naomi's last encounter with her father. The plane crashed at Mount Takamagahara twenty-eight minutes into the flight.

Naomi tried to keep her focus on her aunt's diatribe but couldn't help glancing at her phone every so often. She was supposed to receive a call from Jun Cleo before the end of the month, that's what the HR lady said. Tomorrow would be New Year's Eve.

The call came at the end of dinner, after Naomi fought and lost to Sylvie for the bill. The HR Director said that her first day at Jun Cleo would be in two weeks.

Soon, it would be 2010, the year of the Tiger in the Chinese calendar. In Taipei, as it was in Shanghai, images of tigers and the Chinese character for tiger, *hu*, were adorned everywhere. They could be seen in shop windows, inside malls and restaurants, on TV ads. Naomi continually coached herself—in the upcoming year she would be stronger, wiser. She visualized a fierce tigress as she gave herself internal pep talks.

And maybe that was the appeal of Shanghai too, that she could reinvent herself, re-route her destiny there. In New York she had become too complacent, her only ambition to speak of had been to become Mrs. Seth Ray.

In the new year, Naomi no longer wanted the image of a sad jilted fiancé to trail her. She would be the confident girl at Jun Cleo who had it together, in cosmopolitan Shanghai.

She could be *that* girl.

5

BROKEN BRIDGE

As a successful executive employed with Intel in New York, Gabe Kong was the envy of his peers back in China—he was an immigrant twice-over, first from Shanghai to Hong Kong, then from Hong Kong to the U.S. He had achieved the American dream, had given his daughters Joss and Jamie the world. Of course, it hadn't always been this way. He had rose the ranks steadily to corporate executive VP, but that had come with sacrifices, especially when his wife had passed away. Joss had only been twelve. Long work hours meant less time with his daughters. It also meant Joss assumed parental duties for most of Jamie's life.

Gabe had teared at Joss's wedding. He wished his wife could have been there. He wondered if she would've taken to the Tang family, or if she, like him, would've had her reservations. His peers were constantly congratulating him on his daughter joining a *fuerdai* family, but marrying into a family like the Tangs had its own set of pressures. The wedding had been lovely but only because he had insisted on a pastor presiding over the ceremony, much to the Tangs' annoyance. Personally, Gabe would have preferred Tay to be committed to *any* faith than believe in nothing. He was convinced that, faith, was the cornerstone of a life worth living, and was what had saved him, especially during the dark period of Jillian's passing.

Gabe sighed at the irony of it all—the fact that he had moved his family out of China to the States for his offspring to enjoy better prospects and a broader horizon, and now nearly fifteen years later his daughter was moving back. But he knew they weren't alone. Many of his Asian friends in the U.S. had children who were now taking jobs in cities such as Beijing, Tokyo, Singapore.

Leaving China and moving abroad had been the ultimate goal for Gabe and his peers. And now the next generation was going the reverse route, returning back to their roots.

When Joss Kong had started dating Tay Kai Tang, some had pegged her as a gold digger. But Joss had always been an aesthete, even before Tay came along. Jamie often joked that Joss was a Chinese nobility in a past life, which explained her refined tastes. If Confucius was considered nobility then that would be a credible theory, because all Kongs were descendants of Confucius. That lineage was something her in-laws repeated more often than her own father did.

As much as Joss cared about aesthetics, she made an exception with dining, because to her, taste always trumped looks. One of her pet peeves was a fine dining establishment with mediocre food. Of course she appreciated restaurants with gloss and ambiance and designer decor, but that never distracted her from what was on the plate. If restaurant management invested more in their interior designer than in the sous-chef, then it wasn't an establishment worth going to.

Joss detested the simplistic Chinese fare in America and how it had become synonymous with unrefined takeout meals, especially places like Pan's Express which gave the delicacy of authentic Chinese cuisine a bad name. She believed Shanghai could be just as epicurean as New York or Paris. There was a surplus of excellent French and Italian cuisine in Shanghai, just like in any other major metropolitan city. But what excited Joss the most was the diversity of Chinese cuisine she could savor, now that she was back in China. In New York, even in Flushing, the authentic dishes she remembered from her childhood in Shanghai and Hong Kong weren't easy to come by. Now, she had her pickings of any assortment of Chinese cuisine in this city: Sichuan *mala* hotpot, Xinjiang lamb skewers, Beijing duck, Guizhou *suan la* fish soup, Hunan smoked meat, Shanghainese *hongshao rou*, Shanxi *Maoerduo* noodles, Yunnan mushrooms, Macanese Serradura pudding, Hainan *ji fan*, Guangdong spareribs soup, colorful dongbei dumplings, and all the dim sum she desired. In this city, you had easy access to all the delicacies—hairy crab, ox tail, bird's nest. She had an adventurous appetite.

Born in Shanghai and raised in Hong Kong, Joss grew up on street food. Her dad said she'd always had a keen palate. She was especially fond of *shen jian bao* and still remembered frequenting the stall manned by the hunchback grandmother. Nowadays, her in-laws admonish her to refrain from street food due to the food safety scandals. Joss thought it was a pity that a spate of street food areas had been disappearing in preparation for the World Expo. One of her favorites, the Wujiang Lu traditional food market had just closed down, the breakfast stalls of Tianping Lu and the street food of Dongjiadu had vanished overnight as well. She thought about all the locals whose livelihood depended on income from their modest food stalls and felt sad for them.

Having sharp taste buds and a refined palate didn't mean she particularly enjoyed cooking, however. She was grateful for Ah Ming, who was so much more than their live-in cook and maid.

The Tang residence was in the part of the city that didn't resemble Shanghai, or the idea of Shanghai. There were villas dressed in ivy, gardens framed by marble sculptures, a miniature waterfall cascading off a faux cliff. With several international schools nearby, her neighborhood was filled with expat families that looked like they were from the Hamptons. Tay's parents had bought the six bedroom property for their only son, while they lived in the same gated community in another villa just a couple of doors down. Joss was grateful for the luxurious living quarters, but privacy was desperately coveted, since her in-laws had a set of keys to their villa, and came and went as they pleased.

Joss was just finishing typing up her article when Ah Ming approached. She brought out loquats in a porcelain saucer and set them upon the hand-cut mosaic coffee table.

Joss eyed the fruit resembling a smaller, apricot-colored pear. "Wow is this a *pipa?*" she asked, referring to the loquat's colloquial Chinese name.

"Yes. *Xin xian gang mai de.*" Just bought, very fresh.

Joss smiled and took a sip of pu'er tea from her Wedgewood. Ah Ming was particular about scouting out the freshest seasonal fruits from traditional markets, which were as close to the source as you can get in this city. "Thank you, Ah Ming."

Joss picked one loquat up, taking in the floral note the fruit emitted. She remembered reading about the pipa, which was connected to colorful Chinese folklore. The "gate of the pipa" was traditionally linked with places of forbidden pleasure.

"How do I eat this?" Joss held up the fruit.

Ah Ming shook her head and laughed. "First, you tear off the stem and cut the fruit in half. Then you flick out the seeds and tear off the calyx. Now you can enjoy!"

Joss bit into the juicy filet of a loquat, which resembled a half apricot, and savored its sweetness—a blend of peach, plum, and cherry.

"*Xiao gu niang* you're just like my son. You both have good taste and big appetites," Ah Ming teased, playfully patting Joss's stomach.

"I'm like the daughter you never had," Joss replied in a singsong tone. Joss found it easy to be with Ah Ming, who was about the same age as her own mother, had she been alive.

A flash of sadness seemed to cloud over Ah Ming's face. She paused, speaking tentatively, "*Qin ai de*, my dear, I need to ask you for next Thursday off."

"No problem at all. May I ask why?"

"Because it's the third day before Chinese New Year, and I need to go to Hangzhou. Every year on that day, I go to the Broken Bridge."

"That's real? I always thought Broken Bridge was just a fairytale place in that traditional story White Snake." In the mythological tale, Broken Bridge was the romantic place where Xu Xian and White Lady first meet.

"Yes, it's a real bridge, and it's very beautiful there. I'll take you there one day…" Ah Ming's voice started to choke up. She sat down on the sofa.

"Ah Ming! What's wrong?" Joss went to her, putting her arms

around her.

"I'm sorry. You don't know my story. Most of the Tang family knows." Ah Ming wiped her eyes. "My dear, every year on this day, I go there to search for my daughter."

Joss's mouth dropped open as Ah Ming started telling her the saddest day of her life.

"She was only three months old. She was perfect. Very plump. I had so much milk and I loved feeding her. I loved her so much. But..." Ah Ming's face clouded over. "I had no choice. I left her at the orphanage that day hoping...praying that a good family would find her." Through tears, Ah Ming said she had arrived at the brick-and-wood structure at the crack of dawn that day in 1990. Her daughter was swaddled tightly and sleeping in a large basket where Ah Ming included formula, diapers, and fifty renminbi. Ah Ming had traveled more than an hour to get to the orphanage located near the Broken Bridge. The orphanage had a sound reputation, it was housed in a former Italian Catholic mission and was one of the nicer ones. Ah Ming had placed the basket at the front door and hid behind a nearby bush. She had waited there until she saw a middle-aged woman open the door, peer at the basket, then take her in. Ah Ming remembered that the woman had a compassionate look. She liked to believe that the woman had led her daughter to a good home.

Ah Ming explained that her husband's brother was a village leader at the time, and their family was expected to be exemplary, to be a role model in their region. Her daughter was over the quota per the family-planning policy, and the punishment for those who violated the law was severe, including financial repercussions and forced sterilization. In some cases, the family home would be vandalized and even demolished. They couldn't afford the shame, nor the fines.

"I prayed to the gods that my daughter would be taken in by a loving family, although I had hoped she would remain in China, so I could still find her someday. 1992 was when the Party started allowing international adoptions. On one hand it was a very good thing, I believe many babies had a chance at a better life. On another hand, some of the orphanages in China were connected to crime rings, where babies were seen as commodities that could help these institutions earn money from required donations in the adoption process. I also heard of stories where babies were forcibly abducted from their families then sold to orphanages."

"Oh my," Joss exclaimed. "And this is still going on today?"

"For the most part, no. The government has cracked down on this type of corruption. I have visited many orphanages throughout the years, in hopes of meeting somebody that would have any information on my daughter." She hung her head now. "The orphanage I brought my daughter to was torn down nine years ago."

Ah Ming had left a note inside the basket before she said goodbye: "My precious daughter Xiao Yue, I'm so sorry. I love you. May your life shine bright as a moon, just like your name. After you're grown, after you turn fifteen, I will wait for you at the Broken Bridge every year on the third day before Chinese New Year. Until the heavens reunite us, every year on that day I will wait for you at the Broken Bridge, because that day is your birthday."

Upon hearing the story, Joss had teared even more than Ah Ming. For reasons that confounded her, it made Joss think of her own mother.

6

THE CITY WAS OURS

Naomi peered down the window from her seat in the conference room, where it boasted a view of one of the city's most famous streets. Nanjing Xi Lu was Shanghai's Rodeo Drive. Luxury storefronts lined the street next to gargantuan marketing displays from brand after brand. The street was a luxury marketer's wet dream, designated for ten feet tall towers of Louis Vuitton luggage displays, Dior handbag monuments that lit up, and colossal Ferragamo shoe sculptures. Cavalries of Chinese and foreign women in sunglasses and oversized shopping bags filled the boulevard. Aston Martins, Maseratis and Ferraris dotted the street. White collars dashed in and out of Henglong Plaza, a towering skyscraper with sixty-six floors, home to some of the most coveted workplaces in the city. It was all part of the pageantry of Nanjing Xi Lu.

It was Naomi's second week at Jun Cleo, located on the twenty-second floor of Henglong Plaza. She could hardly contain her excitement when she had received her very first business cards. Embossed on them was her name and title: Assistant Manager, Experiential Marketing. Her first week had been a whirlwind of orientation workshops, meeting with clients, visitations to the brands' shops. She was handed thick files to read, industry reports that detailed how China was minting millionaires at an extraordinary speed and was outpacing all other markets in luxury consumption, with a double-digit growth each year. Within two years, China was projected to become the number one luxury market globally. Jun Cleo was a clear benefactor of this trend, named by AdWeek recently as one of the top marketing agencies catering to luxury brands in the country. The agency's clients were made up of multinational Fortune 500 companies, whose advertising budget for China alone was double to triple that of the North American or European markets. One of the clients, an upscale Italian retail brand, had recently established their flagship store on the Bund, which was larger and more lavish than their Milan counterpart.

Naomi recalled what she had heard at orientation. Fifty years ago, it was considered taboo and bourgeoisie in China to preoccupy oneself with cosmetics and clothes. Now, generations of Chinese were claiming what they had been denied of. Beauty and fashion were this city's obsessions.

The loud chatter that filled the conference room hushed to a halt as soon as a woman stepped in and called the meeting to order. She had sharp cheekbones, long limbs, an asymmetrical bob that was longer on the left side than the right, blood red lipstick, and was in an impeccable ivory satin wide-legged jump suit. There was a glacial air about her.

"Who's that?" Naomi whispered to Frida Du, who was sitting next to her.

"Are you serious? You've never met Nicki? Didn't you interview with her?"

Naomi racked her brain. Then it hit her. She was the VP of Marketing whose schedule was so intense that she had no time for an in-person interview. Naomi ended up being grilled by Nicki Jiang on the phone for fifteen minutes instead. *Do you know who our clients are?* Nicki had asked. Naomi had prattled off the partial list she remembered from the agency's website: an Italian retail brand, a Korean beauty conglomerate, a Spanish handbag brand, a Japanese furniture company, an American sportswear line, a Canadian athleisure label, a French luxury beauty brand, a UK jewelry company, among others. *And do you know what Jun Cleo does for them?* Naomi had answered but it didn't seem to satisfy, so Nicki had corrected her: *more accurately, we're here to create fantasies. Our clients aren't just selling leather clutches, organic eye creams, alligator boots and diamond pendants. They're selling a dream, a lifestyle, an extravagance that was previously unknown to the majority of Chinese. Jun Cleo's job is to curate and distill those dreams into spectacular experiences.*

Nicki threw Frida a stern *be quiet* look. "Frida, why don't you go first then. Give us a report of your clients' Expo programming update."

The meeting was called to discuss *shi bo*, the Shanghai World Expo, which would be opening on May first, in less than four months. There would be nearly two hundred country pavilions straddling the Huangpu river. The entire site had been compared to the size of a thousand football fields, twice the size of the country of Monaco, four times the size of the last expo in Japan. This was the largest world's fair to date, both in terms of size and projected visitor numbers. Almost all of the agency's clients were sponsors of some capacity at the international event.

Frida stood up and cleared her throat. "So far, Loewe will be holding a leather craftsmanship demonstration in the Spain pavilion from June through September, as well as sponsoring the Charles Rennie Mackintosh exhibition in the Scotland pavilion. Jejuka is planning a beauty salon inside the Korea pavilion in May, and bringing over the K-pop group Kosmic for an outdoor concert at Expo's central stage..."

"Kosmic?" Nicki interrupted her sharply. "As I recall, one of its members was photographed with a shirt bearing the Tibetan flag."

"I think that was just a rumor..." Frida replied hesitantly.

"Well you better double check because they will never gain approval from the Ministry of Culture if that proves true. Minyoung from Jejuka did not sing praises at the winter road show, so your team needs to get it right this time." Nicki scanned the room. "Okay next, Cher. Let's hear from you regarding Chantevieve's fragrance exhibit in the French pavilion..."

Naomi leaned forward. Cher Xiang was the Experiential Marketing Director and her direct report. She listened carefully as Cher described Chantevieve's programs for Expo. The French luxury beauty brand was one of the agency's most important clients. Chantevieve's exhibit inside the French pavilion would comprise of a video projection telling a fantastical story of a starlet journeying her way from Paris to Shanghai. Another exhibit would take visitors on an olfactory voyage of the French Riviera by incorporating Chantevieve's fragrances. The fragrances would be sold in the pavilion's gift shop, including the brand's limited edition Expo themed products.

"Fine, fine," Nicki replied impatiently, cutting Cher off. "Just remember to assign a team member to run the exhibit for the entire duration of Expo. It's stated in their contract that we're providing the staffing for this. Next, Margeau, what's the update on the sneaker hip-hop show inside the Brazil pavilion…"

The meeting concluded an hour later. Naomi relished the energy pulsating within the room. The world's fair only happened every five years, and this particular one was supposed to be the most remarkable of them all. It was a thrilling time to be in this city.

"What is your sign" and "where are you from." Naomi quickly learned that in Shanghai, those were the most asked questions upon meeting somebody new. At least that's how she felt. The zodiac was easy, her origins were not. Where was one from? Was it where you were born? Raised? Resided? She had a different answer to each: born in Taipei, raised in Tokyo (until age 5) and Southern California (until age 17), then resided in New York before moving to Shanghai.

There were predictable cliques at the agency: the account executives were friendly with each other, the fashion-forward girls flocked together, the English-speakers went to happy hour. Frida Du was Naomi's only real friend at work, well, Amos Kim could count as a friend, sometimes, whenever he wasn't hitting on her. Although the foreigners had all been welcoming, they were also older, had children, held higher positions than she did, and had negotiated an attractive expatriate package which included housing, airfare to and from their home country, extended vacation time, and tuition covered for their children's international schools. Naomi wasn't privy to any of that, this post being her first real marketing job. She was unperturbed though, in fact she counted herself blessed to have landed this position. Not only did it pay much better than her previous retail job, but for the first time in her life, Naomi felt like she was on track to establish a career.

During her welcome lunch, her teammates had interrogated her about her zodiac sign. Naomi wasn't quite sure actually. Her birthday fell on the cusp of Leo and Virgo, so according to different charts she was either one or the other. Orca Cao said he thought Naomi seemed more like a Leo, who could be headstrong, impassioned and bold, while Fei Hu disagreed, and said Naomi's aura was distinctly Virgo, a quiet but hardline perfectionist. Liya Hu said she hoped Naomi was a Leo, because she herself was a Sagittarius and would be incompatible with Virgos. Pearla Lin smirked that neither Leos nor Virgos got along with their boss Cher, who was an Aquarius. Naomi was amused that they were so overly presumptuous about somebody they just met.

There were two alliances within the Experiential Marketing department. The first belonged to Pearla Lin, a haughty senior manager whose twiggy outline was elongated by pointy pumps, and her "work husband," Orca Cao, who mostly aligned himself with her, at least, according to water cooler gossip. The other clique was Fei and Liya, who shared the same surname and were joined at the hip, although it was obvious that Liya lived in Fei's shadow. Naomi detected a subtle rivalry between Pearla Lin and Fei Hu. Both held the same roles as senior managers who constantly vied for Cher's approval, and both seemed less than enthusiastic about the new hire.

Over the last several weeks, Orca had become friendly with Naomi. He was a fan of mandopop and said Naomi looked a bit like Hsu Ruo Xuan, a Taiwanese musician. Naomi had no idea who that was but was grateful for a friend in the department.

Some of her colleagues had peculiar English names, and sometimes she had to stifle a smile whenever their names popped up in her inbox: Blue, Jobs, Fish, Comet, Walker. Tina, a British colleague, had once poked fun at Orca's name. "Isn't there a singer named Seal?" he retorted. Tina was taken aback. "You're quite right," she chuckled. Orca said he thought his name would make him memorable. He confessed the English name on his business cards changed whenever he switched companies. His previous cards have read "Navy," "Razor," "Zoro." *New start new name* was his philosophy.

Naomi's first three weeks at Jun Cleo felt more like three months; she got off work past ten almost nightly. Her cubicle was right outside of Cher's office, and she sometimes doubled as Cher's assistant, manning her phones, setting up meetings, and once, she had to pick up her dry cleaning. Although secretarial duties were not in the original job description, Naomi was determined to stay on Cher's good side. Cher's perennial office attire was a dark pant suit, which seemed to match her mood most of the time. Her complexion was flawless—probably due to the lack of smile wrinkles.

At first Naomi thought Cher must've been rewarding her for her industriousness, when she announced that Naomi would be the one stationed inside the French Pavilion at Expo, running Chantevieve's exhibit for six months. This brand was one of Jun Cleo's most prized clients; it was a cash cow for the agency. But then she noticed Pearla flashing her a faux sympathetic smile when her new job assignment was announced at the team meeting.

Orca was the one who shed light on the situation. "Good luck. You're going to need it."

"Excuse me?" Naomi said.

"The Expo pavilions open at nine a.m., which means you'll need to arrive at eight to prep the exhibits, which means you'll need to leave your apartment here in Puxi at seven. And the Expo closes at nine p.m. Not to mention that the Chantevieve clients are the most demanding ones of all."

"You're basically being exiled from Henglong Plaza for half a year," he continued.

"Hey quit being a killjoy."

"A what?"

Naomi sometimes forgot that English was not Orca's native tongue. He had such a superb command of the language. Most of her colleagues did, since the agency only hired those who had studied abroad.

"It means stop being negative. You know, buzzkill?"

"Such an optimist. Cher did choose the right person." Orca shrugged.

Naomi smiled. This was a once-in-a-lifetime opportunity. It was an experience that would never be replicated again—to be able to work at a world's fair, in China out of all places, alongside people from nearly two hundred other nations who like herself, had left home and descended in a foreign country, on the Expo grounds, a previous wasteland which had been transformed into a global village.

After receiving her first month's paycheck, Naomi was able to move into a considerably more modern and spacious apartment rental on Beijing Xi Lu, which was only a fifteen-minute walk to Henglong Plaza. Before she had moved in with Seth, Naomi's last real residence in Manhattan had been a cramped flat in the East Village, shared with two others: Lisa and Rex, a couple who had posted a craigslist ad for a "clean female roommate who could double as a dog walker." Compensation for the dog sitting service had been paid in the form of a lower-than-market-price rent, which suited Naomi and her budget, as well as her flexible schedule working in retail.

Now her Shanghai apartment was more than quadruple the size of that closet-sized room in the East Village, which had been just a pop-up room, created via a partition wall that was erected to halve the living room. On the other side of the wall had been another makeshift room for Lisa's aging bulldog, whose odor permeated the entire apartment. Naomi appreciated that her salary from Jun Cleo now afforded her rent in this gorgeous studio space in Shanghai, without having to share it with a quarreling couple or a geriatric canine.

During Naomi's teenage years in California, New York had seemed like the very definition of *The City*. True, she was raised in Tokyo, but Tokyo for her was never the city to aspire to, it was her childhood home, and therefore in essence, was in a different category than the aspirational. Manhattan, in contrast, was the place where magic and romance and ambition were supposed to bloom.

But once she got there, it had been a different reality. All those never-ending avenues, those towering buildings closing in, those elusive opportunities, those suffocating expectations. She had heard all those voices: *You're in New York! The greatest city on earth! Go realize your dreams! Make them come true!* In art school, the halls had been teeming with talented students who were on their way to become prodigies in any industry that required a designer—graphics, interior, architecture, fashion, industrial, toys, product, packaging, publishing. When people talked about the future or envisioned the life they were pursuing, she had felt rudderless, removed. Some of her friends had mentioned creating their own fashion label, working for prominent corporations, crisscrossing the world, or having a handful of children. Whenever Naomi was asked about the future, she had choked. She didn't have a vision, didn't have grand plans.

People in New York liked to say *if I can make it here, I can make it anywhere.* But to thrive in a place like Manhattan, you had to possess immense faith—you had to believe you belonged, that the city was yours, that the dance was yours. New York had never felt that way to her. She'd been at a standstill. The interminable options had all been too much for her to bear.

But Shanghai presented a different story. This city restored a sort of optimism that had eluded her before. She felt a certain kind of liberty in Shanghai, a freedom that evaded her in Manhattan. She didn't feel weighed down here.

Naomi often thought of her past in blocks, each with its own saturation of pigments. The color of jade was the verdant hills of her grandmother's home in Taipei, where Naomi was born. The gentle pink of *sakuras* was her childhood in Tokyo, where cherry blossoms bloomed near their home. Her adolescence took on the shimmering sheen of turquoise green, the color of Orange County's hypnotic beach waves, where she spent much of her time in high school. When she thought of her college years and early twenties in New York, the memories took on a shade of stained maroon—a dye of illicit passions and alarming mistake, after mistake, after mistake. She wondered what color Shanghai would manifest for her. She stared into the faceless gray buildings from her kitchen window. For now, all she knew was that Shanghai was a clean slate, a place where her skeletons were hidden, the pristine palette that for so long, she had desperately wished for.

7

SEVENTEEN IN SHANGHAI

WHEN NAOMI FIRST MET ROXANNE GAO, SHE SAID, "CALL ME ROXY." Her smile was electric and it matched her shiny metallic outfit. She wore a cropped top that looked like it was drenched in platinum glitter, a leather skirt with Vivienne Westwood's signature orb logo embroidered near the hem, and knee high lace-up pink suede boots. She looked part punk, part princess. She was small for seventeen, even in Shanghai standards. When she opened her mouth, you forgot that she was petite. She oozed attitude, talking as if she was the only one in the room, in volume and in presence.

Roxy was the daughter of Mrs. Gao, Naomi's Chinese teacher. Naomi wasn't exactly studious, but she knew she needed these Chinese languages courses. On the first day of class, Mrs. Gao had spouted a statistic: compared to the 300 million English speakers in the world, there were now more than 800 million Chinese speakers, and that number was increasing.

Naomi was glad that she could recognize some Chinese characters from learning Kanji in Tokyo as a child, but even so, she had to re-learn their meanings. The same looking ideogram could have vastly different definitions in China versus Japan.

As Naomi begrudgingly hauled her overtired body to Fuxing Nan Lu for her Chinese lessons on Saturday mornings, she would admonish herself for being persuaded by Logan, yet again, to stay out late on a Friday night. But whenever Friday afternoons rolled around, amnesia inevitably hit and the Saturday migraine became more or less a fixed ailment. As she raced through the shady lanes of Fuxing Park to class, she would pass the usual throng of Chinese grandmothers in rhythmic formation. Although their granddaughters danced the nights away inside the city's glitzy array of clubs, the older generation preferred the regimen in the open air, under shady foliage or starry skies, among gathering onlookers. Any open plaza, courtyard or park in the city was a venue for the city's elderly to blast old Shanghai tunes on their portable stereos while they waltzed, folk danced, or practiced Tai Chi. At sixty or seventy years old, they looked like they had more vitality than most of her office-bound white-collar peers.

One day after Chinese class, Roxy approached Naomi's desk just as she was putting away her books. Naomi was relieved that class was over; her head was still throbbing and she had to keep pinching herself to stay awake during Mrs. Gao's monologue about Zheng He, the Muslim Chinese mariner who lived five hundred years ago and discovered America before Columbus. Mrs. Gao continued to posit that western historians were all in on the conspiracy to undermine China by covering up Zheng He's accomplishments.

Roxy plopped down in the seat next to Naomi. "Where you from?" she asked.

"I moved here from New York," Naomi replied, taken aback by the sudden appearance of the teenybopper.

"You the...most pretty student here," Roxy said in stilted English. Naomi laughed and shook her head.

Roxy passed a note to her. She opened the typed-up message in caps: PLEASE CAN YOU TUTOR ME ENGLISH? I PAY 100 RMB TO YOU.

Naomi glanced at Roxy and saw Mrs. Gao watching them in her peripheral vision.

"Hourly?" Naomi said.

Roxy gave her a blank stare.

"One hundred renminbi per *xiao shi?*" Naomi repeated in Chinese.

Roxy nodded.

"Deal." Naomi smiled and held out her hand to shake Roxy's. She could use the extra income. Prices in this city were becoming frightfully extravagant. A cup of caramel macchiato in Shanghai cost almost double of one in Manhattan now.

During their weekly lessons, Naomi and Roxy would usually meet at one of the myriad of cafes on Huai Hai Zhong Lu. Naomi had a penchant for pastries—egg custard *dan ta* tarts, pineapple buns, sesame balls, or taro mochis—in addition to kumquat boba tea, her favorite. But Roxy almost always only had coffee, black, and didn't consume anything in the color of white, which meant pastries were off-limits. She would say *wo zai jian fei*. Losing fat. Naomi would shake her head at the pint-sized teen. Roxy couldn't have been more than ninety-five pounds. Naomi felt like she was twice her size. She soon learned from her colleagues that for women in this city, dieting was more or less a permanent state of being.

Roxy took Naomi to all sorts of cafes stocked with delectable Asian-style pastries. They would sit for hours, sipping on tea and flipping through her U.S. editions of *Vogue* and *People* while Roxy asked her to translate the latest season's fashions, or the most updated pop culture gossip. In the beginning Naomi had suggested a more serious lesson plan, but Roxy was disinterested in scholastic workbooks. She was much more engaged in learning the latest lingo as heard from her "Gossip Girl" pirated DVDs. In return, Roxy helped Naomi with her Chinese homework. While Roxy's mother gave Naomi structured lesson plans, Roxy liked to provide Naomi with non-textbook Chinese.

Roxy introduced Naomi to *Weibo*, China's most popular micro-blogging site. Roxy herself was also considered a *Weibo da ren*, a moniker she earned for the fact that she had over twenty thousand followers to her site, which made her an It Girl, at least among her own social circle. But Roxy had her sights set on becoming a *wang hong*, an internet celebrity recognized all over the nation.

When Naomi first logged onto Roxy's Weibo site, she was bombarded by images of Roxy in belly baring tops, short shorts and mini skirts posing across all corners of Shanghai. She was in denim cut-offs clutching an armful of tangerine colored balloons at People's Square, in a strapless sundress having afternoon tea at the Pudong Ritz, rollerblading in matching bikini tops with her puppy next to a graffiti wall in Red Town.

Roxy aspired to be the next Queen B, a Shanghainese self-made celebrity through her picture-perfect selfies. Queen B was now an established fashion model, a spokesperson for a national pet care brand, and dating a Hong Kong actor. According to tabloids, Queen B's aging parents could still be found greeting customers at their humble floral shop next to Jing'An Temple every day at six a.m., despite the fact that their daughter had bought them a new apartment and that their retirement was long overdue.

Queen B was so revered for her beauty that plastic surgery clinics were offering cosmetic operations named after her to accommodate all the requests to resemble her. Roxy professed to Naomi that one of her many future goals was to go under the knife to correct her facial features. "Why? You're gorgeous the way you are. You're not afraid of the pain from the surgery?" Naomi asked, bewildered.

"Zhe shi mei de dai jia," Roxy replied. That's the price of beauty.

The following week, Roxy invited Naomi to meet her at Logo, a live music bar located on Xinfu Lu. One would often find scores of lovers posing under the Xinfu Lu street sign. The auspicious Chinese characters *xinfu* meant "happily blissful," and attracted many couples with their cameras.

Roxy was in a dazzling sequined top with the Versace Medusa head logo emblazoned across, a frayed denim skirt and golden high-tops. Her friend, Shannon, was in a bomber jacket, designer sneakers, a cap on backwards, and a choker that looked like a spider web. It was only at close range that Naomi and Joss realized it was a tattoo. Roxy informed them that Shannon was a *tongzhi*, the colloquial term for gay.

On stage, the all-girl band was sporting boy cuts, leather gear, and screaming into the microphone amid cheering crowds. Shannon took Roxy's hand and led her to the front of the stage, where throngs of androgynous looking Chinese teenage girls were swaying and gyrating to the music. At one point the lead singer grabbed her crotch and the mob of Chinese teenage girls shrieked as if she were Justin Bieber.

After the all-girl band exited the stage, the emcee introduced the main event of the night: Rustic, a Beijing punk rock band who had won the Global Battle of the Bands in London several months ago. Rustic was the first Chinese band to win the esteemed global competition. "These boys from Shijiazhuang took first place! They beat out the bands from Iceland, Ecuador, Morocco…they beat out nineteen bands from all over the globe and became the world champion. They are China's pride!" the emcee roared into the microphone. The crowd erupted with gleeful shouts and thunderous applause.

The trendy trio from Hebei province had a glam rock appearance, complete with mohawks, piercings, tattoos, leather pants and blonde manes. They leapt around the stage schizophrenically, and at one point, the lead singer played the clarinet while the bassist played lead and bass simultaneously with his hands and teeth. The music channelled The Ramones and Violent Femmes. Naomi clapped rapturously. Rustic's theatrics and stage chemistry electrified the air.

After the set, Roxy and Shannon joined Naomi and Joss at the bar. Joss spoke to Roxy in Mandarin, "Drinking on a school night? What's the legal drinking age here?"

Roxy threw Joss a look of disdain and ignored her question. "I've been coming here since I was fourteen."

Shannon turned to Joss and gestured for her to get closer, like she was about to share a secret. She said she was looking for a foreigner girlfriend. She wondered if Joss knew any *laowai* lesbian friends whom she could match her up with.

"Why do you only want to date a laowai?" Joss asked. Shannon replied that her parents were unaware of her sexual orientation, and that she hoped to leave China with a foreigner girlfriend to a more gay-friendly country. Her parents were already trying to set her up on blind dates.

"Eight years ago, homosexuality was still classified as a mental illness by the government," Shannon sighed. "But Shanghai has come a long way on this issue." Joss nodded. Just last year the city hosted its first gay pride event.

Meanwhile, Roxy was grilling Naomi about her life story. What was it like living in Tokyo? (Roxy was a big fan of Japanese soaps, especially "Hyoryu Net Café.") What about Manhattan? ("Are New Yorkers really like Carrie Bradshaw?") Did she feel more Taiwanese or more Japanese? ("Because you look more Japanese.") Could she get her an internship at Jun Cleo? ("I'll ask," Naomi promised.)

"How old are you anyway?" The interrogation continued.

"Twenty-seven." Naomi sipped on her cocktail.

Roxy's eyes widened. "Will you get married soon? You don't want to be a *sheng nu*."

Maybe it was the martini talking, but Naomi suddenly found herself confiding in the seventeen-year-old. She told Roxy about Seth, about how she had become a jilted fiancé. Before Naomi could finish her story, Roxy interrupted her. "Does he have *che fang*?"

Naomi had heard that in China, *che fang*, "house and car," was almost a prerequisite for a marriage proposal. Naomi explained that Seth had company housing, not a mortgage. As for transportation, Seth had relied on taxis and the metro in Manhattan, as is the case here in Shanghai. Roxy shook her head, "No house, no wedding. Good thing you didn't marry him." The statement made Naomi laugh. She wanted to explain to Roxy that she didn't care much for the *che fang*, that her conditions for love had a different set of standards, that she just yearned for something true. No matter, Naomi thought wryly, Seth had failed both criterions.

Naomi was amused that at a mere seventeen years of age, Roxy was already so pragmatic. Roxy reminded Naomi again that she needed to find a new boyfriend soon, so she wouldn't remain a *sheng nu*, a leftover woman—a term relegated to women over twenty-six years old who were educated professional urbanites and unmarried.

"So," Roxy continued, "why don't you sign up for Jiayuan?" She explained that Jiayuan was a popular online dating website in China, and that her own cousin had met his wife there.

Before Naomi could respond, Shannon returned with a Chinese boy adorned with tattoos that looked like intricate shirt sleeves. He whispered something in Roxy's ear.

"Do you want to *liu bing*?" Roxy asked Naomi and Joss. Shannon and the boy smiled conspiratorially.

"Ice skate?" Naomi exclaimed, looking confused. She recognized the vocabulary from her Chinese class.

Joss had heard the expression before and knew it had nothing to do with ice. "She's asking if you want crystal meth," she explained to Naomi. Joss knew that Ephedra Sinica, the essential ingredient in meth, was sourced in China. In fact, the plant had a place in traditional Chinese medicine.

"No, drinking is our drug of choice," Joss replied.

Joss and Naomi gave Roxy a concerned look. "How long have you been *xi du?*" Joss asked Roxy. Naomi knew it literally meant "inhaling poison." Doing drugs.

Roxy laughed. "Fifteen? Sixteen? Just like American high schoolers, right?" Roxy said they loved watching "90210."

After they left the bar, Naomi insisted on sending Roxy home. Roxy dozed off in the taxi, resting her head on Naomi's shoulder. She was a decade older than Roxy. To Naomi, Roxy and her friends were foals, bright young things just teetering. In a way, Roxy reminded Naomi of herself when she was seventeen—tried too hard to fit in, oblivious to the fact that actions were not inconsequential, that the real world was not a pop song.

8

SMALL WORLD

ON THE BANKS OF SUZHOU CREEK, NAOMI HURRIED PAST THE Shanghai Post Office and Museum, a nearly hundred-year-old building with stately Corinthian columns. Naomi looked up. Atop the building was an ornate Baroque clock tower guarded by bronze statues of the Greek gods Aphrodite, Eros and Hermes, peering down at pedestrians. Naomi had been to this part of town with Joss before, to attend a sculptural exhibit by a Chinese-Chilean artist. The once derelict warehouses along Suzhou Creek had mostly been converted into art galleries, trendy boutiques and hipster tea joints. Joss said Tay frequented the galleries along Suzhou Creek and Moganshan Lu for work.

Xiu Station Art Gallery was adjacent to the museum. Naomi checked her watch. She was thirteen minutes late. She hoped nobody would notice.

"Naomi! What took you so long? Go assist Pearla in the press room."

"Sorry Cher," Naomi said, her cheeks burning. It was her first client event. She should've spent less time worrying about what to wear and allotted more time to the commute.

Naomi rounded the corner, passed the gallery hall and sprinted towards the media room. She found Pearla Lin in the center of a semi-circle, fielding questions left and right from the media and guests. The clients from the Japanese sneaker brand, Zijuno, were also present. The tension in the room was palpable.

"What did I miss?" Naomi whispered to Amos Kim, the Account Manager for Zijuno.

Amos yawned. "Oh you know, a bunch of disgruntled Chinese journalists. Just another day for a foreign fashion brand in China."

Naomi nodded knowingly. She had learned through her orientation a slew of cautionary tales. One American fashion label committed political gaffe when it sold a t-shirt featuring a map of China. The map elicited harsh criticism for leaving out several disputed territories, which then led to a swift boycott of the brand. Another British brand faced backlash for releasing a marketing video depicting a Chinese model struggling to do the waltz, who then did kung fu moves instead. Even though their PR team had attempted to gloss it over as an ironic and humorous statement, the damage had been done; the brand closed up shop recently.

Naomi glimpsed at the multiple paintings and three-dimensional art pieces hung on the walls. This exhibition was a collaboration between Zijuno and Taka, a celebrated Japanese artist. Naomi took a closer look. Some pieces featured similar themes—a sun rising over the Pearl Tower and dragons. One digital art piece displayed a samurai wearing Zijuno sneakers and pointing his sword in the direction of a panda.

Chinese journalists cornered Cher and Pearla, criticizing the art themes as Japanese dominance over China, evoking the bloody conflict between the two countries during World War Two. Japanese journalists who had flown in from Tokyo for the event appeared to be upset by the commotion and disrespectful commentary towards Taka, who was considered a national treasure. The Yokohama-born artist did not make an appearance himself, staying true to his personal principle of refusing commercial occasions, a stance which appealed to his cult following. Another Chinese journalist interpreted Taka's absence as a sign of contempt towards China.

While Naomi reasoned with the Japanese media, Pearla tried to pacify the Chinese editors. Roxy, who had just started the internship with Jun Cleo by way of Naomi, was using another tactic altogether.

Roxy weaved in and out of the irritated clusters of male dominant Chinese journalists, offering cocktails on a tray. She bowed to each editor as she passed out the beverages, and called them *lao-shi* (teacher), or *ge* (older brother) to the younger reporters. She was wearing a skirt that looked more suitable for playing tennis rather than for a client's corporate function.

"If you ask me," chirped Roxy, "that panda looks barely threatened by the samurai. Just look at the proportions, the samurai is not even half the size of the panda. The panda looks serene and confident, and the samurai is merely waving his sword in a friendly way to get the panda's attention. And look at the claws on that panda and the strength of the bamboo in its hands, the samurai is undoubtedly no match for the panda." Roxy went on to explain that her father was a native of Chengdu, the nation's breeding ground for pandas, so she knew a thing or two about the beloved creature.

Roxy's voice was soft and syrupy sweet. She laughed in a way that sounded like notes dancing off a stringed harp. She skittered around each editor, pouring tea in their cups. The journalists looked momentarily amused by the distraction. Her commentary was so endearingly juvenile that only Roxy could pull it off.

By the end of the night, Naomi and Pearla were able to diffuse some of the tension and bad press by offering more red envelopes to the editors. Red envelopes were stipends, ranging anywhere from six hundred to twelve hundred renminbi. It was the industry norm in China to distribute red envelopes to the press.

Some editors could not be appeased however, and scathing reviews of the exhibition ensued.

But it worked to Zijuno's advantage, since the controversy only boosted the exhibit's ticket sales, bolstering brand intrigue. The clients were marvelously happy about the entire episode.

*

It was so cliché Naomi let out a bitter sigh. There it was on her phone, the text message from Seth she had waited in distress for since their breakup last September. If she had received this even just a month ago, she would've been roused. But now, she wasn't sure how she felt anymore.

Seth's text message asked to get a drink, to catch up "for old time's sake." Naomi didn't respond to him for nearly twenty hours. The next day, Seth texted her again, asking to meet at Park Hyatt's bar in Lujiazui.

Naomi was torn. She had been down this road before, knew this dance, and it usually didn't end well. The rational side of her brain was flashing warning signals, telling her to ignore him.

But as usual, her neurotic side prevailed.

Naomi texted back and said she was only available to meet for half an hour. She knew exactly what she'd wear—the new Helmut Lang cocktail dress she had just purchased. It resembled another dress he had been familiar with, one that he had particularly favored.

Naomi thought she was a in a good place to meet him. She trusted herself to see him and not wilt. She had a respectable new job working with some of the biggest brands in the world, a fabulous new dress (in a shade of white that signified fresh beginnings), a new look (she had recently splurged on expensive highlights), and a new apartment. A certain optimism lingered, and she knew it had put a buoyant bounce in her step, a more assured look in her eyes, a striking refinement to her poise.

She couldn't wait for him to notice.

Naomi took off her bulky parka jacket as soon as she stepped into the cavernous lobby of the Park Hyatt, an eighty-seven-story elevator ride up from the ground floor of the Shanghai World Financial Center. It was only thirteen degrees Celsius outside, and although the jacket was cumbersome, she depended on it to keep warm since underneath it her dress had no such effect. She had paired her backless halter with a sheer cardigan and camel-colored suede boots, her hair in a bouffant-style ponytail. She gave herself another once-over in the elevator mirrors before stepping out.

Seth was already seated at the bar, scrolling through his phone with a glass of Suntory in front of him. He was in a new suit, and his hair looked longer. Watching him, she felt a wave of nostalgia wash over. How many times had she sneaked up on him behind a bar in Manhattan, shielded his eyes with her fingers, whispering *guess who?*

Naomi took a deep breath and approached him. "Hey you," she smiled with pursed lips. He leaned in for an embrace, but she slid past him onto a bar stool.

"You're not going to knock me out again, are you? You're getting good at aiming, real good." He flashed her a wide grin.

She gave a glare that said, *don't start.*

"Too soon, I know. May I say though, you look good...I mean it." He tried to hold her gaze but she turned to the bartender and ordered a drink.

"What do you think?" He gestured at the view. "You're inside the world's tallest hotel right now."

"I've been here."

"Oh yeah?" He gave her a sideways glance. Even though they hadn't spoken in nearly six months, Naomi recognized that tone. He was trying to guess who she had come with.

"How's corporate life? I always thought you didn't like routine office jobs, that's why working in retail seemed to suit you." He swilled his glass of whiskey.

"It's fine. Takes some getting used to. Nothing I can't handle," she replied a little too defensively. "I'm learning a lot, especially about the Chinese luxury market," she kept her tone steady, trying to present an intellectual demeanor. "It's mind-boggling to think that China, still considered a developing nation, is now competing as the number one luxury market in the world." She continued to list her projects for the World Expo.

"Fascinating. My dad's been to a world's fair, the one in Queens. It was in the sixties I think. Did you know Walt Disney tested out his *It's a Small World* ride at that world's fair?"

She suppressed a smile. He was trying to play the *did you know* game with her again. She usually lost because his brain was filled with useless trivia and hers was not.

"Did you know China already held a world's fair a hundred years ago? It was in Nanjing and only fourteen countries participated," she spouted.

He looked impressed. "Did you know there was a serial killer on the loose during the Chicago world's fair? Dozens of festival-goers were killed by a deranged murderer."

"Of course you would know the most gruesome info."

He took a step closer, his voice low. "Did you know…that you're the hottest woman in the room right now?"

His gaze pored over her lips. Her eyes lingered on his for a moment, before she quickly looked away.

Naomi remembered her first meeting with Seth like it was yesterday. It had only been several months after the Rex fiasco. She hadn't been looking to date, but there among clay statues of dead Chinese men, love bloomed.

They were at the Met, at a traveling exhibition featuring the first unified dynastic rule of China, the Qin dynasty. The exhibit chronicled the life and legacy of Qin Shi Huangdi, the first emperor of China, and his terracotta warriors.

After striking up a conversation with her, Seth had asked Naomi out that day, taking her on their first date to Nomwah Tea Parlor in Chinatown. They bonded over the experience of being hyphenated Asians, she a Japanese-Taiwanese-American, he a Chinese-Thai-Canadian. He was unlike any other twenty-eight-year-old she knew. All her other male friends were fattened versions of their college selves, still living to get high and get laid. Seth wasn't like Rex, or any of her exes.

Naomi continued to see Seth, and the following six months had seemed like a candy-colored reverie, all too good to be true.

True enough, it wasn't long before they started arguing about his schedule, his flirtations, or her demands, her insecurities.

There had been moments in their relationship, when Naomi had pondered the ironic reality of being intimate with Seth, of feeling so alienated even when they were in the same room, as if their orbits were made of substances mutually exclusive, never colliding.

Naomi sipped on her cocktail. Across from her seat inside the Park Hyatt's bar, the windows gave a sparkling vista of Lujiazui's multihued illuminations reflecting off the Huangpu River.

Seth held out his hand. "Care to take in the view?" He gestured at an unoccupied corner of the far side of the bar, near the floor-to-ceiling windows.

Unfazed, she ignored his outstretched palm and walked boldly towards the windows, giving Seth a close-up of her backless, flouncing dress. She tried to calm her nerves as she looked down at the city, its skyline an ever-shifting spectacle of lights. She was starting to get dizzy from the heights and could feel his breath on her back. *What now? What am I doing here?*

She had been waiting for this moment. Maybe he was about to tell her how stupid he was, how lucky he'd been, how blind as a bat he was not to cherish her. Maybe she'd savor the victorious moment, tell him it's too late, and then walk away sashaying, head held high, the way the film heroine gracefully snubs the jerk.

He approached slowly, breathing down her bare shoulders, standing behind her. He now cornered her, knuckle tracing her spine. *The nerve,* she thought. It was all so familiar, yet it wasn't anymore. Now, it only made her feel small.

Then, the assault. It came out of nowhere.

Naomi was still trying to decipher her mixed feelings, when a splatter of burgundy abruptly stormed her eyes amidst gasps, dripping down the collar of her Helmut Lang dress. Seth had reached out to block the incoming attack, but in swiping away the hand of the attacker, the glass had inadvertently turned towards Naomi's cheek.

The woman in the vermilion-colored dress doubled over, guffawed something in Chinese, and started pointing and laughing at Seth. Or maybe she was laughing at Naomi. The woman was still holding the now empty wine glass.

The woman looked familiar. Then it hit Naomi in her sinking stomach—this was the sexting girl. Jo.

Naomi felt her throat close up. Jo was flanked by four other Chinese girls who were chortling and taking photos of them. The image of Jo on Seth's phone came flooding back. Naomi shivered from the dampness of her dress and the chilly air. She was now cognizant of the flagrant gawking from bystanders who were hovering around them, as if they were eagerly anticipating a fight to break out.

Jo smirked and started stalking off with her entourage, but then turned around to add one more insult to injury. "By the way," she sneered in English, turning towards Naomi, "he didn't say he was engaged. He said you were a *friend*."

Seth looked like he was about to say something, but the tallest girl in Jo's posse bellowed at him, "Stay away from Jo!" Before Seth could react, the girl made a grand spectacle of spitting in his face. Some onlookers had their iPhones out and were snapping away, others were howling with laughter and clapping.

Naomi willed herself not to cry. DO. NOT. CRY. Even as she was focusing on these three words, pushing through the crowds and sprinting towards the exit elevator, she could feel the shit storm swirling inside her head, the prickly sensation of hot tears welling near her nose, threatening to further undo her disheveled appearance at any minute. She felt herself shaking. She tried to hold back the deluge of emotion that was pooling in her chest as she frantically pressed the elevator button to shut before anyone else could step in.

As soon as she was alone in the elevator, she let the tears engulf her. The wall-to-wall mirrors in the elevator gave an eerie illusion of a never-ending version of herself, bent over and sobbing. Blotches of wine stains formed erratic maroon patterns on the front of her dress, which for a moment, resembled a bloody aftermath of piercing stab wounds.

PART *2*

SHANGHAI TO THE WORLD

Spring 2010 – Spring 2011

"The future was right where you were standing and what was small had become big, the scale had enlarged and you were no longer looking down at it, but standing in it, on this corner of the future, right here in the World's Fair!"

—E.L. DOCTOROW,
WORLD'S FAIR

"You meet the one...amongst thousands and tens of thousands of people, amidst thousands and tens of thousands of years, in the boundless wilderness of time, not a step sooner, not a step later."

—EILEEN CHANG,
LOVE (TRANS. QIAOMEI TANG)

1

LA VILLE SENSUELLE

By May, temperatures had climbed steadily. Scarves gradually came off and skirts had hiked up. It was Naomi's first spring in Shanghai. Tulip fields flourished in the north side of the city, magnolias bloomed near the Huangpu, cherry blossoms saturated Luxun park.

A herculean infrastructure overhaul had radically transformed Shanghai in the months leading up to the World Expo, akin to somebody undergoing a massive facelift. There seemed to be no escaping the fervor and buzz of Operation Shanghai Makeover. The colossal clean-up effort was evident in all corners of the city. Streets and buildings received new paint jobs. Metro lines got scrubbed squeaky sterile. Masses of pirated DVD storefronts and imitation goods shops disappeared. Road signage was checked for English accuracy and misspelled ones were replaced.

A 'round-the-clock sledgehammer noise seemed to live right outside of Naomi's apartment. Raucous machines plowed out canyons, creating clouds of dirt dust. The smell of demolition and the overnight scaffolding was as ubiquitous as the buildings that overran the city. Yesterday, Naomi was almost hit by debris flying out of an abandoned shop on Jianguo Lu. The workers wielding power tools inside had looked oblivious to the pedestrians who were walking less than five feet away, trying to avoid cars on one side and falling into a construction zone on the other. Some of the construction crew held lit cigarettes in their mouths as they worked without hard hats. All over the city, migrant workers dangled off the side of buildings, climbing ladders, jackhammering from dawn to dusk.

Installations of one peculiar looking cartoon character, which resembled the love child between a Smurf and Gumby, had sprouted in arbitrary locations across the city. The blue grinning creature's name was *Hai Bao*, treasure of the sea, and it was the mascot of Expo.

The Chinese characters *wen ming*, "civilized," were plastered on signs hanging on storefronts and street corners, admonishing passersby to remember their manners. The government had issued booklets to the city's residents, a guide on *civil behavior*. The beggars sitting near the entrance of Naomi's apartment—the old woman holding a swaddled infant, the man on crutches—had also vanished overnight. Naomi hoped and prayed that they had at least been subjected to civil treatment.

Non-Chinese mouths emitting Mandarin consonants were no longer a sight to marvel at. At Expo, nearly every country pavilion Joss passed by had a foreigner staff speaking fluent Chinese.

Officially, the French titled their pavilion La Ville Sensuelle. It was surrounded by a moat-like stream and created the illusion of a fantasy fortress floating above the waters. The pavilion was a diamond-shaped, trellis-like structure with gardens, plants, fountains, flora and fauna sprouting everywhere—hanging from the ceilings, bursting on the roof, blooming from the walls. The garden atmosphere was accentuated with video projections of the sights of Paris, Nice, and Marseille, accompanied by the sound effects of French films and lyrical melodies. The structure was conceived to aspire to the Guggenheim, where visitors start on the top floor, and make their way down to ground level.

Joss found Naomi on the second floor, stationed at Chantevieve's exhibit space, gated by a replica of an art nouveau entrance to a Parisian metro. The brand's video projection entertained visitors with digital artistic renderings of the Seine, Notre Dame, Versailles, and featured a fanciful starlet voyaging from Paris to Shanghai, collecting falling stars along the way.

"My shift ends in ten minutes," Naomi said, checking her watch.

"How are you feeling? Tired?" Joss asked as she handed Naomi a water bottle. "You've been on your feet since nine in the morning, right?"

"Eight, actually." Naomi shrugged. "I feel fine though. In a way, I think my retail jobs had prepared me for this gig." She took a gulp of water. "How was lunch?"

Joss recounted the menu at 6 SENS, the Michelin rated restaurant atop the French pavilion: sea scallops carpaccio, gruyere tuiles, langoustine ravioli, shellfish bisque, hazelnut soufflé. "The gruyere tuiles dish here is comparable to the one I had near the French Alps. That's some work perk you have here!" she exclaimed.

"Well the staff menu isn't quite as elaborate, but still, it's been nice. I haven't been dining here as much as I should, there are way too many pavilion restaurants out there to try."

Joss nodded enthusiastically. "So I hear! Which one should we check out first?"

"Here," Naomi gave Joss an Expo map with routes she had highlighted in yellow. "I've already mapped out our itinerary!" Naomi had switched shifts with a colleague so she could accompany Joss at Expo today. They were like giddy schoolgirls on a trip to Disney's Epcot.

Naomi's staff pass and Joss's press pass enabled them to skip the long lines to the pavilions. Navigating through the sea of human traffic at Expo was challenging, even more so as people habitually used parasols to protect from the sun. Getting poked in the head by somebody's "sunbrella" was not uncommon. It also wasn't unusual for people to cut through lines, therefore one had to battle their way through the queues. This meant minimal elbow space in front, lest the person behind conveniently slither through. On peak days, some lines reached interminable lengths of ridiculousness. Joss had heard the line to enter the Saudi Arabian pavilion had been nine hours long one day. Some scheming entrepreneurs made a business of selling scalper "fast-lane" tickets into various popular pavilions. Naomi had witnessed firsthand of other pavilion staff successfully selling fast-entry admission for an equivalent of a hundred U.S. dollars. So, for five times the price of the entire Expo ticket, you could buy a quick pass and gain entry through a secret doorway. Some visitors were undeterred by the long queues and continued to line up once they entered the pavilions to collect country stamps on their prized Expo passport. Collecting the most stamps on Expo passports seemingly became an Olympic game in and of itself.

In the following six hours, Naomi and Joss had made an impressive round of some of Expo's most popular pavilions, including: the Swiss pavilion which gave guests a reprieve from the crowds and heat with their "ski lifts" (cable car ride), hoisting visitors "across the Alps" (faux snow-capped mountains) to a view of the entire Expo site. Spain's key feature was a gigantic animatronic baby named Miguel, which represented future generations, but also appeared to be frightening some children. The United Kingdom garnered much praise for its Seed Cathedral, which housed sixty thousand botanical seeds sourced from Kunming, each illuminated within the darkened sanctum of the cathedral, creating an installation highlighting the luminosity of life. North Korea's pavilion also received much attention as this was the hermit kingdom's first time exhibiting at a world's fair; their LEDs showed "true footage" of the peace, progress and happiness of North Koreans (the good-looking and well-dressed characters in the video were not unlike a Korean TV drama). The Cuban pavilion simply consisted of a lone bar selling Havana club rum drinks and a souvenir shop where one could enjoy a rare Cuban cigar. Denmark had its national treasure, the original Mermaid sculpture, moved from its home in Copenhagen to Shanghai, so she could reign over a sea of saltwater at the Danish pavilion. Cirque Du Soleil performers entertained guests in line at the Canadian pavilion. The Russian pavilion was a fairytale storybook land, and other highlights included a singing robot in the Japanese pavilion, a tea ceremony demonstration in the Taiwanese pavilion, Mexico's sea of kites, Italy's high-fashion exhibit, Belgium's Smurf display, Israel's seashell-like pavilion structure, and the Netherlands' grand lawn with faux sheep and faux grass (where scores of visitors took naps since it was one of the few pavilion resting places with shade, and without a line). Pavilions tried to outdo each other with entertainment and when evening fell, the site was transformed into a neon light show akin to Las Vegas.

But the pavilion that Joss was most excited to see was the one representing the country of her birthplace. The China pavilion was a gargantuan scarlet structure which resembled an ancient imperial edifice, channeling the Forbidden City. Indeed it seemed like the forbidden city of Expo; it was so popular that entering was virtually impossible for most visitors, unless you were prepared to wait in the heat for over five hours. Even with their fast passes Joss and Naomi still waited in line for over an hour. Once inside, Joss made a dash to the main attraction: a wall-to-wall digitally animated version of one of China's most famous art painted in the twelfth-century, "Along the River at Qingming Festival," which featured more than 800 people and 70 animals. The original version was housed in the capital's Palace Museum and to prevent damage, seldom publicly exhibited. The sheer size of the crowd congregated in front of the 3D animated "Along the River at Qingming Festival," reminded Joss of the massive throng of viewers assembled before the "Mona Lisa" at the Louvre.

It was the USA pavilion's rule to permit U.S. passport holders into the express queue, Joss and Naomi were relieved to hear. Some days the lines there were more than four hours long.

When they arrived at the USA pavilion, a staff member explained that the pavilion would be closing early for a special visitor. Naomi wondered which American celebrity was visiting—previously there had been Harry Connick Jr., Hillary Clinton, Miss America, Claire Danes.

It was now eight in the evening. Naomi and Joss were able to squeeze their way into the last batch of visitors of the day. As they were finishing up the tour, Naomi felt an onset of stomach pains. She desperately needed to use the restroom. The lack of available restrooms was one of the biggest complaints about Expo. There were stories of children who could not hold their bladder while waiting in the lines, who had defecated at random Expo grounds.

Naomi was panicking now. She felt her bladder would give out at any minute. As they were being ushered out, Naomi pleaded with a staff named Tim to let her use the pavilion restrooms. Tim looked sympathetic but gave Naomi a firm headshake; the VIP visitor would be arriving soon.

While Naomi was talking to Tim, Joss had turned to a staff with a name tag that read "Gu Kong" manning the stairs to the second floor. She asked him politely in Shanghainese if her sick friend could just use the toilet for a minute. "By the way, you and I share the same surname. I'm also a Kong!" Joss added, giving him her most winning smile. Gu hesitated for a second, then agreed to take only one of them to the restrooms. Tim had already left. Joss grabbed Naomi's hand and thrust her towards the stairs, where Gu was waiting to take her up.

Naomi gave Gu a grateful look and hurried to a restroom stall inside the VIP area. She took a quick glance and saw that people were running to and fro, laying out food and beverages, wiping down tables. She tried to relieve herself as quickly as possible.

Naomi was just finishing up and zipping her jeans when she heard a commotion outside and then clapping. She quickly exited the stall and washed and dried her hands. Just as she pulled opened the door, she ran into a woman with a headset on, juggling a purse, a dress, and two phones.

The woman looked at Naomi like she was a criminal.

"Sorry, I was just about to leave," Naomi explained.

"You're not supposed to be here," she said, looking at Naomi menacingly. She turned around to the woman behind her. "I apologize, Vera."

Naomi peered behind the woman. She did a double take. It was Vera Wang!

"It's such an honor to meet you, Ms. Wang! My name is Naomi, I work at the French Pavilion," she blurted out.

"How wonderful, it's very nice to meet you, Naomi."

"Can I just say that your fall 2003 New York Fashion Week collection meant the world to me? I was a student at FIT and my senior show was based on that collection! I was so inspired by the Asian-influenced pieces, especially the origami-folded ribbons..."

The woman with the headset on was now glaring at Naomi and giving her a you-need-to-scram look.

"...anyway, you are so inspirational. Just wanted to tell you that!" Naomi gushed.

"Thank you!" Vera Wang threw her head back and laughed. "And are you still designing?"

Naomi shook her head.

"Well," Vera Wang continued, "I hope you pick it up again. You know, I started my business at forty years old." She checked her watch. "Okay, I think I'm supposed to be out there right now. You take care, Naomi."

"Thank you!" Naomi waved. She scurried out the door.

Once she exited the pavilion, she squealed at Joss.

"Guess who I just saw!"

"What a day!" Naomi exclaimed, as she and Joss sat down at the Hakuna Matata fast food joint. They had just visited their last stop of the day, the Joint African pavilion. The imposing structure was one of the largest at Expo, housing installations from more than forty African countries. Naomi had been fascinated with its exhibits, including a replica of Ethiopia's Harar Jugol structures and a display of its eight World Heritage sites, Chad's exhibit of the Sahel desert and grasslands, and the Sudanese installation of the Suakin Gate.

"You have enough material for your article?" Naomi asked.

"Got some juicy tidbits. Did you hear about what happened at the Indian pavilion?" Joss replied as she bit into her ostrich meat sandwich.

Naomi shook her head. "What's the scoop?"

"Apparently an Expo bureau official stormed into the Indian pavilion this morning and caused a big ruckus. He tore down all the maps exhibited inside. On top of that, the Chinese government denied a visa to a big-shot Indian General."

"Wow. A political dispute, huh?"

Joss nodded. She explained that the maps at the India Pavilion had exhibited certain parts of Tibet and Arunachal Pradesh as Indian territory, which China considered as part of its Tibetan Autonomous Region.

Joss went on to describe another territorial dispute of a different nature, currently brewing inside the USA pavilion. "This feud between Coke and Pepsi is hilarious, you won't believe how immature these corporate executives are acting." She explained that Pepsi was the official sponsor of the USA pavilion, but because Coke was the official beverage provider of the entire Expo appointed by the Chinese government, Coke was making it extra difficult for Pepsi to conduct any marketing activity at Expo.

"So in the end, a compromise was reached. The Pepsi cart will now be situated near the front door of the pavilion, which is only about thirty-five meters from its original location. A war almost broke out for a measly thirty-five meters!"

"But this feud is so distinctly American!" Naomi laughed. "I mean there is an entire hall in the USA pavilion dedicated to corporate sponsors." *Of course* a conflict of this nature would occur in the American realm of Expo.

Joss's phone buzzed and she picked it up on the first ring. Naomi could tell it was Tay. "Yeah…I know…probably in an hour. Just having dinner…okay then…bye." Joss hung up. "Tay's worried I won't wake up in time for the flight tomorrow."

"Singapore right? Is it for his business trip?"

"Um, kind of. Yes and no." Joss shifted in her seat. "Anyway, how was the date with Amos? He's kind of cute."

Naomi made a face. "And he knows it too." Amos Kim, the pompous Korean-Australian strategy consultant, had asked her out three weeks after she arrived at Jun Cleo, giving her a wink and an obnoxious once-over. It seemed like he was smoothing his hair over with his palm every fifteen minutes. The old Naomi would have welcomed his advances. He was the aggressive, chauvinistic type that she usually decided to date, or as Joss put it, chose to self-flagellate with. But Naomi was not about to let a workplace fling sidetrack her from her first real career opportunity.

"The date was horrific. I think he was flirting with the girl at the next table. Not that I cared. Honestly, I don't know if I'm ready yet."

Joss's tone softened. "Of course, after what you went through? It's understandable."

It's not that Naomi still harbored romantic feelings for Seth. Those feelings had long since dissipated. She was more floored by how far off her judgment had been. Was there ever a moment in which they brought out the best in each other?

Joss had been furious when she learned about the debacle at Park Hyatt. She was ready to storm Seth's workplace and give him blood. But at this point, Naomi just wanted a civil ending. During a good chunk of their relationship, all the on-and-off in New York, the ex prefix had been his title. Now it would be permanent.

Naomi looked at the bare spot on her left hand where the diamond once sparkled. Some days, she had to admit that she missed wearing the ring, more than anything else. Not because she missed that piece of jewelry, but because at that point she had thought she was done with the dating pool, had been ready to shelve all the mistakes and trauma, was proud to proclaim the quest was over——that she'd found love.

Although she no longer wanted anything to do with Seth, she wished there had been a closure of some sort. She had expected just one apologetic call, text, or e-mail. But it had been three months since that disastrous night at Park Hyatt, and still no word. There were times she would ponder how? How could he not call her, after all they had been through? Was she that forgettable?

Joss said that Seth just "didn't have the balls to face her" after what had transpired. But Naomi didn't believe the solitary reason was that he was spineless. No, the radio silence was from something far more spiteful. It was a punishing indifference, a certain apathy.

For the very first time, Naomi saw something she had failed to detect before. She saw that Seth Ray could be cruel.

2

SEA TURTLE

In Shanghai, June was the moody, mercurial sister among her siblings in the calendar. The sixth month, as the Chinese called her, was usually *meiyu*, plum rain season, and her patterns were consistently misunderstood, especially by weather forecasters. It would shower when the prediction was supposedly sunny, shooing throngs of pedestrians underneath pitifully thin awnings of storefronts, sending entrepreneurial umbrella and raincoat vendors to set up impromptu stalls on street corners, leaving pedestrians dodging and children sloshing in pond-like puddles on uneven sidewalks in its wake.

The month-long inclement climate conditions made living in this city an unpredictable affair. Events and gatherings were frequently cancelled or postponed. Then when it was suddenly unclouded and sun-drenched, the whole city seemed to converge out of their homes and offices, crowding sidewalks and terraces with spur-of-the-moment luncheons. Jing'An Park and Zhongshan Park would be packed within minutes, teeming with unrestrained dogs, untethered children, chess-playing geriatrics. But just as soon as they'd laid their picnic blankets on the greens, another downpour would charge in like an unwelcome guest, leaving the parks deserted again, save the forgotten litter. After getting caught in abrupt showers twice, Naomi learned her lesson and kept a foldable umbrella in her bag.

Naomi descended the elevators of her work building on Wukang Lu. She stepped out of the powerfully air-conditioned edifice and snapped opened her yellow umbrella. The evening air felt muggy and heavy. There had been torrential rain earlier, but fortunately now the deluge had slowed to a mild drizzle. She liked that her canary-colored umbrella was a bright speck among the wet gloom, helping her stand out among the rest on the street, making it easier for her to flag down a taxi, especially on rainy days when the numbers of available cabs dwindled. All around her, harried commuters were clomping and clicking down the pavement, whizzing by, rushing past her.

Damn, she was already late. It was Logan's new dessert bar opening shindig tonight, and Naomi had promised to take it on as a pro bono marketing case. She was supposed to be at the venue in five minutes, managing all the lifestyle editors who'd been invited to the event.

As Naomi struggled to close her umbrella while opening the taxi door, Amos Kim appeared and held open the door. "Mind if we share? It's going to take forever to get a cab in this weather." Amos barely waited for her answer before squeezing in. He leaned against his seat and Naomi felt his eyes travel all over her as she gave the taxi driver the address. "What's going on at Xinhua Lu?"

She explained her crisis. In no time, Amos was calling Qi, the media expert on his team to meet him at Logan's venue. "Qi will handle this like a pro," Amos reassured Naomi. "All I need to do is to give Qi tomorrow morning off."

Naomi protested a little. She didn't want Qi to feel pressured to work after-hours when this wasn't even a client that belonged to the agency. Amos shushed her. "It's my pleasure," he waggled his eyebrows.

Jujube Dessert Bar was hidden inside a traditional *shikumen*. Housed in a restored century-old vine-covered villa, the first floor was a patisserie-style cafe that included an outdoor garden, while the bar and lounge area occupied the second floor. Naomi recalled what Joss said about the jujube: also known as Chinese dates, the sweet, chewy jujube is a beloved fruit that had been cultivated in China for thousands of years.

Jujube Dessert Bar was the first of its kind in Shanghai. Almost every dessert, beverage, cocktail, or dish on the menu had a jujube theme or ingredient in it. By the time Naomi and Amos arrived, Qi had already completed the task. The handful of editors that had been invited were sipping on honey jujube cocktails, munching on amaranth black jujube cake, or dipping into their jujube ice cream sundaes, looking visibly satisfied. Logan greeted Naomi warmly, "I owe you big time." She swiftly transferred the credit to Amos.

It was Logan Hayden's first time meeting Amos Kim, and they had hit it off immediately, as if it were a bromance waiting to happen. Naomi had an inkling they'd get along. They were the same type: braggadocious, chauvinistic, with a borderline attention-deficit disorder.

She checked her phone. Joss texted and said she was running late from Tay's medical appointment. Naomi looked around. Amos and Logan were at the bar near the DJ stand now, surrounded by half a dozen women. Naomi's stomach started to grumble. Just as she was devouring some chocolate-covered stuffed jujubes, somebody tapped her on the shoulder.

She turned around, her chocolate-covered fingers flew to her mouth.

It was Dante!

All week long she'd been wondering about Dante Ouyang, whom she had met on a China Eastern airlines flight from Beijing back to Shanghai last weekend. The flight had been delayed, so it was nearly midnight by the time they departed. On top of that, she had a middle seat.

Naomi had fallen into a stupor state of sleepiness immediately after boarding, but had been woken up by loud bickering some moments later. The woman sitting on her right had shouted at the man behind her for propping up his foot on her armrest. The man had hurled back insults. A meek flight attendant had tried to break up the fight to no avail. Naomi had heard of the many disturbing disputes aboard Chinese domestic flights, but this was the first time she had a front row view.

Dante, seated on Naomi's left, had offered to switch places with her. She gratefully accepted the offer. Soon they began chatting but were disrupted by flight turbulence. Morbidly and ironically, they started talking about aviation disasters. Dante remembered that his mother's cousin had been on the fatal China Airlines flight that crashed in Hong Kong in 1996, and Naomi mentioned her father was a victim of a plane crash in Japan.

"I'm so sorry," he had nearly whispered, his eyes soft with sympathy.

"I don't remember it. I was a toddler," she had responded quickly.

"I can't believe one of our first conversations is about plane crashes."

"While we're on a plane!"

"Not the greatest pick-up line."

"Definitely not your finest moment. But you might get a chance to redeem yourself later," Naomi chuckled.

Their conversation on the flight hadn't lasted as long as she would've liked. She'd been exhausted and had napped for the rest of the journey. When the flight landed at Shanghai Hongqiao airport, she was mortified to find that she had dozed off on Dante's shoulder, slightly drooling on his jacket. Dante had laughed it off and said he would forgive her as long as he could see her again soon. They ended up sharing a cab after they had retrieved their luggage. He had insisted on sending her home first, even though his residence was closer to the airport than hers.

She recalled assessing that Dante was good-looking when they had first met. Tonight, he was positively debonair in a simple tee and Topman jeans. He was half a head taller than Naomi's five-seven frame, had strong shoulders, a rectangular forehead underneath a bush of thick hair, prominent brows with intense brown eyes and an angular jawline. The lines of his body were transparent under his white shirt, which looked like it'd been machine-washed a thousand times, the graphic in the front foregone and faded. She noticed the veins visible on his forearms. He was of Asian descent and spoke with a British accent, although his accent wasn't as overt as some of her colleagues from London.

Dante gave Naomi a European style double-cheek-kiss greeting. His lips grazed her chocolate-smeared cheek. "Yum, please tell me where I can get more of that."

Naomi laughed and dabbed her mouth with a napkin. "Dante! What a coincidence! What are you doing here?"

"I came to ask you one thing," Dante said. He looked at her with a mock-serious expression.

"Huh?"

"Your surname."

Naomi smiled. "So you can stalk me online?"

"Yes. That, and I need to know what to put in my phone. See, right now I have you down as Naomi the-girl-who-stole-my-plane-seat." He held up his phone to her face.

She laughed, took his phone, and typed in her full name. "There. Now you're able to google me."

Dante's friend approached. "Is this is the *mei nu* you wouldn't shut up about?" The guy grinned at them. Dante introduced him as Zach Ma, his colleague.

Naomi smiled. "Are you guys here because of Logan?" Sensing their blank looks, she added, "He's the owner of this place."

Zach shook his head. "We came to check out the restoration work of this villa. We might be using the same contractor for another heritage architectural project. We were just about to leave, but he insisted on staying after spotting you."

"Hey mate, don't you have somewhere else you need to be? Like, right about now?" Dante nudged him.

"Right. See you tomorrow then," Zach laughed and bid them goodbye.

"You're interested in the venue's restoration work? I can introduce you to Logan, he might have more information." She craned her neck and looked around. "Never mind, it looks like he's busy at the moment." Logan was encircled by a group of girls, a proud stamen surrounded by petals. She was blabbering now. Something about Dante made her heart skip a beat.

Dante picked up a glass of red jujube wine from a waiter circulating a serving tray. "It's okay Naomi, it's not Logan who I came for tonight." He locked eyes with her.

Naomi felt her cheeks reddened. There was a palpable tension rising between them. She could feel the intensity blooming from her chest, up towards her neck, radiating from her face. Dante led her to an empty booth and left for a minute to gather a drink for her. Naomi shifted in the high-backed leather seats and was glad for the quick moment to regain composure.

She remembered feeling embarrassed about falling asleep on him during the flight, and had been more reticent than usual that night at the airport. Now though, maybe it was the aphrodisiac concoction of liqueur and chocolate stuffed dates that emboldened her. Their conversation, although initially peppered with comfortable pauses, flowed effortlessly.

Their seat next to the window gave a clear view of the historic blue-domed Russian Orthodox Mission Church. Naomi took the time to admire the stunning piece of architecture. Sensing her interest, Dante gave her some background information: more than twenty thousand Russians lived in Shanghai during the thirties, which was when this church had been built. During the Cultural Revolution the church was in danger of being demolished, but locals had saved the building by hanging a large picture of Mao on the roof. The church had ceased religious services since then, and had assumed many identities over the years—a washing machine factory, a warehouse, a government office, a bar and a restaurant. Just recently the government designated it as an architectural heritage treasure to be preserved.

"Wow. How do you know so much?"

"Occupational hazard. I'm an architect, and I'm especially interested in heritage architecture. If you're into stuff like this, there are a number of organizations you can join, such as the Shanghai Art Deco Society, the Royal Asiatic Society. They sponsor educational events catered to people who are nostalgic for Old Shanghai. Zach and I are members."

"You nerds," Naomi teased.

"I'll admit to that. How about you, what do you do when you're not working?"

"I used to sketch a little, but that was ages ago. Right now Jun Cleo and Expo are keeping me busy. I wish I had more time for other things, but I'm fairly new to the experiential marketing industry, so there's lots to learn."

"Hey I'm working at Expo too! Our firm has projects at the Taiwan, Oman, and Peru pavilions, and at the Corporate pavilions zone."

Naomi's eyes lit up. *Another fellow Expo staff member!* They talked more about Expo, sharing mutual stories about dealing with the bureaucracy of Expo officials, and how Expo was one of their most peculiar but most memorable work experiences. Then the conversation veered to a variety of topics: their favorite bootleg TV shows from Shanghai's pirated DVD shops (his: "The Indian Doctor," hers: "Downton Abbey"), best place they'd visited (he: Bordeaux, she: Naoshima), preferred foods (his: Italian, hers: Japanese). They covered the requisite *Who What Where When Why* and were delighted to discover that they had moved to China at the same time—last August.

Although for Dante, it was a homecoming.

Dante had left China for London when he was just a boy. He recently returned to China when a lucrative job opportunity came his way. He had spent the first five months of the new job at the firm's Beijing headquarters, and had moved to Shanghai only in January. The move to Shanghai was also a chance to see his parents and relatives more often, who were still residing in Nanjing.

Naomi was reminded of the local terminology *hai gui*. Translated literally, it meant "ocean" and "return," or "overseas returnee." It was also a homonym with "sea turtle." The slang referred to those Chinese who left the motherland for a foreign education, then returned to contribute to China's workforce. It was an apt nickname; sea turtles typically undertake epic journeys at sea, before returning to their place of birth to mate. *Hai Gui* held a socially esteemed position, possessing the desirable trait of being foreign enough but still retaining the essence of their Chinese-ness.

Besides architecture, Dante's other obsession was culinary. He was in the middle of a story about a pasta class taken at the Castle of Costigliole d'Asti, when Amos and Logan slid in their booth—Logan to Dante's left, and Amos in the space next to Naomi. Dante complimented Logan on his cocktail version of *sujeonggwa*, a Korean tea traditionally made from jujubes, cinnamon, spices, ginger, persimmon, pine nuts. Logan's mixologist had added in rye whiskey, which gave it a delectable kick.

Amos, who seemed even more intoxicated than usual, was whispering in Naomi's ear, "Let's get outta here...whaddaya say..."

"I'm going to wait for Joss," Naomi whispered back, shooing away Amos impatiently. His hand was flirting dangerously at the hem of her skirt, trying to cop a feel under the table. She swatted him away. If Amos thought she'd compensate him with some post-work canoodling for helping her out tonight with the editors, well, he got it wrong. For some reason, she cared intensely about what Dante thought of her—this man whom she barely knew. She knew she didn't want Dante to think she was loose. She'd been called certain names before in what seemed like a lifetime ago—pre-Seth, pre-Shanghai—and it wasn't a reputation she wanted trailing her.

Under the table, Amos's hand roamed her left thigh now, and Naomi instinctively pushed him away. She hadn't meant to use so much force, but Amos was so drunk that he lost his balance and fell out of the booth onto the checkered marble floors. Sprawled out on his back, Amos looked stunned for a second, then burst out chortling in his hyena-esque laugh, convulsing on the floor, hooting and snorting as if he'd just been told the funniest joke in the world. "Get up you moron," Logan hollered.

Naomi tried to smile, but she was rattled by the whole incident now, and wasn't in the mood for any more of Amos's antics. Dante searched Naomi's eyes. "Are you okay? Do you want to leave?"

Naomi nodded. Dante offered to send her home, but she declined. She would find Joss and head somewhere else with her.

Some made relationships with cities through its cafes, its books, its museums, its language, its bars, its women. For Dante, he engaged with a city through its architecture, and those observations were best conducted through strolling its streets, ambling about aimlessly.

Dante especially enjoyed strolling the various *shikumen nongtang*, the historic alleyways where local communities have lived for generations. Plenty of shikumens in this city were home to the geometric shapes, symmetrical lines, and rich ornamentation characteristic of art deco design. The Yuyangli nongtang was a favorite, so were Bugao Li (Cite Bourgogne) and Kongjia Nong (Confucius Lane). In Asia, Shanghai boasted the most art deco inspired architecture. Although art deco was traditionally a western motif, in Shanghai there was an abundance of hybrid art deco with Chinese-influenced designs in their nongtangs, incorporating feng shui as well.

Dante found that strolling through these alleyways was a way to completely immerse himself in local life. He got a haircut in Wangyima nong once, where the barber didn't even have a storefront. He had several chairs lined outside his home with some hair cutting bibs and scissors. The haircut had cost him five renminbi, less than one euro. It wasn't the best haircut he'd ever had, but it wasn't bad either.

Although Dante had hoped to try the street food in the shikumens, or the skewered barbecue lambs sold by Hui Muslims in white caps on street corners, he was well aware that he had a sensitive stomach. He didn't entirely blame the locals who wanted to scrimp on cooking oil though. They led a hard life. When Dante had first arrived in Shanghai, he often walked past walls in various stages of dereliction—the crumbling brickwork and condemned buildings which were spray painted with a big red Chinese character for "tear down." These were people's homes, some of whom had lived their whole life there. But they had been resettled by the government due to the Expo. The Expo slogan "Better City, Better Life" was slapped in their face when they were served the resettlement notices, but in reality, it wasn't better for everybody.

Dante had heard of the injustices inflicted on some of the nongtang residents. Once, as he strolled through Xingping Li nongtang, he heard a loud commotion as a gang of what appeared to be migrant thugs harassing an elderly couple. A younger man, a relative maybe, was defending them against the gang. Then Dante realized that the gang was actually a demolition team. The nongtang was slated to be demolished for Expo, and although the elderly couple protested, the demolition team threatened to remove them forcefully. The younger relative had shouted angrily, "We'll get a lawyer!"

At Jiu An Fang nongtang, Dante had befriended Lao Zhou, a balding middle-aged man with thin gold framed eye glasses, who was a tailor and cobbler all in one. He had repaired a pair of shoes for Dante and afterwards they were as good as new. Lao Zhou had once said that some people were grateful for the government-imposed resettlement because the new housing assigned to them was modern, and much more livable. However, Lao Zhou also knew friends that were irate at the arrangement, not wanting to leave the place where they had grown up in, where generations of family and ancestors had raised their children. But most people just placidly accepted their fate. They were accustomed to being jostled around by the government and its surprises. Lao Zhou recounted how his own parents had been harassed by the Red Guards fifty years ago during the Cultural Revolution, right here in this very nongtang, where teenagers bearing red armbands had vandalized and destroyed his home.

Dante was no stranger to such stories. He had grown up hearing them from his own family. He was grateful to be near them now, to be back in China. Although China today bore little resemblance to the one from his youth. In fact, at times Shanghai seemed altogether like a foreign country.

Dante was relieved that Shanghai, like London, was a walkable city, or at least Puxi, the territory west of the Huangpu River, was mostly walkable as long as you knew how to navigate the dangers of cars ignoring traffic lights. Dante preferred Puxi over Pudong, the land mass east of the river. Pudong's boulevards were more like parade routes than pedestrian friendly streets. But Pudong was where his work was, and nowadays he was spending quite some time at the Expo site where he led architectural projects at a number of pavilions.

For an architect, Shanghai was an artist's canvas. Within the last two decades Pudong had morphed from farmland to one of the most concentrated clusters of skyscrapers the world had seen. It was a city within a city. Then, there were the mind-boggling statistics—currently the government was in the midst of more than a hundred airport projects around the country. In fifteen years, China would've built an astronomical number of skyscrapers enough to fill ten Manhattan-sized cities. Dante was astounded with China's efficiency in erecting infrastructure, a feat that other countries were unable to achieve at such neck-breaking speed.

At the same time when he'd been contemplating whether to take the Expo job, he had also received a job offer from Hong Kong, which he eventually declined. Hong Kong was the world's most vertically congested city. Architecturally, Dante felt Shanghai was still developing in many fascinating aspects, while Hong Kong was already a mature market.

It was a stroke of great fortune that he decided to tag along with Zach at the last minute to Jujube Dessert Bar, where he ran into Naomi Kita-Fan again. And the fact that she also worked at Expo! That was a definite sign.

It was strange, the simultaneous contradictory feeling of nerves stimulated by this beautiful creature, and the ease in which he felt he could open his soul to her. Before meeting Naomi, it was a feeling that had eluded him for a very long time.

3

IN THE MOOD

As Naomi ambled her way to work, the symphony of cicadas rang in her ears. The humming of these five-eyed creatures was their mating call, and it formed the soundtrack of summers in Shanghai. The sun prodded away the polluted grayness and the skies were enveloped in resplendent hues of blue, with verdant foliage from plane trees lining the streets. The heat rendered the ordinarily fast-paced city languid. People slowed down to slurp on their iced drinks, to fan themselves, to wipe their sweat off. Stylish millennials roamed in skirts and gladiator sandals, middle-aged local women stepped out in ankle socks and pumps. Old Chinese grandpas, shirtless and toothless, waved their delicate paper fans while lounging in bamboo chairs in front of their nongtangs. Western cafes filled their outdoor pavements with tables and chairs, and patrons wreathed in smiles sipped their chilled coffees or iced boba tea drinks. Hotel pools re-opened and would try to outdo each other in throwing the best pool parties. People seemed to be in a better mood. The once crabby taxi drivers would swear a little less, honk a little less fervently.

By July, Dante Ouyang was texting Naomi regularly. At first, it started out as brief, witty messages. She never texted back right away, although Joss encouraged her to. It had been nearly a year since the broken engagement.

One sweltering Wednesday night, instead of his usual text message, Dante had called her out of the blue. Naomi let it ring for five seconds before picking up and taking the call out to the patio where there was a slight breeze, plugging her electric fan on full blast. Her air conditioning had broken down yet again.

They talked for a solid hour. Naomi was surprised that the time flew by, how easily their conversation flowed. But she was sweating rivulets. She looked down, her sweat had now threatened to render her white shirt completely transparent. She was about to say she needed to hang up and jump in the shower, when Dante inquired if she was up for meeting.

"Right now?" Naomi replied incredulously. It was eight, she was in her pajamas, and she had an early morning meeting. "I don't think so."

"I don't mean it like that. I just think there is a great place to go right now. C'mon, I'll text you the address."

Half an hour later, Dante and Naomi were in thick parka jackets and gloves. They held fist-sized cherry-flavored vodka cocktails in glasses which were custom-designed from frozen Danish artesian water. The temperature inside Igloo was a crisp zero degrees Celsius. The walls, tables, and bar were constructed with ice derived from the Torne River on the border of Finland. Chandeliers made from ice hung in a corner, while a dragon ice sculpture guarded another. A rainbow of LED lights shimmied off the ice walls, creating a spectrum of radiance inside the compact venue. The DJ was spinning beats from a mix of techno and mandopop.

"Great way to escape the heat, right?" Dante grinned, shouting above the music.

"Brilliant," Naomi smiled.

He took another gulp of the vodka as nerves suddenly besieged him. *Keep it together man!* He felt like a fumbling idiot in the ridiculously bulky jacket, which he cursed, but simultaneously appreciated for making her look extra adorable.

Dante thought Naomi was probably among the best-looking girls he had ever seen. The swell of her lips looked delicious enough to eat. When she had fallen asleep on his shoulder on that fateful flight where they first met, Dante had taken advantage of his view. Her soft curls cascading across his shirt, he had to resist the urge to trace the arc of her nose.

He didn't dare move—he didn't want to awake her. But he did take the liberty of looking at her, of taking in her scent, which evoked a garden of wildflowers. Naomi reminded him of an art gallery painting, an exquisite Pre-Raphaelite nymph.

The word he would use to describe her was *ravishing*. She wasn't merely pretty, or gorgeous, or arresting. She was all of those things. But he knew plenty of beautiful women, Europe had been full of them. What Naomi was—ravishing—brought out the gentleman and animal in him. He wanted to admire her, ravage her, then be wrecked by her.

After two shots, he started swaying to the beats in front of the DJ stand on the makeshift dance floor. Naomi joined him, then they both doubled over with laughter. They looked ludicrous dancing in their cumbersome thermal jackets, the fur lined hoodies covering their heads.

Dante could feel the tangible heat and combustible energy radiating between them. It was as if they had brought along summer into this freezing sanctum.

After they exited Igloo, Dante proposed bowling near Shilipu Pier. Naomi hadn't bowled in years. She seldom went bowling in Manhattan, so the last time she held a bowling ball was probably when she was a teenager in California.

It wasn't the most popular choice as a first date activity in this city, and she wasn't exactly dressed appropriately for the game. Within ten minutes however, Naomi realized why Dante had suggested bowling. He was an exceptional bowler. He knocked out four consecutive straight strikes and was upgrading splits into spares left and right. Even as they were flushed with beers, he bowled well. They joked around as he pulled out the kiddie rails for her so her ball wasn't perpetually in the gutter, and he poked fun at her dress flying in all directions as she bowled.

After one game, Dante suggested a jazz club. "One of the city's signature offerings," he said. They took a cab to a dimly lit blue-black club where jazz floated out of the venue. Naomi recognized the place, it was only a ten-minute walk from her apartment.

The Cotton Club was enveloped in nostalgic bars of a big band ballad, full of chatter escaping the lips of shimmering cigarette holders and chic champagne imbibers. For a moment, Naomi felt transported to the raucous era of Old Shanghai, in the generation of gramophones and qipaos and opium, when opulence and menace cohabited. She was dressed for the occasion, in an eclectic ensemble found in a boutique by a local designer. This city had made her more daring in her fashion choices. Tonight, she was in a dress with many hybrids. From the waist up, her attire was demure, proper; it had a Peter Pan collar and buttons that lined neatly to her naval. From the waist down, her dress drifted into a gradient of sheerness, like the wing of a cicada.

The jazz band songstress started crooning Gershwin into the microphone and couples began moving to the intimate makeshift dance floor. Dante held Naomi by the waist. Her back was against his chest, her scent strong on her flesh—notes of vanilla, citrus, rose. He stretched out his hand. The glorious, languorous night expanded in front of them, beckoning with its infinite possibilities. Locking his fingers with hers, his other free hand held her close. Back arched, head thrown back, and silky hair fanning, she was flooded with the adrenaline of incensed summer nights.

They drained their drinks, exited the club, re-entered the charcoal night, casting shadows underneath the halogen lights that lined the streets. Dante was conscious of their surroundings: flashing lights, blaring horns, billowing smoke, but he was only mildly bothered. He was so focused on Naomi—the way her eyes shone when she smiled, the way her giggle sounded like bells, the way she tucked stray strands of hair behind her triple-pierced ear—everything else was just background noise that faded whenever she spoke. Her iridescent dress flapped suggestively against her outer thigh. At certain angles and lighting, her derriere was just ever-so-slightly visible. Under the street lamps, their dancing shadows bounced across the asphalt.

Then one of Naomi's heels broke off. "This is what I get for buying cheap Jimmy Choo knock offs," she wailed.

Dante knelt down, took off her heels, and chucked them into the nearby trash bin. "There!" he grinned.

Stunned at first, Naomi stared at her exposed feet on the street, then burst out laughing. Dante suddenly picked her up, and she draped her arms around his neck, her bare feet dangling over his arms. She giggled as he carried her the rest of the way.

He didn't put her down until she fished the key out of her purse, and unlocked the front door. Then, as he laid her to her feet, he took her hand, drew her close, and kissed her. He hadn't planned on doing it tonight—it was only their first date. But the moment felt right, ripe with romance.

When he kissed her, she had looked surprised, her eyes wide with curiosity. Then her long lashes lowered, and she responded in kind, her arms encircling his neck. Her tongue was a butterfly, flitting beautifully against his. The elevator made a ruckus as it traveled up and down, then a howling siren raced down the street as indistinct conversation came from the staircases.

But Dante didn't hear a thing, was only lost in the lingering sensation of Naomi's soft lips.

Although initially she had told him to take things slow, Naomi gradually welcomed Dante's advances. Maybe it was because of the explosion of carnal energy brought on by the swarm of foreigners who had descended onto the city to visit or work at Expo. It seemed to Naomi that everywhere she went there were couples.

Or maybe it was because of the sizzling Shanghai heat emanating a certain sparkle, beckoning a summer fling. Whatever the reason, Naomi came to appreciate Dante's phone calls, the Calla Lily bouquets, the homemade lunches he delivered to her at the French pavilion. He usually worked at Expo grounds twice a week. He would wait until her shift was over, and they'd flock to different pavilions like children at an amusement park.

For the past year, Naomi had told herself to focus on her career, to avoid any distractions, but maybe this season would be different. Although sometimes, in the still of the night, resting on her tear-soaked pillow, she wondered if she was really ready for somebody like Dante Ouyang, somebody who was so...well-adjusted.

Before Seth, there was a time when Naomi treated men as mere accessories, as if they were fashion trends that could be discarded seasonally. That was when she had no qualms about charming the pants off of borderline strangers or waking up next to no-strings-attached men. Growing up without the other gender in her home (her mother's intermittent boyfriends didn't count), she sometimes dehumanized men, as if their anatomical differences made them an entirely different species. She had played the game of push and pull, reeling them in and spitting them out. She had been the perpetrator of too many hit-and-runs.

In retrospect, the malice and manipulation she directed at some men was astonishing. At the time, she probably went through four to six guys per year, disposing boyfriends whenever another one caught her fancy. She was in her early twenties at the time, her physique svelte yet buoyant—fresh rubber that bounced off walls. She was the girl always up for a good time, radiating that school's out type of vibe. There were one-nighters, week-long flings, affairs that carried on for months, there was Rex, then there was Seth.

Some of the men had been genuine. They had truly cared, had been tender. They had envisioned a future with her, had rallied for her. Some had pampered her with enchanting gifts, but the ones she felt guilty about were the ones who had been generous with their emotions. Like the one who had turned to her during his parents' acrimonious divorce, or the one who had opened up about his childhood trauma. They were the ones she shouldn't have deserted. She hadn't been kind, been ruthless even.

She didn't think much of her myriad, messy liaisons at the time. She had thought of herself as a protagonist in her own rom-com, coming-of-age and bright-eyed and forgivable, just stumbling and learning how to adult in New York City. It was clear now, as she thought back to those years, that as much as she was preyed on, she had also been the predator. Rex once said that Naomi was like an azalea—vivid, alluring. However, its nectar was also venomous, and her toxic side surfaced when things went south.

It's still painful to remember. There is a part of her that never wants to go back there. And that's exactly how she feels about New York now, that it's a petulant cupid's paradise, a jungle littered with broken hearts and full of daggers ready to pierce unsuspecting men and women.

*

Shanghai Scene had gradually expanded Joss Kong's assignments. There had been positive feedback to her articles, so she had recently been promoted to a lifestyle columnist. Joss didn't mind the extra responsibilities. She was grateful for the day job, for somewhere to be while Tay was at work. Although she was pleased to be Mrs. Tay Kai Tang, she never wanted that to be her sole identity. Tay's circle had started treating her as a mere afterthought, as if his voice took precedent over hers.

She was also appreciative of the magazine work for filling up her schedule, so that she wouldn't be relegated to the beck and call of Ruiling Fong, her mother-in-law. Joss didn't spend much time with her father-in-law. She saw him once every several months even though they lived five minutes away. Ruiling however, was constantly requesting Joss's company.

Joss understood there was probably either an *ernai* or *xiaosan*, or both, in her father-in-law Tang Zhaoyi's world. Both were colloquial terms for mistresses, although generally an ernai was in a more respectable position than a xiaosan. The difference between the two was that an ernai knew her place, was content to be the "the other woman," was not unhappy that her man had his real wife and family and that she was the girlfriend who reaped financial benefits of the arrangement—an apartment, monthly allowances, luxury gifts and regular dates. A skilled ernai could even convince her man to buy an apartment for her aging parents. A xiaosan was a different story. She wasn't as pragmatic. She was in love with her man. Her emotions ran the gamut—jealousy, possessiveness, elation, depression. She was often labeled a homewrecker because she would pursue a position for herself, demand a separation from the wife and kids, and was adamant about making herself seen and heard.

It would be naïve to think that Tang Zhaoyi didn't have at least one ernai. The majority of Chinese men in his position did. Naomi once asked her whether she was worried Tay would stray like his dad, after all, it was no secret that Tay sometimes entertained clients in questionable venues. The thought had crossed her mind before, but she knew Tay was fundamentally cut from a different fabric than his father. They never did get along and recently, their conflicts had been intensifying.

It wasn't that Joss was overly confident. She knew there were plenty of conniving *hulijing* in this city that found her husband attractive—he was educated abroad, had benevolent eyes, and most importantly, was economically among the top ten percent in China.

Joss might not be the most striking or most accomplished or the most *wen rou* (a *wen rou* woman was submissive and gentle in the most feminine way possible, traits that inspired desire in Chinese men). No, Joss's advantage was that she was Tay's best friend. True friends were hard to come by in Tay's world, especially when that much money was on the line.

She, and she alone, knew her husband inside and out, his deepest vulnerabilities, his sealed-up secrets. She was understanding and compassionate towards her husband, she'd always been. And for that, she knew Tay loved her back, immensely, and would never betray her.

4

MANY MOONS AGO

The perfectly spherical moon was looming low, glowing in the September evening sky. It was technically still several days until *Zhongqiu Jie*, the Mid-Autumn Festival, the annual Chinese lunar celebration dating back three thousand years. But most of the city had already commenced the celebration starting Friday evening, setting off orange and violet fireworks, exchanging and hoarding boxes upon boxes of *yue bing*, mooncakes. Multinational brands had been promoting their mooncakes and cashing in on the holiday for weeks now—ice cream mooncakes from Häagen-Dazs, Earl Grey and coffee flavored mooncakes sold in Starbucks, rose hibiscus mooncakes from the Shangri-La Hotel. Naomi's favorite flavor was still the one she savored from her trips in Taiwan: *lianrong*, lotus seed paste.

Naomi and her colleagues had been preparing for the occasion for months. It was customary for brands to send important editors, publishers, VIPs, and government officials mooncakes gift sets as a cordial, relationship-building gesture. Brands competed with each other in producing the most winning mooncake and gift box designs. Last year, Fendi custom-designed a drawer-style mooncake gift box, with a built-in projector that displayed its logo. Tiffany & Co. sent editors mooncakes in a signature Tiffany's blue jewelry box that required a miniature Tiffany's silver key to be opened. While the brands maintained those relationships, Jun Cleo's Experiential Marketing team was responsible for providing the goods.

This year, Naomi managed the project for one of the agency's biggest clients, Chantevieve. She worked with a vendor to produce mooncakes that tasted of fragrant jasmine, osmanthus and dates, a flavor reminiscent of their Chantevieve Blossoms fragrance. She also came up with the idea of the mooncake box resembling a music box with a lantern motif. Inside, a tiny figurine in a qipao twirled and emitted a pink glow. She had sketched the concept and designed the emerald-colored qipao herself.

It took two months for the vendor to get the prototype of the mooncake and the music gift box just right. The first prototype had been thrown against the wall by Cher. "Wait until it's absolutely perfect to present it to her," Frida had advised Naomi. When she finally presented the finished product to Cher and Nikki, they had seemed pleased. Cher was usually more critical, but even she didn't have anything negative to say. Nikki had nodded in approval, saying it was *fine*. When Auguste Reynaud requested to keep a sample of the gift set in his office, Naomi knew she had done better than fine.

While locals convened with family to savor *yue bing* and *tang yuan* (glutinous rice balls with sesame filling in syrup), there was a plethora of events across Shanghai for foreigners who found themselves without family on this holiday.

Joss had dinner obligations with her in-laws. Dante had a family feast to attend but promised to join Naomi later. Frida said she'd introduce Naomi to the city's festivities, after an early dinner with her relatives. She still lived with her parents, as was customary for many single, twenty-something Shanghainese until they wed. She said she would skip the usual *ta yue* tradition with her family this year—moonwalk, or a leisurely stroll to observe the full moon.

For their first stop, Frida led Naomi, Amos and Logan to Zhenlao Dafang on Nanjing Dong Lu, a snack market founded during the Qing dynasty. The line outside the shop snaked around the corner. Their savory pork mooncakes, freshly baked, were four renminbi each, less than one U.S. dollar. The group decided to purchase ten in total, in a variety of flavors. While they stood in line, children were entertained by someone in a rabbit suit, a nod to the mythological bunny who in the *Zhongqiu Jie* folklore, was the companion of Chang'e the Chinese moon goddess. Afterwards, the group headed toward Jinmao Tower in Lujiazui. On the eighty-eighth floor of the pagoda-topped skyscraper, they enjoyed panoramic views of the city, and the moon, mesmerizing, was in full view.

At nearly midnight, Logan corralled the group outside of Jinmao Tower. "Let's head to Shelter!" he hollered. The venue was a former bomb shelter turned underground nightclub on Yongfu Lu, where the strip of bars was a haunting ground for foreigners, and the target of complaints from locals residing nearby.

Inside the club, the ceilings hung low, the thumping bass was deafening, the floors felt as if they were shaking. It was packed, wall to wall, bodies spinning and spiraling and falling left and right. Naomi and Frida huddled close to the bar, where they ran into Frida's other friends. Logan and Amos roamed the room like vampires under the full moon, fangs tucked and eyes sharpened, seeking out their next conquests.

"There you are!" shouted Dante. He elbowed his way through the ocean of warm sticky flesh grinding and dry humping to pulsating music and took Naomi by the hand.

"How was dinner?" Naomi asked.

Dante furrowed his brow. "Fine, except…well, let's talk about it later."

They struggled against the incoming tide of bodies. Dante held Naomi close and led her to a slightly roomier dance spot near the deejay, whose jerking head motions made him look like a mad turkey.

Naomi shook off what she imagined to be the shackles of Jun Cleo work life formalities and let her inner animal loose. All around them, people looked like distorted, untamed creatures underneath the flashing strobe lights. It was as if mating rituals had been heightened to the max in this jungle—howling and panting and gnawing and strutting; feathers splayed, chests puffed, claws out. It was so overcrowded that there was no way anybody was actually *dancing*. People crammed against each other while swaying, arms and legs brushing up on each other, masses of warm bodies against sweaty ones—that was a more accurate description.

Dante led her to a darkened corner. Her awareness dimmed as his kisses enveloped her, the intensity building by the second. Naomi pulled away momentarily, to catch a breath, to freeze-frame this memory. She wanted to immortalize this moment.

She wished the summer would never ever end.

*

From the living room windows in Joss's villa, the skies were cotton-clouded, rosy and opalescent. Inside, the room was enveloped in a shade of jade with rose gold accents from the hand-painted House de Gournay wallpaper. The floors had been polished to a brilliant sheen. Layers of the couple's travels were present everywhere—Flemish tapestries, Venetian sculptural art, a restored Italian grand piano, Lebanese rugs made of sheep's wool, Dutch Chinoiserie cabinets, a sofa draped with Pakistani quilts. A massive spiraling column of horns from deer, considered a symbol of prosperity in China, protruded from the wall. Naomi thought the deer horns were a bit morbid. Joss agreed but couldn't do anything about it since her in-laws had gifted the piece.

Naomi was appreciating a Zhang Daqian splashed-ink landscape piece on a wall, when a lion-like creature came bounding through the hallway, lunging at her. Naomi let out a bloodcurdling scream as she got pushed down onto the floor. The animal let loose a guttural bark.

"Xiao Wang Zi, no! No, get down," Joss yelled. Naomi managed to get away from the lumbering, slobbering creature as Joss tugged on its collar.

"Sorry. Xiao Wang Zi is staying here for the week, while MIL is in Macau again." Joss explained that Ruiling Fong dropped off her *Little Prince* with her whenever she traveled, which was at least once a month.

Naomi took a good look at Xiao Wang Zi, who resembled a chestnut-haired bear with a lion-like mane. He looked like he weighed more than a hundred pounds. His size was terrorizing, but up close, Naomi now saw he was harmless.

"He's precious." Naomi gave him a hearty rub on the back. She had heard that the Tibetan mastiff, originally from the Himalayan Highlands, was the largest dog breed in the world. This was the first time she came face-to-face with one.

"That he is. He also cost as much as a Lamborghini. Although I think Xiao Wang Zi is worth much more than that. He's part of the family," Joss said. "And I mean that literally. MIL spoils Xiao Wang Zi like a grandson. His meals and haircuts are fancier than mine."

"Not that I'm complaining." Joss wrapped her arms around Xiao Wang Zi. "The more MIL's attention is focused on him, the less it's directed toward me."

"Are things getting better with her?" Naomi asked.

"You know, I don't mind Ruiling. Sometimes, I even feel bad for her. Her husband is never around. I would like to spend more time with her, if she weren't so obsessed with my uterus," Joss said.

"You've only been married a year!" Naomi exclaimed. "Although, I know both you and Tay love kids. You two would be excellent parents. Also, would the one-child policy apply to you guys? Tay is on a Chinese passport, right?"

"Yes, he is," Joss replied. "I should probably look into the details of the birth policy. We do want to start a family at some point. But…it's just not the right time…not yet."

"Anyway," Joss said quickly, "how's your mom? Still at Corsica? Or is it Crete now?"

"Who knows?" Naomi shrugged. "I haven't heard from her in weeks. I can't believe she cancelled her China trip…"

Joss was relieved the conversation had been steered away from pregnancy and children. She'd had enough conversations about these dreaded topics with Ruiling alone. She couldn't stand Ruiling's nagging about grandkids and inquiring into the frequency of their copulation. Last week, she had insinuated that Joss was still not pregnant because she'd been too busy fraternizing with friends, or too preoccupied with the magazine work. Not once did Ruiling question her own son, consider the fact that maybe he was the problem, not she.

Joss *almost* blurted out the truth about Tay then. But she had promised him she wouldn't tell a soul, and she loved Tay enough to honor that.

Naomi was a bit bothered that her mother's e-mails and postcards had dwindled as of late. When Naomi decided to move to Shanghai last year, Reina Kita was still reeling over their last big fight, e-mailing her daughter once every couple of days in hopes of reconciliation. Naomi responded only occasionally.

The last time Naomi made the long distance call to Reina, they had, predictably, found something to fight about. There seemed to be incendiary topics littered everywhere. Naomi tried to tread lightly around them, but with her mother, her usual easygoing mood became a pendulum, a sensitive ticking time bomb.

Naomi was especially upset when Reina abruptly cancelled her trip to Shanghai in May. Last year, Reina casually mentioned she was interested in seeing the World Expo, so Naomi had arranged to get her fast passes to the pavilions. Two weeks before her flight, Reina postponed the visit—she had met someone. Naomi recalled her mother's e-mail about him: Bryan Shawnberg was dashing, divorced, and so very talented—fluent in Spanish and French, semi-fluent in Japanese and Chinese. He was assigned as Reina's tour partner in the travel agency they both worked at. It was somewhere in Cyprus where sparks flew between them. In an e-mail, Reina had enclosed a photo of them in front of the Roman ruins in Paphos, along with the caption: "According to lore, this city was founded by Aphrodite, the goddess of love!"

Naomi had rolled her eyes at the e-mail. *Here we go again.* Two years after Wesley Fan's passing, Reina Kita had started dating again, and hadn't stopped since.

When Naomi was younger, she remembered distinct things about each *uncle* her mother had introduced to her. There was the uncle whose head of black curls fascinated Naomi. She loved to climb on his shoulders and tug on them. There was the tall uncle in Reina's salsa dancing lessons, and the one who would always buy Naomi new dresses.

Up until the age of sixteen, Naomi worshipped her mother. But

Naomi's relationship with Reina went downhill with the appearance of Jay Sampert. He was the father of Pam Sampert, a senior at school whom she recognized only because Pam was the student body president.

Pam and two other seniors cornered Naomi in the girl's restroom near the library one day after school. Pam tossed several pieces of paper at Naomi, screeching at her to "tell the homewrecker to back off" and to "go back to where you came from." The two other girls shoved Naomi against the wall before leaving the restroom. Crouched on the cold tiled flooring, Naomi picked up the crumpled papers and scanned them. They were print outs of e-mails Reina had written to Jay—love letters of sorts. For Naomi, that singular moment in a high school restroom was the watershed point.

Naomi confronted Reina and pleaded with her to halt the affair, not just because of Pam's threats, but because Naomi truly believed her mother deserved better, more than being a mistress. It would be another full year, after Naomi had already completed her college applications and decided to move across the country, before Reina ended the relationship with Jay.

By then, Naomi was already on a plane to New York.

5

ONE YEAR ANNIVERSARY

Roxy Gao was off somewhere flirting with Chester Wu, when she was supposed to be stuffing the promotional gifts bags. Naomi sighed and scrambled to finish Roxy's job. It was less than an hour before the launch event and Naomi still had a checklist of tasks to complete. She made a mental note to sit down with Roxy and go over the internship Dos and Don'ts again. DO follow instructions especially when you're at a client event. DON'T make your boss finish your job while you flirt with the VIP.

Nearly fifty KOLs—key opinion leaders—were invited to a skincare salon inside the French pavilion. They were bloggers, designers, socialites, and other movers and shakers who had a following among Chinese netizens. When Roxy heard that Chester Wu would be in attendance, she literally squealed. Chester, an Oxford-educated French national who had a Chinese face with a K-pop wardrobe, was coined the most eligible bachelor in China after he appeared on the dating show "If You Are The One," the most-watched television show in the country.

Naomi checked her watch, there were still some KOLs who hadn't arrived yet. Naomi handed Roxy the list of phone numbers and instructed her to begin calling the absent ones.

Several minutes later, Roxy ran towards her, out of breath. "Emergency! Agnes Sung detained in airport! She is very very angry." Roxy briefed Naomi on the situation. After Agnes deplaned her flight from Taiwan, she was prohibited from exiting the Hongqiao airport and was currently detained for wearing a questionable shirt. Roxy showed Naomi an image Agnes had posted to Weibo before boarding the plane. She was in a cropped magenta-colored t-shirt that had the Chinese characters *zhai nu fan kang dui* splashed over her bosom.

"What do these characters mean?" Naomi asked.

"Maybe 'nerdy girls protest team' or something like that," Roxy replied. "Maybe that word 'protest' is the problem."

Naomi took the phone and tried to console Agnes. She was howling about being interrogated on the meaning of her tee. Agnes explained that she had bought the shirt from a night market in Taiwan because she thought the slogan was clever. She didn't think it had any political leanings. The officers had been even more alarmed when they'd learned she was attending an event at Expo.

"Why am I being treated like this? It's just a stupid shirt!" Agnes was hysterical now.

Naomi asked Agnes to hand the phone to an officer. In a syrupy voice, she pleaded with the grumpy man to let Agnes go, but he was resolute. Naomi had no choice but to call her boss.

Cher dispatched Pearla to the airport straight away after Naomi explained the crisis. An hour later, Pearla accompanied a distraught Agnes into the French pavilion, who was no longer wearing the controversial shirt.

"How did you get her out?" Naomi wanted to know.

Pearla shrugged. Naomi was a foreigner, even if her Mandarin was not too shabby. There were many instances in this city where Naomi's foreign-ness would have yielded the upper hand; people loved English speakers in this town. In this situation, however, Pearla's advantage was that she spoke the local dialect. Shanghainese was the language of over ninety percent of the airport staff, and of people who worked for the city. Pearla would not be divulging her secrets to Naomi, although it wasn't as if it had been a solo effort. Kang Lu, the VP of Government Relations for Jun Cleo, did most of the negotiating—in Shanghainese, of course. In the end, the request was simple: Agnes had to relinquish the shirt. And the packages of cigarettes and Chantevieve products

Pearla brought also helped.

Kang Lu said the characters on the shirt were sensitive due to the character *zai*, which may have meant "nerdy," but used in another context, meant "home." The other controversial characters were *fan kang*, resistance. Kang Lu speculated that the airport officers linked the phrase to the sensitive issue of government-forced demolition of eighteen thousand homes in order to make way for the Expo site. There had been protests, and now that Expo was well underway, the government took all precautions to prevent anything that might deter from positive coverage of the country's biggest event of the year.

After the skincare salon ended, Naomi sent Roxy to accompany Agnes and Chester to various pavilions, equipping them with VIP passes so they could skip the long lines. Naomi quickly packed up her work bag and headed towards the Expo exit. She had a meeting at Henglong Plaza with Nicki Jiang.

Inside a conference room adjacent to Nicki's office, Naomi laid out photos of each model on the table. Chantevieve would be holding a product preview at the French pavilion next week, but this time, it would resemble a runway show with the models "wearing" the brand's cosmetics. As the Event lead, Naomi felt she had a good handle on the event logistics already, but Nicki insisted on overseeing all of the last-minute details.

Nicki examined each of the model's photographs and profiles closely, then started flinging several of the photos out of the lineup. Without any explanation, Nicki said two of the models should be switched out. She picked up two photos from the "second choice" pile and told Naomi to use them instead.

The two models Nicki wanted replaced, was Sarima, the Nigerian model, and Tanvi, who was from India. Nicki studied the photos of Yana, the haughty Ukrainian model, and Hualing, a model from Dalian who appeared to suffer from stage fright.

"Yana and Hualing will now be in the show," Nicki announced.

Naomi explained the reasoning for her selection of certain models over others. She had conducted several rounds of auditions and had narrowed down the list to the top twelve with the best work ethic. All of the models were gorgeous, that was a given. But since the show entailed cooperating with the makeup artists and audience on live demonstrations, Naomi wasn't just looking for a decent strut. The chosen models also needed to be flexible, smart, and quick on their feet. This would be the brand's first show at Expo, and the Chantevieve clients had expressed high expectations for it.

Nicki held up her hand. "I've made myself clear."

Naomi flinched. "Look, I conducted personal auditions with Tanvi and Sarima, and they have an excellent work ethic. Trust me, you'd be happy with their performance." Naomi tried to keep her tone even but could feel a migraine on the rise. The show was in four days and she still had a mountain of work to do. The last thing she needed was for Nicki to turn it into an avalanche.

Fei raised her eyebrows, Orca shot her a meaningful look, and Pearla looked like she was stifling a smirk. The irritation on Nicki's face was apparent. She wasn't used to being backtalked to.

Cher stepped in. "The whitening line is one of their bestsellers, so how do you suppose that would work on those *hei gui?*"

Naomi paused to see if anybody else had a reaction. Nicki was sitting at the head of the table, while the rest of the team had their heads down, buried in their laptops. Nobody acted like anything was out of the ordinary.

"Nicki," Cher continued, "please excuse Naomi. She is still new to China."

Naomi could feel her cheeks flushed from anger. "The foreign models were not assigned to represent the whitening line, remember? Besides, Sarima and Tanvi have earned their spots—"

"I should not have to spell out everything for you," Nicki cut her off. "We are here to put on a show to sell products. It's not a charity hire."

Frida tried to calm down a fuming Naomi after the meeting. "I know you feel bad for Sarima and Tanvi, but it's inappropriate for you to talk back to Nicki."

"And it was appropriate for Cher to use racial slurs? Also, I didn't select them out of pity, I hired them based on a fair standard during the auditions," Naomi shot back.

"Why are you getting so worked up? No need to lose your job over this. Have you heard of 'Singing Angels' and Lou Jing?" countered Frida.

"That talent competition? I've watched several episodes. Is Lou Jing the African-American on that show?" Naomi had watched a gratuitous amount of local television last autumn before she was employed. She remembered being mesmerized by the powerful voice of Lou Jing, who was sometimes called by her western name, Vicky Lou, on "Singing Angels."

"Lou Jing is not African-American, she's African-Chinese. She was born and bred in Shanghai. But people here were very cruel. They called her names and many wouldn't accept her. That was probably the real reason why she lost the competition, even though she was very talented," Frida explained.

Naomi was quiet for a moment. She thought about the momentous election just two years ago when Barack Obama won the seat of the U.S. presidency. Obama's greeting filled the big screen inside the USA Pavilion at Expo, and her heart had welled with pride watching his address, knowing that in 2008 she had voted as a U.S. citizen for the very first time, and had cast a winning vote, contributing to electing the first black U.S. president.

She realized she had at times felt very Japanese when she was in the U.S. but felt very American now that she was in China.

"What Cher said was unacceptable. But ultimately," Frida continued, "our end goal is pushing sales for the Chinese market."

That evening, when Naomi recounted the whole episode to Dante, he told her of a news piece he had once read, about the author Martin Jacques, and his wife, Harinder Veriah.

"Harinder was Indian. She said she didn't receive adequate care at a Hong Kong hospital and experienced racism there. She later died in the hospital."

"That's heart-breaking!" Naomi's hands flew to her mouth.

"It is." They were both momentarily silent.

"Allegedly the case had a part in Hong Kong passing its first ever anti-racism law. But mainland still lacks any specific bill on racism," Dante added.

Naomi sighed. "I feel terrible for Sarima and Tanvi."

"Didn't Joss say her magazine needed models?"

"Oh good thinking! I'll ask her. And I'll still pay Sarima and Tanvi for the amount they were supposed to earn for the Expo show. Out of my own pocket."

Dante kissed her now. "That's the right thing to do, isn't it."

*

Naomi was due in Beijing for business. Her client, a Japanese sportswear brand, was holding an all-agencies meeting. Jun Cleo represented the below-the-line activation vendor. Numerous agency representatives from around the region would also convene in Beijing to present on their respective marketing and advertising disciplines: above-the-line, out-of-home, digital, social, PR.

Since her work obligations would be completed by Friday, Naomi decided she would extend her trip until Sunday evening, and use the weekend for sightseeing. She had traveled to Beijing at least three times now, but on previous business trips she'd never had the time to visit the capital's sites. "Let me come with," Dante had suggested. "I've been meaning to visit anyway." It was a milestone—their first trip together.

Compared with Shanghai, Beijing felt soot-stained, more industrial. Everywhere reeked of dust and car exhaust, and the air tasted like sawdust swirling in her throat. The culprit was the sandstorms originating from the Gobi Desert that swept up more than a million tons of sand, depositing them in Beijing. Dante came prepared and had packed Naomi an extra mask.

Not so different from Shanghai, were the contrasts that abounded everywhere in Beijing: towering skyscrapers adjacent to low-rise historic *hutongs*, heritage dynastic pagodas that stood side by side with American fast food chains. Other similarities with Shanghai: Beijing's ubiquitous seething of mass crowds, the barking of jackhammers, blaring of car horns, and the thicket of glass and steel, each daring the other to crack the colorless sky.

Dante was thrilled to be back in his old stomping grounds. He had lived in Beijing for five months when he first moved back to China last year. His childhood friend from Nanjing, Yen Deng, who went by Ed Yen at the multinational pharmaceutical company he worked at, had resided in Beijing for the past decade. He was now married to a woman from Busan and they had a toddler son.

Ed was Dante's oldest friend in the world. Even if they had lost touch in their youth while Dante was in England, they had quickly reconnected in their twenties, especially when Ed started traveling to Switzerland on business trips. Then when Dante got posted in Beijing, he was at Ed's apartment near Sanlitun almost weekly.

Ed planned a comprehensive itinerary for Dante and Naomi, including a tour of *hutongs*, a labyrinth of alleyways that were un-gentrified and still looked and smelled like Old Beijing—gamely, garlicky, greasy. Afterwards, they strolled along Chang'an Avenue, and did the requisite Tiananmen tour: The National Museum, the Forbidden City, the Imperial Palace, the Great Hall of the People. They took a tour of the Three Birds Buildings: The Birds Nest (Olympic Stadium), the Birds Egg (National Theater), the Birds Legs (CCTV Tower). They ran out of time for the Summer Palace, the Ming Tombs and the Great Wall; those would have to wait until the next trip.

Dante had mentioned how special Naomi was, how completely different she was from the other girls he had dated before. Now that Ed had finally met her, he had to agree. Of course she was stunning, Dante usually dated exceptionally attractive women. Naomi was arresting, sure, but she was also very down-to-earth, and once you started spending time with her, that slight demureness and whimsicality so many Japanese exuded would manifest itself. All throughout the day, Ed couldn't help but notice how utterly euphoric his friend looked. He certainly hadn't been this way with Esme or Giorgina. Dante seemed so infatuated, that at times Ed had felt like a big *dian deng pao*—a light bulb—a term the Chinese used to describe "the third wheel." Being around a couple so immersed in that initial blissful phase had a contagious effect. Ed suddenly missed his wife very much.

That night, his wife and son joined them at Da Dong, one of the most coveted Beijing Duck restaurants in the city. From the open kitchen, Naomi admired the chefs roasting the shiny birds over a wood fire. The glossy duck was then brought over to their table, sliced into pieces of crispy skin and tender fowl by the staff, then sprinkled with sugar, garlic and hoisin. Dante showed Naomi the proper way to consume *bei jing kao ya*: he wrapped a piece of the crispy meat in a paper-thin pancake along with some leek shreds and folded it up like a mini burrito. Naomi said it was one of the most exquisite things she had ever tasted.

The next day, Dante and Naomi lunched at Nanluoguxiang, the historical Drum and Bell Tower district dating back nearly three hundred years. He led her to a traditional Chinese courtyard, where festive lanterns were strung all around and the menu featured over fifteen kinds of dumplings to choose from. They ordered an assortment in a rainbow of colors, served in steamer baskets.

At the Confucian Temple, Naomi appreciated that Dante provided the unaltered version of history, the parts not displayed on the brochures and plaques of the sites. Dante told her about Lao She, one of China's greatest novelists of the last century, and how he had been nearly beaten to death by the Red Guards at the Confucian Temple during the Cultural Revolution. He had committed suicide shortly after.

"Lao She's fate is not unique. There are many stories like this from that era. I grew up with these stories, some of which occurred in my own family." Dante's expression turned somber.

"You can tell me," Naomi whispered, holding his hand. "I'm all ears."

He kissed her forehead. "Another time."

On their last day in Beijing, Dante suggested some more sightseeing before lunch. They rode rickshaws around Houhai Lake in Shichaihai

Park while munching on candied crab apple. Afterwards they made a quick stop at a mall to escape the midday heat. They mulled over whether to take a taxi or stroll to the special restaurant where Dante had made lunch reservations. He had called weeks in advance to secure seats at a tiny restaurant that served up imperial dishes from recipes handed down from the owner's great-great-grandfather, who'd once been a senior courtier in the Qing Dynasty.

But after twenty minutes of trying to hail a taxi to no avail, they decided they would trot to the restaurant on foot. It was supposedly only an eighteen-minute walk. Dante had brought a lightweight, portable electric fan the size of his palm, which he held to their faces as they strolled.

As they passed by Liangmaqiao Lu, their leisurely walk was interrupted by a commotion coming from throngs of demonstrators gathered around a gray edifice, shouting, chanting, and holding signs. Some were throwing eggs and plastic bottles at a building flying a Japanese flag.

Dante held Naomi's hand tightly as she pressed him about what was going on at the Japanese embassy. Dante explained that it was the seventy-ninth anniversary of "the Mukden incident," a plot by the Japanese Imperial Army who had provoked the Japanese invasion of Manchuria. The demonstrators were protesting about a recent collision between a Chinese skipper and the Japanese coast guard near the Diaoyu Islands in the East China Sea.

Naomi nodded, she knew the disputed islands were referred to as the Senkaku in Japanese. China, Taiwan, and Japan all laid claim to the islets, likely due to the gas and oil reserves in the surrounding seabed.

Dante gripped Naomi's hand as they navigated the rowdy crowds. Their restaurant reservation was in ten minutes, and they needed to cross over the next street to get there, which meant there was no way to avoid the protests. They had no choice but to hunker down and pass through the thick of it. He wished he had planned this better. They should've just waited a little longer for a taxi.

Dante looked around him in all directions, trying to see if he could flag down a cab. But the protesters had blocked off most of the traffic routes and the taxis that were in sight were all occupied.

A woman approached them and stuffed a brochure in Dante's hand. The headline on the front page was *wei an suo*, comfort stations—military brothels established by the Japanese Army that forced countless women into sexual slavery during World War Two. The brochure stated that Shanghai had the most *wei an suo* of any city: 172, but the war crime committed by the Japanese Army had spanned all throughout China, Taiwan, Korea, Vietnam, Thailand, Philippines, Malaysia, Burma, and beyond.

Naomi took the brochure from Dante's hand. "Let me keep this." She placed it in her purse.

He wasn't sure if Naomi could make out the Chinese characters on various banners the protestors were holding up: *Boycott Japanese goods! Defend Diaoyu Islands to our death! Japanese get out! Fight Japan!* Dante cringed at a particularly profane one: *Take a Japanese wife, then beat her if she doesn't obey.*

Now crowds started to congregate around a Japanese branded car parked in the heart of the protesting zone. It looked like it had been intentionally placed there for display. Men waving metal rods shouted for onlookers to stand back. People cheered wildly as they started smashing in the windows.

A group was holding up a portrait of Mao and singing the Chinese national anthem now. In another corner, another faction was stomping on a Japanese flag before lighting it on fire amid applauding crowds. Naomi clutched Dante's hand tightly, a horrified expression on her face.

A Chinese woman suddenly approached him. "Is that your girlfriend?" She pointed straight at Naomi's face. Dante stood in front of Naomi. He didn't know what this woman wanted, but it didn't sound good. The whole atmosphere around them was intensely hostile. They needed to get out of there as fast as they could.

The woman didn't wait for Dante to answer. "Why is she wearing a kimono? She is a Japanese sympathizer! Look at her!" The woman was making a scene now, yelling in Chinese and pointing at Naomi.

Naomi was baffled at the aggressive woman pointing at her; she recognized several Chinese words spouted from the woman's mouth: *he fu* (kimono), *pan tu* (traitor). Naomi suddenly understood. It was her silk wrap dress, which had a modern-day kimono look, with billowing sleeves, an empire waist, cherry blossoms pattern, complete with a vintage Obi belt. Japanese characters spelling the designer's name were visibly sprawled on the back. The dress was a gift from her relatives in Osaka, and its lightweight fabric made it one of her favorite outfits.

The antagonistic group was growing and chanting something at Naomi now. "*Tuo xia lai! Tuo xia lai!*" Suddenly a man grabbed the edge of her garment and shouted, "Ugly dress! Take if off!" It was one of the men who had smashed the car windows.

"*Zou kai!*" Go away! Dante growled at the man and shoved him in the shoulder so hard that he toppled over another woman who fell to the ground and yelped in pain. The man got up and snarled at Dante, clenching his fists, and a cluster of men behind him followed suit.

Dante grabbed Naomi's hand and started sprinting in the opposite direction towards the assembly of police cars that were now pulling in. The men who were following them slowed down as they saw the anti-riot police armed with shields and batons. Dante and Naomi scurried past them onto Dong Jie.

Not wanting to take any chances, they ran as fast as they could to deter any followers. Naomi was soon out of breath and said she needed to stop. Her toe was bleeding. She was in open toe sandals and somewhere amidst the chaos, somebody's sharp heels had dug into her foot. Dante spotted a Lawson's convenience store and hurried in to get some bandages. They walked the remainder of the way to the restaurant.

Naomi was reticent for the rest of the day. After lunch, they gathered their belongings and rushed to the Beijing airport, settling into their flight. On the plane, she closed her eyes, turning away from Dante, saying she needed some shut eye. In truth, she just wanted some solitude to gather her emotions.

She felt shaken up from being singled out, pointed at, chased after at the protests. She wondered if this was a one-off, or if she would be subjected to more incidents like this if she decided to stay in China further. Very rarely had she questioned whether coming to China had been the right move. But today, the question left her feeling unsettled.

She had recently passed her one-year mark of moving to China. Dante had insisted on celebrating this momentous date. Thus on her moving-to-China one-year anniversary, they had toured Expo, including the China pavilion. Inside, they'd been enthralled by the various Chinese exhibits. It seemed fitting, on that day, to pay homage to the country that had given her so much in the past year—a solid career, a beautiful apartment, a Chinese man whom she was head over heels for. She remembered thinking that the single best decision she had made last year was staying in China, even when things had gone south with Seth. She thought about all the friendships she held dear in Shanghai: Joss and Tay of course, but also Frida Du, Roxy Gao, Orca Cao, and even her juvenile male friends Logan Hayden and Amos Kim. But most of all, she felt supremely blessed that she had met Dante Ouyang. And what happened today at the demonstrations, how Dante had led them out of harm's way—that feeling of being protected was foreign to her. It made her realize that she was in the midst of experiencing something extraordinary.

Naomi turned and laid her head on Dante's shoulder as the plane continued to rumble. He put his palm on her hand and squeezed it. They looked out the window and at all the dotted twinkling lights.

Soon, they would be touching down in Shanghai, to their home.

6

HYPHENATED

Dante was usually obliged to dine with his parents and extended family in Nanjing for lunch on Saturdays. When he joined Naomi on Saturday evenings, more often than not, his usual easygoing demeanor would appear agitated and rattled. Naomi knew it had something do with his parents, but he never elaborated.

Still, Naomi couldn't help but pry a little. Last week, she found out that his parents had set him up on a blind date without his consent. He had arrived at a dim sum lunch expecting the occasion to be a family affair. Instead, he was forced to sit next to a girl and her parents, absolute strangers who were also coercing small talk out of him. Dante said the girl was "the typical Nanjing type," that her mannerisms and mentality were so similar with his own parents that she might as well have been their daughter.

Naomi now spent more than half of her time in Hongqiao district, where Dante resided, instead of in her own apartment in the French Concession. The two districts almost felt like separate countries. The French concession was rife with Caucasian faces, American cafes, European languages and restaurants. Her neighborhood felt younger, hipper, while Dante's was bursting with children, pets, families, and international schools. In Hongqiao there were distinct enclaves of Japanese, Korean and Taiwanese communities, and Naomi savored the variety of East Asian restaurants there: Korean barbeque, samgyetang ginseng chicken soup, teppanyaki, omakase, izakaya, shabu shabu,

Taiwanese shaved ice, and even the cuisine served at Pyongyang Restaurant, where Naomi had been fascinated with the live singing by the North Korean waitresses.

Dante lived just a block from the North Korean restaurant, at a residential high rise in Gubei called Moderna Gardens. The doorman, Lao Kang, a Shanghainese man in his sixties, was familiar with Naomi by now.

To Lao Kang, Naomi was one of the most attractive women he'd seen come and go in this building. Lao Kang was impressed with Dante, although he wasn't necessarily surprised. Dante had money, that much was obvious from the fact that he was a homeowner in this luxurious residence. But Lao Kang also knew Dante came from humble origins. That was apparent when Dante's parents had visited. Lao Kang identified with the worn expression in their eyes, recognized the excessive lines on their faces that exposed the years beyond their actual age. It was the residual effect of a generation who had endured the severe sorrows of humanity: hunger, torture, war, loss.

The fact that their son could achieve so much, that their fortunes could be turned around in just one generation, was not unique. It was happening all over China now. His former roommate, Lao Liang, had been a penniless factory worker decades ago in the Anhui countryside. Then, he decided to collect scraps of paper and start a paper factory. Today he's a philandering factory boss with a wife, two girlfriends, three cars, and who-knows-how-many children.

Luck didn't shine on Lao Kang the way it did on Lao Liang. He never had the opportunity nor the acumen to strike it rich. But life wasn't bad at Moderna Gardens. He'd been working here for almost five years now. The residents here were far classier than those in the high rise he used to work at in Hongkou district. Lao Kang was fond of Dante. Dante always greeted him in Shanghainese and was generous, even giving him a fat red envelope during Chinese New Year.

Naomi raced down the stairs of the metro station on Shaanxi Nan Lu towards Line Ten. She checked her watch. There were seven stops until they would reach Gubei, which meant she would be fifteen minutes late. Her phone was out of battery or else she would've texted Dante about her tardiness. Her thoughts were momentarily interrupted by the roaring wind blowing in her face. The rumbling train rattled and hurtled through the station as people elbowed their way towards the car doors, forming what resembled several queues, making it a challenge for passengers to exit the train.

As Naomi arrived at the sleek lobby of Moderna Gardens, she smiled at Lao Kang, who held open the door for her, and Eko, the concierge. "Good evening, Naomi," Eko greeted her. "Have a seat, I will call Dante now. His parents just arrived ten minutes earlier." No matter how familiar Eko was with a visitor, she took security protocol seriously and always rang the residents for permission before letting guests up the elevator.

Naomi was pleasantly surprised to hear Dante's parents were there. Did that mean he would be introducing her to them today? That signaled a whole new phase in a relationship. They had been seeing each other for five months now, though had never addressed their "official status." Tonight, however, she was not dressed properly to meet his parents for the first time. She was in her favorite Seven jeans. The jeans were so ripped and frayed that she knew his parents would not understand that the tattered look was intentional.

Just as she was ruminating whether to purchase a simple skirt at the discount store down the street, Dante called the front desk. Eko handed Naomi the phone.

"Hey sorry, something came up…"

"Something? You mean your parents?"

Dante paused, then sighed. "Yes, they just unexpectedly showed up."

"Okay I'll meet you guys at the restaurant, I just need to get something really quick. Are we still going to Luigi's? Or I guess your parents might want Chinese—"

Dante cut her off. "Can we meet next week? Sorry love, I'll make it up to you next time."

"Oh…" Naomi was taken aback.

"It's just that my mom brought groceries, and she's about to…well, cook dinner..." Dante paused.

Naomi waited for him to continue, to tell her they would all be staying in, instead of eating out. He stayed silent. She suddenly understood that she was not receiving an invitation to come up.

"Alright, see you later then." Naomi hung up before he could say bye. She waved at a confused Eko and Lao Kang, and quickly left the building.

She had just spent close to forty minutes on the metro to get to his place. Usually Dante was so thoughtful, this gesture seemed unlike him. Then again, when it came to his family, he sometimes seemed completely out of character.

The following week, Naomi tried to broach the subject of his parents, asking him how they were doing, joking about them trying to set him up with another girl. She talked about her strained relationship with her own mother, hoping the topic might induce him to share more about his family. Each time, Dante seemed to tense up and switch subjects.

Later, at a noisy teppanyaki restaurant, Naomi felt her temper and patience slip away from her. As the Japanese chef flipped shrimp and scallops amongst tall flames, Naomi let loose her annoyance. She recounted how the other day, he could've at least invited her up to exchange pleasantries, unless, there was some reason he didn't want them to meet her.

Dante sighed. "I probably should have explained things better. We needed to take care of some family stuff that day. Some banking stuff."

"Huh?"

"I wire a portion of my paycheck to my parents. I always have. But that day they found out that their account was compromised. Some sort of fraud issue. Anyway, it's all taken care of now."

"Oh. Okay. Why didn't you just say so?"

He shrugged. "Sometimes things are complicated with them."

"Okay. So, it's not like, you're embarrassed of me or anything," she half joked.

He sipped his sake and didn't say anything for a minute. Then he turned around and held her hand. "It's...the other way around."

It took a moment to register, and then it all made sense. Dante had mentioned how eccentric his dad was. He rarely mentioned his parents, but when he did, it was always with a tone of resignation. Naomi softened her voice. "Why? You don't want me to meet them?"

Dante sighed. "The issue is that my dad's side is...originally from Nanjing. In fact, our lineage in Nanjing goes way back...generations even..." He paused.

Naomi furrowed her brow in confusion and stared at him blankly. "What are you getting at?"

Dante took a big sip from his glass, and for the next hour, he took Naomi through his paternal family saga.

In the 1930s, Dante's grandfather, Ouyang Langzou, was the principal of a primary school in Nanjing. One mid-December morning in 1937, Japanese troops stormed into the school. It was later revealed by some of the surviving students that Langzou had hidden the children behind locked closets in the school basement, before being fatally wounded. Dante's grandmother, Minlei, was pregnant when her husband died. She escaped to a nearby village, and Dante's father was born three months later. Minlei's harrowing escape nearly resulted in a miscarriage, and Minlei often said she had aged prematurely from that arduous journey.

Dante's father, Ouyang Zhangjie, never forgave the Japanese for killing his father. Tragedy seemed to plague Zhangjie's life over and over. His mother passed away from a hemorrhage shortly after giving birth to his half sister, and his first wife died from tuberculosis. For a long time, Zhangjie could not bring himself to marry another, not until he met nineteen-year-old Pan Jinsung when he was already nearly forty.

Dante paused, and swilled the sake from his glass. He recounted to Naomi a memory from his boyhood. Every year on December thirteenth, sirens would sound all over Nanjing as a reminder of the atrocities the Japanese Army had inflicted on their city. It was a grim reminder of what the people of Nanjing had suffered through.

Dante had never seen his parents shed a tear. Sometimes he thought his parents must've cried every last tear from the war and the Cultural

Revolution, when scores of their loved ones died from the hysteria and chaos of the times.

"Do you know Iris Chang's book?" Naomi asked.

"Of course. Most of my friends in Nanjing know it. Have you read it?"

She nodded. "I have the book."

Naomi was well-aware of the brutality of the Nanjing Massacre. In Tokyo, she rarely heard the Japanese reference it, but Iris Chang's book, *The Rape of Nanking: The Forgotten Holocaust of World War Two*, had changed all that. The best-seller brought the massacre into the forefront of public discourse, including inside Japan.

Naomi remembered some of the backlash she had heard about the book when she visited her relatives in Osaka during the late nineties. Naomi had picked up the paperback but was unable to finish it due to the graphic descriptions of war violence. She had read the part about how the Imperial Japanese Army had tortured even children. That chapter alone made her put the book down. She had wept, and the horrific churning of her insides would return whenever she thought about what she had read. She believed wholeheartedly in Iris Chang's research and reporting. Naomi thought it was despicable that the *uyoku dantai* or some members of the Japanese government and population went so far as to deny the war crimes had happened.

"I'm curious. Do you find yourself identifying most as Japanese, or Taiwanese, or American?" Dante had asked.

For Naomi, the answer wasn't so straightforward.

Once, when she was vacationing in Okinawa, a local had sneered at Naomi and her mother. By then, Naomi was in middle school and had moved to California. Later, Naomi learned that there were anti-American protests demanding that the American military withdraw from Okinawa. U.S. bases took up nearly twenty percent of the island. The year prior, the island had been embroiled in a horrific scandal when three American servicemen had raped a local Okinawan. It was one of those crimes the locals still talked about, felt haunted by.

In high school, she had gone on a road trip to central California one summer with her mother. Reina had accidently cut off another driver, and the woman had stuck her head out of the car, flashing her middle finger, yelling at Reina to "go back to China" with expletives in tow. In Orange County, Reina was an active member of the Japanese community, some of whom were third generation Japanese Americans, whose grandparents had endured the internment camps in the 1930s. Naomi had heard from her mother's friends about the harrowing conditions they lived through.

Last week, Naomi was met with mild hostility on a taxi ride when asked about her country of origin. Out of curiosity, she replied that she was from Taiwan, instead of from the U.S. or Japan. The driver didn't seem to appreciate her response. He proceeded to admonish her on how her answer was "inaccurate" and "unpatriotic" because China and Taiwan were one country after all, and she had now insulted her Chinese brethren by separating herself from them. He had weaved in and out of lanes, barely missing a biker from a U-turn, running a red light, all while giving her a historic lesson on how Chiang Kai-shek was a traitor to China who had sold his country and soul to America. It was an interesting theory, and Naomi would've paid more attention, had she not been paralyzed by fear of getting hit by a truck that came barreling out of nowhere. She held on for dear life as the driver sped and swerved, spitting and gesticulating. At another terrifying point, their taxi had been among the three cars jostling aggressively for position in a two-car-lane. The driver, unfazed, was still lecturing her by the time they had reached her destination.

For Naomi, existing on the hyphen—balancing her Japanese, Taiwanese, American identities—feeling neither here nor there, a drifter among homes and countries, was a perpetual state of mind.

7

GOLDEN PINE

BEFORE DANTE ADOPTED HIS ENGLISH NAME, HE WAS KNOWN AS
Ouyang Tian. It was emotionally wrenching for Ouyang Tian to leave
Nanjing in the late 1980s, at age eleven for England. He didn't want to
leave his family, his home country. But after years of meticulous planning,
his mother had finalized arrangements with her cousin in England to take
Ouyang Tian in.

Ouyang Tian's mother, Pan Jinsung, came of age during the Cultural
Revolution. Although her peers were brainwashed to extol the
omnipotence of Mao Zedong, Jinsung was inclined to believe otherwise,
especially after her father died in a prison cell, when she was a mere
nine-year-old.

Pan Jinsung's father, Pan Mengru, was inexplicably jailed on
suspicions of spy activity in the sixties. In the mid-forties, Mengru's
siblings and cousins had left for Taiwan, Hong Kong and Europe, before
the communists came into power. Mengru was an ardent believer in
communism and the promises of New China. He had refused to leave
his country. Mengru's resolve only strengthened when he attained
the prestigious job of Secretary to Police Chief in a fierce competition
against many other applicants. By the time he started his new job at the
communist police headquarters, his wife was pregnant with their third
child, a daughter they named Jinsung. *Golden pine.* The pine tree was
traditionally revered as a symbol of luck and longevity in China. All of
Jinsung's siblings had the character *pine* in their names.

Mengru's post at the communist police headquarters entailed much political maneuvering, as there were recruits from all over the nation who did not trust each other, at a time when there were constant suspicions of spies lurking around. Because Mengru's direct superior had favored him by granting him perks and pay raises, Mengru's peers grew increasingly hostile as jealousy and tensions rose. When Mengru's boss was reassigned to Beijing, Mengru's peers in Shanghai seized the opportunity to slander him. They had heard that Mengru's siblings were settled in Europe, and that he regularly received overseas letters. His peers reported this to another police chief, who promptly had Mengru arrested on suspicion of spy activity.

In prison, Mengru was interrogated and forced to confess to the crimes he did not commit. Beaten, starved, and most of all, disillusioned by the system and the job he was at first impassioned with, Mengru finally succumbed to self-defeat and allegedly committed suicide in his cell.

Jinsung would never forget the stony-faced officer who arrived at their home to deliver the news of her father's death. It happened on the day before her ninth birthday. Because Mengru was considered a criminal, the police didn't even give his family a chance for a proper burial. Mengru's wife was left with a death certificate stating he had committed suicide, which the police intimidated her into signing, to acknowledge that her husband's death was self-inflicted. But she refused to sign the paper until they would let her claim the body. It was a demand left unanswered.

Jinsung is now the keeper of the unsigned death certificate, and she still laments that her father does not have a grave which the family could honor and visit. Jinsung remembers the week her father died, the towering tree plant they kept at home in a gargantuan pot started sprouting white blossoms. The plant had been in the family for a decade, and had never grown flowers. Everyone in the family was convinced that this was a manifestation and sign of Mengru's ghost.

After Mengru's death, his wife Yang Anqing, doubled her hours as an accountant at a privatized food processing plant on the outskirts of Shanghai to make up for the loss of her husband's income. Anqing had once been the envy of her peers; she had graduated with an economics degree from the prestigious Eastern University, where she had met her husband. But during the height of the Cultural Revolution, all privatized companies and white-collar workers came under scrutiny. Anqing was forced to endure the beatings by her peasant neighbors and Red Guards. Her past "crimes" included but was not limited to: being a capitalist, graduating from university, and having relatives that had immigrated to Europe.

As a single mother of three, Anqing had no choice but to send her youngest daughter, Jinsung, to be raised by her colleague and his wife, who were barren. Jinsung's memories with the Xu family were mixed with good and horrendous times. Uncle Xu had spoiled her like the child he never had, but Auntie Xu periodically punished Jinsung for having a growing girl's appetite, and would starve her further whenever Jinsung complained of hunger. She was finally able to return to her mother's side in her teens, when she could work for wages. All three of Anqing's children were forced into intensive farm labor due to Anqing's status as "bourgeoisie."

But Anqing had considered herself fortunate that the harassment she experienced was nowhere in the league which others had endured—those who had previously been teachers, business owners, landlords. There were scores of people who had been humiliated and assaulted to death by the Red Guards. At least she had been able to keep her children alive.

In the seventies, when a matchmaker mentioned Ouyang Zhangjie, a widowed glassware factory worker in Nanjing who had been left heartbroken for years over the death of his wife, Anqing recommended her youngest daughter, Jinsung, who had just turned nineteen years old. Anqing didn't mind that Zhangjie was nearly two decades older than her daughter. From what she knew of the Ouyang family, they were considered proletariat, and thus in good standing with the communist government.

When Jinsung first met Zhangjie, she thought he looked quite handsome, even if he looked older than forty years old. He must've aged from mourning his first wife, Jinsung thought. Plus, he was from

Nanjing, a place that experienced the terror and carnage of war not too long ago. For whatever reason, Zhangjie's bleak smile reminded Jinsung of her own father's. Both of Jinsung's brothers were married, and she was also eager to find the stability of a proper marriage.

Ouyang Zhangjie and Pan Jinsung were married in Nanjing. Their only son, Ouyang Tian, was born in 1977, a year after Mao's death and the subsequent conclusion of the Cultural Revolution. Zhangjie and Jinsung affectionately nicknamed their baby *Xiao Tian*, their little slice of heaven.

From when Xiao Tian was just a boy, Pan Jinsung had been plotting to get her son out of China. Her father's siblings and their families had left Shanghai before the communist takeover in 1949, and were dispersed in Taiwan, Hong Kong, and London. She discussed with her husband about buying their son a one-way ticket abroad, but Ouyang Zhangjie didn't agree with his wife. He already experienced enough separation and destruction of families in his lifetime, and was determined to keep this one intact.

But Jinsung was plagued by paranoia, by thoughts of the communists taking away her son, just like they took away her father. In the 1980s, applying for a visa abroad wasn't as stringent as it had been in the seventies. The fact that her relatives were already established abroad helped. By the time Xiao Tian turned eleven years old, Jinsung had saved enough for her son's travel expenses. Jinsung's wealthy cousin, Pan Yaning (who went by the western name *Anne*), and her English husband, Matthew Wickshaw, enthusiastically agreed to care for him until he was of age to fend for himself. Anne and Matthew's only daughter had left home to attend university in Boston, so they welcomed the company of Xiao Tian. There was an excellent boarding school just in their neighborhood, in North Yorkshire, England. Eventually, Xiao Tian came to call Anne his *gan ma*. Godmother.

Jinsung saw in Xiao Tian a resilient and inquisitive child. He was praised by his school teachers for strong mathematical skills, but was told he liked to draw during lessons, and that he asked too many questions. Compared to the other children, Xiao Tian didn't cry as much. When he fell or hurt himself, Xiao Tian's instinct was to get back up on his own. Jinsung was comforted to see that her son turned out to be self-sufficient. She was confident he would be able to make a life for himself in England.

The month leading to her son's departure she cried every night. Although Zhangjie was at first furious at the arrangements his wife made, he knew he couldn't deprive their only son of the coveted, golden ticket out of China. That was the dream that his peers had for their children.

Xiao Tian adopted the name Dante when he started at Thomford boarding school. Uncle Matt, his gan ma's husband, a literature professor, provided a sheet of names to choose from: Herman, Oscar, Earnest, Dante, all of whom uncle Matt said were respected writers.

Xiao Tian liked the way *Dante* sounded, which was a relief for Matt to hear, since Dante was easier to pronounce than *Xiao Tian*. Matt provided Dante with intensive English instruction. Anne wrote letters to her cousin Jinsung: her son was a fast learner and Matt was impressed with the boy's determination. Matt Wickshaw knew an ambitious student when he saw one, and in Dante Ouyang, he saw a boy who yearned to excel.

Dante recognized how fortunate he was for the opportunity to stay with uncle Matt and his godmother Anne. The idyllic English countryside was a far cry from his childhood home in Nanjing, where they didn't even have modern plumbing, where his family and their neighbors would share just one telephone. He saw how privileged his peers at Thomford boarding school were, how they never lived in discomfort, not even for a single day. Dante vowed to work hard, to make a glorious amount of money someday, to give back to his parents for their sacrifice, to make sure his parents would one day live in similar comforts.

It would be six long years until Jinsung and Zhangjie saw their only son again, after he had left Nanjing in the late eighties. By that time, he was no longer a boy. Dante was able to save enough from his part-time job to afford his first round-trip ticket back to China. Thereafter, Dante visited his parents every two years. Jinsung always cried profusely at the airport whenever it was time to bid goodbye again.

Every time Dante visited, Zhangjie repeated the same lectures to his son—after you have saved up enough, move back home to China, marry a good girl from Nanjing, and start a family. But Dante would laugh off the counsel, much to his father's irritation.

In London, Dante achieved career stability at some of the city's most renowned architectural firms. By then, he was dating all types of women, but few were Chinese. It wasn't intentional, it just so happened that the ones he was attracted to were mostly of different cultural backgrounds.

Still, deep in his core, Dante had great reverence for his aging father. He vowed one day to make good on his promise to return to China, to care for his parents, to make up for time lost.

8

FLOATING PALACE

For his thirtieth birthday bash, Logan invited around twenty friends to the Floating Palace. It was one of the secret KTV Lounges hidden in a dark alley near the Bund, adjacent to a sordid row of windowless hair salons, which everybody knew were "dirty massage parlors."

Naomi had heard of these infamous KTV lounges in China. Not to be confused with karaoke venues (sometimes locals referred to karaoke as KTV too), these KTV lounges sold services unavailable in karaoke venues. Expats sometimes referred to them as "dirty KTVs."

"What? Why would you want to go there?" Joss asked Naomi, crinkling her nose in disdain. Joss had been to these type of establishments with Tay and his business acquaintances. These places were only tolerable if you were able to look past the demeaning behaviors of everybody there.

"C'mon, it's Logan's birthday. He treated our entire party at his restaurant last month for your birthday, remember?" Naomi countered.

"I didn't ask him to," Joss retorted. "Fine," she sighed. "I'll go. But only if we leave within one hour."

"Dante will come too," Naomi added. Although at first she was hesitant to attend the affair, curiosity got the better of her. Dante said he wasn't interested in these type of venues, but would go to keep her company.

Some would say Floating Palace was aptly named. It was pronounced *Piao Gong* in Chinese, and the character *piao* for "floating" was also a homonym for "prostitution." Therefore, a slight change in intonation meant that instead of Floating Palace, you got, well...Prostitute Palace. Humor of the homophonous kind was lively in Mandarin.

The hostesses, all in various curve-hugging qipaos, appeared in the room and lined up in formation. Logan made a show of examining the lineup in detail before selecting his date for the night. Yards of glossy skin fanning out of petite hemlines stood before him. They were all good-looking, as was expected for the damage done to his wallet; this place was criminally overpriced compared to other similar venues. One of the women in particular was staring at him seductively—the tall one with an inhumanely narrow torso, long schoolgirl braids, a mischievous smile. He'd like to climb that mountainous rack. All at once she looked delicious, diabolical, magical. *Ni jiao she me ming zi ya*, he asked, taking her hand. What's your name?

"Angel," she replied back in English. Logan flashed his kilowatt smile. He'd heard of a popular Chinese expression: the face of an angel with the body of the devil. Yes, this one would be his undoing tonight.

A mixed group of local and foreign men, including Amos Kim, and Logan's business partner Vincent Tu, took turns making their date selection. Dante and Tay sat out, sitting firmly next to Naomi and Joss in a corner while enjoying their beer. The ornate room was outfitted with black leather sofas, strobe lights, bar stools, cocktail tables, microphones, a plasma television, a miniature stage and a dancing pole. Trays of appetizers were laden on the tables: pork dumplings, edamame, roasted peanuts, spicy cucumber, sliced watermelon.

In no time, the qipao-clad hostesses began pouring drinks and putting song orders into the computer. They circulated the room and asked for everybody's song choices, everybody except for Naomi and Joss. The hostesses had also skipped over them when pouring drinks.

Naomi's eyes widened at the blatant show of rudeness. "They're not going to serve us because we're not here to solicit their *special* services," Joss explained.

"Ladies, bottoms up!" Logan came over, holding a bottle of Grey Goose by the neck. He squeezed himself in the seat between Naomi and

Joss, leaving Angel pouting in the corner.

He turned to Naomi when Dante left for the restrooms. "Where's my birthday present?"

"My presence is present enough," she smiled sweetly.

"Touché. And might I add, you look incredible tonight. They've got nothing on you," he cocked his head towards the hostesses. He was being honest. Naomi was still the most stunning woman in the room, even in her simple black tube dress. If anything, the simplicity of the dress accentuated that incredible figure.

Naomi laughed and shook off Logan's hand draped over her shoulders. "Hey did you call your brother?"

Logan made a face. "What for?"

"It's his birthday too."

"Right. I'll send him a message later." He shrugged and looked around for Angel. "Now where are those sake bombs?" he bellowed.

"That Angel of yours is giving me the death stare. You better get back to her," Naomi chuckled.

Then Dante was back and Logan quickly got to his feet to rally the group to *ganbei*. The hostesses scrambled to lay out the required ingredients for the sake bombs: chopsticks, shot glasses filled with sake, pint glasses filled with beer. They balanced the chopsticks on top of the pint glasses, then precariously placed the shot glasses on top of the makeshift chopsticks bridge. Then everybody started hollering, pounding and slapping the table until each sake glass had splashed into the beers. Following the goading of his friends, Logan downed five successive sake bombs.

Joss deliberately moved in front of the computer to put in Mariya Takeuchi's "Plastic Love," a Japanese song she and Naomi both loved. Kitty, the hostess selected by Amos as his date for the night, didn't hide the annoyed look on her face.

When "Plastic Love" appeared on the screen, Joss picked up two microphones for herself and Naomi. The song evoked memories of their college days, when Naomi had taught her the Japanese lyrics of "Plastic Love." Joss had become addicted to the tune, putting it on repeat and blasting it as they'd get dressed and ready for their nights out on the town in New York.

Joss and Naomi were up on their feet now, simultaneously laughing and singing, sashaying and bringing back old dance moves. But before they could finish the song, Kitty shouted "my turn!" and grabbed the microphone out of Naomi's hands, smiling spitefully. Warbling into the mike, wagging her backside and gyrating to the music, Kitty's barely-there dress shimmied, giving the crowd flashes of her undergarments. The men whooped and hollered. Joss looked like she was about to say something but Naomi just shook her head and mouthed "it's fine."

"Are you sure?" Dante asked. Naomi nodded.

Next, Amos rapped to a Korean hit and the hostesses all applauded rapturously like he was Rain, the current reigning K-pop king. After his performance, Amos grabbed Kitty and led her to another room. "Go easy on him!" Logan snickered.

Dante's song came on then. He picked up a mike and started belting a Chinese ballad. It was a hit mandopop song this past summer: *Wo...wo... wo...he ni mei wan mei liao.* Me and you, 'til no end.

Naomi had been to karaoke lounges with Dante before, but had never heard him croon a solo. When he sang, his voice was delectable, like velvety rich butter. Everybody clapped at the performance, surprised at his talent.

Before Dante could finish, Logan grabbed his mike and cut him off. "Alright, that's enough. No offense, it's my birthday and I didn't come to hear men sing."

"What a douche," Dante grumbled as they left. After seventy minutes at Floating Palace, Dante, Naomi, Tay, and Joss said their goodbyes. Nobody seemed to care when they did.

Naomi sighed. "Sorry you had a bad time. With Logan, you just never know. Sometimes he's dreadful, sometimes he's a friend."

"And you know *why* he's friends with you, right?"

Naomi shrugged.

"Don't tell me you've never noticed the way he pines after you," Dante glowered.

It's true, Naomi had noticed. She never told Dante that she and Logan had kissed once, when they had first met. But that had been a slip. After that, Naomi swatted away any further advances from him, and Logan had acted as if it'd never happened.

Logan had his faults, but he was also one of the first friends she made in Shanghai. Didn't that count for something?

After they left Floating Palace, Naomi and Joss decided to continue the night at New Star, a Korean bathhouse located in the K-Town neighborhood of Hongqiao.

"How are Tay's TCM visits going?" Naomi asked carefully as she toweled herself off. Joss mentioned that Tay was trying traditional Chinese medicine for his health issues, but she had been reluctant to detail the specifics. Naomi hadn't pressed further about it.

"Well we hope the treatments are working, but we don't know if they actually are," Joss said, stretching out her legs on the lounge chair inside New Star's state-of-the-art restrooms and showers. The bathhouse was complete with saunas, steam rooms, cold plunge pools, cooling rainforest showers, and a gym. Naomi favored the *tui na* massages. Joss liked to lie in their brick kilns and dine in the Korean restaurant attached to the complex.

Joss explained that they had been visiting Dr. Xie and his renowned traditional Chinese medicinal practice on Xizang Nan Lu. According to Dr. Xie, Tay's kidney energy was deficient. He prescribed a cocktail of herbal roots: renshen (ginseng), gancao (licorice root), dangshen (Codonopsis root), huangqi (Astralagus) and ling zhi (Ganoderma mushroom). He ordered Tay to come in for three sessions of acupuncture weekly.

Tay was also balding prematurely, which Dr. Xie said was another side effect of a weak kidney meridian. The doctor had instructed Joss to "buy black sesame seeds and black soybeans. Mix them in his dishes, such as in his soup, rice bowl, vegetable or meat dishes. Make sure your husband eats these at least once a day." Joss had worked with Ah Ming to revamp Tay's meals and diet. Organic produce was not easy to come by in China, but there were markets for imported goods. Before Tay's diagnosis, Ah Ming usually shopped at the traditional markets. Now, Joss accompanied Ah Ming to the grocer's and picked out some of the produce herself.

Joss hoped Tay's health would improve soon. The TCM treatments were their last resort. They were running out of options.

She excused herself and said she needed to find a toilet. She blinked back tears and hoped Naomi didn't notice.

*

Naomi felt like wearing her sunglasses on her walk to work this morning, even though there were no sun rays to be shielded from. The sky was a dreary gunmetal hue, the fog of pollution looming ominously, lingering at eye level and in her nostrils.

The morning news released a report from the Shanghai City Weather Bureau: the haze was a combination of "dust, fog, and airborne particles rolling in from the north." It was just another paraphrase for pollution. The particulate matter was 416 micrograms that day. She felt wistful for the World Expo days when the government was steadfast in ensuring the PM stayed close to 100. Although in North America this level would've still been categorized as "unhealthy," it was considered a relatively breathable day in China.

Naomi pulled her 3M mask over her nose and mouth. She quickened her pace alongside the congested traffic, her ears ringing with the hum of vehicles against the asphalt. She was reminded of a statistic she had heard, of how among the country's many achievements, China was also now the world leader in carbon emissions.

She passed by the street sweepers with bamboo brooms and pushcarts. The masks on people's faces were like a funeral-esque uniform, eulogizing the end of autumn, the hazy gray air a premonition of the eventual fall of winter. The winds had picked up and golden gingko leaves floated off en masse to the grounds.

It was early December. The Expo had been over for a month now, but the city was still basking in its afterglow. The government published statistics that pointed to the unprecedented fanfare and scale of the extravaganza. It's as if Expo had been an exercise in Chinese superlatives—the largest number of visitors (72 million), the greatest number of pavilions (246), the largest territory of any world's fair in history (over 1300 acres).

"Glad to have you back!" Frida smiled as she passed by Naomi's cubicle.

Naomi hugged her friend. "It's nice that my commute is back to under fifteen minutes." Although she had felt a pang of nostalgia on her last day at the French pavilion, it was also somewhat of a relief to be able to resume her former route to Henglong Plaza, which was an easy walk from her apartment. Now that Expo was over, she would no longer be required to make the hour-long commute from Puxi to Pudong.

Just then, they heard a commotion coming from the reception area—loud shouting in Shanghainese, then the sound of glass shattering and women screaming. Naomi and Frida hurried over to Lingyu, the receptionist. She was hiding under her desk crying, her hand bloodied. A fist-size rock stood among shards of glass scattered over the marble floors.

"Lingyu!" Naomi helped her up. "Are you ok? What happened?" Frida grabbed the tissues on the desk to cover Lingyu's bleeding forefinger. Droplets of blood trickled onto Lingyu's ivory slacks. "Somebody get the first aid kit!" Naomi shouted out. Her colleagues scrambled from their cubicles and were now hovering over the reception area, gasping. Somebody from HR emerged with the first aid kit and helped Lingyu apply gauze to her fingers.

"A crazy man…threw a rock…at the door," Lingyu said in between sobs. "He said Jun Cleo and Chantevieve should be kicked out of China because Angelique supports Tibet…"

Over the weekend, footage of a media interview with American starlet Angelique Ford had gone viral and caused an uproar in China. In a rambling interview, Angelique extolled the virtues of the Dalai Lama, describing her "utmost admiration and respect" for him, and how she believed "karma would haunt those who hurt the Tibetans." Angelique was Chantevieve's brand ambassador for the Vie skincare line, and her face could be regularly spotted in glossy magazines worldwide, in department stores, and wherever Chantevieve's billboard ads had a presence, including the ones in China.

Naomi dabbed at Lingyu's eyes with a tissue. "Are you ok? Did the glass get you anywhere else?" Lingyu looked visibly shaken. "I don't know…"

Auguste Reynaud was by Lingyu's side now. He told her to get to the hospital and take the rest of the week off. He quieted the crowd. "The police and building security have been alerted. There will be an investigation to arrest the man," he announced solemnly. "You can all take the rest of the day off. You don't need to worry about your safety when you come back tomorrow. There will be heightened security here, effective immediately."

Naomi heard some of her colleagues cheer under their breath at the unexpected day off. As the crowd began to shuffle out, Pearla approached Auguste. "I can stay back and help out today."

"Thanks Pearla," Auguste replied. "But I'll get Naomi since she's been working on Chantevieve's account." He turned to Naomi now. "Please gather all the relevant team members. We need to hold an emergency con call with Chantevieve's Paris HQ."

An hour later, Naomi was seated in a conference room with Auguste, Nicki, Frida, Margeau Leroux, an Account Director, and Louis Liu, Chantevieve China's Sales Director. They were on a conference call with a host of Chantevieve executives based in Paris.

Auguste did most of the talking in French, while Margeau translated on the side into English for the rest of the group. Auguste was noticeably frustrated at the stalled responses from the other end. Naomi, acting as minutes secretary, was typing furiously.

As he continued the call, Margeau explained that Auguste was currently requesting that Chantevieve officially denounce Angelique Ford from her role as brand ambassador immediately. "But HQ responded that the contract should still be honored until year end—"

Louis cut her off in an urgent tone. "We can't wait that long! Our daily sales have already tumbled more than forty percent. Our beauty consultants are receiving threats and somebody threw a rock at our makeup counter in Baisheng mall——"

"There's a movement to boycott Chantevieve on Weibo and newspapers are still publishing the interview with zeal," Frida chimed in. "The PR team has tried to sweet talk the editors out of the negative coverage and we've sent them tons of free products already, but the reception has not been very warm——"

"Yes," Nicki interrupted authoritatively. "What should happen immediately is an official apology from Angelique, a simple statement released by her publicist that she misspoke. They need to take this seriously. After all, China is Chantevieve's number two market, only slightly behind the U.S., isn't that right, Louis?"

Louis nodded. "Our profits are on track to surpass America by next year. Well, hopefully, that is if HQ doesn't hire anymore ignorant celebrities that say idiotic things——"

"Yes, of course." Nicki cut him off and turned her attention to Auguste. "And HQ needs to conduct better celebrity management, and provide all the brand ambassadors with a crash course in cultural sensitivity, especially with any issues pertaining to China——"

Auguste held up his hand, indicating for Nicki to quiet down so he could continue the call. Nicki rolled her eyes and folded her arms, lips pursed. Everybody went mute for a few minutes as they listened to the back-and-forth in French. Margeau continued to translate: "HQ said they will urge Angelique's team to issue an apology, however there are no guarantees." Margeau quieted for a few minutes as she listened in some more. "Now Auguste is suggesting that the China market use a local influencer as the official brand ambassador, so Angelique can still continue on in the other markets until the end of the year."

Nicki nodded. "I already have a list of potential collaborators. And I think the market is mature enough for a local face." The majority of Chantevieve's ads featured white faces—celebrities from Europe or North America. They were, after all, a French company, and that was part of their appeal in China. But Nicki had seen competing companies increasingly employ Chinese ingenues as the face of their brands. She had long advised Auguste to take on such a move, but he had previously hesitated to bring it up to HQ. She was glad he was *finally* standing up to them now, but they were definitely considered late to the game.

Ten minutes later, Auguste finished the call. "It's done. Effective immediately, Angelique Ford will have nothing to do with China. Frida, please draft a press release about Chantevieve's severance with her in the Chinese speaking regions: China, Hong Kong, Taiwan—"

"What about Japan, Korea and the Southeast Asian countries?" Nicki interrupted.

"No, they will continue the relationship. Angelique is still popular with the Japanese, Koreans, Malaysians, Indonesians, et cetera. But I doubt HQ will renew Angelique's contract next year after this fiasco blows over."

"Frida and Naomi, have the bilingual release ready for my review by four," he continued. "I'll need to send it to APAC and HQ afterwards. If all goes well, it will be distributed to the press first thing tomorrow."

Auguste turned to Nicki now. "Have the print team recall all the Angelique ads for the spring and summer issues, prepare for the tear down of all of Angelique's images in all stores, and destroy all the promotional materials for the Vie product line. Start working on replacing all of Angelique's images, especially the—"

"I know," Nicki cut him off sharply. "The OOH billboard in Xujiahui."

"Devise a plan and timeline to review with me at five," Auguste replied curtly.

Auguste dismissed the group and the meeting was adjourned.

9

CHINESE VIRTUES

PEOPLE OFTEN UNDERESTIMATE PAN JINSUNG WHEN THEY FIRST MEET her. She was in her fifties, but some people thought she looked much older. Her skin was wind-beaten, her knees weak. Years of malnutrition and farm labor during the Cultural Revolution had left their mark on her complexion, not to mention the terrible fall she had endured on a mountainside in her youth that scarred her forehead. She had tried to cover it up with one of those fancy makeup bottles she bought at the Super Brand Mall, but usually two hours after application, the scar would be visible again.

No matter though, she was no longer ashamed of the scar. It was the mark of a survivor. There was much attention drawn to North Korea's poverty, but she still remembered a time when the Chinese were more impoverished than the North Koreans, when her brethren ate tree bark mixed with sorghum. The Great Leap Forward allegedly caused the world's worst famine, with estimates that it had killed over forty million people. Jinsung recalled how skeletal people had fought over measly kernels of corn. She recited her *amitabhas* and thanked the Goddess of Mercy Guanyin Buddha that she had been able to endure the hunger pains of her youth.

But what she went through was child's play, compared to the ordeals her husband Ouyang Zhangjie had endured. He was two decades her senior, so the second world war and the Japanese atrocities in Nanjing had a much more lasting effect on him. She admired Zhangjie's resilience.

Sometimes she thought the foundation of their prevailing relationship was rooted in the shared pains they had sustained, something the younger generation could never comprehend nor fathom.

Still, Jinsung and Zhangjie had a breadth of differences, one of them being their private opinions of Mao. Zhangjie had a miniature plaster bust of Mao on his bookshelf, and it made her cringe. Once, when Zhangjie was out, she had *accidentally* dropped the plaster while cleaning. There was a chip on the right side of the face now, but Zhangjie displayed the cracked figure all the same.

Sometimes Jinsung thought she and Zhangjie were as disparate as night and day. To Zhangjie, the greatest villains were the Japanese that killed his father. For Jinsung, she blamed Mao's policies for the death of her own father.

Her husband thought Mao's policies, though errant and brutal, had been *a necessary evil* in strengthening the country, and in paving the way for a New China. In her mind, Deng Xiaoping was the true hero of this country, the one who guided its economic miracle, the one they should thank for the successes of modern China. But she could never utter these unpatriotic thoughts out loud, especially not to Zhangjie.

Some of her female friends agreed with her husband. They were eternally grateful to Mao for the gender equality policies he had instituted. Mao had established the One Wife rule, ending thousands of years of concubine tradition. Many women had been "upgraded" from concubine status to wife, under Mao's policies. He had also outlawed prostitution, but Jinsung scoffed at the thought. Everybody knew the government largely turned a blind eye towards prostitution. Some estimates said there were as many as ten million sex workers in China now.

Jinsung sighed. Her own father should've lived as long as her mother. She had passed away only last year, at the ripe age of eighty-nine. But these were all futile thoughts. Her dad had been a victim of his time, but he was only one among the millions and millions.

Nowadays, most people didn't think Jinsung spoke any languages other than Mandarin, Shanghainese and the Nanjing dialect. But she was also semi-fluent in Russian, since she'd taken classes in her youth when the language had been heavily promoted. In the last decade, Jinsung had been working as an admin at a small publishing house that distributed Russian literary works translated into Chinese. Her goal now was to learn English, the language her son used with his peers.

Her husband had retired from managing the glassware factory six years ago, leaving her to fend for their income. They had saved up over the years, but if it weren't for Dante wiring a chunk of his paycheck every month, they could never have afforded their current apartment. The cost of living in Nanjing and Shanghai had surged recently, and Dante didn't protest when they had asked him to increase the monthly amount into their account. He said it was his filial duty to ensure his parents led a comfortable retirement. Her brother, Pan Desung, hadn't been so lucky.

Desung's only son, Shilong, worked in sales at a Japanese automotive company in Beijing, and had married a virtuous wife from Tianjin who bore him a lovely daughter. But after Shilong started excelling in his sales job and receiving hefty commissions, he became arrogant. He started an affair with a Japanese woman he met through work, and last month he had secretly divorced his wife without informing his parents.

Jinsung couldn't believe the shame Shilong was inflicting on his family. Now Shilong was even considering moving to Japan with that *hulijing*. Jinsung was sympathetic of her brother, but it was obvious he had spoiled his only son. Shilong was clever, but selfish as well. He didn't send money home to his parents. He probably wasted it all on his mistress.

The Qius who lived next door were in a similar predicament as her brother. They seldom heard from their son, Weiyong, whom they had sent to Canada in his teens. During his university days in Quebec, Weiyong fell in love with a Dutch exchange student, then had married her without the blessing of his parents. Weiyong was settled in Toronto now. The Qius lamented that their daughter-in-law had no interest in getting to know them. Even their children, who didn't look at all Chinese, only spoke French, Dutch, English. Mr. Qiu was enraged with his son's ineffectual parenting. "French? Dutch? What a waste of time. Don't they know Chinese is the most spoken language in the world right now?" Mr. Qiu often muttered.

Jinsung had invited her neighbors to join her in her English classes, as she thought it might do them good to learn some English basics. It would be especially helpful when they traveled to see their son. The Qius had visited Canada once, but Mrs. Qiu returned in tears saying the trip was a disaster, that their grandchildren had no respect for them, and that they felt useless in a land where they couldn't comprehend anything. Jinsung could understand their frustrations. They were similar to her husband, who had emphatically refused to learn a foreign language.

Ouyang Zhangjie didn't see the need to expend energy on studying a new language—he was too old for that. The only connection he had outside of China was their son. Zhangjie had always trusted that Dante would eventually return to the motherland to settle down. Yes, he had taught his son well, especially in the importance of *xiao shun*, filial piety—love and reverence for one's parents and elders—which was an essential Chinese virtue.

*

Dante had visited Japan several times before, mostly for business. He had never mentioned these trips to his parents. Nor did he tell them about his plan to accompany Naomi to Japan for Christmas this year. He told them he would be traveling to Macau for the holidays, which wasn't a complete fib, since he and Naomi would be stopping by Macau after their trip to Tokyo and Osaka.

Dante sighed. He respected his parents deeply, but sometimes wished they were more open-minded. His father wouldn't even buy anything Japanese branded. No Sony or Hitachi. Only Guomei or LG was allowed in their home. His parents had assumed he would be traveling to Macau with friends, and Dante hadn't corrected them.

In the Ebisu district of Tokyo, Dante met Naomi's cousin, Kouji Nishizawa, and Ruri Kita, the sister of Naomi's mother. Kouji treated them to dinner at the Yebisu Garden Place among the Christmas illuminations, while Ruri fawned endlessly over Naomi. It had been at least four years since they'd last seen each other. They spoke mostly in Japanese, until Ruri surprised Dante by suddenly apologizing to him in Mandarin—*dui bu qi wo men yi zhi jiang ri wen, wo yi zhi hen xiang nian ta!* Sorry that we keep speaking in Japanese, I've missed her so much!

The following morning, Ruri and Kouji accompanied Naomi and Dante on their train ride to Osaka, where Naomi's other relatives resided. They packed the day with family activities: visiting the Sumiyoshi Taisha Shinto Shrine, sightseeing at Osaka Castle, shopping at Dotonbori and Shinsaibashi.

For dinner, Naomi and Dante were whisked to a posh restaurant, one of the top rated in the city. Enka singers in exquisite kimonos performed while patrons dined. The dishes were a vibrant burst of colors: bright orange uni spoonfuls, juicy cuts of Kobe beef, pink slices of yellowfin tuna, mozuku seaweed in vinegar, seared beef carpaccio, tuna with grated mountain yam, roasted gingko nuts, miso marinated cod and grilled rock shrimp.

Dante could see plainly how much affection Naomi's relatives had for her. They laughingly recounted anecdotes of her childhood, how bold and somewhat naughty she'd been in her youth. An aunt reminisced about her "rebellious stage," when a young Naomi had harbored a wild streak. Another uncle said she had always been a talented painter and called her the family's *geijyutsuka*, artist. Naomi reddened at her relative's overzealous stories.

The relatives who spoke English asked Dante about his work, his family, about China and England. The ones who could only speak Japanese tended to him as if he were the guest of honor, making sure his tea was filled, his plates were cleared, his comforts were met.

Dante felt a certain privilege, to be in this position, that it was he—*him!*—whom this woman was fond of, enough to show him her family, her past, her love.

He hoped he would have enough courage to one day, do the same.

It was past nine in the evening. Naomi and Dante were sprawled comfortably on the pool lounge chairs. Besides them, the Miyako Osaka

Hotel's indoor pool was almost empty. There was a couple wading in the shallow end with their toddler, and a middle-aged man doing laps as if he were racing with himself. Dante and Naomi themselves had already swam laps, synchronizing their strokes in adjacent lanes.

"Tell me something you've never told anybody," Naomi murmured, eyes closed.

Dante was quiet for a moment. "Only if you'll do the same."

Naomi nodded.

He closed his eyes. "I've never told anybody about good ole' Rick. Rick Pitcheta. He basically beat me up once a week my entire sixth grade year."

"What?!" Naomi gasped, sitting up.

Dante explained that Rick had been his neighbor in North Yorkshire. Rick's parents had befriended Dante's godmother and uncle, and urged the boys to become friends after discovering both were in the same grade at school. Dante eventually became a punching bag to Rick's frequent moody episodes.

"Oh my. How bad did it get?"

"It was bad. The bruises were bad. He gave me nightmares. My grades dropped that entire year."

"Why didn't you say anything to your godmother or uncle? Or at least steer clear of him?"

"I don't know, pride? Ego? Stupidity? In my twelve-year-old brain, I thought it would be uncool to tell on him. He was a popular guy in school, and I was the lone Asian kid who'd just arrived from China. I kind of thought it was a rite of passage you know—to get beat up, like it was some kind of training to manhood."

"And the adults didn't detect anything?"

"Once I came home with a bloody nose and my godmum freaked out a little. She kept asking who the perpetrator was, but I didn't say anything. Uncle Matt just said *boys will be boys.*"

Naomi squeezed his hand. "I'm sorry you had to go through that."

He shrugged. "It's ancient history. Stronger in the broken places, right?

Well that's me. Your turn."

Naomi took a deep breath. She had never told anybody about Rex. Not even to Seth. Only Joss knew the full story from the night of the crime.

Something about Dante made Naomi feel at home, vulnerable enough to unwrap the gauze from the tender wound. Naomi closed her eyes for a moment, transporting herself back to Manhattan, back to 2007. "Okay," she whispered, as she looked into Dante's concerned eyes. "I'll tell you."

It was the tail end of summer of 2007 in New York. It was breezy out, the stifling heat waning. Naomi should've been strolling along St. Marks to her favorite ramen joint, or lounging in Bryant Park, or at happy hour with Joss in Midtown. Instead, Naomi was under the covers in her apartment, but not in her own bed. She was in her roommates' room, in their bed, except Lisa was at work. Rex had been planning this, waiting for this moment. He had called Naomi and said he was only working half the day. So there they were, at five in the afternoon. Lisa wouldn't be home until past seven p.m.

The first time with Rex had left her breathless, pounded her with guilt, until she shrugged it off, over and over again. Then these covert meetings became routine. They had kept up the charade in front of Lisa for months.

Naomi doesn't remember when exactly it all started between them. At first it was just a glance, at his gym-toned abs as he paraded his shirtless body day in and day out, or a brushing of elbows as they all sat on the cramped couch watching Korean dramas, him sandwiched between her and Lisa. Then one morning he accidentally walked in on Naomi as she was about to shower. The bathroom lock had been broken, unable to be securely locked. Rex had found a guy to fix it, who apparently didn't do a very good job.

It wasn't as if she was in love with Rex. He was attractive, as brawny and charismatic as most personal gym trainers were, but the whole affair started more out of spite toward Lisa, who always acted superior for some reason. Rex and Lisa were college sweethearts who moved from

Florida to Manhattan for Lisa's new job as a research assistant at the United Nations headquarters. In their East Village apartment, Naomi's shoebox of a room was half the size of Rex and Lisa's master bedroom. The walls were thin. She knew the couple weren't getting along, that the move to New York strained their relationship, that Lisa's career was going immensely well, and Rex's job trajectory was stagnant.

In the beginning Naomi was cordial with her new roommates. She was determined to make a friend out of Lisa. And they did have some good times together. They invited each other to birthdays and dinners and parties. But Naomi was aware of the wall Lisa raised between them. Sometimes she was subtle about it, other times, less so, such as the time Naomi opened up to her about being fatherless, and all Lisa could say was, "Well, that explains some of your issues."

Rex's theory was that Lisa felt threatened by Naomi, the way girlfriends do with other beautiful women. Naomi blushed when Rex said she was beautiful. She had been complimented many times before, but it was the way he said it, the way he stared at her when she did the most mundane activities—make coffee in the kitchen, do yoga in the living room, fold laundry, brush her teeth, vacuum. The way he looked at her intently filled some sort of void inside, a cavity that had never left her.

It wasn't just a physical relationship, even if it had started out that way. Rex and Naomi talked about their dreams, their past, their family. Rex's mother was Japanese, and had met her American husband at Miami Beach. Naomi and Rex bonded over having Japanese mothers, of mutual frustrations with their dead-end jobs—hers in retail, his at the gym.

Rex didn't want to work at Fitness Planet forever. After he had enough savings he planned on traveling, working abroad, going as far as Kyushu to visit his mother's hometown. Naomi's stories of Japan fascinated him.

In the winter of 2007, Manhattan was blanketed in snow, and Naomi was counting down the days to her trip back to California. She was relieved to escape the chill, not just outside but within the apartment too. The guilt of her routine trysts with Rex was weighing on her, and one afternoon, after she confided in Joss about the whole sordid affair, Joss urged Naomi to end it. But the more Naomi pulled away from Rex, the more obsessed he became.

By December, Naomi was sleeping over at Joss's more frequently, to evade Rex and Lisa altogether. She had been gradually moving her belongings to Joss's. While she still felt lost, she was becoming more and more convicted of *what she didn't want*—to be in a committed relationship with Rex. But when she said "let's take a break," he had been anything but deterred. Naomi would turn her phone off at night to avoid his barrage of text messages.

On a snowy Thursday afternoon, she returned to the apartment to pack up the remainder of her possessions. It had been about three weeks since she last saw Rex. The time away from him confirmed for Naomi what she suspected all along—that she had no intention of being Rex's girlfriend. She e-mailed Lisa and Rex about officially moving out that week, saying that she would drop off her last rental check. Naomi was careful to select a time when she knew she would have the apartment all to herself. No messy goodbyes necessary.

Naomi was in the middle of packing her toiletries in the bathroom when she heard the front door slam. Her heart sank. She knew the sound of those footsteps. She was just about to close the bathroom door when Rex elbowed his way in.

His face was beet red and Naomi knew immediately he had been drinking. He lunged at her and pulled her in.

Naomi shook him off. "Why aren't you at work? How much did you drink?"

Rex loomed over her and nuzzled her neck. "Gawd I've missed you. Where've you been? You're not taking my calls now?" His hand was already on her back, digging under her shirt.

Naomi pulled away. "I've made it clear…we need some distance. I never meant for you and Lisa to break up."

His eyes looked glazed and he didn't seem to hear her. He didn't let go of her waist. She was still in her work attire—a knee-length navy pencil skirt, a white button-down and a high ponytail. He began to yank the zipper of her skirt from behind, tugging it down.

Naomi shoved him hard. "I mean it Rex, cut it out!"

He snickered and didn't let go. Then he had her left arm twisted behind her back and her right arm pinned to the wall, his groin pressed up against her. "That's it? I lost my girlfriend and my job because of you, and now you're just walking away?" he sneered.

"What do you mean? What happened?" And then Naomi knew. He had probably been drinking too much, upset at Naomi's disappearance, missing work and frequenting their usual bar haunts.

He shoved her to the floor and tore off her shirt with such a force that the buttons popped. "Stop it! You're hurting me!" Naomi was screaming, pounding his chest, kicking him away. He held her down and quickly lowered himself on her, crushing her under his weight.

He shoved her on her back. Naomi grabbed at whatever was within reach, the tub curtain, the steel bar on the wall, the toiletries hook. She hit his head with a bottle of shampoo. It was useless. He had torn through her undergarments, pressed his hips against hers. He grunted with pleasure.

When he tried to kiss her, she bit into his shoulder as hard as she could. She tasted blood.

"Argh!" he roared as he rubbed his shoulder. That was when he let go of her, pushed her away, slamming the door behind him as he stumbled out of the apartment.

Still crouched on the tiles, her clothes strewn all over the floor, Naomi cried for a while. She then willed herself to get up, grab her bags, and get the hell out of there.

When Joss saw Naomi's bruises, she was ready to call the authorities and report the crime. But Naomi just wanted to calm the vicious storm brewing inside. She felt simultaneously livid, guilty, fearful. A part of her wanted to violently inflict pain on him, a part of her felt the colossal guilt lifted from her shoulders, now that it was over with Rex. She knew the courageous thing, the *right* thing to do was to go to the police. But for reasons she couldn't elucidate, she didn't want to go through the ordeal of filing a report, and getting the police involved. For what? Justice?

Truth? She wasn't in the mood to face all of the interrogation, to have her body examined, to provide evidence and fluid samples. The truth was, she wasn't supposed to be with him in the first place. He had been Lisa's, but Naomi hadn't cared. Naomi hadn't been that into Rex, while he had fallen for her completely—and she had known all along that was going to happen.

The only thing Naomi wanted was to run far, far away—away from Rex, away from that goddamned city.

PART *3*

SLEEPLESS IN SHANGHAI

Spring 2011 — Spring 2012

"I don't ask you to love me always like this, but I ask you to remember. Somewhere inside me there will always be the person I am tonight."

—F. SCOTT FITZGERALD,
TENDER IS THE NIGHT

"…Shanghai was a waking dream where everything I could imagine had already been taken to its extreme."

—J.G. BALLARD,
THE KINDNESS OF WOMEN

1

EROS AND PSYCHE

NAOMI ADJUSTED THE BUTTONS ON HER QIPAO. A QIPAO WAS NO EASY feat for any figure to pull off; it could accentuate all the wrong areas and complimented only certain body types. She should've had her garment made by the more experienced and expensive seamstress at the fabric market, instead of at the cheaper stall. The craftsmanship was shoddy in the sleeves of the qipao and a size too snug. Still, it looked decent enough in photos, the midnight blue with silver blossom patterns shimmering nicely against the vintage movie sets at Chedun Shanghai Film Park. Frida had told her about the tourist attraction located in Songjiang, an hour away in the outskirts of Shanghai. Naomi yelped in excitement when Dante agreed to accompany her there, especially after she learned that scenes from Ang Lee's "Lust, Caution" had been filmed there.

After they snapped what seemed like hundreds of photos in front of replicas of Old Shanghai landmarks—Waibadu Bridge, Bund Peace Plaza, Moller Villa, the Nanking Lu tram—Naomi was famished. They left the film park and sat down at Yu Xin, a Sichuan restaurant.

All day long Dante had been quieter than usual, Naomi noticed. He barely made eye contact, and constantly looked like he was hesitant to say something.

"Is something the matter? You're not yourself today," Naomi looked at him, agitated. He was fidgeting and on edge, as if he were sitting in a job interview, and not on a date.

"Nothing's the matter, it's just…it's just that I…I have something to tell you," Dante stammered. He took a deep breath as Naomi held hers. A slew of questions spun in her head. It sounded like he was about to divulge terrible news. Was he ill? Was he about to break up with her? Did he meet someone else?

"You know how I was insanely busy about a month ago with that pitch?" Dante asked. He took a gulp of water.

She nodded. Since Christmas they had barely seen each other because he'd been preoccupied with work and she had traveled to Taiwan for Chinese New Year. "Yep. Why?"

"Well, we won."

"Isn't that good news?" Naomi breathed an internal sigh of relief. She took a sip of her *Tieguanyin* tea.

"It's good news for the company. We're opening up a new office too. I've been asked to head up a new project there. Well, at least initially."

"Wow congrats, that sounds like a big promotion!"

"I guess it kind of is. It's definitely a good career step. I mean, the compensation is unbelievable, it's an almost thirty percent salary increase. Any less and I wasn't going to consider." He was quiet for a moment.

"Okay…then why do you look like that?" Naomi asked, as she wolfed down her *liangfen*—chunky jelly-like noodle strips dipped in Chongqing spicy sauce.

"Like what?"

"Like that day we ate at Dacosta. You were thrilled that a celebrity chef from Tarragona came, but you had this look after your first bite of the Catalan Fricando. Like you were underwhelmed."

"It's just that I'm…conflicted." He looked down now. "The new office is in Palo Alto."

"Palo Alto, California?" Naomi shrieked. She nearly choked on her noodles. She coughed and lowered her voice now. "So…what does that mean? Are you moving?!"

"It's not permanent," he said quickly. "At least, that was my request.

I told them I'd only be interested in this one particular project. I led a similar development back in London. Which is probably the primary reason they've asked me to lead this one." He had a pained look.

"So how long are we talking about?"

"At least eight months." He sighed. "Could be longer."

"Oh." Naomi paused, trying to keep calm. "So you knew all this time that you might be leaving Shanghai."

"I didn't want to say anything at first…I wasn't sure whether we'd win the pitch or not."

"Okay. I wish you had kept me in the loop."

"I should have. I'm sorry."

She took a deep breath. "Well, I'm happy for you."

"Really?"

"Like you said, it's an incredible opportunity." Naomi tried not to look disheartened, after all, they had never properly delineated their dating status. They only met a little over half a year ago. Each time she thought they would approach the subject—either at the restaurant in Beijng, in the pool at Osaka, or during any of the myriad of moments in Shanghai—something always seemed to come up. She had an uneasy feeling that he was hesitant to move forward with her. And now, they were going two steps back.

Dante reached across the table for her hand. "Naomi, I'd still like to call you or video chat from time to time, if that's okay with you."

Naomi looked down. Seth had traveled extensively for work, and at one point he had been posted in Hong Kong for months. It was her first taste of being in a long-distance relationship, and it did not go well. They had fought on almost every single international call between Manhattan and Kowloon.

She crumpled a napkin in her hand and forced a smile. "Yeah sure, whatever. We'll keep in touch."

*

From: ouyangtian@gmail.com
To: naomi.kitafan@yahoo.com
Date: March 2, 2011 23:42
Subject: keeping in touch

Dear Naomi,

Many apologies are in order.

The first one is for waking you up in the middle of the night with my ill-timed phone call. I've somehow mixed up the time zones. I have to say though, hearing your adorably groggy voice really made my day, even if it was only for a minute.

The second one is for my work schedule, which I know you had asked about, so we can figure out some video chatting time slots. The schedule is horrid. The company has me shifting between multiple time zones for the next several months. I'm in the Bay Area now, but will have meetings in Chicago, Boston, New York, London, Brussels, Vienna, Dublin, then back in the Bay Area again after the meetings in Europe. I thought I'd be spending the majority of my time in Silicon Valley, where the client's corporate headquarters is, but looks like they want us to meet the various other stakeholders in the other offices too.

Yesterday I had some free time and made a point to visit the SF Palace of Fine Arts and the Legion of Honor museum. Have you been there? The Palace of Fine Arts was built for the 1915 World's Fair, and the Legion of Honor is a replica of the French Pavilion from the same exposition. The whole day made me nostalgic for our Expo days. Remember when we snuck into the VIP lounge at the China pavilion and hobnobbed with Chinese film directors? It was pretty special now that I think about it—that we had the opportunity to work at a World's Fair, to be, in a small way, part of that history.

This is only my second time in California. The first time was years ago, on a layover in L.A. I quite enjoy SF and the Bay Area. People are cheerful to a fault. Coming from London and Shanghai, this takes a bit of getting used to. But now I see where you get that hopeful glint in your eyes, that optimistic sparkle. Do you miss your home state?

So here I am, about to hop on a red eye at SFO, thinking about what you're up to in Shanghai. Did you eat at Yuanyuan this past week? Please have some *niangao* for me, I've been craving it and even went to a Shanghainese restaurant in Chinatown here asking for it. But it didn't taste the same.

I have an idea. Remember that night we got near-alcohol-poisoning pissed and played that game "Top Three?" Can we continue playing? Even if it's in e-mail form? Here, I'll go first.

Top three things I miss about Shanghai:

1. Clean subways (the bart is crap)

2. My mom's *hong shao rou* (she makes a mean one)

3. You

Dante

From: naomi.kitafan@yahoo.com
To: ouyangtian@gmail.com
Date: March 8, 2011 18:11
Subject: Re: keeping in touch

Wow, I come AFTER food and transportation? I guess I should be flattered that I made it into the top three, although I've never tried your mom's cooking. I'm sure that's exactly where you learned your gourmet culinary skills from.

I should apologize too, for hanging up so soon. And thank you for calling my grouchy-slash-angry-three-a.m. voice "adorable."

To answer your question, no, I haven't been to Yuanyuan's lately. Because I'm not even in Shanghai. I was summoned to Tokyo. Remember that colleague I told you about, Pearla? She was supposed to go to Tokyo for a client's event. At the last minute (and I mean literally six hours before her flight), her travel visa was denied by the powers that be. Apparently single women in China are currently a flight risk because the government assumes they may jump ship and never return. So Cher sent me on this last-min business trip without so much as a proper brief, but it turns out I didn't really need one, because the most interesting thing the client said to me all day was, "Is the wi-fi working here?"

I shouldn't complain. I was put up in the Otani at Roppongi Hills, and I had a chance to see aunt Ruri and cousin Kouji, and to treat them to dinner via the corporate card. Kouji looked even worse than he did at Christmas. Remember how I said he must've lost ten pounds? He looked even skinnier this time. He said he doesn't have much time to eat, and that he's been working twelve-hour days.

I'm worried for Kouji. I told him he should switch jobs. Did you know there is a Japanese term for people who die from being overworked? Karoshi. It's common enough in this country that it even gets its own vocabulary. The suicide rate is another sad phenomenon in Japan. I grew up hearing tales of the haunted forests at Aokigahara near Mount Fuji, a well-known suicide site. I am a proud hafu (half-Japanese), but being here this last week, I've realized that I wouldn't enjoy working here.

It's mind-boggling to think about how much time is wasted at work. Yes, we're compensated for our time. But it's also time we'll never get back. I think you're the one that has it all figured out. Architecture moves you, (in fact, I don't think I've ever seen anybody linger longingly at an early twentieth century art deco building like you do), and that's what you get to do, day in and day out.

I'm grateful for Jun Cleo, for the opportunity to work at Expo. But sometimes I look at Pearla, Cher, Nikki, and wonder if they're thriving, and whether I like being a "marketer." I don't know if you're right, if I'm always an optimist, but a girl can dream.

My top three dream jobs:

1) A couture dress designer
2) One of those artists who sketches on the side of the street
3) A florist

I'll add in a number four: a traveling World's Fair worker. Is there such a thing? How fun would that be, to be a part of all of the World's Fairs? In the meantime, I like what you're doing—visiting the monuments that commemorate these historic events. Today I visited the Tsukuba Expo Center, home to 1985 World's Fair. Of course it reminded of me of our time at the Japan pavilion watching robots play the violin.

You asked if I miss home. It's strange, in Shanghai I'm called an expat, while back in the U.S., I'm viewed as an immigrant. Either way, we're not fully accepted, not really. I think maybe Taipei and Tokyo are the places I have the most nostalgia for. They're the most dependable, magical places when reminiscing my childhood. Is it ironic that I can't remember much of it, except for the moods it evokes? But maybe that's what home is—somewhere warm and safe and wonderful.

Miss you too,
Naomi

From: ouyangtian@gmail.com
To: naomi.kitafan@yahoo.com
Date: March 8, 2011 22:39
Subject: keeping in touch

I still have the doodle you did at that restaurant in Beijing. I can't believe you sketched me with such accuracy within those nine minutes of us waiting for the dishes. If you decide to go back to the fashion industry, I have no doubt your designs would find a following. You are easily the most fashionable person I know.

A florist? I never would've guessed! But it makes sense now, your place always looked and smelled like a garden. And I agree with you. A permanent World's Fair worker sounds like a dream job.

Being overworked is certainly a tragic phenomenon in many cities in Asia. I hope your cousin finds a solution. My parents also worry about me working too much, but most of the time I don't really think of my job as "work." You're right that architecture is an obsession. I think it started when I left Nanjing and moved to England, where I suddenly went from a communal urban ghetto without so much as a toilet, to a picturesque Yorkshire prep school with all the trappings of an English country club. The stark contrast in my living situations really prompted me to examine the frames and shells that shelter and shape us.

I think every edifice houses multitudes of stories. And conversely, every building or structure affects our stories, maybe even alters them.

My top three favorite structures in Shanghai:

1. There is a secret garden and villa on Julu Lu, called Eros' Garden. You may have passed by it before, not knowing that it's behind those imposing gates. The garden is a gift from 1920s coal magnate Jisheng Liu to his wife Rose Chen. Jisheng commissioned Hungarian architect Hudec to design the garden, and Hudec was so moved by the affection between the couple, that he thought only the Greek myth of Eros and Psyche could compare to their love. A statue of Psyche adorns the fountain of the garden, which was miraculously unharmed during the Cultural Revolution. I hope I can take you to see it someday. It's closed to the public, but I had a rare chance to see it with the Shanghai Art Deco Society once.

2. On Yuan Mingyuan Lu there is an eighty-year-old art deco building, home to the former Young Women's Christian Association. It has Ming and Qing dynasty architectural elements, such as carved lotus petals shapes, sea waves and cloud patterns. The building was

designed by Lu Yanzhi, one of my heroes. He was the first Chinese to start his own architectural firm. My maternal grandmother had briefly been a member of the YWCA, involved in various social reform initiatives, such as campaigning for anti-foot-binding.

3. Your apartment. Definitely a top contender of a favorite place in Shanghai.

Homesick,

Dante

2

CLOCKS IN THE CITY

From: ouyangtian@gmail.com
To: naomi.kitafan@yahoo.com
Date: March 11, 2011 06:33
Subject: ARE YOU OKAY????

I tried calling you, but nobody picked up. I'm in Boston now and have been monitoring the news. Looks like transportation and most flights are grounded in Japan now. But hopefully you left before the earthquake struck? Magnitude 8.8...wow I can't even imagine...

Please let me know you're okay when you get this. I'm worried.
Yours,
Dante

From: naomi.kitafan@yahoo.com
To: ouyangtian@gmail.com
Date: March 15, 2011 14:47
Subject: Re: ARE YOU OKAY????

I'm okay. Well I mean I'm still shaken. I left Tokyo on 3/11 morning, so fortunately, I narrowly missed the earthquake. When I heard what had happened, I tried to get in touch with Kouji and aunt Ruri and the rest of my family in Tokyo and Osaka, but no calls were going through. It looks like most of the internet was down too. Kouji returned my e-mail two days later. He said he had walked over ten hours to get home from work on 3/11 when the earthquake had struck, since all subways and trains had halted. I was finally able to reach all of my family members. So thankful that they are all accounted for. But Kouji said his colleague's family was not so lucky.

The hysteria has extended to China as well. Everyone here is in a mad dash to buy potassium iodide, which purportedly fends off residual radiation effects, likening this Fukushima Daiichi nuclear plant disaster to Chernobyl. The salt aisle is all out and people are wearing heavy-duty masks. It feels surreal, like we're living through a pandemic.

It's been a really crazy week. You'll forgive me if my responses become intermittent...to be honest, at a time like his, I'm not really in the mood to be typing or pouring my emotions out to a screen.

Wish you were here.

Stay safe. Be well,
Naomi

From: ouyangtian@gmail.com
To: naomi.kitafan@yahoo.com
Date: March 17, 2011 09:12
Subject: ARE YOU OKAY????

I get it. And I wish I was there for you. I really do.

I'll try to call you soon.

From: naomi.kitafan@yahoo.com
To: ouyangtian@gmail.com
Date: May 22, 2011 14:43
Subject: Re: ARE YOU OKAY????

I saw news of the Grimsvotn volcanic eruption and that many flights in Europe have been cancelled. You mentioned that you would be traveling in Europe in late May. Are you there now? Is everything alright? Please reply to this and let me know you're well.

I'm sorry we've been missing each other's calls, and that I haven't been good with responding to e-mails. Cher has been piling on my workload, so it's been hectic around here.

Remember that movie marathon night, when we watched "Before Sunrise" and "Before Sunset" with Joss and Tay? You made a comment about how Jesse and Celine could've saved themselves nine years of angst and heartache had they just exchanged e-mail addresses. Maybe you're right. But I think the ease in digital communication and the prevalence of devices have made us all less present, not more. I don't know, maybe I'm too retro.

Three reasons why I think e-mails would've downgraded Jesse and Celine's story:

1) So, in an alternate universe, they start e-mailing each other after they bid goodbye to the most romantic twenty-four hours they've ever had. Everything seems fine at first, but then, one of them takes too long to reply, and then the other stops responding, eventually. I mean the year was 1995 and they were in their early twenties. Why would they sit around a dial-up computer all day? If they had, then they wouldn't have been the Celine and Jesse that fell for each other in the first place. Because Jesse and Celine, in 1995, lived for the moment. That was a fundamental reason why they took a chance on each other.

2) Since they're both very philosophical people, eventually they would've started arguing through their e-mails, had they started e-mailing each other regularly. The difference between fighting in person versus online, is the power of immediacy and making up. Remember that fight we had that day I came all the way to your place and you changed plans on me at the

last minute because of your parents? Well I'm guessing you remember the following day better, when we made up. ALL. DAY. LONG.

3) If they had e-mailed each other all along, then Jesse would not have felt compelled to write a book in order to track Celine down. Now what's more romantic than writing a book in order to find the love of your life?

You know, I wrote you a letter. A hand-written letter. Who does that nowadays, right? But you don't have a permanent address for me to send it to, so you'll just have to read it when you get back here.

Sealed with a kiss,
Naomi

From: ouyangtian@gmail.com
To: naomi.kitafan@yahoo.com
Date: May 23, 2011 16:57
Subject: Re: ARE YOU OKAY????

It's funny you mentioned the films. I was in Vienna two weeks ago and thought about you, thought about our "Before Sunrise" and "Before Sunset" movie night. There's actually a "Before Sunrise" film tour in Vienna, where one can trace Jesse and Celine's footsteps. I ended up spending an hour near the Albrecht statue. I sat at the exact same spot where Jesse recited that W.H. Auden poem to impress Celine. I ate my lunch there, then looked ridiculous as I attempted to take some selfies to commemorate my "Before Sunrise" moment with an imaginary you.

Been stuck in Dublin for the past two days. My flight to Portugal has been moved to the 26th now, although we're not sure if that one will be re-scheduled again.

The week before Vienna I was in Brussels. As much as I appreciate the institution of World's Fairs, there were many that were on the wrong side of history, including the 1897 Belgian one. In King Leopold II's colonial palace in Tervuren, there was a Congolese human zoo, a folly they senselessly repeated in the 1958 Brussels World's Fair too. There was also the Temple of Human Passions, constructed for the 1897 World's Fair as well. I made a point to go see it. The pavilion houses a controversial marble relief on the theme of humanity's pleasures and pain. There are all manners of passions displayed here: seduction, motherhood, debauchery, rape, war. The rawness was simultaneously moving and disturbing.

I want to address something I don't think I adequately expressed when you told me what happened to you in 2007. Thank you for trusting me enough, to share with me your story. I heard the anguish and regret in your tone, all while knowing you were trying to dial it down. I can only imagine what kind of trauma you had to endure. I get the sense that you have a certain idea of yourself. But I think sometimes you forget how resilient you are.

Responding to your third point: How about giving up a plane seat? That's just as romantic right?

Hang on to my letter, I'll be coming for it.

Romeo a.k.a Dante

From: naomi.kitafan@yahoo.com
To: ouyangtian@gmail.com
Date: June 15, 2011 15:46
Subject: Re: ARE YOU OKAY????

Sorry for the delayed response. I just returned from Suzhou for a client's conference. Then I stayed behind for a day and took a city tour. Suzhou is gorgeous. It has the most UNESCO recognized gardens in the world!

Your selfie is hilarious. You probably haven't had a haircut in a while. I like this new look! Your descriptions of Vienna sound captivating. I wish

I could've been there. And yes, I've heard of that shameful history of the Belgian world fairs.

Cher has me traveling to various regions in China for the next several months. It's the job assignment that everybody else on the team dreaded, but I'm excited about it. I'll have the weekend in some of the cities for personal leisure. So Joss and Tay will meet me in Lijiang, Frida is working with me on the project in Jilin, and Amos and Logan are meeting me in Qingdao.

Work will be insanely busy this summer. I'm not sure I'm up to the task of playing phone and e-mail tag.

If that sounds harsh, I'm sorry. It's not that I want to hit pause on us. But I'd rather pick up from where we left off once you're back.

That said, here are the top three things I miss about you:

1) Your food factoids. "Ice cream is one of the most beloved foods in the entire world and was invented in China during the Shang dynasty. It's a travesty that most people attribute the treat to Italians."

2) Your strange obsession with durian. Yes, I'll admit I miss the durian stench you carry with you. The other day I read in the news that a flight had to be evacuated in Germany because of an unidentifiable odor. It turned out to be a durian. When I read that I thought maybe you would be on that flight.

3) I love how your right eye is bigger than your left, ever so slightly. It's visible mostly when you laugh. I miss your smile.

Be well. In the meantime, I'll be guessing... wherefore art thou, my Romeo?

Naomi

3

DIVINE INTERVENTION

SOME WOMEN HAD THAT MATERNAL, INSTINCTUAL, EMOTIONAL CORE that drew them to miniature fingers and toes. They cooed and sighed at the sight of infants, made peek-a-boo faces at toddlers and rushed to console weeping babies. Joss was one of those women, but she didn't wish for her in-laws to know that.

Ruiling and Zhaoyi were becoming increasingly impatient with their son and his wife. The other day, they had commented on Joss's *aging eggs*, now that she was over thirty years old. "You've been married for over two years now! What are you waiting for? The longer you wait, the more problems down the road," Ruiling said.

Joss tried to deflect with "Tay is focusing on his career right now," but Zhaoyi waved the excuse away, saying he had purposely lightened Tay's workload recently. He gave Joss a stern look, and emphasized that he was itching for grandchildren, specifically a grandson. "Daughters marry into other families. We need sons to continue the Tang name and the family business," Zhaoyi said.

Joss rolled her eyes internally at the archaic preference for boys over girls. She couldn't wait to terminate this conversation. It was futile, not to mention, premature. She and Tay were nowhere close to conceiving. They had seen a variety of fertility specialists, but none of the doctors had been able to prescribe an effective remedy for Tay's problem.

At first they had taken secret jaunts to Singapore to see a leading fertility expert in the region. Tay had heard about the famed Singaporean doctor and his high success rate of helping couples conceive. When that didn't work they had started TCM treatments. But after rounds of testing, even this doctor didn't seem so optimistic about their prospects anymore.

Joss felt at a loss. She decided to do something she hadn't done in years. She went to church.

It had been at least five years, six maybe, since Joss had last step foot in a church. That was when her dad had insisted that they attend Christmas service as a family. But Christmas was precisely the time when Joss tried to avoid all things Jesus. Mother's Day, too.

Jillian Liao had passed away the day after Christmas.

Joss still remembered being on her knees in the waiting room at the New York Presbyterian Hospital. She was twelve years old. All her life she'd been told that Jesus performed miracles, that God heard prayers, "seek and it shall be given to you, knock and the door will open." She had never knocked so hard, had never prayed so fervently. *Please Jesus. Please bring my mother back. I'll do anything. Anything.*

The Shanghai International Church service was held at a hundred-year-old building on Hengshan Lu. The historic building was an anomaly on a boulevard lined with dive bars and mediocre western restaurants. Vines were entwined along the church's bricked walls, and a large golden cross greeted visitors at the corner of the church on Wulumuqi Lu. Chinese beggars congregated at the front of the entrance, bobbing paper cups in their hands, hoping to catch the spare change of parishioners who were seemingly at the height of their compassion, their spirits stirred from hearing a moving sermon.

Joss had quickly taken to pastor Luke Chang's impassioned sermon style. The Taiwanese-American pastor and his Caucasian wife hailed from New Jersey, and had adopted a Chinese girl.

"Look around you," Pastor Chang bellowed. "We have represented here more than thirty spoken languages and a hundred nations of origin. This congregation is a microcosm of the world and gives a glimpse of what heaven will look like."

"China, and the Chinese, figure greatly in God's plan," Pastor Chang continued. "Just look at some of the earliest Chinese characters, which are pictograms that date back thousands of years ago." He then detailed a biblical school of thought that the ancient Chinese were originally a monotheistic people worshipping the same God as the Hebrews. In *Shu Jing* (Book of History) and *Shi Jing* (Classic of Poetry), Confucius recorded how Emperor Shun performed the border sacrifice to *Shang Di* (God), a ritual of vast parallels with the ancient Hebrews. There are scholars that found the first ten chapters of Genesis featured in a number of Chinese characters. For example, the character *chuan* (boat) points to the story of Noah's ark.

Sometimes Joss forgot China was anti-religion. From what she could see, churches were expanding rapidly, at least in Shanghai. She had heard that another English-speaking church was opening in Hongqiao, and another in Pudong. She had also been invited by a colleague to a house church, which differed from regular churches in China. Unlike regular churches, which were recognized by the Three-Self Patriotic Movement and the China Christian Council, a house church was not sanctioned by the Party, essentially making it illegal to attend one. Yet house churches were growing exponentially, Joss had learned.

"It is not a coincidence that you're here," Pastor Chang continued to address the congregation. "You're all here by design. You're now in a country where Christianity is growing at a faster rate than anywhere else in the world! It's truly an extraordinary time to be in China."

Joss hadn't anticipated the feeling of serenity, of respite, inside the church. It was almost like coming home. The familiarity of the praise music calmed her, grounded her.

Somehow, Joss felt her mother's presence, right there with her.

Joss's spiritual journey began with her father, Gabe Kong, a devout Christian who preached to his daughters about the New Testament, about strong work ethics, about an empathetic disposition. But Joss was stubborn. Though she attended Sunday school as a child, once her mother had passed away, Joss held out on any religious services save Easter. Gabe did not pressure Joss on the issue. He believed the journey with Christ was deeply personal, that the matter was out of his hands and rested with their savior's. It was an incident that occurred in Joss's senior year of college, that nudged her a bit closer to the faith of her father.

Joss thought back to that disastrous trip in Thailand, planned by her college senior year boyfriend, Stan Tsien. Her dad hadn't known about the visit, had only been aware that Joss was Stan's date at his cousin's wedding in Hong Kong.

After the wedding, Stan insisted that they fly to Bangkok to join the infamous Full Moon Party on the Thai island of Koh Samui with his friends, Ken and Rio. Joss did not hesitate. She was twenty-one and in love.

On the boat ride from Bangkok to Koh Samui, Stan gave Joss a bucket as big as her head, a straw sticking out of it. Everybody on the boat was imbibing out of their own buckets. Joss sipped on the sweet-tasting drink, which reminded her of spiked punch from high school prom. When they docked, Stan took Joss's mobile phone and wallet, and said he would keep them safe for her, after all, she had no pockets on the strapless sundress she was wearing.

That was the last memory Joss had before midnight. When she woke up, Joss found herself lying in the sand near a throng of other partygoers canoodling on the beach. She looked around, and started to panic when she realized Stan, Ken, Rio were all nowhere to be found, and that she also didn't have a cell phone. She vaguely remembered that the last boat would be leaving at four a.m. She ran as fast as she could to the dock, hoping it wasn't too late. When she arrived, she began to break down in anxiety when she remembered that she didn't have any cash to purchase the boat ticket.

A local woman in a yellow t-shirt approached and asked if she was alright. Her voice cracking and tears rolling, Joss incoherently told her what happened. The woman took out a cardigan from her tote bag and urged Joss to wear it since the boat ride would be windy. The woman then purchased her ticket. She too, was leaving the island and heading back to Bangkok. She said she would make sure Joss returned to her hotel safely.

True to her word, after they docked in Bangkok, she accompanied Joss on the taxi ride back to the Marriott.

"Thank you. Please, can you wait a moment? Let me pay you back for the boat and taxi fare," Joss pleaded with the woman as they arrived at the hotel lobby.

"Don't worry about it. Just do me a favor and watch what's in your drink from now on. Okay?" She was already making her way back to the taxi.

"Okay. Thank you...wait, I'm sorry, I don't even know your name."

"Jillian," the woman shouted, as she waved from the moving taxi.

Joss waved feverishly. She felt warm all over. A lump formed in her throat when she heard her mother's name.

Stan was fanatically upset at Joss about the whole incident. He said she had disappeared and wandered off into the crowds while he was buying a round of drinks, leaving him worried sick and unable to enjoy the party for the rest of night. Furious at Stan's reaction, Joss blamed him for giving her a questionable drink and for departing the island without her. She suspected the bucket Stan gave her on the boat was laced with substances.

"Of course I didn't drug your drink! What kind of person do you think I am?" Stan yelled back at the accusation.

"I didn't say you did it. I'm just saying somebody did!"

Joss broke up with Stan shortly afterwards. The core of their relationship changed, mutated into something she no longer recognized, nor trusted.

Joss's father said he had tried to call her multiple times on the night of the party. When Gabe hadn't been able to reach his daughter, he had felt an ominous feeling in the pit of his stomach. He couldn't sleep a wink, and had prayed for her, all night long.

Years later, when Joss recounted the episode to Tay, he would tell her that she should thank God she was even alive. He mentioned the human trafficking, the scores of missing girls, the notorious reputation of those

Thai beach bacchanals. He said more than fifty percent of the alcohol served at Koh Samui was considered illegal by U.S. standards. "Instead of ethanol, the alcohol served at those Thai beach parties contain methanol. And dangerous levels of it," Tay said.

Joss knew that she was fortunate, that things could have turned out badly. It was from this incident, that she began to believe she was protected, she was blessed, albeit undeservedly. She liked to believe the woman in the yellow shirt had been some form of an angel, that her own mother was watching from above, that a higher power, who her father called *Yehehua*, was divinely intervening.

4

KARMA

September 25, 2011

Naomi re-tied her ponytail and adjusted the straps of her floral jumpsuit. She fanned herself with the exhibition brochure and tried to determine the direction of the weak air conditioning. Willfully ignoring the gallery's signs and recommended route, she decided she'd start viewing the exhibit in the coolest area first, and maybe stay there until Joss and Tay were done. Tay had described this installation as a "thought-provoking piece from one of China's up-and-coming artists," but the heat bouncing off the myriad of mirrors was distracting her from the art.

Installations of ginormous rotating cubed mirrors of varying sizes were scattered throughout the space along with dilapidated doors. Some of the doors were hanging, some were affixed to the floor. Some of the doors had antiquated Chinese door handles, not knobs. The brochure stated that the cast-off doors were all rescued from traditional buildings in Shanghai that had been demolished for Expo. The effect was akin to a Chinese cubist-themed funhouse labyrinth.

Naomi thumbed through the brochure. A description suddenly caught her eye. One of the doors was from Shanyin Lu nongtang.

Naomi looked around and tried to locate this particular door. She snapped a photo when she finally found it. She knew Dante was fond of this nongtang and frequented that area.

"Genius, right? What do you think?" Tay asked, as he and Joss approached.

"One, I think this gallery needs to upgrade the air conditioning," Joss replied, as she continued chewing. "Two, these crème fraiche and caviar tartlets are the best hors d'oeuvres I've had at any of your artsy shindigs."

"I was talking about the art," Tay grinned.

Naomi took a step back to find an optimal photography angle. "The effect of the rotating mirrors makes it a moving experience, like we're passing through homes of various states of abandonment," she said. She stood in front of one of the mirrors, mesmerized.

"It's a remarkable installation," Naomi continued. "Like a critique on urbanization maybe, and the obliteration of memory, or home."

"Interesting," Tay said, contemplatively. "Or maybe it's a reflection on the opportunity costs of commerce and globalization. In any case, it's one of the best artists debuts I've been to in a while."

"Look," Naomi pointed to a door, "this one is from Shanyin Lu, the nongtang where Lu Xun used to live." She looked at her phone. "Dante would've appreciated this exhibit."

"Why couldn't he make it today?" Joss asked.

"He's in Nanjing. At his parents' place." She checked her watch. Dante wouldn't be back in Shanghai until midnight.

"He just returned from California, right?" Joss asked, as she munched on a cheese gougère.

Naomi nodded. "Just last week."

"So, you two are okay now? I thought you were upset at him."

"I guess I was. I mean we had a good thing going on, and he just up and left. Then all the e-mail and phone tagging had been wearing on me, so I had to take a break from it." Naomi looked pensive. "You know that week I went to Qingdao with Amos and Logan?"

"For the beer festival?"

Naomi nodded. "It's funny. Several days after that trip, Dante e-mailed, texted, and called, saying that he was requesting a transfer back to Shanghai."

Joss laughed. "Sounds like he felt threatened. So the company granted his request then."

"I didn't think it would be this quick! Originally he wouldn't have been able to fly back until Christmas." Then Naomi was gushing about how Dante had surprised her by phoning her out of the blue last weekend, asking her to meet at Laris on the Bund. "He asked me to be his girlfriend. Exclusively. He said being away made him realize what he wanted!"

"So it's official!" Joss shrieked.

"It's official," Naomi echoed. "He even asked me to meet his parents next month."

Joss's eyes widened. "Now that's a huge development."

"We'll be meeting at a fancy crab place. Is there some sort of etiquette I need to know when eating hairy crabs?"

Joss nodded. "Hairy crab is a local delicacy and one of my favorite foods. But it can get very messy. Don't worry," Joss linked her arm in Naomi's. "I'll coach you."

Ouyang Zhangjie was a plainspoken, intimidating man in his seventies. His face was riddled with age spots, his teeth tea-stained. His once ramrod posture was now wilted and his torso round, yet he carried an air of dignified authority.

Dante remembered for years that his dad would wear the same ill-fitted rumpled coat that had always been too tight. It was a thick cotton blue jacket, a ubiquitous uniform from the Mao era. It was only when Dante started wiring portions of his paycheck from London to his parents, along with a package containing a new Burberry jacket, did his dad have a change of look. Tonight, at a family banquet, Zhangjie was wearing his favorite navy tartan-patterned scarf, and that very same jacket his son had gifted to him all those years ago.

They were at Xinguang Jiujia, a seafood restaurant that had been serving eight hundred pounds of crab meat a day since it opened twenty years ago. Naomi fingered her bracelet nervously at the banquet table. She hoped she had made a good first impression so far.

It was a seven-course dinner and they were only on the third. Naomi glanced at her watch discreetly. It felt as if they had been there for hours, but it'd only been fifty-three minutes since they sat down. They had already feasted on crab meat wontons, steamed okra stuffed with crab meat, and braised crab with chicken in a clay pot. She read the English printed on the menu card placed in the center of the table for the tenth time. The next courses would be steamed seabass, fried crab roe with mung bean noodles, followed by steamed whole hairy crabs, and lastly, hairy crab soup dumplings.

Dante and Naomi sat at the outer edge of the roundtable, their backs toward the aisle, where the waiters edged in while setting down the dishes. Ouyang Zhangjie and Pan Jinsung sat across from them, their seat perched against the wall. Joining them was also Dante's cousin's family: Nie Hengmin, his wife Ying, their son Huan Huan, and Nie Hengmin's parents, Uncle Nie and Auntie Nie, who was Ouyang Zhangjie's half-sister. Dante translated back and forth between Chinese and English for Naomi's benefit.

"The service is too slow here, we should've gone to Wang Bao He, like we usually do. You know the original Wang Bao He opened in the Qing dynasty and has a history of over two hundred and fifty years! They have the plumpest hairy crab sourced from Yangcheng Lake. All the modern places, like this one, are too expensive and slow," Zhangjie grumbled. Uncle Nie nodded in accord.

"The crabs from Yangcheng Lake are no longer rated number one due to their contaminated waters. The ones from Taihu Lake and Chongming Island are much more coveted. This restaurant gets their crabs from Taihu," Dante countered.

Naomi chimed in. "I also read that there are many 'shower crabs' now in Yangcheng Lake, meaning the farmers source the crabs from elsewhere and just dip them into Yangcheng Lake. So, in reality, they are considered counterfeit Yangcheng crabs." Dante quickly translated for his relatives, calling the shower crabs *xizao xie*. Naomi was glad for the opportunity to contribute to the conversation. After the initial pleasantries, she had run out of topics with the rest of the table.

Zhangjie harrumphed. Jinsung shot Dante a don't-back-talk-to-your-father look. A waiter interrupted them by showing them the seabass, alive and slithering in a bucket, sauntering off only after Zhangjie had nodded in approval.

Dante sighed internally. Why was his dad perpetually grumpy or complaining about something? Dante knew the reason for his moodiness tonight: Naomi, and the fact that she was not from China. This was the first time he had brought a girl to meet his parents.

"Dip it in the sauce, Naomi." Jinsung pointed to the small bowl laden with rice vinegar, sugar, and ginger. Naomi smiled and shook her head slightly. "Thank you, but I don't like ginger." Dante translated for Naomi and put up his hand gently as a gesture for his mother to back down.

"But the ginger is yang, and the crab is yin, so you must eat the ginger for balance," Jinsung insisted.

"In Chinese culture, ginger is considered a food that warms up the body, and crab is a cold food, so usually it's eaten together to balance the yin and yang of the body," Dante explained. He squeezed her hand and whispered, "You don't have to eat it if you don't want to."

"Naomi is drinking the Shaoxing rice wine which has the same effect as ginger," Dante repeated, seeing the looks his parents were exchanging. He could read what they weren't saying. The polite thing for her to do is *ru jin sui su*—adapt to and respect local customs.

Naomi learned that there were eight different tools used to deconstruct the hairy crab, each designed for specific parts. Joss had told her that it was almost a show of status, to be able to eat crab without cracking the exoskeleton, and then reassemble the crab with its shell.

Naomi wished she hadn't worn her newly purchased pomelo-colored collared dress. She had thought the conservative yet pretty knee-length dress resembled something she saw Kate Middleton wear once in a magazine. She had hoped the dress would deliver in making her appear elegant and graceful. At the moment, however, she felt anything but. Although Joss had prepped her for the banquet by demonstrating how to crack open a crab, Naomi could not recall the steps anymore. All she could remember was Joss's warning not to eat the heart and lungs of the crab, but right now everything seemed congealed into a glob of mess. As she attempted to handle the pair of fur-clawed crustaceans crouching on her plate, pieces of shell flew in all directions, landing in piles next to her plate and leaving visibly oily stains on her dress. Pulling open the legs and claws had been easy enough. It was the excavation of the shell that was daunting. Joss had said the real treasures inside the shells were the golden semen of the male crab and the orange roe of the female crab, sprawled atop the custardy meat.

Out of the corner of her eye, she saw Dante's cousin, Nie Hengmin, smiling at her. Dante said Hengmin's English was not bad, since he had once worked in the IT department of an English tutoring center. His wife, Ying, was busy admonishing her son to finish the food on his plate. Ying was an exquisite Shanghainese woman who looked like she could grace the pages of a fashion magazine. Naomi looked over at Ying's plate. One minute the crab was in disarray as she chopped it open, the next minute she had miraculously assembled the crab shell perfectly back to its original form, as if the crab had been untouched and could at any moment come back to life, leaping off of her plate.

The adjacent table was engaged in a loud tug-of-war with the check. The two friends first ran around the table chasing each other for it, before one started sprinting toward the cashier counter, and was followed by the other, who ran after him like his life depended on it.

After the hairy crab soup dumplings were served, the mood at the table turned somber. The conversation had veered toward a deceased family member—Ouyang Huajie, whose favorite dish was soup dumplings. "Uncle Huajie is my dad's cousin, but they had been like brothers to each other. He passed away three years ago," Dante whispered to Naomi.

Ouyang Zhangjie turned his gaze to Huan Huan who was busy coloring, noting how clever and neat Huan Huan was, and how he colored within the lines, a noteworthy accomplishment for a three-year-old. Zhangjie mentioned that Huajie was also *you tiao you li*, a neat and a notorious rule-follower. The table quieted, and Ying exchanged odd glances with Hengmin. Then Huan Huan broke out in giggles, amused by his own coloring creation of a purple crab. "See how joyful Huan Huan is," Zhangjie said, "just like my cousin, *yong yuan le guan*, forever the optimist." The table grew silent again, and then there was murmur of how late it was. Then, despite Hengmin's gestures in protest, Dante paid the bill.

Dante later explained the odd episode to Naomi. "Father believes that everybody you meet in this life, is somebody you had known in a past life." His dad had mourned Uncle Huajie's passing by visiting the Buddhist temple daily, praying to a bodhisattva for the safe passage of his cousin's soul. Two months later, when Huan Huan was born, Zhangjie was convinced Huajie's soul had journeyed back, reborn into a gleeful baby boy.

The family was simultaneously amused and annoyed at these remarks. Ying found the comments deranged, Dante often rolled his eyes, while Jinsung would whisper, "*Jiu rang ta ba.* Just let your father be. These thoughts give him peace."

Zhangjie was a staunch Buddhist who believed in the six realms of the afterlife. There was the one of gods, akin to heaven. Then there were the worlds of demi-gods, of human mortals, of animals, of hungry ghosts, and there was hell. Hungry ghosts were often those who died violently, unjustly. They awaited reincarnation.

Zhangjie believed that his father, Ouyang Langzou, died a hungry ghost, but was eventually reincarnated into somebody great, living a life of luxury. His father had been a respected teacher beloved by all, before he was violently killed by the Japanese. As a teacher he had passed down wisdom and had protected students. Zhangjie took comfort in knowing the laws of karma ruled this world—that even though his father had suffered greatly in this life, he must've been compensated for his good deeds in the next.

5

MATCHING DOORS

NAOMI THUMBED THROUGH THE STACK ABSENT-MINDEDLY. THE NEXT big work project was a collaboration with the Shanghai Museum on a joint exhibition exploring the art of incense and fragrance spanning two thousand years of Chinese history, from the Three Kingdoms period, Wei, Sui, Song, Ming, Qing dynasties, to last century's jazz age. From ancient incense tables, fragrance burners, ceramics, bronzes, to art deco inspired Chinese perfumes, there was an abundance of historical artifacts the museum possessed which were suited for the multi-sensory exhibit, designed to engage visitors in an olfactory and visual experience. As the title sponsor, Chantevieve would be allocated prime installation opportunities. The brand had commissioned Yan Xi, a celebrated contemporary Shanghainese artist, to begin creating an installation incorporating the brand's perfume bottles. Naomi made a mental note to phone Yan Xi's assistant about the current progress of the art piece.

She was so engrossed in the research that she nearly missed the e-mail buried in her inbox, an explosive announcement about Auguste Reynaud's departure. She gasped as she read the e-mail espousing his virtues while wishing him well in his new post. Auguste Reynaud would be heading back to France to run the Global Corporate Social Responsibility department. The new appointment was undoubtedly a step down from leading the agency's largest and most important market.

During lunch, Frida informed her that Auguste had been forced to step down, stating underperformance as the primary cause. The agency had been enjoying profitable double-digit growth in China until recently, and the government's anti-corruption crackdown may have been a factor.

The new president was now Nicki Jiang, his nemesis. Nicki had a signature speaking style—she spoke in deliberate tones, often leaving pregnant pauses for effect, making eye contact with each person while the rest of the room held their breath during these intense intervals.

Nicki's appointment was setting two precedents: she was the first local to helm the China office's president position, as well as the first woman. Since Jun Cleo's entrance into the Chinese market a decade ago, the agency's China president position had been held exclusively by white males, mostly Europeans. There was a significant morale boost in the office after Nicki's promotion. Most seemed to appreciate the fact that the highest position in the office was now rightfully held by a Shanghainese.

As soon as Nicki moved into the presidential office, the changes to Auguste's former office were striking. Where Auguste had been a minimalist, preferring muted colors and clean walls, Nicki now had vibrant thangkas covering a side wall. When Naomi had been summoned into her office for a meeting, she had heard a stream of low humming, chanting noise that she thought was drifting in from the open window. Later, she learned that the sounds had been streaming from a Buddhist chanting CD inside Nicki's office. Naomi wondered whether the religious music was supposed to create a zen atmosphere inside her workspace, a stark contrast to what actually happened in there. Everybody knew that Nicki was abrasive and foulmouthed. Most of the curse words were screamed in rapid fire Shanghainese, which Naomi didn't understand a word of, but could detect in her gruff sense of tone.

While Auguste had provided Cher's department with an adequate berth and budget, Nicki was now moving a significant amount of the department funding elsewhere. There were rumors swirling that sooner or later, somebody from the Experiential Marketing department would have to be sacked. The speculation put the entire team on edge.

Halloween was in three days. Jun Cleo's HR department had sent an announcement about the mandatory company-wide social a month ago.

The theme was Masquerade Ball, and the much-anticipated affair would be held at the Peninsula hotel on the Bund.

Naomi was aware not to let her guard down during company socials. The consequences were harsh for those who were not well-prepared and well-groomed for the occasion. The typical cheap or DIY-looking Halloween costumes would be unacceptable. No, this was couture Halloween.

For her attire, Naomi settled on an androgynous cat-woman suit. She had on fitting leather pants, a tuxedo jacket, cat ears, and heels with spikes that were reminiscent of the Christian Louboutin fall collection. Once she had arrived at the event however, it was quite clear that her costume was among the least interesting.

Some colleagues had showed up in elaborate period costumes dressed as renowned historical Chinese figures. Pearla came as Princess Wencheng of the Tang dynasty (who eventually became a queen in the Tibetan empire), Liya dressed up as Empress Wu Zetian (the only female sovereign ruler of dynastic China), Fei channeled Diao Chan (from the literary classic *Romance of the Three Kingdoms*). Cher turned into the celebrated Shanghainese writer Eileen Chang, carrying several paperbacks, with her hair primped roaring twenties style. Nicki arrived in a show-stopping gown and wig as Marie Antoinette. Orca was dressed as Karl Lagerfeld, and Frida came as, of course, Frida Kahlo.

The ballroom was transformed into a Venetian themed masquerade ball, with nearly two hundred costumed employees, a vast pasta and gelato bar, a performance by a Chinese soprano, and waist-coated hotel staff in Venetian masks passing out Bellinis and Prosecco.

Frida told Naomi what she had heard, that the gala had been Nicki's idea. It was no secret that Nicki had complained about Auguste being an uptight bore who skimped on employee team building events. Her distaste for the last company social under his leadership had been apparent; it was a trip to the outskirts of Shanghai, where Auguste had arranged for staff to volunteer at a university's eco-awareness conference.

Other than team building, the gala served another purpose. The PR team had been instructed to invite a plethora of reporters to the event.

All throughout the evening, Nicki was seen being interviewed by TV outlets and various media about her historic appointment as Jun Cleo's first Chinese female president.

*

"May I remind you there are twenty million more men than women under thirty years old in China." Dante had gleaned this statistic from the news. This was the effect of the one-child policy and the traditional preference for male children, which had led to innumerable abortions of baby girls. There were actual rural villages in China devoid of single women.

Dante was at his parents' place. That morning he had met his parents for lunch at a restaurant on Hanfu Lu in Nanjing. When he had arrived, he discovered that the elderly Pengs and their daughter, Min, had also been invited. The lunch had been painful. It was obvious his parents had led him to a *xiang qin* event, where one meets prospective marriage candidates. Min had looked just as irked as Dante and had barely glanced his way.

When they had returned to his parents' apartment, Dante pleaded with them to stop meddling in his relationship with Naomi.

"Don't get smart with me!" Ouyang Zhangjie had shouted in response to his son referencing a stupid statistic. "With your qualifications, you know very well you can have any Chinese girl you desire."

Dante laughed at the absurdity of this assertion. "Thank you for your faith in me, but that's not the point. I'm not interested in dating some girl from China you approve of. I'm with Naomi now. I don't care if her family is from Japan. And who knows? I might ask her to marry me someday." Dante surprised himself by blurting out such a declaration. He was just so agitated that he felt like issuing a statement to squash this discussion. The truth was, he had only met Naomi about sixteen months ago, and they were both in no hurry to tie the knot, at least, they had never spoken of it. Not that it had never crossed his mind. He was approaching his thirty-fourth birthday and his relatives never ceased to remind him that at this age, he should consider *ding xia lai*. Settling down.

But most importantly, Dante had never been this content in a relationship. When he was around Naomi, he wanted to be the most optimum, the most kind, the most attractive version of himself, and he wanted to give every part of himself to her. Nobody else had ever inspired him to feel this way.

Dante observed his parents' dismayed expression, which incensed him even more. "Bottom line is, *ru guo ni zhen de yao wei wo hao*, if you care about my happiness, you'd understand. This conversation is done." With that, Dante slammed the front door behind him.

Zhangjie fumed. What kind of statement was that? *If you care about my happiness?* Hadn't they done enough to make him happy, to demonstrate their love for him? They had sacrificed everything for their only son, working multiple jobs and saving up every single renminbi to pay off the debts to his wife's cousin in England for taking Dante in as a child. Didn't he know he meant the world to his parents? How could he disrespect their judgement, especially in matters as important as courting and eventually, matrimony? Furthermore, it was an affront to Zhangjie's family if Dante married somebody whose veins flowed Japanese blood. How could that woman ever understand the trauma the Japanese had inflicted on his family?

Jinsung sighed. It was just typical of this generation! To be so entitled that they would only accept things from their own point of view. Had they spoiled their only son too much? In her generation, people only married with the blessing of their parents. It was a basic sign of filial respect. Jinsung knew her son was intelligent; he had always excelled in his academics. How could he be so gullible in an area as crucial as marriage? Doesn't he know that marriage does not just run on love alone? It is a partnership that is so much more complicated than that. Marriage is never between just two people—it's a merging of many.

Before Naomi, in a previous life, Dante had dated a wide spectrum of women in Europe. Some were Asian, some were not, but seldom were they from China.

The only Chinese girl he had been steady with was Giorgina Wei. They had met in a culinary school in Italy, and had been pleasantly surprised when they discovered they both resided in London, and were both born in China. Her parents were from the capital, and though she had never specified her parents' profession, or the source of her wealth, Dante knew Giorgina was most likely a *fuerdai*, and that her parents were affiliated with the Chinese government one way or another. He had gathered that much during their three years of on-and-off dating.

Giorgina was sweet-natured, if not a little timid. She seemed genuinely afraid of most things, and Dante had felt the urge to protect her somehow. She was never overt in displaying her wealth, though she did have an affinity for the high-end boutiques on Bond Street. Her overbearing cousin also lived nearby, and her parents had visited frequently from Beijing. Giorgina never did introduce him as her *boyfriend*, she had reasoned with Dante that her parents didn't approve of her dating at such a young age, even though she was already in her mid-twenties. Dante didn't take offense at first. Giorgina had always seemed extra anxious around her family.

Later, Dante figured out the real reason he was treated with no more deference than a bus boy by the Weis, someone only good for holding open doors or carrying bags for their precious Giorgina. Once, Giorgina had used his laptop to send some e-mails. Dante hadn't meant to snoop around, that is until he spotted his name.

In an e-mail to her daughter, Mrs. Wei had admonished her for running with "types like Ouyang Tian," referring to him in his Chinese name. She said that she had already checked out the Ouyang family background in Nanjing. Mrs. Wei had concluded that Ouyang Tian's parents were nobodies, poor backwater peasants and mere blue-collars. Mrs. Wei ended her e-mail with a simple lecture: *men dang hu dui*. The four-character Chinese idiom literally meant "corresponding windows and matching doors," which alluded to the pairing of a couple who were in similar educational and socioeconomic standing. In certain contexts, the saying was a compliment about a couple's matching attractiveness. But Dante had no illusion about Mrs. Wei's insinuation—this had nothing to do with his appearance or any other factor within his control. It made no difference to Mrs. Wei that Dante was regarded as more educated than Giorgina since he had a Master's degree and she a B.A., or the fact that in many parts of the world, Dante would be considered a very rich man for the salary he commanded, or that in many circles, he would garner the utmost respect for having achieved what so many of their Chinese brethren aspired to—he was a classic rags-to-riches case, a shining model of Chinese perseverance, the Chinese dream personified.

No, this wasn't about any of that. This was about bloodlines, status, class, lineage. Mrs. Wei had made it clear that Dante was *beneath* them, that her daughter would one day be matched with somebody *born* into the same strata as the Weis.

After the horrible fight that morning, Pan Jinsung headed toward the Guanyin shrine at Jiming Temple near Xuanwu Lake. Dante had never slammed the door or huffed and puffed at his parents before today. She sensed that the Naomi issue would not be resolved easily.

Jinsung took out the joss sticks and lighted them from another burning one. As she stuck them inside the urn, she bowed. With her palms joined firmly together, Jinsung implored Guanyin to have mercy on her family.

At first she had thought Naomi would just be a phase. Jinsung was not naïve, she knew her son had dated all types of women when he had been abroad. They had rationalized that Dante and those women were just *wan wan*—playing, casually dating, which was what young people did nowadays before marriage. And they had thought Naomi would be just another one of his playthings too. But then they started to notice the way their son gushed about her, how she increasingly accompanied him to family gatherings. That was when Jinsung and Zhangjie became alarmed.

It wasn't that Naomi was terrible. No doubt she was beautiful, but she was almost too attractive. There was a Chinese saying: *hong yen mei ren duo bo min*. Beautiful women have thin lives. Women who looked like that invited unwanted attention that wasn't good for anybody.

But the main issue wasn't just the way she looked, but where she was from. Or *not* from. They had hoped their son would marry a Nanjing or Shanghai girl, and there were so many eligible ones to choose from! Jinsung and Zhangjie had visited the marriage market at Shanghai's People Square, and there had been a wealth of enthusiastic responses to the ad they'd put up for Dante. Their son had the most competitive package: western education, impressive salary, a homeowner, not to mention he was handsome. She had shown her son's picture at the marriage market and the women had swooned. Jinsung had gathered many phone numbers that day, all from parents who had practically begged her to consider their daughters.

Another thorn was the Japanese heritage issue. Jinsung cursed their luck. Out of all the women in China, why did their son have to pick *her*? He knew how his cousin Shilong had broken his parents' hearts by cheating on his wife with a Japanese woman, and then there was her husband's family history. How could Dante ask his father to overlook a painful past that still haunted his dreams at night? It was asking too, too much.

Jinsung prayed to Guanyin, hoping that it wasn't too late to change Dante's mind. Had her son become too anglicized? Maybe they should have sent for him to return earlier. Yes, she had felt blessed that they had the great fortune to send him abroad in his youth, but times have changed. Now, China was one of the most powerful countries in the world. Everybody said the twenty-first century belonged to China, to the Chinese. Dante had made the wise decision to return to his homeland, where his future in Shanghai would undoubtedly grow in prosperity.

But what if this Naomi yearned to leave China? All the foreigners eventually left. If things continue the way they do, Naomi might persuade Dante to leave with her. No, Jinsung couldn't bear the thought.

Her son had finally returned home. She couldn't lose him again.

6

CHRISTMAS

THE SHANGHAI SCENE OFFICE WAS ON THE FIFTH FLOOR OF A FIFTEEN-story building on Maoming Bei Lu. In reality, they were situated on the fourth floor, but the Chinese avoided the number four, since the number was a homonym for the word "death" and considered unlucky.

Nearly thirty people were crammed in the conference room for the staff meeting called by Trina Akerston, the editor-in-chief.

"I'm pleased to announce that this year our holiday charity drive partner is the Shanghai Children Welfare Institute, a local orphanage. Our project leader will be our beloved lifestyle columnist, Joss Kong. Now, Joss has already been prepping for the event, so I'll give the floor to her." Trina sat down as Joss started explaining the charity drive action plan to her colleagues.

"We're scheduled to volunteer at the Children Welfare Institute on the fifteenth and sixteenth. On Wednesday morning, there will be a training session conducted by Kenna Dai, the director of the orphanage. I've spoken with Kenna already, and we've worked out various stations and a schedule. We'll be divided into groups and rotating among the different stations over the two days. Here is a sample of some of the stations and responsibilities," Joss said as she gestured at the wall where a slide was being projected. It was an image of the layout of the orphanage. "They'll need food prep help in the canteen, cleaning the children's playground, teaching English to the older kids in the classrooms, and also volunteering in the nursery with the babies." Joss paused as a buzz of chatter filled the room.

Joss started passing out the fliers Kenna had provided. "This sheet lists the types of donations the orphanage needs: hygiene items, kitchen supplies, new toys, books, et cetera. I've prepared boxes for each of us to take home and fill up. Please circulate the fliers among your community, friends, relatives, and rally them to donate something from the list. All boxes need to be back in the office by the fourteenth."

Every year, since its inception in 2005, *Shanghai Scene* has sponsored a charity drive to coincide with the holidays. Last year it was a toy drive to benefit migrant children, the year before that, a fundraiser for a local literacy program. Weeks ago, Trina had approached Joss to inquire her interest in leading this year's holiday charity drive. Joss had initially declined due to the fact that her sister would be visiting from New York that week.

But maybe it was the Yuletide spirit. Joss had felt uneasy about her response for days. She later told Trina that she would gladly lead the charity drive this year as long as Jamie could participate as well.

Kenna Dai was a petite Shanghainese in a colorful Christmas sweater, red framed eyeglasses, and a curious British accent when she spoke English. "I spent some years in Manchester," she explained. When Kenna returned to Shanghai, she picked up her father's post at the orphanage. He was finally retiring after over eleven years at the Shanghai Children Welfare Institute.

After Kenna finished conducting the volunteer training for the group, Joss handed out the printed schedule and announced the assigned teams. They had more foreigners than locals working for the magazine, but Joss made sure that each team had at least one Chinese speaker for ease of communication.

Joss and Jamie's first station of the day was the baby nursery. They were introduced to Weili, the supervisor of the nursery. Joss tried to concentrate during Weili's demonstration, but couldn't help staring at Nini, the two-month-old baby girl in her arms. Nini was wearing a pink top and yellow polka dot pants, her feet bundled in yellow socks with patterns of smiley faces. A pink bow rested on her head among her wisps of hair. Nini's long lashes framed her eyes, which were wide awake as she stared at Joss. When Weili positioned the bottle in Nini's mouth, Nini opened her mouth wide, showing a large gap from the roof of her mouth to the base of her nose.

"It is very challenging to feed babies who have *tu chun*," Weili said, as Nini squirmed in her left arm. With her right hand, Weili picked up a bottle with a long teat. "This special bottle is specifically designed for them. It's like an eyedropper and is easier for these babies to use. Here, you try." During the volunteer training, Kenna had said that the majority of children in China's orphanages suffered from some sort of birth defect or disability. Cleft lip and cleft palate were one of the most common.

Without much warning, Weili placed Nini in Joss's arms, thrusting the bottle and a pink bib in Jamie's hands. "Try to get Nini to finish this bottle. She'll have surgery next month for the *tu chun* so she needs to be as healthy as can be. After Nini is done, come find me and I'll bring you to the next baby."

"*Hao de*," Joss called after her as Weili walked off, trying to sound as confident as possible, even though her heart was racing. Nini seemed so fragile, as if she could break at any moment.

But Nini proved to be an apt eater, even if her bib was getting soaked with milk dribbling down her chin. Joss and Jamie stared as Nini drank. When she was done, Jamie clamored to hold her. When Nini started whimpering, Jamie handed her back to Joss.

"I think she likes you better."

"Well, I do have more experience." It was coming back to her now. All those years ago in middle school, when her life consisted of bottles and diapers and raising her infant sister.

They both went quiet for a moment as they looked at Nini's drooping eyelids. Joss started rocking her in her arms.

"You're thinking about her, aren't you? Mom's sister?"

Joss nodded. They never knew their mother had a sister, even up until her death. It was their father who revealed the family secret—that their mother's sister had been born with a cleft lip, then left at a market in Wenzhou in the sixties. It was sad, thinking about a relative you could have known, a person that could've been a part of your life. Joss closed her eyes momentarily and said a prayer in her head. She hoped her mom's sister was okay, wherever she was.

Nini was sound asleep now. Joss hugged her close.

Trina Akersten was grateful for Joss Kong's leadership at the charity drive. Trina had handpicked the Shanghai Children Welfare Institute as their charity partner this year. It was a cause dear to Trina's heart.

Trina looked more like Joss, than she did with her own parents. Well, her adoptive parents. She didn't know her biological parents—they had abandoned her when they discovered she had a high-risk form of hydrocephalus at five months old in Pingtung, Taiwan.

Luckily for Trina, Jeremy and Erin Akersten from Pittsburgh came along. They had her operated at the Johns Hopkins neurosurgical unit, and had raised her as their own. The surgery outcome was wildly successful. Aside from the occasional migraine and the surgery scar on the sides of her skull, shielded by her long jet-black hair, there was no indication that Trina had been born with an abnormal neurological condition.

At the orphanage, the caretakers had called Trina *Xiao Dan Dan*, Little Egg. The nickname was born partly in reference to her egg-shaped oval head, also partly due to the fact that another Chinese character which sounded like *Dan*, was in her given name.

The character *Dan* in her Chinese name was made up of a water sign, and two fire signs, Trina was told. She thought it was fitting, since she often felt engulfed by contradictory forces. On one hand, she didn't think of herself as anything other than American. On another hand, there was a spark inside her that flickered now and then, urging her to dig into her biological heritage, though she knew Erin especially, had never been enthusiastic about her doing so.

It's not that Trina had never probed. When she had turned twelve, the questions she heaved at Erin and Jeremy had intensified. They told Trina everything they knew—the story goes that Trina's grandfather had traveled two hours from their rural village to the nearest orphanage in Pingtung, where they believed the conditions were better than their local orphanages. Her parents had no money for her medical conditions.

Trina had revealed all of her personal history to Joss the other day at Kaiba Bar, when Joss asked why the orphanage was the chosen benefactor this year.

"Wow I had no idea. Thanks for sharing, Trina." Joss paused. "So… are you curious about them? I mean, do you think you'll try to track down your biological parents some day?" she asked tentatively.

"I have thought about it, once or twice. But I ended up here in Shanghai instead. I still haven't been to Taiwan yet. I don't know, maybe I'm not a hundred percent ready yet."

"Well, it's a giant step already, moving out here."

The truth was, although sometimes Trina yearned to come face to face with her bloodline, it was a desire that was waning as the years passed. Did it really matter what had transpired the first year of her life? Or whose blood flowed in her veins? Maybe the emphasis shouldn't be on that story, because the real heroes had been by her side all along, through it all, tending to her, loving her. They had never abandoned her, and would never dream of doing so.

Erin and Jeremy would always be her beloved mother and father, that was a certainty Trina knew to be as true as the sky was blue.

*

It took Naomi almost half an hour to reach Xin Jesse due to halting traffic, a side effect of the rain showers. Although Naomi would have preferred Japanese food on any given occasion, Xin Jesse was one of Dante's favorite Shanghainese restaurants, and Naomi was quickly becoming addicted to their Eight Treasure Duck.

Once seated, Naomi rattled off their usual orders: sweet red jujubes filled with glutinous rice, crab marinated in Shaoxing wine, a braised fish head covered in fried spring onions, Beggar's chicken baked in lotus leaves, Grandma's braised pork in red sauce, pea shoots in white wine, stir-fried bitter melon, and of course, Naomi's favorite duck dish.

"Did your parents like the Christmas presents?" Naomi asked eagerly as she took a sip of the *Longjing* tea.

"You really didn't need to. I'm sure they loved it." Dante kissed her now. "They didn't open them in front of me, but my mom said on the phone that it was appreciated."

Naomi had returned to Shanghai several days ago. She had spent a week in California with her mother and her boyfriend, Bryan Shawnberg. Naomi had been surprised that their relationship was still going strong; she had pegged Bryan to be history by now. It'd been wonderful to be back in Orange County for the holidays, to bask in sunny weather, to stock up on drug store items she normally couldn't get in Shanghai, things like her favorite brand of deodorant and essentials such as tampons, which were difficult to get in China.

Naomi took the time to select a Christmas gift for Dante. He loved molecular gastronomy gadgets—induction cookers, immersion circulators, digital scales. She settled on an infusion siphon coffee maker. Dante was a big coffee drinker. She knew he would adore the vintage looking gadget, which by itself looked like an art piece, complete with a rose-gold-plated hook handle, a wooden base, and a borosilicate glass brewing flask.

Afterwards, she spotted a scarf draped over a mannequin in a luxury shop window. She went inside the store and asked to see it. It was a classic military tartan scarf in navy, green, and black. She felt the fabric, its softness and knotted fringes. It resembled the one Dante's father had worn at the crab dinner. She remembered how tattered and frayed it looked, how his wife had mocked it, saying she couldn't wait to get rid of the old thing.

It was pricey for Naomi's taste. She had never bought a scarf for over a hundred dollars before. The saleslady insisted it was pure Alpaca yarn, made in Peru. "Plus," the saleslady continued, "Alpaca fibers are elastic, hypo-allergenic, have microscopic air pockets that trap heat, and are also thicker than cashmere, so it insulates better."

Naomi was sold. Nanjing winters could be brutal. Later at a holiday bazaar, Naomi was thrilled when she found something for Dante's mother, who she heard was semi-fluent in Russian. It was a collectible egg-shaped music box that played Tchaikovsky's "The Nutcracker Suite March." Inside the egg was an enameled sculpture of the Nutcracker Prince. The porcelain music box was adorned with the lacquer artistry of the Russian Palekh masters, depicting classic scenes from The Nutcracker Ballet.

Naomi had carefully gift-wrapped each present. Just like Japanese people, Naomi knew the Chinese placed great significance on gift giving. She hoped her efforts would pave way for improved relations between her and her boyfriend's parents in the new year.

7

VICTIM OF LOVE

REINA KITA HAD NEVER TAKEN HER DAUGHTER TO VISIT TAIWAN, the island Naomi's father had called home. Even though Wesley Fan's relatives encouraged the visits, even begged for them, Reina harbored a long-held grudge, one that stemmed from various disputes with the Fan family all those years ago.

The summer after junior year of high school, after a particularly horrendous fight with Reina, Naomi had written to Aunt Sylvie in Taipei, who then purchased her roundtrip flight to Taiwan. Naomi ended up spending the entire summer getting re-acquainted with her father's family and culture.

One of Naomi's favorite memories from that summer was visiting her *Nai Nai*, her paternal grandmother, at her modest apartment on Muzha Lu, near the zoo. Nai Nai's primary language was the Taiwanese dialect. While Mandarin had four tones, the Taiwanese dialect had seven. Naomi appreciated that she had Aunt Sylvie to translate for her. Aunt Sylvie said that the Taiwanese dialect, similar with Hokkien, was a language that incurred minor changes in the last three thousand years. "If Confucius was alive today, he would most likely understand those speaking Hokkien and Taiwanese, not Mandarin," she said.

Naomi had adored the embroidery of her grandmother's silk satin, apricot-colored cheongsam blazer, and its colorful patterns of floral detailing, the frog buttons, the Mandarin collar. She had also loved thumbing through Nai Nai's old photo albums. The blush pink paper that wrapped the album cover was yellowing and torn at the edges. The dusty black and white photographs spoke of an era bygone, when cheongsams were the everyday attire for women, and the interior of houses were fitted with Japanese-style tatamis, a legacy of the Japanese colonization of Taiwan. Nai Nai had remembered some basic Japanese phrases, and would say them to Naomi.

Nai Nai had told stories of her own father, whom she'd said Naomi should address as *Ah-Tzou*, the reverent title for great-grandfather in the Taiwanese dialect. Ah-Tzou had been a journalist at the eminent Taiwan *Minpao* newspaper in the 1920s.

Nai Nai also liked to reminisce about the people she knew. One of these people was Xu Zhimo, one of the most acclaimed Chinese poets of the early twentieth century, who was at one point, a friend of Ah-Tzou. Among all of the stories Nai Nai had told, the ones about Xu Zhimo left the most lasting impression on Naomi.

Xu Zhimo's personal relationships were just as legendary as his poetry. Among the three women he loved, his affair with artist Lu Xiaoman was the most well known. Xiaoman and Zhimo divorced their spouses to marry each other, which caused a scandal among Shanghai society in the 1920s. Their marriage became a symbol for passion and freedom, of choosing one's own destiny against arranged marriages. Their relationship polarized literati society; they were brave, progressive, romantic, or they were reckless fools disrespectful of tradition.

But Nai Nai hadn't cared much for Xiaoman; she was familiar with the descendants of Zhang Youyi, Zhimo's first wife through an arranged marriage. The day Zhimo's plane went down, Xiaoman wasn't with him. "She was probably at home with the opium pipe," Sylvie had commented.

It was Zhimo's first wife Youyi who handled the majority of his funeral arrangements, and it was Youyi who cared for Zhimo's aging parents even after their divorce. It wasn't a secret that Xiaoman and Zhimo's marriage became troubled after the nuptials. Xiaoman had a male friend who provided a constant supply of opium. And the day Zhimo died, his flight had been returning from an ex-girlfriend's lecture at a university in Beijing.

So, Hui Hui, who do you think understood true love? Nai Nai had asked. She liked to call Naomi by her childhood Chinese nickname, *Hui Hui*. Nai Nai was the one who had given Naomi her Chinese name, *Fan Jianhui*—it meant wisdom, chosen.

Naomi thought about Zhimo's choices, how he had left Youyi to be with Xiaoman, a borderline drug addict, who had allowed another woman to handle her husband's funeral. Naomi knew the correct answer to her grandmother's question was the noble first wife, poor Youyi, who so loved her ex-husband, that she even financially provided for his widow after his death.

But what about Xiaoman, the most famous one among Zhimo's lovers? She was admired for her beauty, her artistry, and her notorious marriage to one of the most prominent poets of her time. Xiaoman had been the victor, never the victim. And wasn't that worth celebrating too?

Nai Nai had stroked Naomi's hair gently. "My silly Hui Hui, one day you will understand, true love is not judged by what you can get, but measured by how much of yourself you can give."

Naomi had stayed silent. She didn't want her grandmother to know that her stories scared her, that she was so, so frightened to be a victim of love.

*

Naomi was practically sprinting as she stepped out of the elevator. She had woken up late, thrown on a coat, and half-ran to the office. It was already ten. For the past week, most of those in her department had been arriving at work late, taking advantage of the fact that Cher was on an extended vacation, a rarity. In the last two years at Jun Cleo, Naomi could recall only once when Cher took a vacation longer than three days. This time, Cher would be gone for *three weeks*. And she hadn't responded to any e-mails. It was unprecedented.

As Naomi scurried quietly to her desk, she heard audible gasps spewing from neighboring cubicles. Naomi peeked over to where Orca was sitting. "Tian ah!" he exclaimed, an expression akin to *oh my*. The look on his face was pure shock and horror.

Her curiosity piqued, Naomi peered at his computer screen. "What's wrong? You look like somebody died."

"Did you read this?!" He was pointing at an internal job posting sent from HR. Naomi scanned the e-mail. It was an announcement about the search for a new Experiential Marketing Director. The job would be open to internal and external candidates.

Naomi and Orca stared at each other wide-eyed, then started trading theories about what had happened with Cher. It was well known that she wasn't the biggest fan of Nicki. Was she heading to one of Jun Cleo's competitors—Rochay or Weber or Zhen Lux? Fei would be starting at Weber soon. Was she leaving voluntarily or was she being let go? Was this why Cher was taking an extended vacation?

Then Naomi started gathering her notes for a meeting. "Meet at the usual place for lunch okay?" she called out to Orca before scurrying off.

Naomi sipped on her black truffle potato soup at Kee Aqua, the Dunhill brand's restaurant and bar lounge hidden inside their retail shop on the second floor of Henglong Plaza. The venue was adorned with dark leather, oak paneling and polished brass, giving an air of swanky old-world English opulence.

"So what do you think? Are you applying?" asked Orca, as he dug into his linguini.

"Applying? For what?"

"For the director position of course!"

The question stunned Naomi. She hadn't given it much thought. She was still in shock at the idea of Cher leaving the department.

"Should I? Well, why don't you?"

"Don't be silly. I have no intention of reporting to that witch Nicki Jiang. But, I think you two would work well together."

"Um, thanks?"

"Well it's apparent that she likes you. At the last marketing summit she had praised you in front of Severine Chenot. That's kind of a big deal, to be recognized in front of the clients. She hasn't said a nice word about Cher yet."

Naomi sipped her Darjeeling tea quietly. Could she succeed in the director position? Could she do Cher's job? Even if she could, was that what she wanted? Cher's schedule was inhumane and the probable reason she never took vacations.

"I guess I'll think about it? Although it would be fun to boss you around," Naomi joked.

"Better than being bossed around by Pearla," Orca muttered.

"Are you saying Pearla is applying for the position?"

"I haven't spoken to her about it yet, but I am a hundred percent certain that she will. Since Fei is leaving, Pearla thinks she's a shoo-in."

"Isn't she though?"

"Not if you can help it. Also," Orca leaned forward, "there's something else you should know. You're probably well aware that Pearla doesn't like you very much—"

"Are you kidding, she's been unfriendly since day one."

"Exactly. She's not going to make your life easy if she becomes your boss. In fact, I'd even say your career here may be in jeopardy..."

"She can't do that! HR wouldn't allow it, would they?"

"Maybe, maybe not. She'll take care of the thorn in her side, one way or another."

8

WATER DRAGON

JANUARY 22, 2012

THE FIREWORKS SENT ROSY SPLASHES AND ENDLESS BURSTS OF COLORS alight in the dark starless sky. Dante held her close, his face emitting a soft glow from the streetlights. Naomi had never seen the aurora borealis, but she thought these fireworks could possibly be as magical as the northern lights.

Afterwards, they went to bed early, entwined with each other. His touch relaxed her. She was wrought with nerves about what would transpire the next day—it would be her first time in Nanjing spending Chinese New Year with Dante's family. She had been anxious at the thought of staying with his parents and was pleasantly surprised when Dante said he would break with tradition and book a hotel instead.

Chun jie, Spring Festival, was a weeklong Chinese celebration akin to the American Thanksgiving, where people traveled far and wide to get home for meals and reunions, to stuff themselves silly, to enact family rituals. It was a holiday that elicited a range of emotions and behaviors— joy and bliss, sure, but also abnormalities. The strangest thing Naomi had heard about Spring Festival were the trending escorts-for-hire. It was a rising craze among Chinese singletons to hire an actor to play their significant other during family reunions to deter the *san gu liu po*, gossipy relatives, who would otherwise chastise and embarrass them for being *still* unmarried.

It would be Naomi's first Chinese New Year in China. The last two Spring Festivals she had traveled, as most foreigners did. Last year it was to Taiwan to visit Aunt Sylvie, and the year before that it was to Penang with Joss. For this year's *chun jie*, Joss and Tay were in Sicily on a Tang family trip.

This year was linked with the element of water, thus designating 2012 the year of the Water Dragon, an event that only came around once every sixty years. The Water Dragon symbolized advancement and confidence, and that was exactly what Naomi had high hopes for this year.

Mr. and Mrs. Ouyang's apartment complex was decked out in festive *chun jie* decorations. The lobby entrance was adorned with *chun lian*, Chinese New Year couplets with auspicious messages. Gold lettering laden red envelopes hung on faux tangerine and kumquat trees. Outside, sidewalks were covered with dust and red casings from the crackling explosions of firecrackers.

Taped to the door of their fifth-floor apartment was a red squared-shape paper with a calligraphic character scrawled across. Naomi looked perplexed as she tried to make out the character. That's *fu*, blessings, Dante pointed out. But it's hung upside down, Naomi noted. She recognized the character from her Chinese class. Dante explained that the right side of the character was a pictogram of a jar, thus when hung upside down, meant that luck shall soon pour out to bestow blessings upon the household.

Then they removed their shoes, went inside, and a flurry of activity ensued as introductions were made. There seemed to be more people than Dante had expected. He had told Naomi that it would be an intimate family affair, with only his parents and his cousin's family attending, minus Nie Hengmin's parents, who had joined a tour group to Cebu for the week. But a family of five had also arrived several minutes after Dante's cousin.

Naomi watched as a girl in a glistening qipao ran up and embraced Dante. "Ge!" she shrieked. *Big Brother.* Dante looked caught off guard. Then they were smiling and speaking in Chinese rapidly, in the Nanjing dialect, which Naomi rarely heard him speak.

Naomi shifted her feet. Everybody in the room was talking animatedly or sipping tea, everyone except for her. She tried to greet Ying and her son Huan Huan; she hadn't seen them in several months, since that *da zha xie* dinner at the crab restaurant. But Huan Huan had started crying unconsolably once Naomi approached, until the shiny qipao girl presented him with a red envelope. Everybody laughed at the fact that Huan Huan had immediately cheered up after being handed some cash.

An elderly grandfather figure, who looked about Dante's father's age, stared at Naomi unabashedly as he took his tea in the armchair. Dante pulled Naomi over and was about to introduce her to the qipao girl when a middle-aged woman cut him off, ushering her daughter into the kitchen to give Dante's mother a hand. Naomi instinctively approached Pan Jinsung as well, asking her *xu yao bang mang ma?* Can I help with anything? But Jinsung waved her away.

The girl's name was Yuna Xia, Dante said. She was the granddaughter of his dad's best friend, Xia Rong. Dante gestured toward the elderly man in the armchair. The Xia family were all in attendance today: Xia Rong, his wife, his son and daughter-in-law, and Yuna. Dante said he didn't know Yuna all that well, although she was considered a family friend. Over the years, whenever he had visited Nanjing, he'd see Yuna from time to time by way of his parents.

Naomi tried to appear discreet as she took a closer look at Yuna. She was in a princess pink modern qipao, her hair in a high bun with a fastened sparkling lotus-shaped hair clip. She was so graceful that she looked like she was floating most of the time. Naomi looked at her own loose-fitting red sweater dress. She had thought it appropriate to wear the *lucky* color for Chinese New Year. She was a full head taller than Yuna, and felt like a clumsy, crimson giant next to her.

Pan Jinsung had outdone herself, and that was an understatement. The round table was laden with an array of colorful dishes: mustard greens *jie cai* sautéed with tofu skin, golden *chun juan* spring rolls, duck blood *ya xie* soup with vermicelli, white cut chicken, sticky *nian gao* rice cakes, stir-fried bok choy, pork *jiaozi* dumplings, fried *luobuogao* turnip cakes, lion's head *shizitou* meatballs, radish *luobuosi* pancake, hand-pulled scallion oily *la mian* noodles, Yangzhou fried rice, an entire steamed rock cod *yu* with its fish eyes intact. Dante beamed at his mother's gourmet spread.

Mrs. Xia announced that her daughter had a song prepared for the occasion, which they could enjoy before the feast commenced. Yuna settled herself behind the piano, and asked Dante if he could stand beside her and assist with turning the sheet music. The rest of them gathered in a semicircle around the piano. Yuna asked everybody to sing along as her fingers danced on the piano keys. Then everybody started crooning to *Moli Hua*, a song about jasmine flowers. Naomi was familiar with the tune, it was an ancient Chinese folk song which Puccini had popularized by including it in one of his operas. From time to time Naomi saw Yuna glancing up and smiling at Dante. The flash kept going off from Mrs. Xia's camera.

After thunderous applause, everybody gathered in their seats. Ouyang Zhangjie was seated at the head of the roundtable, next to Xia Rong. Yuna sat next to her mother. As Dante started pulling out the chairs next to his cousin, Jinsung steered him toward the seat next to Yuna. Dante took Naomi by the hand and held out the seat next to his for her. Dante's cousin Nie Hengmin took the seat on Naomi's left.

All throughout the meal, Zhangjie kept spooning heaps of food into Yuna's bowl. Yuna seemed to have endless questions for Dante. Of the ones Naomi understood: What is England like? How do you like being back in China? How's your job at the architectural firm? You must be very busy and very important.

Dante had initially been translating everything in English for Naomi's benefit, but Yuna began to interrupt as he was translating. Naomi gave him a reassuring smile, a *don't-worry-about-me* look. Then Dante and Yuna were speaking too rapidly for Naomi to follow, so she tuned out completely. She was grateful for Hengmin, who tried to engage her in conversation in his halting English.

An abrupt frigid chill enveloped the air. Jinsung groaned and asked Dante to help her look at their heater, which had been malfunctioning lately. "I'll be right back okay?" Dante squeezed Naomi's hand as he followed his mother.

Then everybody was getting up from their seats and putting on jackets. Naomi went to retrieve her fleece zip-up. That was when she noticed Yuna knotting an oversized scarf around her neck. Naomi stared. The scarf looked exactly like the one she had gifted Dante's father. What was happening? Had Ouyang Zhangjie given away the present she had painstakingly selected and bought for him? She tried to calm herself. Maybe she was mistaken. The tartan pattern was very common. Or maybe Yuna was just borrowing it.

Then she saw Yuna approaching Zhangjie, and heard her thanking him. The words *xie xie* kept floating out of her mouth as she fingered the scarf. Zhangjie darted a glance at Naomi, then shifted his eyes as she met his gaze. Naomi nudged Hengmin, who was standing next to her.

"What did Yuna say to Mr. Ouyang just now?" Naomi asked.

Hengmin shrugged. "She was just thanking him for the gift. The scarf."

Naomi sucked in her breath. She could feel her cheeks burning and the onset of hot tears threatening downpour. She excused herself and headed toward the bathroom. Then some of the background noise sharpened and she found herself overhearing an exchange between Yuna and her mother, who weren't exactly speaking discreetly.

"Yuna, ta shi sei?" *Who is she?*

"Ta sei ye bu shi. Guo jie ta mei di fang qu." *She's nobody. She had nowhere to go for the holidays.*

Naomi's face reddened. She had been taking regular Chinese lessons for more than two years now. She had become accustomed to people underestimating her Mandarin abilities.

Naomi glared at Yuna, then ran to the bathroom.

Dante looked at his watch. He had been in the bathroom consoling his girlfriend for the last twenty minutes. Earlier, after she had told him what happened, Dante had led his father into the bedroom and asked him why Naomi's gift to him was now in Yuna's hands.

His dad, initially looking sheepish, said he didn't realize Yuna would wear it *tonight*. He started becoming defensive, saying that he was entitled to give gifts to whomever he pleased, that he already had the exact same scarf, that he didn't need a new one, that he liked things just the way they were. Later, Jinsung burst into the room and shushed them, urging them to keep their voices down.

Dante tried to coax Naomi out of the bathroom, but she was bent on returning to the hotel and taking the train back to Shanghai the next day. Dante tried to sound empathetic, assuring her that her anger was well-placed, but also pleading with her to calm down. It was only the first night of the weeklong holiday, and there were other family festivities planned for the week. Sure, they had started on the wrong foot tonight, but tomorrow, when he had the chance, he would straighten out his parents, and all would be well.

"I can't control how they act," he told her. "Look, they're old. My dad is over seventy. It's going to take them time to adjust to things. But they'll come around."

"How do you know that? I've tried with them. I really have. But your parents have been fawning over that girl non-stop since I got here."

"I know you have, and I appreciate that. But like I said, they are set in their ways, and it will take time. They can't unlearn some of the historical trauma overnight."

"I get that. But it's also unfair to me. So just don't ask me to spend time with them anymore. I'm done making an effort!" Her voice had risen an octave.

Dante could feel his patience wearing thin. He took a deep breath and steadied his voice. "Look, I've apologized. I don't know what else I can do. Chinese New Year is a special time for my family. I can't just leave. But if you don't want to be here, well, then don't feel forced to stay."

"Are you asking me to leave?"

"No. I'm asking you to calm down and start enjoying yourself."

"You're right. It's my holiday too. I should enjoy myself."

With that, Naomi pushed past Dante, grabbed her shoes, and darted out the door.

Tear-stricken, Naomi picked up her phone and texted Logan. It was nearly eleven p.m. and she had just returned to her apartment. She hadn't even bothered picking up her luggage at the hotel in Nanjing. From the Ouyang residence, she had taxied straight to the Nanjing high speed train station and purchased the next available ticket to Shanghai.

Her girlfriends were currently unavailable. Joss was in Italy, Frida was at a family feast. Most shops and restaurants were closed during the first several days of Chinese New Year, and there seemed to be a dearth of taxis. Shanghai felt unusually muted.

Naomi knew Logan probably had plans somewhere in the city, somewhere loud and impersonal and ruinous, along with ten other guys. She could use a dose of Logan right now. She could always count on him for some mindless raucousness and ridiculous diversion. His idiocy and insensitivity would distract her from Dante. Logan texted her back to meet him at APT, next to Shelter.

Naomi found Logan easily in the crowded venue. His group of guys were boisterous, loud, and congregated near the right side the bar. As soon as Logan spotted Naomi, he pulled her next to him and bought her two shots which she downed swiftly.

Naomi felt the dual demons of vodka and tequila coursing through her veins, boiling in her bloodstream, burning behind her earlobes, traveling down her chest, searing a hollow in the pit of her stomach. It had a sedating, paralyzing effect. She could feel her mind numbing, becoming impervious to the pandemonium and pain spinning inside. Her phone buzzed from Dante's stream of text messages. She didn't feel like dealing with him right now. Logan was rambling about something, asking her questions, but Naomi wasn't really listening or answering. She put up her hand to get the bartender's attention to order more drinks. *Allow me*, Logan said.

Logan's friends milled around nearby, scanning the crowds, looking like they were on the prowl. The only other female in the group was a local named Ling. She looked like a supermodel who couldn't be bothered by matters as trivial as buttoning her shirt. Maybe because Naomi was already tipsy, but Ling had started taking on caricature-like features. Her legs flowed underneath her Daisy Dukes and were further enhanced by her silver stilettos. Her only modesty was her hair obscuring her chest.

Her side swept fringe was shielding her left eye, framing her cheekbones and pouty lips, making her look like a real-life Chinese version of Jessica Rabbit.

Ling was draped all over Amos. They were both visibly inebriated, and Naomi wondered if she looked like she was too. She knew she was getting there. Logan took Naomi's hand and gyrated his hips against hers. She swayed to the music, letting his musky cologne overcome her senses. Then, Amos was grinding against her, with Ling behind him, as if they were a human sandwich in this feast of bodies.

Logan suddenly grabbed Naomi's coat and led her out the door. "Hey let's head to Craft. My friend is spinning there."

"Why?" Naomi whined. "It's fun here..." But he had already flagged down a taxi and was pulling her inside.

Inside the cab, Naomi rested her head on Logan's shoulder. He didn't have a chance to properly study her outfit in the dark bar, but now he could see that she was dressed completely inappropriately for this glacial weather—a tank top underneath a thin coat, no socks, tennis shoes, and holes abounding in her frayed jeans. Her eyes looked blotchy, as if she had been crying. And she still looked amazing. That was the thing about this girl—her beauty required no effort.

Logan tried to make small talk, but she looked away, clearly not in the mood. He rubbed her thighs, trying to keep her warm. She didn't protest. Then she nestled her head on his shoulder. He wondered if she was giving him hints that he wasn't entirely out of her league. It was turning out to be a happy new year indeed.

At Craft, the DJ was thumping techno-house-electronica at a hundred decibels. There was a guest mixologist who hailed from Sweden, or was it Switzerland? Naomi wasn't sure. The muscled bartender was juggling bottles in the air, catching them and mixing drinks, pouring shots that were being set on fire. He brought a flight of shots to Logan, and another to Naomi, setting the trays on the low table in front of them.

Logan sat close to her on the loveseat. She felt cold. She asked Logan to get her coat, but he just sat closer and rubbed her arms, *I'll keep you warm,* he said. Her vision rendered everything soft-edged, spinning, prismatic.

She felt like dancing. She wanted to shake away all the wretchedness that was congealing inside of her, this bitter, maddening glob of misery and dejection. She wanted to shake off everything that made her feel small, unseen. Dante flashed through her mind again, and she willed herself into the teeming pit.

Logan was becoming more and more aroused by the minute. Unlike normal women, Naomi only looked more gorgeous as the night deepened. If she was sweating, then she was glistening. If her makeup became subdued, then her natural beauty radiated. She was acting as if it were her last dance, writhing and dancing with an abandon he had never seen. Her body was on a super kinetic, super sexy, supersonic adrenaline. Her lustrous hair fluttered, her glorious breasts bounced, her sculpted legs shook and flexed, her ass jiggled with the vibration of the throbbing beats.

Logan came up behind her grinding, his hands roaming under her shirt, just above her waist. They danced like that for another five minutes, or was it forty-five? Naomi had no idea. She was just focused on the rampaging tempo, on the pulsating music. She closed her eyes. Why couldn't it all be as simple as this? Just energy, melody, rhythm, release, freedom.

Then two women suddenly grabbed Naomi, leading her up a step to the bar top. The trio gyrated to the crowd's delight. The two women started what looked like an ad hoc striptease, undoing the buttons of their shirts one by one. The men hooted and goaded Naomi to follow suit. Before Naomi could react, Logan pulled her down.

By now, Logan was so turned on he could hardly stand it. He put his jacket on Naomi, took her hand, and led her out the door. The night air was crisp. At some point in the evening, somebody's gum had wound up in her hair, and she was pulling at it furiously now. He tried to help her, but it was clearly a lost cause. He laughed hysterically at her, and she giggled too. He said he'd help her wash it off later, and she nodded. They passed through an alleyway and were confronted with scents of someone's perfume, someone's dinner, someone's urine. Their own footsteps echoed behind them. The street was almost deserted; only shadows, no bodies, came into view. None of the usual suspects were lurking, no delinquents, no beggars, no drunkards, no lovers. The narrow alley suddenly belonged to them only—he, the desperate offender, she, the tangled lush. He kissed her, she parted her lips. Then she nearly tripped.

He led her toward the Howard Johnson, which was usually a seven-minute walk from Craft, except it took them a good fifteen minutes, since Naomi could barely walk straight. He hoisted her up, then piggybacked her to the hotel reception.

9

UNLUCKY

Although Naomi can't say she was completely floored by the announcement, she was disappointed. She had genuinely believed she was a strong contender, that the portfolio she had put together of her cases in the last two years was nothing short of remarkable. But was Pearla's portfolio even more impressive? Had Cher given Pearla a better review?

Nicki had ceremoniously announced Pearla's promotion to Experiential Marketing Director at the all-staff meeting on the Tuesday after Chinese New Year holiday. Pearla was beaming, gloating, and maybe it was Naomi's imagination but it seemed like Pearla was smirking at her during the announcement. All week long, Naomi tried not to panic as Pearla moved into Cher's former office and began delegating projects for the upcoming quarter. Naomi knew what was coming. The dreadfully difficult program of overseeing the store launches for a demanding German client at dreary third tier markets such as Jinan, Hefei, and Zhengzhou was the least favorite job, and of course Pearla had assigned that to her, smiling at her gleefully when she did so.

Naomi sighed and peeked at her watch now. 5:45. She closed her laptop and marched toward the elevators, ignoring the incredulous looks her colleagues were throwing at her. Nobody at Jun Cleo left before six-thirty. But Naomi didn't care to adhere to these unwritten rules anymore, especially since she was already on Pearla's bad side.

Pearla's power-tripping antics seemed to reach new heights every day. Yesterday she had demanded Naomi sort out the vendor billing spreadsheet, which was typically the intern's duty. *The intern is out sick, and somebody has to do it*, Pearla had reasoned, *so why not you?* Naomi had rolled her eyes. She knew that Pearla was relishing these moments. After Naomi had completed and laid out the document on Pearla's desk per her request, Pearla had taken one look at it and tossed it on the floor, nitpicking and criticizing inane points.

Just as she was about to enter the elevator, Liya approached her. She had a message for Naomi: Pearla was sending her on a last-minute business trip to Jakarta. There was a product launch for Gemvea, their German client. Initially Pearla was expected to attend, but "something had come up," and now Naomi was to go in her place. It was to be a brief trip, no longer than forty-eight hours, including flight time. The plane would depart at six in the morning.

Peeved at first, Naomi soon felt grateful for the unexpected exodus from Shanghai. She was still devastated about what had happened with Dante, and with Logan. She had cried profusely over her recklessness. As soon as Naomi settled into her plane seat and closed her eyes, she was glad for the excuse to be alone, for the time and space to think.

For her return flight, she was scheduled to fly out of Soekarno-Hatta International Airport at midnight on Thursday. Her red-eye flight would land in Pudong at eight in the morning. Pearla said she needed Naomi to be back in Henglong Plaza three hours later, by eleven a.m. for the Friday team meeting.

Naomi felt utterly exhausted as her flight landed at Pudong airport on Friday. She barely slept a wink due to the snoring passenger next to her, and as soon as the plane touched down, her phone was bombarded by Pearla's calls regarding the client event report. By the time it was her turn to face the passport control customs officer, Naomi felt completely beleaguered.

She handed over her passport to the male officer. The officer flipped through her navy blue passport, then narrowed his eyes at Naomi accusatorily, "You cannot enter China without a visa. What is your purpose for visiting?"

"There must be some kind of mistake," Naomi mumbled, perplexed. "I work at Jun Cleo, and I've lived in Shanghai for two and a half years now."

The male officer called out a female colleague and spoke in rapid

Shanghainese to her. Naomi fished out her Jun Cleo business card and presented it to both officers. The male officer ignored the gesture and raised his voice. "Where. Is. Your. Work. Visa."

"My visa is in the passport!" Naomi exclaimed, exasperated.

Naomi eyed the increasingly irritated male officer as he flipped through each page of her navy passport, then slammed it down on the desk. "No, it is not here. If you do not have a proper visa, you cannot enter China." The female officer cast Naomi a sympathetic look but stayed mum.

That was when Naomi realized her critical mistake. "I'm sorry, I gave you the wrong passport!" She fumbled through her purse and took out her green *Tai Bao Zheng* visa booklet. She'd been in such a daze, that she forgot she was supposed to enter China with her visa booklet for Taiwanese, and not her U.S. passport. The Jun Cleo HR personnel had explained that it was more convenient and cost-effective for the company to apply for Naomi's *Tai Bao Zheng*, rather than annually renew her work visa on her U.S. passport. Therefore, Naomi could use her U.S. passport whenever she was entering and exiting other countries, but must use her *Tai Bao Zheng* to go in and out of China.

"Do you understand that it is illegal to use two different identities in China?" the male officer admonished her sternly.

"But it was a mistake. I handed you the wrong passport by mistake," Naomi pleaded.

Ignoring Naomi, the male officer said something in Shanghainese to the female officer, then exited his seat.

The female officer took his colleague's seat. "I'm very sorry, but you will not be able to enter China today."

"What?" Naomi gasped.

"Because of your mistake, you need to enter China on another day."

"But...but where should I go right now? I just landed!"

The officer looked at her computer. "Most foreigners go to Hong Kong to sort out visa problems if they are denied entry here. I think there is a flight to Hong Kong in one hour." She offered to lead her to the sales office where Naomi could purchase the roundtrip airfare and book a hotel in Hong Kong. Naomi would be permitted to enter China twenty-fours from now, no earlier.

Naomi flashed the officer her most charming smile and pleaded with her to overlook her *hu tu*, her carelessness. "It won't happen again," Naomi promised. She really hoped the officer would give her a break and just let her in.

The officer sighed and shook her head. "I wish I can help, but *jin tian suan ni dao mei*." You are just unlucky today.

She doesn't know when, but the streets of Shanghai had ceased to be a novel composite of sights and sounds: the screeching raucous of car honkers, the impatient commuters jabbing her as they rushed past her, the intermittent spitting from drivers who would hang their heads out of vehicles, the burdensome mask pulled over her nose to protect against the hazardous air.

Naomi's not in the mood to talk. An hour ago, Joss had suggested dinner. She hadn't seen her in weeks, since before her business trip to Indonesia, and the subsequent airport fiasco that took her to Hong Kong for a night. Joss herself had been traveling as well with Tay.

Naomi declined the dinner invitation, saying that she would head to bed early.

She continued ambling along Nanjing Lu, through the thicket of crowds. There was a group of spirited white men up ahead who seemed high on something, a gaggle of teenagers gossiping and clutching their milk tea drinks to her left, and a throng of twentysomethings behind her chattering away about the newly opened club. Naomi muted the noise internally. It was nine p.m. All around her the artificial lights were beckoning, as if the city was just waking up. But all she felt was a sense of suffocation and the city closing in on her.

Sometimes, Naomi was unsure she had ever rooted herself here. Sometimes a place never becomes home, not even after an accumulation of years, of stuff, of jobs, of boyfriends. But sometimes, a place can seem so familiar, so essential, that nothing else is needed to validate belonging there.

Naomi continued her solo stroll. For one Saturday evening, she let herself be the loneliest woman in Shanghai.

10

PEKING SOLEIL

VALENTINE'S DAY FELL ON A TUESDAY THIS YEAR, ACCORDING TO the Gregorian calendar, that is. The Chinese Valentine's day, called *Qixi*, was in the summer, on the seventh day of the seventh month of the lunar calendar. A third version of Valentine's Day in China, was on the twentieth of May, a trend started by Chinese millennials who grew accustomed to mobile texting the numbers "520" to their significant others, since the numbers were homophonous with "I love you."

On this frigid February evening at seven p.m. sharp, Dante was already waiting outside the offices of Jun Cleo with a bouquet in hand. The Calla Lilies were multihued, dyed in royal blue, lavender, peach, pink. He had made a reservation at Hatsune, one of her favorite Japanese restaurants.

The couple had made up several weeks ago, after not speaking for six days from when Naomi had left Nanjing abruptly during Dante's Chinese New Year family feast.

After what had transpired with Logan, Naomi hadn't been able to sleep properly. For days she had ignored Dante's calls and apologetic texts, because she was unsure of how to respond. She knew the respectable thing to do was to tell Dante the truth about her transgressions, but she also knew that would herald the end of them. She still loved Dante deeply, and what had happened with Logan was a grave mistake.

She had felt even more guilt-ridden when Dante had unexpectedly showed up at her doorstep, apologizing. Naomi had started sobbing, apologizing with even more intensity. They had made up right away, trembling with a zeal as if they had been separated for years, and not the six days they had endured.

The next day at work, Naomi confided in Frida. "But Dante doesn't need to know right this minute, maybe wait for better timing," Frida offered.

Naomi nodded. But when was it ever an ideal time to reveal a betrayal?

Frida thought that Naomi needed to distance herself from Logan, indefinitely. Naomi didn't need further convincing. She was infuriated with Logan for crossing the line, but most of all, she was angry at herself for allowing him to. She wouldn't point fingers, she was an adult, and even though she had been under the influence, she couldn't fairly say it was un-consensual.

Logan seemed to have taken a hint when she didn't pick up any of his calls or respond to his e-mails. He tried to get in touch with her for about three weeks in the aftermath, before all communication ceased.

*

Naomi checked her watch. She was fighting traffic to get to the Le Corbusier's 1933 Slaughterhouse, located in Hongkou district. It was Shanghai Fashion Week and the show by the Lebanese-Korean designer Shuna Koury would begin promptly at four p.m. LunaSong, one of Jun Cleo's most prized K-beauty clients, would be sponsoring the backstage makeup artists and cosmetics for this show, and Naomi had been assigned as the Event Lead.

After Naomi positioned the press photographers on the hydraulic platforms perched near the end of the catwalk, she quickly ran backstage, where a chaos of models, makeup artists and minions milled about. Naomi ran around with her clipboard and headset on, making sure the LunaSong's group of makeup artists—flown in from Seoul—were each on schedule at their stations, working on the looks for their assigned models.

The fashion show coincided with the brand's launch of Peking Soleil, a one-off, limited edition fragrance catered to the China market, with only a hundred vials available worldwide. A fraction of the models would be holding the perfume as they strutted down the runway.

Naomi was able to snag Dante a seat to the show. Although most came for the fashion, Dante came for the architecture. The 1933 Slaughterhouse was built as an abattoir. The gargantuan geometric façade was a unique labyrinth of angular bridges, an array of beams and maze of staircases. The original design was intended to easily usher workers and cattle throughout the building into the circular inner structure. It was a one-of-a-kind art deco building, and Dante was eager to finally see it.

Inside the VIP Lounge, Naomi exploded into a tirade at Roxy Gao. Liya Hu turned around to see what the commotion was about as a tearful Roxy ran towards the restrooms. Liya went over to Naomi, took one glance, and understood the reason for Naomi's reaction. The product display was in complete disarray and disorder. The product display case exhibiting all of the brand's fragrances was supposed to be set up according to the flavors represented in the ice cream cart. As the most prestigious sponsor of the show, the VIP lounge had been transformed into a whimsical, LunaSong-branded ice cream parlor, serving customized artisanal flavors complementing its product scents, in flavors such as ylang ylang, lavender, lemongrass, lychee, coconut, citrus, pistachio, peppermint. The ice cream would be served to VIPs in branded miniature jars which resembled LunaSong's product containers. As the Event Lead, Naomi had worked on this VIP lounge concept for months, collaborating with Ms. Park Hye-kyo, the brand's Olfactory Creative Director based in Seoul. She was currently backstage and would be stepping into the lounge any minute now to make final inspections.

"Oh hi Liya, I thought you would be at the hospital today," Naomi said, flustered. She was surprised to see Liya. Everybody knew her three-year-old was undergoing hemangioma removal surgery.

"I was there this morning. My husband is with my daughter now." Liya had initially planned to take the entire day off work to be with Lulu in the hospital. But Nicki had put her foot down and said Liya needed to be present at today's event. Most of her colleagues had been sympathetic when she described Lulu's condition. Only Nicki had sounded dismissive, calling it a cosmetic surgery, questioning whether it was necessary, even asking Liya to reschedule the surgery date.

Liya knew the value of a girl's appearance in China, and the unsightly strawberry birthmark on Lulu's forehead would undoubtedly be a detriment to her daughter's future. Even if she couldn't stand her boss, Liya knew she had to endure. She needed the paycheck from this job to fund the ever-increasing bills associated with raising a daughter in Shanghai.

Liya knelt down and starting sorting through the product boxes with Naomi. "Thanks," Naomi mumbled. "Sorry, this was supposed to be the intern's job. She seriously drives me crazy sometimes!" She slammed a box down forcefully.

"She's just a kid. Calm down, Naomi, it's okay."

"It's not okay. Now I have to re-do the entire display case, and we are already half an hour behind."

"I'll give you a hand. Are you not feeling well? Did you throw up in the bathroom earlier? I've never seen you so anxious."

Naomi reddened, waving Liya away. This was the first time Pearla had assigned her as Event Lead and things were not exactly going as planned. "It was probably just something bad I ate."

"Not the ice cream I hope," Liya joked.

Naomi mustered a smile even though her head was spinning. She was appreciative of Liya's calm demeanor; it had a soothing effect. Among the team, Liya was probably the least put together on the surface—she always looked a bit harried, her hair unbrushed, her makeup half done—but Naomi now saw that Liya was actually the most composed. Naomi thought about her panicked state and suddenly felt silly next to Liya, who had much bigger things to worry about at home.

Roxy approached tentatively and started assisting Naomi and Liya with the product cases. Naomi reached for Roxy's arm and pulled her aside. She took a deep breath. "I'm sorry about earlier. I shouldn't have yelled. You're doing great."

Roxy smiled, then uttered her apologies and thanks all at once. She counted herself lucky to be working with Naomi, who was usually generous and collected. Her boss was acting out of character today, but Roxy had heard Naomi throwing up in the bathroom twice this morning, so maybe that explained it.

11

CATKIN

THE STREETS OF SHANGHAI WERE LINED WITH ABOUT ONE MILLION poplar and willow trees. April to mid-May in this city was peak season for catkins—the airborne, white fluffy stuff that from a distance, could either resemble snowflakes on a good day, or depending on your sensitivity, allergens gone wild on a bad day. Joss loved this city zealously, but her only gripe stemmed from her allergies to pollen. She learned to avoid Hengshan Lu, Fuxing Lu and Shanxi Lu during this season, where whole streets were filled with flying flurries of catkins.

For dinner tonight, she had purposely chosen a restaurant inside a mall near People's Square. Thanks to Joss, Hunan House was no longer just a neighborhood gem, but a crown pearl which attracted people across the spectrum—smartly-dressed locals, wealthy expats, well-informed tourists, government officials, women looking to impress, men hoping to score.

Hunan House paid plentiful homage to Mao Zedong, who had hailed from Hunan province. Walls were plastered with various portraits of Mao, including an enormous piece from Icelandic pop artist Erro. The menu was rife with Mao's name, such as *Mao's Steamed Hams, Zedong Cucumber Eel, The Chairman's Red-Braised Pork.*

"Hunan cuisine is actually spicier than Sichuan food. The Sichuanese use peppercorn so after a while everything starts tasting the same because your mouth becomes numb. But the Hunanese use vinegar in addition to the pepper, that way your taste buds are stimulated so you can taste all of the ingredients and spices," Joss said, as they munched on the preserved eggs with roasted chili peppers.

Inside the low-lit restaurant, Joss scanned Naomi's outfit. Lately, Naomi had taken to more and more flowy maxi dresses. She still looked like a goddess, and the average observer probably couldn't tell Naomi had put on weight, but Joss had an eagle eye for details.

Naomi savored all of Dante's culinary creations and home-cooked meals. Sometimes he would pack lunch for her in a stainless steel thermal tin lunch box, which kept the meal piping hot. In the last week he had packed her stir-fried tomato beef, oyakodon, soba noodle salad, garlic chicken, clam linguini, pumpkin bread. She often received questions about which restaurant had catered the meals. *Nan peng you*, she'd say, eliciting envious exclamations. My boyfriend made these.

But lately, Naomi hadn't been able to fit into several of her jeans. She jokingly chastised Dante the other day, but he just shrugged it off and said, "You've always been too thin, and hey," he reached for her then, "you've put on weight in all the right places."

After Naomi had hurled out most of the *Mao's Fish Head*, she sat in the bathroom stall heaving. She had just puked up three hundred renminbi worth of food. She felt miserable and needed to head home.

"Naomi?" Joss was knocking on each bathroom stall now.

"In here," she croaked.

Joss pushed her way into the stall. Naomi's head was resting on her arms spread out over the toilet bowl. Joss retrieved a hair tie from her purse and gathered Naomi's curls up into a ponytail. She examined the situation. This didn't look like food poisoning. After all, they had consumed the same dishes. Something was off.

Then Joss noticed the bulge underneath Naomi's dress. It was slight, but it was there.

"You know, maybe you should get tested," Joss said, as she handed Naomi a bottle of water.

"For what?" Naomi whispered tiredly. She wobbled to the couch in the resting lounge adjacent to the sinks, taking a big gulp of water.

"Pregnancy, my dear."

*

Naomi stared at the pink line, her breathing quickening. Memories of that night at the New York Presbyterian hospital maternity ward flooded in. That February morning in 2008, she had awoken with dread when she discovered a pool of blood on her bed. Joss had quickly rushed her to the hospital. When the doctor broke the news to her—that she had miscarried her eleven-week old baby—Naomi had clutched Joss's hand, weeping out loud. It was a reaction that even surprised herself. When she learned she had conceived a baby with Rex, Naomi had been overcome with disgust, fear and hatred. The last time they saw each other Rex had forced himself on her against her will.

But Naomi had never considered abortion. Although she hadn't been raised in any particular religion, she secretly subscribed to Catholicism, the faith of her *Nai Nai*, her paternal grandmother. She didn't attend mass regularly, but she had taken to praying to Saint Mary whenever she was in a crisis. In a way Saint Mary took on a maternal role for Naomi. So she had decided to keep the baby.

But the heavens had taken away the baby from her in the end. Maybe Saint Mary in all her infinite wisdom had spared Naomi. Maybe she had spared the baby. Naomi was Reina's daughter after all, so who knew if her motherly gene was completely intact?

These thoughts plagued Naomi right now as she left Shanghai Lenai Hospital. Dr. Tseng had printed the black-and-white photo of the ultrasound results and explained that the fetus was currently the size of a *mei zi*, plum, and would eventually grow bigger than a *xi gua*, watermelon. She gave Naomi the conception date range and a tentative due date, since Naomi couldn't produce the exact date of her last menstrual cycle. Her cycle had always been irregular.

At first, Naomi had wavered whether she was making the right decision, but she was resolute now. She put her hand to her abdomen. She would keep the baby, and she would love her baby, fiercely. In this moment of clarity, she closed her eyes and gave a quiet thanks to Saint Mary. She rummaged through her purse to retrieve her cell phone. She wondered whether Dante could step out of his office momentarily, she wondered what his reaction would be.

Then it hit her.

She stared at the conception date range the doctor had just printed for her. Hot tears fell as reality sunk in, and she hung her head. She admonished herself again, at how irresponsible and foolish she had been. That, yet again, she had committed another bad decision to add to the books.

The identity of the baby's father was, in fact, unresolved.

PART 4

LOVE AND OTHER MOODS

Spring 2012 – Spring 2015

"Because of a great love, one is courageous."

—LAO TZU,
TAO TE CHING

"To love someone means to see them as God intended them."

—FYODOR DOSTOYEVSKY,
THE BROTHERS KARAMAZOV

237

1

MEANT TO BE

ONE OF THE THINGS JOSS MISSED MOST WAS TAY READING ALOUD TO her. It was their thing. They would curl up on the couch, her head on his lap, him stroking her hair. He would use different voices for each character, pausing for effect, making ominous *dun-dun-dun* musical notes for suspenseful chapters. They were fond of Haruki Murakami, Jhumpa Lahiri, Yan Lianke, Wu Danru, Mohsin Hamid. Sometimes they wouldn't get around to finishing the book. He'd get distracted, she'd get excited.

They hadn't read together ever since Tay had started the fertility treatments. It had been physically stressful, not to mention emotional straining to keep the treatments a secret from everybody. Male infertility wasn't spoken of in China, and especially not in a family such as the Tang's.

Dr. Zhuang had officially diagnosed him with Klinefelter Syndrome, a condition which in turn had caused Azoospermia. His body was devoid of the sperm needed for conceiving, and they had exhausted all medical options. The diagnosis was a final declaration, a pronouncement of the failure after nearly three years of injections, surgeries, and foul-tasting Chinese medicinal herbs.

After Tay had received the devastating diagnosis, he had disappeared for three days. He did this sometimes. He would get agitated at work, at his parents, at Shanghai, then retreat to their vacation property in neighboring Hangzhou. Unlike Shanghai, there were pockets of Hangzhou where the skies went on forever, where one could catch glimpses of soaring egrets and verdant mountaintops, like vague brushstrokes in a classical Chinese painting.

When he returned, Joss had a jar of *shao xian cao* waiting for him. The jello-like herbal treat was Tay's favorite dessert, but he had avoided it for the past several years while undergoing fertility treatments. One of the TCM doctors had said the herbal drink was considered *han xing*, too "cooling" for his body, and may negatively affect the treatments.

"Let's eat this out in the garden," Joss said, as she brought a tray to their outdoor patio dining table.

He sat down next to her. "I'm sorry," he said. "I just needed to get away."

Joss nodded. "I know."

"Do you think the universe is telling us something?" Tay said.

"Hmm?"

"Maybe it's just not meant to be."

Joss paused, seeing the burst capillaries in her husband's eyes, sensing the desolation. "No," she shook her head. "We will have a family, I know it."

"But my condition is hopeless. And you never wanted to give birth anyway." Although Joss was fond of babies, and had always envisioned having some, she'd been fearful of childbirth ever since her mother died of pre-eclampsia while delivering her sister.

Joss was in the seventh grade at the time. It became the defining year which distinguished the *before* and *after*. Before seventh grade she had just been another normal tween. Then, in an instant she went from pre-teen to parenting.

"There's still hope," she said quietly.

"How? Surrogacy? But you don't want to do the egg retrieval, remember?" It was true. She was adverse to hospitals and any physically invasive procedures, a residual effect of waiting in the hospital at twelve years old for her baby sister to arrive, only to go home without a mother.

"I want children," she said firmly. "I know you do too."

He sunk into the sofa, his head in his hands.

"What about...adoption?" She was almost whispering.

"What?" He looked up.

"Adoption." Said out loud, it didn't seem so implausible anymore.

"No...no."

"Why not?"

He looked at her incredulously. "There are a ton of reasons not to. The kid might not be healthy, or might be psychotic, or might not even want us. Have you ever thought about that? That the child may end up searching and going back to the biological parents when all is said and done? Plus, my parents..." his voice trailed off.

She touched his arm. "I know they wouldn't approve. But this might be the only way. And they do want grandchildren."

"Look," she continued, "why don't I just make some calls first? See what I can find out."

Tay looked at the moving clouds above. The sky, a glorious azure vault, looked limitless today. Common elsewhere, fluffy clouds were hard to come by in this city, where pollution mostly rendered the skies slate gray, cloudless. Today's sky was like the ones from his childhood.

Tay pored into his wife's pleading, hopeful eyes, and took her hand. "Okay," he whispered. "See what you can find out."

*

Party World was a popular karaoke establishment which featured private rooms, plush sofas, buffet dinners, and endless song choices in Chinese, English, Japanese, and Korean. Naomi learned early on that similar to Japan, karaoke was one of China's most beloved pastimes. Even her shyest colleagues had no qualms channeling Beyonce and shaking their behinds once they clutched to a microphone in a karaoke room, their larynxes lubricated with the locals' drink of choice—whisky mixed with iced green tea, a curious concoction that was popular in Shanghai.

Tonight was another marathon karaoke night. It was now nearly eleven p.m. Naomi was ready to head home, but everybody else looked as though the party was just getting started. While not exactly a Mandopop or Cantopop fan, by now Naomi could recognize the most requested tunes, such as songs by Fish Leong, Eason Chan, Elva Hsiao, David Tao. When she was put on the spot, Naomi's go-to song was Utada Hikaru's "First Love," one of the most recognized songs from Japan. Even some of her Chinese and Taiwanese colleagues could sing along with her in perfect Japanese.

Amos Kim was clearly the closeted pop star in the room. His impeccable dress and pompadour hair style coupled with his dance moves while he crooned to K-pop hits and rapped to Jay-Z made him a pseudo celebrity at Jun Cleo. The female colleagues screamed and hollered and flashed cameras like groupies.

Naomi's colleagues had already finished off two bottles of Chivas and had been singing for the past three hours. All night long she had been declining alcohol, feigning sickness. It wasn't a complete fib. She was in her eighteenth week of pregnancy. The only person at work who knew she was expecting was Frida.

Tonight's occasion was a send-off for Frida, who was quitting her job as Senior Account Director at Jun Cleo, much to Naomi's dismay. Frida was moving to the country's southernmost province located in the South China Sea, the tropical Hainan Island. She'd been working at Jun Cleo for seven years, a respectable amount of time considering that on average, people left the agency right around the two-to-three-year mark, either for in-house marketing positions, competing agencies, to get married, or to have babies. Frida was deemed accomplished for her age. She was only thirty, the youngest Senior AD at the company.

Frida's friends and colleagues were baffled by her choices. Her parents especially were against the whole plan. "What type of men can you meet in *Hainandao?*" Mrs. Du had exclaimed.

Naomi had been just as surprised when she heard of Frida's resignation, and was even more shocked when she learned that Frida was leaving the company for a charity foundation in a backwater province.

Frida never made rash assessments. She had thought this life-changing decision through. When her friend, Yuzong, had started a charitable foundation dedicated to victims of leprosy, most of his peers had mocked him behind his back. But Frida admired Yuzong's audacity. He had come from a well-to-do family and his parents had even bought him an apartment in Shanghai, to lure him into staying close to them in the city. But Yuzong could not be dissuaded. He had grown his foundation into a sizable operation, and had moved the headquarters to Hainan Island to be closer to the state-run leprosarium, a rehabilitation colony for leprosy patients. Yuzong had even secured endorsements and donations from high-profile Chinese film celebrities.

When Frida learned Yuzong was seeking a VP of Operations and Marketing, she had e-mailed her old friend asking for more details of the job. "The job is yours if you'd like. We'd be honored to have you," Yuzong had replied instantly.

Most of Frida's peers envied her hefty salary and esteemed position at Jun Cleo, and her parents liked to boast about how successful she was. It was a "fun" job, no doubt—she regularly attended fashion shows and was invited to the trendiest events—but she still felt a nagging sense that something was missing from her life.

To her parents, what Frida lacked was indisputably a husband. But she didn't feel quite ready to settle down yet. She still had much to offer the world, before the inevitability of becoming somebody's wife and mother. Three weeks ago, Yuzong called and said he had found another qualified candidate for the VP position, but his first choice was still Frida. She had an *it's-now-or-never* moment, and determined in that instant, that she would join her friend in contributing to this deserving cause.

Frida's colleagues joked that she had joined the *wenqing* tribe, a term referred to China's urbanite youth who were disillusioned with the standard profit-driven rat race, and who rejected commercialism and consumption. Wenqing sought artistic, cultural or spiritual fulfillment, and were not overly concerned with the national obsessions—money and status. There seemed to be more and more stories of Chinese millennials leaving their lucrative corporate jobs in Beijing or Shanghai, and moving to places like Dalian, Dali, Qingdao, Qinghai. Her friend, Zhan, had left his teaching job in Beijing for one in Tibet. "The Tibetan children are simpler and want to learn, unlike the spoiled kids from the capital who are glued to their cell phones," Zhan had said.

Frida wasn't quite sure if she could be described as a typical wenqing, after all, she was not a die-hard critic of commercialism. She had been a benefactor of Shanghai's profitable economy, concocting marketing campaigns for Fortune 500 multinationals at Jun Cleo. But she was ready for a different pace of life now.

Frida looked forward to using her talents and creativity for a good cause, for something that mattered, for people that mattered. She was enthralled by her new job, as much as she was eager to trade the crowded and polluted city life for some serene sun and sand.

Naomi checked her watch. She was ready to hit the sack. Another colleague was warbling a saccharine Mandopop hit, and Amos had drunkenly stumbled to the karaoke suite next door where "the girls are hot."

Naomi said her good nights to the group and gave Frida a fierce embrace. She was so proud of her. She thought Frida was just about the bravest girl she had ever met.

"You take care of yourself, everything is going to work out, you'll see." Frida chirped, hugging her friend back.

Naomi smiled as she fought back tears. She would miss her terribly.

2

YOURS

"What are you going to do? I mean, who do you think is the dad?" Joss asked as she petted Tuo Tuo, the friendly alpaca who had sauntered over to their table.

Joss and Naomi were at the grand opening of *Xiao Fang Zhou*, Little Ark, a newly opened cafe in Minhang district. Close to Qibao Water Town, Little Ark resembled a petting zoo set up in a picturesque garden, where people sipped their teas as rabbits, piglets, guinea pigs, hedgehogs roamed near their picnic blankets. Joss had been invited by the owners for a review in *Shanghai Scene*.

"Obviously I hope Dante is. But…I'm not a hundred percent sure." Naomi buried her face in her hands.

"Things will be okay. But you know, I have to say that I thought you turned over a new leaf in Shanghai, put all those wild romps behind you in New York."

"Not now, Joss." Naomi sighed. "And don't talk to me the way you talk to Jamie."

"Fine, but, Logan?! Sometimes I don't know what's going on in that head of yours. I thought you knew better. We're not college kids getting smashed all over New York anymore—"

Joss was interrupted by the beeping of her cell phone. It was Tay. Joss listened as an irritated Tay complained about the adoption research paperwork being strewn around the study, when she knew full well that his parents sometimes dropped by their villa unannounced. *What if they had seen the files?*

"Okay okay. I'll put them away later," she snapped at him, before hanging up.

"Put what away?" Naomi asked. She re-adjusted her sitting position, rubbing her belly. The checkered picnic blanket looked so inviting. She just wanted to lie down and sleep away her troubles.

"Oh, um, nothing important. Where were we? Oh right. I can't believe you didn't tell me about what happened with Logan earlier. How could you keep this from me all this time?"

Naomi crossed her arms. "This is exactly why I didn't tell you in the first place. And when did you get so smug and judgmental? Not everybody has it all figured out and leads the perfect *tai tai* life like you, where your biggest problems are in-laws who want to spend time with you."

"You've got it all wrong. You know nothing about my problems."

"Well, how could I when you're keeping things from me. You're always so hush hush about everything now. I mean I get Tay is from some powerful family and you can't talk about some stuff or whatever, but it's like sometimes I don't know what's going on with you. At least I've always been honest."

"If you're so honest then you wouldn't have found yourself in this mystery-father predicament," Joss muttered.

"My predicament," Naomi stood up now, "is no concern of yours anymore."

"Naomi—"

But Naomi was already out the door.

Naomi lined up the shiitake mushrooms and sliced quickly. She was behind schedule since she was wiping down the kitchen counter every ten minutes, while attempting to cook up a grand feast. She needed to contain the mess. Dante took great pride in this kitchen. He had it painstakingly renovated last year, and now it was home to stainless hardware and a state-of-the-art limestone slabbed workspace designed for grilling, steaming, frying, baking, braising, broiling, poaching, roasting, scrambling. Usually she was relegated to the eating, and sometimes, the cleaning. But tonight, they would switch roles.

She glanced at the digital clock perched at the edge of the counter. Dante would be home soon and she still had much to do. She had promised him a spread of his favorite Japanese dishes: *omuraisu* omelet rice, pork *shogayaki* with shredded cabbage, soy-glazed mushrooms, *agedashi* tofu, grated daikon.

The recipes hadn't seemed too difficult at first, but now she wasn't confident she could pull this off. The pork had come out burnt, the tofu not as crispy as she would have liked, the omelet not shaped as nicely as the online photos.

Naomi wasn't a natural in the kitchen, that was Dante's turf. She loved that he experimented and relished being the first to try out his new creations. He was an expert improviser. Watching him cook was like being treated to a jazz concert.

She took out some fresh tomatoes from the magnets-and-photos-laden refrigerator. A polaroid caught her eye. It was a silly picture of them making goofy faces, taken on their trip in Beijing. In the photo, his tongue was out, like he was about to lick her face raw. She was giggling and the camera had caught her in mid-laugh. Memories of the trip came flooding back—them enjoying a fantastic gastronomic tour together, wandering that city hand in hand, him protecting her during the dangerous riot in front of the Japanese embassy.

Then her mind drifted toward that disastrous evening when she had recklessly stormed out of his parents' place and straight into Logan's arms.

She shook herself out of the nightmare, her hand instinctively rubbing her stomach. Tears glistened at the corner of her eyes. She was determined to make things right, for herself, for Dante, for the little one growing inside of her. She needed to come clean. Tonight's dinner was the first she had ever cooked for him.

She hoped it wouldn't be the last.

Naomi was so engrossed in the kitchen she didn't even hear Dante tiptoe in, surprising her as he encircled his arms around her from behind. She turned around, her hands holding his cheeks. She kissed him longingly. She wanted to fixate on this split second. She was petrified of letting this moment go, dreading what would come next, what she would have to reveal, and what would soon unravel.

Dante was in a chatty mood tonight. He opened a bottle of cabernet, but she declined, saying she was too tired to be inebriated. That part was true, she was plagued with fatigue almost all the time now, even though at five-and-a-half months pregnant, she was barely showing. Dr. Tseng had said that her extreme fatigue and morning sickness was to be expected. She urged Naomi to continue taking her prenatal and folate supplements, and reassured her that the baby was growing normally. When Dr. Tseng had asked about the father, she hastily replied that he was busy, and then she had closed her eyes, citing exhaustion. The doctor seemed to have taken the hint and hadn't pressed further.

Naomi let Dante do most of the talking at dinner. She decided that breaking the news after dessert would be the most ideal. Dante was always in the best mood after dessert.

"Still not talking to Joss?"

Naomi shook her head.

"Wow. What was the fight about again? I don't think I fully understood the last time you told me."

"She said some things. Well, I did too. I don't know, we just need some time to cool off I guess."

"This should cheer you up. I just received an invitation to Joe Ong's wedding. You remember his fiancé, right? The Sri Lankan woman you met at the company banquet?"

Naomi nodded.

"Well, guess what? Their wedding is in Maldives in November, apparently at the same resort the Dubai Crown Prince vacations at," Dante said enthusiastically. He remembered Naomi mentioning her desire to visit Maldives on multiple occasions.

Naomi's smile faltered. She looked pensive. "What's wrong?" He reached out across the table and held her hand.

She shrunk back in her chair. "I...I won't be able to travel in

November…it's my…my due date…"

"What's due in November? A work thing?" He pressed, confused.

She looked into his eyes. How she loved those eyes. They drooped slightly at the edges, crinkled warmly when he smiled, gleamed when he brooded.

"What's wrong? Is everything okay?" He had been so sure that she would be more than thrilled about the prospect of traveling together to Maldives.

"No." She didn't meet his eyes. "I…I can't go because…because of the baby. The baby is due in November…" Her voice trailed off.

Dante stared at her, dumbfounded. Then he jumped up from his chair. "Are you serious? I'm going to be a dad? Are you for real or are you joking?" How could he have been so careless? He remembered hearing Naomi vomit the other day, but she had shrugged it off as a stomach bug, and he hadn't given it a second thought.

She looked down. "I'm not kidding."

He knelt beside Naomi, staring at her stomach. "But your belly looks normal sized. Is it healthy? Is it a she? Or a he?"

Naomi closed her eyes now and took a deep breath. It was now or never. She had to get this over with.

She turned to face him now, tears brimming in the corner of her eyes. She took a long look at him, at the worry lines that formed on his beautiful forehead. She adored him, in fact, she didn't think she had ever loved anybody this much. She hated herself for what she did, and what it would do to them, to him. Her heart felt like it was about to splinter into a million pieces.

"I'll find out the gender soon. But Dante, I…I have something to say…" She lowered her eyes. "I…I don't know if…if you're the dad…or if…" she stammered.

Dante's face went pale.

"…if Logan is…" her voice croaked.

His face, drained of color just a moment ago, now reddened. His fists clenched up. His eyes took on a steeliness she had never seen before.

She reached out for him, but before she could, he released a primal, guttural cry that was foreign to her. He swung his fists into the wall, causing a framed picture to hit the floor and explode into fragments of glass.

Naomi was crying hysterically now, holding onto Dante from behind, burrowing her tears into his back. Dante looked numb, like he was being drained of air, of hope, as if he was being suffocated. He tried to shrug off Naomi's embrace and shoved her arms aside.

Naomi fell backwards, her head hitting the edge of the sofa. Dante scrambled to her side. "Naomi! Are you ok?" His hand instinctively went to her stomach. Then he hunched over, back against the wall, head in hands.

She reached out to caress his face. But his face darkened and he turned his head.

"Please Dante, say something..."

She looked longingly at him now. How she wanted to run her fingers through his thick mass of hair, massage the skin in the back of his neck, a move which usually relaxed him. Sometimes it had doubled as foreplay, but she knew she had no right. Not anymore.

Dante refused to look at her. "You need to go. I can't talk to you right now."

Her chest heaving from crying, Naomi fell down to the ground, knees first. "No, please...it was a mistake...I love you...I'm so sorry..."

Dante lifted her up onto the couch. "If you don't go, I will." He hung his head and rushed out the front door, leaving Naomi bent over, sobbing.

3

SYMMETRY

JUNE 23, 2012

NAOMI SHIFTED HER CROSSBODY BAG IN FRONT OF HER BELLY, A protective shield as she thrashed through the elbow-to-elbow crowds on the riverbanks of Suzhou Creek. If it had been up to her, she would have opted for a quiet afternoon at a tea shop. But her mother was only visiting for six days, and had insisted on attending the annual celebration of *Duanwu Jie*, Dragon Boat Festival. This year, more than twenty teams from five nations had entered the dragon boat race.

A stage on one side of the riverbank featured traditional *Kunqu* opera performances, a *zongzi* eating competition, and earlier, a musical play on the legend of *Qu Yuan*, a renowned poet who had lived over two thousand years ago, and for whom the holiday was celebrated.

Reina took out her camera and focused the lens on the dragon boats racing down the river amid loud cheers. The paddled long boats were ornamented with a dragon's head at the prow, the tail at the stern, and intricate dragon scales painted on the body of the boats.

"Should we find a place for tea or coffee?" Naomi pointed to the cafes up ahead.

"Why don't we take a stroll? I'm still very full from lunch. Joss was much, much too generous." Reina patted her stomach.

Joss had called Naomi last night. It was the first time they had spoken since their fight. When she heard Naomi's mom was in town, Joss had insisted on treating them to Yao Li, the city's only three-star Michelin restaurant, recognized for luscious dishes such as Jiangsu Kurobuta pork, codfish in Qimen tea, king crab noodles, roasted suckling pig, and for Duanwu Jie—a specialty zongzi filled with Yoshihama abalone, dried scallops, sakura shrimp, salty duck egg yolk, and black glutinous rice wrapped in lotus leaves.

Naomi recognized the olive branch Joss was extending. "It wasn't my intention to be judgmental, I'm sorry. And I'll tell you all about what's going on with me and Tay," Joss had said, near tears, when they had a moment alone. They had hugged it out, and Reina hadn't even noticed anything amiss between the girls.

"Wow, this is even more exciting than the rowing festival in Venice, the Vogalonga Regatta," Reina said as she snapped more photos of the dragon boats. "You absolutely need to visit Venice someday. It's the most romantic place on earth. The funniest thing happened to me and Bryan there—"

"You already told me. You almost fell out of the gondola but Bryan caught you before—"

"Wrong! He almost fell out but I saved him! Naomi, you need to pay attention more. Sometimes you're not a very good listener." Reina opened a fresh bottle of water. "Drink some before you get dehydrated."

Naomi dutifully complied. The temperatures were unforgiving today, though a breeze brought some reprieve. There were kites of all shapes in the sky—swallows, fishes, peacocks, dragons.

"I was hoping to meet Dante on this trip. Why don't you call him?"

"You're calling me a bad listener? Do you not remember the part where I said he hates my guts now?"

"There is no indication of that."

"The fact that he refuses to speak with me? You didn't see his eyes when I told him the truth. I'd never seen that look before."

"He's hurt. Doesn't mean he hates you. From what you've told me about him, he's a stand-up guy. He will do what's right."

"Mom," Naomi spotted an open bench under the shade now and sat down. They had wandered onto a side street, away from the crowds. "How did you know Dad was the one for you back then?"

"To be honest, I didn't know. Your dad and I...we weren't the type to settle for convention. So we got along in that regard. But you know, every relationship has its seasons," Reina said wistfully.

"It's strange. Those years with your dad, they're the ones I remember most clearly. Maybe because they were the happiest? I don't know. There is so much joy in the infant days, that first year with your baby. You won't sleep of course, but the blissful days outweigh the bad. And your dad was so good with you. He was always racing home after work to see you."

Naomi burst into tears now. She leaned into her mother's chest. "I screwed up so badly. Now my baby won't have a father."

Reina held her daughter, the way she used to when she was a little girl. "Listen to me, Naomi. Your daughter has *you.*" She held her daughter's face now, wiping her tears. "I know you. Your baby will never suffer because you're going to give her your all." Reina looked into her eyes now. "And that's all we can ask of anybody."

*

The day was pierced with sunshine, vivid with light. The clouds looked sculpted against the terrain sliced by skyscrapers. Naomi pushed her sunglasses down from her head to her eyes, shielding herself from the sharp rays. She made her way to Jujube Dessert Bar on a Sunday afternoon, fully expecting it to be packed. She hadn't been here in more than seven months, and had avoided all of Logan's other restaurants as well.

Naomi was determined not to let her nerves get the best of her. She knew it would be an extremely uncomfortable and awkward meeting, but Logan deserved to know that there was a possibility he may become a father soon, as much as she wished it were not so.

Naomi arrived at the entrance of Jujube Dessert Bar and took a deep breath. She swung open the front door, and was surprised to see the interior in shambles, devoid of people. Tables and chairs were stacked haphazardly along a wall. The lush vegetation and fresh flowers that once adorned another wall were wilting, as if it were a purposeful display of decay. The lights were out and the windows looked dusty. The checkered marble floors were filled with muddy footprints leading to the kitchen in the back of the venue. Naomi followed the light coming from the crack of the kitchen door left ajar.

"Hello?" She knocked several times. "*You ren ma?*" Anybody there?

She heard footsteps coming her way and then came face to face with Sola Tan, the Shanghainese woman Logan had hired as manager of Jujube Dessert Bar.

"Naomi, wow look at you! *Gong xi! Hao jiu bu jian!*" Congrats, long time no see! Sola greeted Naomi warmly.

Naomi returned the embrace affectionately and inquired whether Logan was around. He was usually here on Sunday afternoons, that is, if he wasn't nursing a hangover.

Sola shook her head and lugged over a stool from behind the bar, offering Naomi a seat and a glass of water. Sola had not seen Naomi since last year and her visit astonished her for two reasons. The first, that Naomi didn't know Logan had already left for Philadelphia weeks ago. Secondly, the fact that Naomi's usually slim figure had now ballooned. She must be about six months pregnant. As a mother herself, Sola could take a good guess.

"This place is shutting down. Also closing down Napa Kitchen, Britannia Vintage, and Tong's," Sola said nonchalantly, referencing Logan's other F&B establishments in Shanghai.

Naomi gasped. "Why? What happened?"

Sola lit a cigarette, leaning against the open windows. She made sure there was a healthy distance between herself and Naomi.

Sola was puzzled as to why Naomi was in the dark. She had thought Naomi was a close friend of Logan's, at least, that's how it had appeared. She had seen Naomi stop by here with friends more than a dozen times, and each time Logan had showered them with complimentary drinks, which Sola thought was excessive, given that the staff was already underpaid. Each time Sola tried to broach the subject with Logan, mentioning a pay raise, he'd say they would re-visit the issue if she could improve the bottom line. But how could she, when he was constantly giving away free food and drinks?

Logan must've had a falling out with Naomi too, Sola guessed. Just like he did with Vincent Tu, his former business partner.

"You mean Logan did not tell you he left China?"

"He did?!" Naomi squealed, her brows furrowed in confusion.

Sola launched into the full scoop. She had told it so many times by now that she could predict the horrified expressions her audience was about to exhibit.

A bewildered Naomi listened as Sola explained in stilted English, that Logan had a falling out with Vincent, because apparently the financial records were in disarray. She didn't know all the details but she had heard some gossip from a waitress who Logan had fooled around with. Apparently Vincent had accused Logan of mismanagement of company funds—in other words, embezzlement. Then, a month ago, Logan was at Gongdi night club, and had been beaten up by a gang there, badly. He had been hospitalized at Ruijin Medical Center for a week, and was now back in Philadelphia for facial reconstruction surgery.

"I don't think Logan will be coming back to China anytime soon," Sola concluded.

Naomi held a hand over her mouth, her expression in utter shock. "Who hurt Logan? Why, why would they do that?"

Sola shrugged. She told Naomi that rumors were swirling around the episode. The official stance of Gongdi was that they were unaware of the incident, but Logan maintained that one of the Gongdi staff had locked up the private room into which two hulky men had thrown a very drunk Logan down, to be attacked by what Logan described as "at least seven Chinese men." There was talk that Vincent had hired the gang, while another rumor was that Logan had slept with the girlfriend of the gang boss.

"Did anybody call the police about this?" Naomi asked, still in disbelief.

Sola shook her head matter-of-factly. She tried to explain that this was a dead end case. There were no witnesses, or at least no one who dared to come forward as one. And Logan himself had been so drunk that his side of the story and version of the night kept changing. The gang probably had ties with the police force too, who had turned a blind eye. Shanghai was not a city of complete lawlessness, but it wasn't exactly a model for justice either. There were many powerful people in this city, and if one was wise, one did not get on their wrong side.

Sola probably could and should be a bit more sympathetic to her former boss. She had worked for Logan for almost two years now. But the truth was, the guy was an asshole. He had sexually harassed at least a handful of waitresses that she knew of, he was cheap about their wages, and Sola had a much higher opinion of Vincent Tu than of Logan Hayden. Vincent was one of their own, a local man from a humble background who had built his restaurants from the ground up. Logan was the lucky one for having partnered up with Vincent, and no doubt he probably took advantage of Vincent, just like he did with scores of other people. Sola was a devout Buddhist and believed zealously, *what goes around, eventually comes around.*

Sola checked her wristwatch. It was time to get home to her son. As she locked up and walked Naomi out, she gave Naomi a parting hug.

"Good luck to you and the baby!" Sola guessed the father was probably Dante Ouyang, a handsome Chinese man whom she had seen Naomi with a number of times. But you could never be a hundred percent sure. Foreigners were loose, especially in this city.

"Come visit me at the Langham! I'll be starting there next month!" Sola hollered as she waved goodbye to Naomi, who stood there still looking shell shocked.

Naomi was still in a daze after leaving Jujube Dessert Bar. She walked along Xinhua Lu trying to clear her head. Dante hated her and Logan had left town. Her eyes welled up thinking what this meant for her unborn child.

At her last appointment, Dr. Tseng had said she was measuring kind of big, had advised her to do some light work outs such as walking, yoga and doing her Kegel exercises. She thought about this as she started power walking, trying to force herself to do *something good* for her baby, before fatigue set in and she stepped into a cafe for something to drink.

The espresso machine rumbled and growled. The dull murmur of conversation filled the cafe. A couple at the table adjacent to the cashier counter caught her eye. Naomi feigned interest in her phone, but peered over at the silver-haired couple from time to time. Both had on beige tops and matching canvas hats. There were several Shanghai guide books strewn on their table. At times they were silent, both engrossed in their own pages. Then, they were discussing something comical, and her eyes would light up as she laughed. They had a youthful mirth, even if their skin had been desiccated by time. He held her hands across the table sometimes, over hers, as she cupped her coffee mug. They both had kind eyes, weathered by a lifetime of sweetness, of storms, of enduring walks with each other, it seemed.

Their symmetry was enviable and Naomi wondered how they had become this way. Was this ease with each other always this natural, or had it been hard-won? Had they ever kept secrets? Lied? Had they pardoned each other? Naomi once heard that the key to a successful marriage was forgiving your spouse every day. She wondered if she was built for marriage, and if she would be lucky enough someday, to grow old in symmetry with somebody, if that somebody could be Dante, or if she had already lost her chance with him.

During the past two months of separation from Dante, Naomi had seen him often, but only in her dreams. Last night she had felt him again, while she was asleep. She had felt the distance and the space between them shrink, the lines between their bodies blur. She was one with him and he held her like he was anchoring himself, tracing her collarbone with his thumb and the hollow beneath her throat, planting hard kisses on her neck as she faded into him, their breathing synchronized. Her back hit the pillow as her long hair came tumbling and she was a mermaid, swimming in the sheets, in the sea of him. In the eclipse, she needed to gasp for air. Then, she lost his grasp, felt him slipping away, adrift toward the other end of the ocean, away from her, until he was just a tiny speck.

Naomi knew they were from different worlds, and she was far from confident about whether they would work out. She thought of Reina and Wesley, how her mother had loved him so, but knew so little about him. They had spent only several years together before he died. Thereafter, Reina had a succession of boyfriends, some which have lasted a lot longer, but not necessarily happier. She said she never had the urge to get married post-Wesley, that he had been the only true, great love of her life.

Sometimes, her parents' story gave Naomi a tiny ember of hope. Reina and Wesley's worlds were even more radically divergent compared with Naomi and Dante's. At least Naomi and Dante spoke the same language. But love, Reina had said, can be a language in and of itself.

But what did Naomi know about love? Hot tears formed at her irises now. She had botched her chances with the man she was in love with, with somebody who had truly cared for her. Maybe she was kidding herself about having a future with him.

Naomi gulped down the glass of juice and hurried out the cafe before her eyes could inundate.

4

MERCY

NAOMI WAS WALKING SLOWER NOW. HER BRAIN FELT FOGGY AND grainy, and she suffered sudden onsets of dizziness and headaches. Although she had tried her best to conceal her pregnancy at work, she could no longer hide her mushrooming bump. And she was a regular fixture in the restrooms now, trying but failing at containing her frequent urges to urinate.

That morning, Human Resources had summoned her. Huiyi, the HR Director, had sat her down and solemnly announced that the company was downsizing due to a recent scandal: Nicki Jiang had resigned amid allegations that she had created a slush fund, charging existing clients exaggerated amounts in their contracts, and producing a fund in excess of millions of U.S. dollars. She'd been accused of using the slush fund to bribe clients including a tobacco producer. The news had caused an exodus of existing clients and now the agency couldn't afford as many employees. Naomi's last day at the agency would be two weeks from today.

Huiyi reassured Naomi that the severance would be three months, which would also act as her maternity leave payout. She handed her a file of legal documents, asking her to read and sign them within the hour.

Was she the last to find out? She hadn't heard the rumors. Ever since it became apparent that she was pregnant, Amos—her usual source of company gossip—had started distancing himself from her. Not that she was surprised. She knew Amos only imparted his charm and time toward the single and available, and she welcomed the peace and quiet anyway. But she had to admit she missed having him as a confidante at work, especially since Frida had left.

The environment at work had become increasingly toxic. Though her expat colleagues were the first to congratulate her on the pregnancy, she noticed some of the local colleagues whispering and darting strange glances at her, then shutting up as soon as she approached. Later, Orca informed her that people had been gossiping about the fact that she was unmarried and pregnant, which was still considered a social taboo in China, especially in client servicing companies. Pearla had since scaled down her client facing meetings, relegating her to back office work, which, truth be told, she didn't mind much. She had been leaving work at six on the dot for the past month, finding her office chair not nearly as comfortable for her mammoth girth.

Naomi checked her China Union Pay account online every week now. She had a decent amount saved up ever since joining Jun Cleo. In New York she had lived paycheck to paycheck therefore had virtually nothing in her U.S. accounts. But the renminbi in her Chinese bank account would be enough to hold her over for a while, maybe at least until the baby was about six months old.

She probably should've started panicking a long time ago, being pregnant and a soon-to-be-single mother in a foreign country. But the gravity of the situation hadn't really hit her until now—now that she was officially unemployed. She'd had plenty of setbacks in New York, but right now, at this very moment, she felt truly at a loss. She was no longer just making decisions for herself, but for another human being too.

After her meeting with HR, Naomi returned to her cubicle, feeling numb. A torrent of tears came tumbling. She had cried countless nights over the mess already. It wasn't the sort of childhood Naomi had planned for her future offspring. She didn't wish for her child to experience that ache for a father figure, just like she had growing up, and still did.

Naomi wiped away her tears and rubbed her belly. She read in her birthing books that sometimes the baby had surprisingly excellent hearing in the womb. She hoped her baby could hear now. *From here on out, it's just us two, just you and me. I will give you everything, I promise.* She hoped somewhere out there, Saint Mary or some divinity was listening too, and would grant her mercy.

More than a month had passed since meeting with Sola at the now defunct Jujube Dessert Bar. The news about Logan haunted Naomi. She had told Joss right away, who had been shocked as well. It was strange that none of them had heard a peep about Logan and the Gongdi incident. Later, Joss would recall that one of the editors at *Shanghai Scene* had mentioned in passing that some white guy nearly got himself killed at a club near Fuxing Park.

Naomi thought she should get in touch with Logan somehow. She genuinely hoped he was okay. This man was possibly the father of her baby. She didn't have his U.S. number, so she had sent him a quick e-mail asking for it. She didn't know what sort of reaction to expect. The only thought running through her head was that *if* the child was his, she needed reassurance that he would be open to supporting them, and not merely financially. She needed to know whether he desired to be a part of her child's life, and the extent of his involvement. Although she knew Logan could be morally vacuous at times, she was also somewhat confident that he still retained shreds of basic decency. At least she hoped so.

These thoughts plagued Naomi as she left the hospital. The sonographer gave her the option of revealing the gender. Fetal gender scans were considered illegal in China, but foreigners were not subject to such laws. She declined the sonographer's offer, yet again. It didn't seem right to know the gender of the baby before knowing the identity of the baby's father.

Naomi completed the paperwork, paid her bill, and exited the hospital towards the drizzle outside. She crossed the street and ducked inside the mom-and-pop grocers. Their prices were cheaper than Carrefour or City Shop or the Japanese supermarket she frequented. She needed to penny-pinch now.

As she finished up her shopping, worries continued to batter her relentlessly. Should she leave Shanghai and go back to her mother's in California? But Reina was rarely home. Or maybe to her aunt's in Taiwan or in Japan?

Naomi sighed. She liked Shanghai. She loved the life she had built here. She had been content in this city, with Dante, until she had messed it all up. She touched her belly. She always did now, as if this touch could somehow protect her unborn child. Naomi sometimes feared she needed to protect her baby from herself—from her wild, unwise decisions. *Please,* she often prayed now, *please shield this child from harm, especially harm from me.*

Naomi checked her purse for the envelope containing the letter she had written to Dante. It had been sitting there for a week now. Today was the day she would hand deliver the letter, she decided. No more delays. She zipped up her jacket. The rain was coming down harder.

She might have noticed the red light, except there were no cars and she had jaywalked a thousand times in this city, and her flats were now wet from the puddles, and she was fumbling with her umbrella and heavy grocery bags, and there were a million little things contradicting themselves in her head, threatening clarity.

Without these distractions, she might have noticed the man on his speeding motor scooter, helmet-less in a makeshift trash bag poncho, operating the scooter on one hand, talking loudly into his cell phone on the other, zooming full speed ahead.

The thing she sees before she blacks out, are her newly bought groceries strewn over the crosswalk, soaked in rain—the cabbage, carrots, oranges, bananas. One of the tomatoes is squashed, and the can of oatmeal is rolling around. She is at eye level with her torn bag of groceries, cheeks wet and hurting on the cold, damp ground. Then, a searing pain envelops, first at her temples, then on her left hip.

She peers down. Blood, on her bare legs. Then, darkness.

When Naomi confessed her transgressions two months ago, Dante had wanted to murder Logan. It had been a long and miserable summer.

He couldn't concentrate at work, his parents continued their routine nagging about his love life, and he had felt depleted of the energy or drive to do anything. He hadn't even felt like cooking. He probably lost four kilos already. One night, he had staggered into Britannia Vintage, one of Logan's restaurants. He went inside shouting his name, drunk out of his mind, but Logan hadn't been there. And when he called Logan's cell, nobody had picked up. He had been so enraged that he knocked over a row of cups to the ground. Thankfully, they were plastic. Before the restaurant staff could call the cops, Zach had prudently dragged him home.

His parents noticed that he was spending less time with Naomi and had clandestinely tried to set him up with other women. It was always the same scenario—he would attend a family function of some sort, and then the daughter of his parents' friends would "coincidentally" be there.

He was at such a low point that he almost entertained the idea of hooking up with one of them. A striking Nanjing girl, Yang Jin, who liked to be called Jinny, had been coming on to him aggressively. After dinner, Jinny had invited him to join her friends at a bar in the Gulou district. Dante had obliged to the delight of both sets of parents. After nearly an hour though, Jinny's friends still hadn't showed up. He was about to head home, when Jinny had suggested *xiao ye*; she'd like to fix him a late-night snack, and her place was just around the corner. Jinny had heard that Dante was quite the foodie.

As soon as they arrived at Jinny's apartment, she led Dante to the living room couch, poured him a glass of wine, then mauled him. She straddled him, pressing her chest against his. For a moment, he relented. He let Jinny unbutton his shirt while she wiggled out of hers. But in that split second, Dante's mind wandered to Naomi, to her unborn baby, to the fact that maybe it was *his* baby. Or maybe not. A simultaneous rush of desolation and hopefulness washed over him. He felt so flustered that he pushed Jinny off, then apologized profusely when Jinny yelped in pain from hitting her leg on the coffee table.

The next morning, Dante received an hour-long lecture from his parents about "how to be a *jun zi*." A gentleman. They were dismayed that the impeccable Jinny now wanted nothing to do with their son.

Dante was of semi-sound mind when he had caught himself, before any damage was done with Jinny, but he hadn't been so careful two weeks later at Saleya. Dante had ducked into the bar after crossing the street from Jun Cleo's front door. It was six in the evening, and Naomi would be exiting her work building soon. He was already buzzed when he had arrived, although he still had the restraint not to run up to her floor and cause a scene. He hadn't planned on this, he had walked over here on a whim, after taking the afternoon off from work, citing illness. He didn't know what he was expecting, he hadn't even been ready to have a conversation with her yet. Still, he wanted to see her, to see that she was well.

Or maybe subconsciously he wanted her to see him. Dante positioned himself at the window seat of Saleya, directly across from the front doors of her work building, where he had a prime view of the people coming in and out of the brass doors. He had sat in that exact spot while waiting for her before. The patrons behind Saleya's windows were easily visible from across the street.

At approximately twenty-three minutes and two pinots later, he saw her. She was in an ankle-grazing olive green dress, her bump visible from the belt she had cinched underneath her protruding belly. The breeze blew her soft curls away from her face, which seemed fuller, as did her breasts and hips. She looked radiant, beautiful, luminous. What was it that people said about pregnant women, that the prenatal vitamins gave them a glow?

For a second, his heart leapt when he thought she had met his gaze. Then a bus came barreling down the street, parking and obstructing his view. He quickly got up to move seats. But when he looked out the window again she was no longer there. He ran outside the door, looked up and down the street among the harried pedestrians, but her green dress was no longer in sight.

For a moment he stood transfixed in front of the bar, angry. The ugly feelings from their last encounter came rushing back. Did she see him? If she did, how dare she just run away? Did she even know what she had done to him? How shriveled he felt, how bleak his world was now, how he couldn't sleep without drinking anymore. That was when he realized he had left his wallet on the table and hadn't paid the bill at Saleya yet.

He rushed inside the bar and saw that his table had been cleared, replaced by a couple looking like they wanted to devour each other. He approached a waitress about his wallet, and the bored girl pointed to a pair of women lounging on the ruby couches. "Ni de peng you fu le." *Your friend paid already.*

Dante spun around and saw a blonde woman holding up his wallet, smiling at him like he was in trouble. As he approached the women, the brunette next to blondie rose from the couch and chided him to sit down, despite his protests. Then she winked at blondie and left.

Blondie's name was Lottie Magyar. She was visiting from Budapest but was seriously contemplating moving to China. Dante nodded absentmindedly. He just wanted his wallet back and head out.

But Lottie was playing some sort of game. *I paid for your bill and saved your wallet, the least you can do is have a drink with me,* she had pouted. Dante gave up resisting and downed a vodka shot with her. Then she insisted on absinthe, followed by soju, and after that, she was starving, and suddenly he was too.

Dante recalled licking his bowl clean at Pho King, and Lottie commenting that it was her first time trying Vietnamese noodles. Then because Lottie had charmed the owner, they were treated to complimentary lemongrass-tinis. Later, Lottie was laughing and helping him up as he tripped over something, stumbling his way into the throbbing beats of G Plus Club. He vaguely remembered thinking that under the flashing disco lights, Lottie was looking particularly seductive, then he wondered if it was because of his beer goggles. Everything in the club was out-of-focus, a hazy cinematic blur, and he can't even recollect how they got to Lottie's hotel room.

What he does recall is that the room was furnished in gaudy embellishments, such as entwined golden swans on the bedposts, shimmering window curtains, and an actual hot tub, which Lottie had immediately filled with frothy bubbles, after she had magically stripped down within a minute of arrival. Not that Dante took much notice. The only things that interested him at that point were the fluffy pillows and the inviting mattress. His head was pounding, as if a sumo wrestler had taken his skull hostage.

Before he could process what was happening, Lottie had wrapped her limbs around him. She started undoing his buttons, leading him toward the tub. Her lips tasted like cigarettes.

Dante didn't know if it was the steam ascending to his temples, the foul puddle of liquor in the pit of his guts rising up, or the sudden thrashing of her tobacco-tasting tongue inside his jaw. In any case, he had an abrupt urge to regurgitate. Before he could react, the repulsive pool had forcibly surged up his stomach, and shot out his mouth. Most of it had landed among the iridescent bubbles, including the vermicelli, but some of it also got tangled in Lottie's unruly blonde curls. He had reached for her, wanting to pick the stray pieces off her head, but was so swiftly repelled by her ear-splitting shrieks that he wondered if he had just risked permanent hearing loss. Then Lottie was in the shower, scrubbing and cursing. Dante apologized as he bolted out the hotel room, sans shoes, reeking of stench, forgetting his shirt.

He had sprinted down the stairs as fast as he could, bare-chested and barefooted, toward the hotel lobby. Out of breath, he stopped to check his pants pocket.

He let out a sigh of relief. At least he had his wallet.

Dante appreciated Zach for attempting to take his mind off of Naomi. Zach continued dragging him to the Shanghai Art Deco Society meetings, even though he was rarely in the mood nowadays. These monthly meetings consisted of a speaker accompanied by a slide show, and though topics largely centered on architecture in China, presentations on Chinese history, literature, art were also included. When he had first arrived in Shanghai, Dante had also given a presentation at one of these meetings. He had talked about his grandparents, showing some sepia photographs of his grandfather when he had been a principal at the school in Nanjing.

Tonight, the meeting was at the Pei Mansion on Nanyang Lu. This heritage building was the former family home of legendary architect, I.M. Pei., and now operated as a boutique hotel. The building retained its geometric art deco features combined with Chinese ornamentation, including an elaborate carved dragon stone spiral staircase.

Dante found a seat in the back, near the "longevity wall." The wall was covered with a hundred of the Chinese characters *shou*, long life, each character stylized a different way.

Bei Caizeng, a distant relative of I.M. Pei, started the meeting by showing slides of another art deco jewel in Shanghai that had been demolished by the government eleven years ago. Bei Caizeng recounted how I.M. Pei himself had penned a letter to plead for the preservation of the building—a structure that had survived world wars and the Cultural Revolution—but had been met with rejection. Bei Caizeng's family now took solace that at least the Pei Mansion was a functioning hotel, more or less guaranteeing its preservation.

It was all very interesting, and normally Dante would've been riveted by these historical tours. But tonight, his mind kept wandering toward Naomi. No matter how hard he fought it, he was still etched with the memory of her. When they were together, she made him feel like the world oscillated back on its axis, that all was the way it was supposed to be.

That was when he got the call from Joss.

Dante picked it up on the first ring. He listened to what she said, then abruptly stood up in the middle of the meeting.

He dashed out the front door, as fast as he could.

5

BREATHLESS

WHEN SHE AWOKE, THE FIRST THING SHE HEARD WAS THE FUSILLADE of furious raindrops beating against the windows. The next thing she saw was Dante asleep on the side of the hospital bed, his head rested on his arms, next to her thigh. She tried to get up but her left arm was hooked to an IV. She didn't mean to wake him, but she couldn't help stroking his cheek. She yearned to touch him, to confirm that she wasn't dreaming.

He opened his eyes. She saw a crimson nick in the cleft of his chin. The half-moons beneath his eyes were more prominent than usual. His eyes were bloodshot. They reminded her of shattered shards haphazardly pieced back together.

"Naomi! You're awake! Don't move baby...don't move." He cupped her face and held it tenderly. "Joss just left and said she'll be back later to check on you."

Naomi nodded and smiled meekly. Then a sudden onset of migraines hit her and images of the last twenty-four hours started flooding in: the sonographer, the grocery shop, the scooter that had zipped out of nowhere. She felt a burst of anxiety and was sobbing now, garbled questions rushing out of her mouth. *What have I done? Is the baby okay? Where is the doctor?*

Dante held Naomi close, stroked her hair and reassured her that she and the baby were in stable condition. The doctor had already put her on hours of fetal monitoring.

Earlier, a nurse had asked him if he was "the dad." Dazed and anxious, he had nodded without thinking. Then the nurse had thrust him a clipboard thick with paperwork, asking him to promptly fill them out.

Dr. Ye, a stern Shanghainese woman, admonished Dante to take better care of his wife, lecturing him on how Naomi shouldn't have been carrying such heavy grocery bags in the first place. Also, Dante should remind his wife about the perils of Shanghai's crosswalks.

"Green doesn't always mean go. In this city, you need to let the cars go first if the drivers insist on running the lights," Dr. Ye said.

"Bao bao hai hao ma?" Dante blurted, interrupting the doctor. *Is the baby okay?*

"She had a mild concussion and a scraped knee. She appears okay for now, but for peace of mind, we can schedule an MRI. You can discuss with your wife whether she'd like to have one," Dr. Ye continued. "You should thank your lucky stars. She's very fortunate that a placenta abruption or hemorrhagic shock didn't occur. That could've been extremely dangerous for both your wife and daughter."

Dante nodded as he tried to calm the flood of emotions swirling in his chest. Things could've been so much worse! How blessed they were! How blessed *he* was, that she was here and well.

He smiled faintly. He now knew Naomi was having a girl.

It was nine in the evening. Dr. Ye informed Dante that it would be fine for Naomi to eat something. "Gei ta mai tang," Dr. Ye advised. *Bring her some soup.* She especially recommended fish soup with red dates and figs, which would replenish her spleen and blood flow. The nurses gave Dante the address of a Guangdong soup shop around the corner, dispatching him to fetch his wife dinner.

The doctor and nurses weren't actually sure if he was this woman's husband or just a boyfriend, but earlier when they had referred to her as his wife, he had not disputed, even though they hadn't seen a wedding ring on either of them. What was indisputable was that he was in love with her.

Dante returned with his hands full, carrying three different kinds of soup. The nurses chuckled. He couldn't decide on which one to get and the shop owner had sold him on three of their most popular soup offerings: black chicken chestnut soup, pork bone broth with lotus, and the doctor recommended fishtail soup.

Dante held out a spoonful of broth and gently nudged Naomi to open her mouth. Naomi pulled herself upright by the guardrails and dutifully swallowed the soup. Then she clutched his hand. "Please forgive me Dante..."

"Shh...shh...don't talk...just rest..."

"No, I need to know that you forgive me..." she held his hand ardently, tears rolling down her cheeks. "I...I wrote you something." She motioned for him to bring over her purse and retrieve the envelope from inside. He opened the letter.

Dante,

I don't think I've ever told you this. The day my dad died, my mom said I just shutdown. I went somewhere nobody could reach. I was two years old. By then I was already talking a little, but when the plane went down, my mom said I lost all of my speech. It would be a year before I uttered another word.

My mom repeated this story often, with emphasis on how my two-year-old self had crumbled under the trauma. I grew up believing in how fragile I was, how fleeting relationships are.

When we first got together, I don't think I'd ever known such happiness. But it all seemed too good. Then when you left Shanghai last year, I was almost certain that was the end of us, that you weren't coming back. But you proved my theory wrong. Even though I didn't quite believe it at first. I kept looking for you to fail us.

I want to say I'm sorry for that, for the deficient faith in you, in us, in the first place.

I was in a really bad place last month. I was paranoid about everything and wondering whether the baby would really make it. A part of me was scared that it *would* make it.

Then the baby started kicking. A lot. And it kicked me really hard one night, and it felt like it was trying to kick some sense into me, to wake me up.

I've come to realize that my baby and I are going to be fine. I had dreamt about the baby smiling, little fingers and toes stretched out towards me. I was a mother in my dream. I *am* a mother.

Then one day it just occurred to me: I'm built for this. I don't have to fear the fragility of life and relationships.

I'm sorry for what I did. I have so, so many regrets. But I also have so much hope. That's the thing. It's a tall order, and maybe inconceivable that I even ask this of you, but I think you should forgive me.

I don't know how our future will play out, I have no clue how we should move forward. But I do know this—We're right for each other, we make sense. Even if we're the only ones that believe it.

I love you. And I think I always will,

Naomi

Dante wiped her tears away with his thumb, kissing her tenderly. "I...I forgive you, but only if you'll forgive me too. I'm so, so sorry," he whispered into her ear. "We're in this together."

Several days after the Lottie debacle, Dante had made up his mind. He knew now, more than ever, that he wanted Naomi. Needed her.

He forced himself to think about their predicament rationally, tried to filter out all the messy moods. He might be the father, and if he was, he'd gladly, wholeheartedly take responsibility. And if he wasn't? Dante had pondered that painful possibility too. After tormenting himself for the past couple of months, he arrived at the conclusion that the unforeseen circumstances didn't change the outcome. He was still in love with her, plain and simple. And if that meant loving her child too, so be it.

Then Dante heard about the Gongdi incident, learned that Logan had fled China. It was then that he knew Logan was out of the picture, that any chance of reconciliation between Logan and Naomi was slim to none.

Even so, could he really love and raise a baby that was not his own, that would forever remind him of Naomi's infidelity?

He surprised himself. He didn't know he had it within him.

When Joss had frantically called about Naomi being hospitalized, that she'd been in some type of traffic accident, Dante had felt momentarily breathless, like the life was being squeezed out of him. He had immediately raced out of Yuan Mingyuan Lu towards Huashan Hospital.

He felt as if Naomi had forced a resilience, a bravado, faith even, out of him. He never knew he had it in the deep recesses within him—to forgive, to love in such capacity. It had been dormant all this time. But now, Dante understood what he was capable of, what they could realize together.

After Naomi's MRI results showed that she was ready to be discharged from the hospital, Dante was adamant about her moving into his place straight away. In the following week, he helped her pack up, clean out her French Concession apartment, and assisted in negotiating with the landlord to discontinue the lease.

6

SECOND CHANCES

JOSS FOUND HER HUSBAND ON A BENCH IN ZHONGSHAN PARK, NEAR the camphor trees and magnolias. Off to his left, a man with a gray beard was writing calligraphy. To his right, a group of teens were in colorful cosplay costumes taking selfies. In the distance, a band of elderly men were playing *erhu*, the traditional Chinese two-stringed violin. This park was one of his favorite green spaces in the city. His childhood home was just around the corner. He grew up coming here.

"How did it go at the Biennale? Rough day?" She sat down next to him, snuggling her head in his chest.

"The exhibition went well. That is, until Father showed up." He sighed.

"What did he do this time?"

"He botched the deal I was working on, an acquisition of one of Lei Chuyang's work."

"That young ink painter from Changsha?"

"Changchun," Tay clarified. "He does ink on silk."

It was one of their long-standing conflicts. Tang Zhaoyi's focus was exclusively on antiques, while Tay studied forecasting trends that saw benefits to acquiring up-and-coming Chinese contemporary art. The issue with Chinese antiques was the rampant forgery, which made the authentication process difficult, and often caused buyers to default on payments. The company was suffering because of such disputes.

"Father is losing clients and he doesn't care. It's costing me my reputation in the industry too."

Joss gave him an empathetic look. Tang Zhaoyi was not the easiest personality to work with. He was stubborn, authoritarian. When she first moved to Shanghai, Joss had assisted Tay at the family business for a week, before coming to the conclusion that she could not work with her father-in-law. "Do you remember what you told me years ago, when we were in New York and you were in business school?"

"That you were going to be my wife?"

"Besides that." She smiled. "You said you were going to run Tao International Auctions one day."

"Well, that is the plan. That's what my parents have always expected." He stared into the distance. His tone made it sound more like a prison sentence.

"But plans change. God knows how much our plans have changed."

"Okay." He paused, looking at her cautiously. "What are you trying to say?"

"I'm saying that the life we so carefully planned is not panning out that way." She looked at him meaningfully, and knew that he understood. She had quit her job in New York and followed him to Shanghai, and they had both thought they would lead a certain life here. She loved her life with him, but she also knew that he wasn't thriving. Not the way he used to. The last three years of miserable medical treatments, job frustrations, secrecy…it was all crashing down on him now.

"Tay, you're allowed to change course," she said gently, "especially when it comes to your livelihood."

"Just like how we're changing course with our…our own family. Remember?" Joss continued. She took out a manila envelope from her tote bag.

"Are those the files?"

"Yes." She took a deep breath. "Are you interested in looking at them now? Or later?"

He was quiet for a moment. "Before we do that, I just wanted to know. Would you…would you have considered getting pregnant and giving birth, if my body had functioned differently? I'm not trying to diminish what happened to your mom. I know it's a traumatizing subject, and you have every reason to reject pregnancy."

"It's been a journey for me too. I know when we first met I wasn't forthright about my fear of giving birth. I'm sorry about that. But at the time I truly believed I would eventually become brave enough and come around." She held his hand now. "I want a family with you. And to answer your question, yes. I would've been open to pregnancy and delivery. But after all we've been through in the last three years, I think…that's not our path."

She handed him the files now. "But maybe this is."

"Maybe it is," he echoed. A fallen leaf had landed on his shoulder. Joss picked it off, kissing him.

And there in the middle of Zhongshan Park, as people walked dogs, kids flew kites, and the elderly danced, a couple sat together. They read through each document, marveled at the photographs of each child, and wondered whether the destiny of their future family was in one of these files.

A labyrinth of stalls filled with vibrant textiles stretched out before them at the Shiliupu fabric market. Joss linked her arms with Naomi's, conscientious about slowing her pace to match her friend's pregnant waddle. Getting customized apparel tailored—or pieces copied from the high-fashions as seen on the runway—for a fraction of the usual price, was one of those distinct only-in-China experiences. There were foreigners at almost every stall, most had some sort of picture on hand to show the tailor, either torn from a magazine or printed from a website.

Joss didn't frequent the fabric markets. She was considered a VIP at her favorite branded stores. But Naomi came often. She adored these markets, and not just for the quality knockoffs. She enjoyed perusing the fabrics, fingering the textures, imagining the possibilities when she asked for a one-of-a-kind creation she had designed. Just last month she had visited Ding Ayi's stall to have a maternity dress made. She couldn't find anything she liked in the mall maternity section, so had showed Ding Ayi photos from the Miu Miu cruise collection and the Opening Ceremony Spring Ready-to-Wear line. Drawing on her fashion school experience, she had sketched a rough silhouette of an open back silk maxi with sleeves in an elegant Japanese *seigaiha* wave pattern. Using the visuals Naomi provided, Ding Ayi was able to produce three summer dresses in two weeks, all fit to accommodate her bump.

Joss reached for the bag full of purchases on Naomi's arm. "I'll carry that," Joss said as she peered inside the bag. "Really? Did you buy the entire rack of scarves? In every color?" Joss joked.

"They're such a steal! And yes, I absolutely need all of these twenty renminbi Escada scarves," Naomi replied in a mock-serious tone.

As Naomi examined the swatches in one stall, Joss revealed her main preoccupation for the past six months. She and Tay had agreed to keep the news between themselves until they had submitted the adoption paperwork, which they finally did last week.

Naomi looked stunned, before she squealed and gave her friend a fierce embrace. "I'm so happy for you two. That's incredible news! Are you ready? Are you scared?"

Joss nodded. "Yes. Adoption is very scary. But I also know it's what Tay and I need to do. It sounds silly, but I know it's meant to be."

"How do you know?"

"Because we've been praying for a child, and this is the door that God opened. And after visiting the orphanage, I'm even more convinced. Those children..." her voice trailed off. "They need good homes."

"Wow so you're going to be a mom soon!" Naomi held her hands to her stomach. She was bursting with elation and her baby was probably feeling it too.

Joss laughed. "Yes, we both are! But you'll be first. We've just completed the paperwork. It will take another eight to twelve months before we're matched."

Naomi suddenly jerked to her side and her hand flew to her stomach, her other hand holding onto Joss for balance.

"Are you okay?" Joss asked as she steadied her.

Naomi nodded. "She's a kicker. She seems to do that when I'm emotional. Yesterday she kicked like crazy."

"Right, you had that call with Logan yesterday. It must've been intense."

"It was...interesting," was the only thing Naomi managed to say, as she drank a mouthful from her water bottle. She took a deep breath, then proceeded to tell Joss the incredulous conversation she had with Logan.

Naomi had tried to call Logan several times in the past week, but he hadn't answered the phone until yesterday. At first, he sounded pleasant and happy to hear from her. Naomi asked about the surgery, about how he was doing. He said he was on bed rest at his brother's place, that his nose and mouth had needed major reconstruction surgeries, and that he now required dentures for the teeth that had been knocked out. He didn't mention the fight at Gongdi nightclub, and Naomi didn't bring it up. By now, most of the expatriate contingent had heard about the incident, and it served as a cautionary tale. Varied versions of the story floated around the city, each one more appalling than the other, like an urban myth gone wildly out of hand. She knew some Chinese who rejoiced at the news, at the locals-beating-up-and-kicking-a-white-guy-out-of-China essence of it.

Hearing Logan describe the gruesome injuries made her despondent. Yes, he could be a jerk, but a part of her still cared for him as a friend. When Naomi finally delivered the big news, that the child could be his, Logan had immediately, vehemently denied that it was possible. "I used protection that night, Naomi, I always do."

But Naomi remembered things differently. Although she had been intoxicated, she distinctly recalled Logan cursing that he forgot to bring protection. "That's when I ran downstairs to the store," Logan reminded her. "I went to Lawson's, and I also bought us snacks. Remember?"

No, she didn't remember. It was then Naomi wished that she could see Logan face to face, so she could detect the level of his sincerity. She'd only known Logan for the last three years, and she didn't know him to be a liar, but then again, he could be conniving when he wanted to be.

"Look, if you don't believe me, I'm happy to take a paternity test. And if evidence proves the kid is mine, I will take responsibility."

Naomi insisted she wanted this declaration in writing, and the conversation ended shortly afterwards.

It was incredulous that Naomi would accuse him. True, he could be unscrupulous, but that didn't mean he lacked his own set of principles. It was a standard Logan held steadfast to, especially after some of his friends had contracted diseases in Shanghai, or had endured the ordeal of paying for an abortion. These were exactly the type of situations Logan took pains to avoid. That was why no matter how high or how drunk he was, he never did the deed unprotected.

For a moment, he felt a wisp of sadness that their friendship or whatever they had, had whittled down to this—business-like correspondence, and even that would quickly come to an end. He would probably never see her again, now that she and Dante were starting a family. But just as quickly as the thought creeped into his mind, it slipped away in a flash.

Women came and went. That was just the way it was.

Logan had been back in the States for nearly three months now. The first month he had been in excruciating pain and had practically lived in the hospital. Of course he appreciated his brother for putting him up, and it had been nice spending time with the nephews. But everything else here was exactly where he'd left it—his drunken father, friends and their nests of rugrats, the utter monotony of suburbia.

He missed his old life and was itching to get back. Shanghai was out of the question, he could never go back there, not after what Vincent Tu and his barbaric friends did to him. But he didn't rule out Beijing, Shenzhen, Macau, or Hong Kong. He spoke decent Chinese, knew his way around the system, and it'd be a dreadful waste to just give that all up. He would have to start his businesses from scratch again, but if he was able to do it the first time, he was confident there would be a second chance.

That's what he loved about China—it was a forgiving place, a vast country full of opportunities for reinvention.

7

SITTING THE MONTH

NAOMI WAS MOSTLY WADDLING NOW. HER LEGS AND ANKLES HAD never felt so swollen. Still, she clung to a daily routine to keep herself sane. In the mornings she took walks in the city, usually in Hongqiao. She took care of errands, bought the groceries, stocked up on baby essentials here and there. Last week Joss had hosted a baby shower for her. All the baby gifts were still in a pile in the guest room, which Naomi vowed to get down to organizing soon, not to mention all the baby furniture that was still waiting to be installed.

Naomi had just returned to Dante's apartment from a checkup. The doctor said the baby was the size of a pumpkin now, and that the itchy belly was a normal sensation. As she set down her bags on the sofa, she was surprised to see Dante there. It was only five p.m. and Dante usually didn't get off work until seven.

He grinned conspiratorially, then said he had a *surprise.*

He tied a silky sleeping mask over her head as a blindfold, then led her gently by the elbow as they crisscrossed through the living room. He took off the blindfolds once they reached the guest room.

She gasped as soon as she was able to open her eyes. In front of her was an exquisite ivory-colored crib with a mobile hanging low. A pink diaper changing table and a toy chest filled with stuffed animals lined the wall on the right. Inside the closet hung precious baby onesies, and a shelf underneath displayed a row of baby shoes.

Tears brimmed in her eyes. "Thank you," she whispered. They had talked briefly about prepping the baby room, but in the last few weeks Dante had been tied up with a major project in Luwan district.

Dante held her chin up and kissed away her tears. "Naomi, last year when I was abroad, a part of me regretted the decision because I thought you were going to move on. Then this past summer, I really thought I would lose you."

He took a deep breath. "I won't make the same mistake again—I don't ever want to be without you again. I love you, and," he rubbed her bump now, "I already love her."

Dante fumbled for the turquoise palm-sized box from his jacket pocket. As he opened it, he knelt before her. "Naomi Kita-Fan, will you do me the honor of being my—"

Before he could finish, she threw her arms around him. Her trembling lips met his now.

*

It was a popular dish at Court Waitan: wagyu oxtail rice with shaved black truffles and a side of carpaccio nestled in pickled kohlrabi. Joss tried to savor each succulent bite, while Ruiling droned on and on about her recent trip to a luxury *ryokan* in the Hanazono woods of Hokkaido.

A middle-aged woman in a Saint Laurent silk crepe suit approached and pulled Ruiling away for conversation, much to Joss's relief. Across from her seat, Tang Zhaoyi and Tay were debating some work-related issue.

Court Waitan was a members-only club, housed in a former bank with soaring ceilings, granite columns, marble floors, towering mirrors. The club's banquet room was Zhaoyi and Ruiling's favorite place to dine. Billowy drapes framed half-moon windows, crystal chandeliers sparkled from each corner. Upstairs, the rooftop lounge boasted panoramic views of the Bund.

"Was that your friend?" Joss asked, as Ruiling returned to her seat.

"You don't know Zhang Yahui?"

"Oh! I didn't realize that was her." Joss had heard of the "Shanghai property princess," one of the wealthiest real estate moguls in the city.

"Tay used to go to school with her daughter. Too bad they never liked each other. Well, she only dated Europeans anyway." Ruiling gestured at her son now to get his attention. "That was Jia's mother. She was just showing me photos of her grandchildren. Did you know Jia just gave birth in Geneva?"

"I think I heard something about that," Tay replied nonchalantly.

"*Long feng tai*," Ruiling added. Dragon phoenix twins. It was the desired twin set of one child of each gender.

Zhaoyi took a long look at his son. "So when will we be able to *bao sun zi*?" Hold our grandchild.

"About that...Father, Mother, we have an announcement to make."

Ruiling's eyes lit up. "Good news?" Her attention turned toward Joss's stomach.

"Well, yes, it is. We consider it very good news." Tay inhaled sharply. "Mom, Dad, we are going to *ling yang*." Adopt.

Ruiling looked confused. "*Ling yang she me?*" Adopt what?

"*Hai zi!*" Joss and Tay said in unison, almost shouting. A child.

Zhaoyi, who was sipping on sake, doubled over and started coughing. Silence filled the table.

Then, both Ruiling and Zhaoyi began raising their voices, talking over each other.

"Why would you—"

"You can't be serious—"

"No, not a good idea—"

"What's wrong with you two—"

"I don't understand—"

Ruiling turned to Joss now. "Did you put him up to this? This was your idea, wasn't it?"

Joss gave her a firm look. "We made this choice together, as *fu qi*." As husband and wife. "We've thought this through, very, very carefully."

"But why? Why would you do this!"

"It's very simple. Because it's physically impossible for us to have biological children. And the reason doesn't end there. There are countless children who need people like us——"

"Keep your voice down, Joss. People know us here," Ruiling half-whispered, urgently.

Ruiling looked around before continuing. "And what do you mean it's impossible? What's wrong with your body? I know you haven't been taking the *dong chong xia cao* and *du zhong* I gave you. Do you know the trouble I went through to get those? I took a special trip to Sichuan to buy the purest, most authentic kind."

Joss tried to calm her irritated nerves. Ruiling had been nagging her for months to ingest the Chinese herbs that purportedly helped to induce fertility.

Tay put up his hands now. "Mother, stop. It's not Joss, it's...me." In one fell swoop he told them about the past three years of surgeries and fertility treatments with the best doctors in the region, and how it had all been painful, costly, futile.

Ruiling and Zhaoyi looked momentarily shocked.

Zhaoyi shook his head. "It will be better for you to remain childless then."

"And why is that?" Joss said through gritted teeth.

Zhaoyi scowled. "You don't know what type of seed you will get."

"You just don't get it." Tay shook his head. "And to be clear, we were asking for your blessing, not your permission. We've already started the paperwork."

"Son, you do not know what you're doing. As usual."

Tay stood up now. "For once, I know exactly what I'm doing." He took his wife's hand. "C'mon Joss, dinner is over."

*

Born at 10:14 a.m. on November 5th, 2012, in the Shanghai Lenai Hospital, the baby's birth certificate read Mitsue Ningxin Ouyang. The baby's grandmother, Pan Jinsung, had chosen her Chinese name, Ningxin. It meant *peace and prosperity*—her two hopes for her granddaughter, and for their family.

Under normal circumstances, Pan Jinsung's husband should've been the one to name their grandchild. He had named their son, Ouyang Tian, and he had also been consulted for an ideal name when his nephew was born. Ouyang Zhangjie attached great significance and privilege to the act of naming his descendants, but it was a privilege he had forfeited when he ceased speaking with his son.

In the last month of Naomi's pregnancy, Jinsung had been secretly making the trek to Dante's apartment in the mornings, bringing pots of snakehead fish red date soup, radish chicken, fig and black sesame congee. These were traditional Chinese recipes known to nourish the mother's body and boost the baby's development.

Zhangjie was further incensed when Dante and Naomi had obtained their marriage certificate without his consent. Dante said the official wedding banquet would be held later, when things have settled down after the baby was born. Zhangjie had been infuriated with the idea, calling it improper and scandalous.

Although Jinsung concurred with her husband's sentiment to some degree, she still agreed to act as a witness at the Marriage Registration Bureau of the Civil Affairs Office, so the couple could obtain their marriage license. She had wept a little and some might have thought of her a sentimental mother, tearing, now that her grown son was becoming a married man. That was part of the reason, but it was also because of the sorrowful relationship between her husband and son. It made Jinsung sad with resignation. On one hand she was disappointed with Dante for blatantly disregarding his parents in such a monumental life matter such as marriage. On the other hand, she was frustrated with Zhangjie for being so obstinate, for not stepping with the times, for pushing their only son away.

For weeks, Jinsung didn't dare bring up Naomi's name. If she did, her husband's mood would sour on cue. But on the day of the baby's birth, Jinsung had walked up to Zhangjie, looked at him straight in the eye, and announced that she was going to the hospital to see their granddaughter. She had implored him to come too, reminding him that he was getting old and that this could be a once-in-a-lifetime occurrence. Who knew how long they had? Dante would only get busier and busier, now that he was starting his own family. Zhangjie had seemed moved, and for a second Jinsung thought this might've been the turning point. But then his eyes clouded over and he waved her away. Jinsung shook her head and left for the hospital alone.

The birth had been smooth. Naomi had already dilated to five centimeters by the time they reached the hospital. Three hours later, the baby was here, wailing from her healthy set of lungs, screaming her momentous arrival. Jinsung had not seen her son tear in years, decades maybe. It was a wondrous sight for Jinsung to see—holding his baby in his hands, Dante's eyes had welled. And Jinsung couldn't help but cry too. His daughter looked exactly like Dante when he'd been born.

All day long, Naomi kept asking Dante to make the long-distance call to her mother, Reina Kita. But the call only went to voicemail, so Dante had sent a quick e-mail instead. Dante showed Naomi the e-mail response from Reina, who apparently was now somewhere in the Balkans with bad reception. Jinsung had heard that Reina was a full-time travel tour guide, who Naomi seldom saw. It was heartbreaking to see Naomi yearn so dearly for her mother, and Jinsung felt her heart soften for the poor girl.

After the delivery, an exhausted Naomi had reached out for Jinsung's hand, held it, and asked her to give the baby a Chinese name. A wave of guilt consumed her for whatever ill thoughts she had once harbored toward Naomi. She had never told Naomi how much she treasured the delicate Russian music box she had gifted her last Christmas.

At the hospital, Jinsung grilled her son on whether he had prepared for adequate postnatal care. "Xiao Tian, sei yao bang Naomi zuo yue zi?" Who is going to help Naomi with *sitting the month*?

Dante's face drew a blank.

Jinsung sighed impatiently. Her son had become too anglicized and had forgotten many traditions. She explained that *zuo yue zi* was a Chinese regimen which dated all the way back to the Han dynasty, thousands of years ago. The practice restored the mother's beleaguered postpartum body. There would be some lifestyle restrictions and dietary requirements: no cold foods, no showers, no leaving the house.

Jinsung decided she would be the one to make sure that Naomi received the best postnatal care possible. She made a mental list of groceries she had to purchase soon for her postpartum meals: pig's feet, black chicken, papaya, goji berries, dates, rice wine, black vinegar, dang gui, huang qi. If followed correctly, *zuo yue zi* would help the new mother heal faster and produce more milk, directly impacting the health of the newborn. Grandparents in China were highly involved in raising their grandchildren. Jinsung had friends who had expressed joy in experiencing parenting again, but some had also grumbled at the work it entailed. One neighbor had complained that the grandson lived with them for five days a week, and the parents came to visit only on the weekends. This was a normal practice in China, where work life reigned supreme over home life.

Jinsung looked forward to this new chapter in all of their lives. She hoped her son and husband would reconcile soon. Their granddaughter was just perfect, and Naomi would make a fine daughter-in-law, Jinsung decided. She would make a conscious effort to fill the void in Naomi's heart, a vacuum no doubt left by her absent parents.

8

DRAGON GIRL

THE BABY'S FIRST NAME WAS *MITSUE*, A JAPANESE NAME MEANING "RIVER of light." Naomi and Dante called her *Mitsy* for short. Jinsung took to calling her granddaughter *Ningning*, from the first character of her Chinese name. Her relatives nicknamed her *Xiao Long Nu*, little dragon girl, since she was born in the year of dragon.

Indeed, Ningning had the feisty spirit of a dragon. At almost three months old she was already grabbing Jinsung's fingers and swiping away toys she didn't like. When she cried, it was as if the whole house shook.

Jinsung checked the calendar. She had been so consumed with taking care of Naomi and Ningning that she would often lose track of the date. Next week it would be February, and the week after that it was *chun jie*, Chinese New Year.

They planned on spending a quiet chun jie in Shanghai this year. It would be her first one not spent in Nanjing in decades. Zhangjie still hadn't agreed to come, but Jinsung was confident he would yield, eventually. She had been uploading Ningning's videos and photos to their shared computer, and she knew Zhangjie was obsessively poring over them when she wasn't home.

Ouyang Zhangjie was wholly unprepared to meet Ouyang Ningxin. He hadn't anticipated being completely captivated by her, with her thick shock of licorice-black hair, her round, curious eyes, her button nose and tiny toes. She was the spitting image of his son when he had been an infant. He still remembered the birth of his son like it was yesterday—how he had pedaled his bicycle to the hospital with Jinsung holding onto him while heaving in pain, how her birthing cries had scared the daylights out of him, how vulnerable and joyous he had felt holding his newborn baby.

Zhangjie positioned himself on the armchair so he could hold little Ningning more comfortably. His arms were starting to feel sore but she was fast asleep now, and he didn't wish to wake her. Jinsung came over and tried to extricate her from his arms but he shook his head. He would be going back to the hotel in two hours and wanted to spend every minute with his granddaughter until then. Earlier, he had posed for photos with Ningning, placing her very first Chinese New Year red envelope into her palms. She had held onto the envelope with her tiny fingers, while her parents had clapped with glee and snapped photos.

It had been over eight months since Zhangjie was last in Shanghai and inside his son's apartment. The last time he was here, it'd been under a very different context. That was when he had been sure Dante and Naomi were on the brink of *fen shou*, breaking up, because Dante had agreed to meet the daughters of Zhangjie's friends. But then Zhangjie had heard that his son was misbehaving during these *yue hui*, either acting disinterested or rude. To this day Zhangjie was still avoiding Mr. Yang, after the debacle that had transpired with his daughter Jinny. Zhangjie had given up on the matchmaking after that.

All throughout the day Zhangjie observed the exhausted new parents. Dante was doting and hands-on and *ti tie*, to both Naomi and the baby. Fatherhood suited him very well. He looked blissful. He reminded Zhangjie of himself when he became a dad.

Zhangjie sighed. Sometimes in life we just needed to *sui yuan*, let the fates guide. His son was infatuated with this woman, and now they had borne this perfect baby. Maybe they knew each other from a past life. Sometimes that was the explanation for the inexplicable attraction one felt. And who could argue with that?

The apartment was virtually unrecognizable. The guest room, where Zhangjie and Jinsung usually stayed in when they visited Shanghai, had now been converted into a nursery, outfitted with pastel pink wallpaper, dolls, an ivory crib.

Jinsung had been staying over for the past month, helping Naomi *zuo yue zi* and cooking her postpartum healing meals. Jinsung slept on the single bed in the study. Dante had offered to switch out the single for a double bed so Zhangjie had the option of staying over too, but Zhangjie had declined. He was happy to be in a hotel around the corner. It was better this way. He still needed his space, needed time to adjust to this new reality, to a new baby and a new daughter-in-law. Who was part Japanese.

Sometimes his own son seemed like a foreigner too. Dante and Naomi only spoke in English with each other. Zhangjie sighed. He hoped his son would see to it that little Ningning learned to speak Chinese properly in the future.

Throughout the day Zhangjie tried to stay out of Naomi's way—if she needed the kitchen to sterilize the baby bottles, he would step into the living room. If she wanted to watch TV while the baby was napping then he would retreat to the study. It was only during dinner that they had all sat down in the dining room together for a family meal. After dessert, he approached the subject of *jie hun* gently, but sternly. Zhangjie wasn't sure Naomi understood his Chinese, so he pronounced the English word "wedding," which he had specifically looked up. Naomi's eyes widened at the mention and she and Dante exchanged glances. Then she nodded and said *hao de*. Understood.

Dante already anticipated this conversation. He knew how his father's mind worked, how he felt about his grandchild being born out of wedlock. It was always Dante's intention to give Naomi the wedding of her dreams. He just hoped that his parents were prepared to accept that it might not be the same wedding they had in mind.

*

In this city there was a plethora of childcare options available. Night nannies. Day nannies. Nannies who were talented cooks. Nannies who would sleep with the newborn at night. There were Chinese nannies who hailed from all over the country, but the ones who commanded the highest rates were the ones who spoke Shanghainese. The nannies who spoke English were even more expensive. They were mostly Filipino or Indonesian and catered to the expat crowd.

Dante had mentioned these choices to Naomi, plus the additional option of having his mother take a larger childcare role, since she was eager for the job. But Naomi knew what kind of mother she wanted to be. She couldn't bear the thought of handing off her baby for somebody else to care for, for what she thought came naturally to do herself.

But having some help with the chores and cooking in those early postpartum days was a privilege she couldn't pass up, so Dante's mother had moved in temporarily since Mitsy's birth, going back to Nanjing every two weeks or so for a couple of nights.

Joss was incredulous when she had heard about Naomi's mother-in-law moving in. She herself could never stand such an arrangement with her own mother-in-law.

Naomi felt differently. Although she was initially worried about clashing with Pan Jinsung, all her anxieties were swiftly relieved after she scarfed down the first postpartum meal. Like her son, Jinsung was an incredible chef, and mealtimes had become Naomi's favorite time of the day now.

Naomi kissed her daughter on the forehead, gazing into Mitsy's half-opened eyes. She never thought she could love a person this much. She loved Dante of course, it was visceral, and it was a sentiment of feeling blessed, content. The attachment she felt with Mitsy was natural, like this miniature human was connected to every fiber of her existence. She marveled at how this tiny being could radiate a joy that was larger than life, a wonder so pure and unadulterated.

She had once learned through her Chinese classes, the numerous idioms about how children are born in debt to their parents, how filial piety and honoring one's parents were the ultimate virtues. Dante said he had grown up hearing these sayings.

For Naomi, she felt a boundless gratitude to whatever force of universe had granted her Mitsy, had given her the privilege of being Mitsy's mother. She felt submerged in an all-consuming need to give her child everything she had, anything that was within her capacity: her body, her attention, her priority, her utmost, her love. Sometimes it would cross her mind whether Reina had ever felt this way about her, but only momentarily. She knew the answer. She had been her mother's world, once upon a time. Naomi hoped that she would always feel the ferocity of love for her daughter, for all time.

Because of Mitsy, Naomi felt as if she had ceased her tendencies to self-destruct. Mitsy had, in her own unintentional way, saved her mother.

9

NEW NORMAL

JOSS STUDIED NAOMI. THE WEIGHT GAIN HAD ROUNDED OUT HER face, the angles were now a little less sharpened. Her arms and thighs were more robust, her once flat midriff was now contoured with bumps and mounds. Her eye bags had darkened, her wavy hair was more knotted and tangled. Her engorged breasts at times leaked milk, forming damp marks on her shirt. She was baby scented, the way a tired new mother smelled. Her once too-carefree demeanor was not as intact. There was a new set of worry lines on her forehead, underneath her eyes. It was the ageing of a soul, the mark of a mother. Joss appreciated this. Naomi looked more like herself this way, of who she was always meant to become.

For Naomi, her new normal was sleep deprivation. She felt like a bloated, walking zombie. She had grown two sizes up, and her moods alternated between being merry and being crabby.

Joss was hovered in the corner of Naomi's living room, poring over the lists of to-dos for the wedding. The couple had decided on a date in September, after Dante had went through rounds of discussion with his parents. It was rushed—pulling off a wedding in six months—but they didn't want to put off the nuptials any longer. Joss had introduced the couple to Mira Cheung, a wedding planner who came highly recommended. Naomi was grateful, but with a baby constantly latched to her body, she also felt overwhelmed with Mira's incessant texts, e-mails, and calls regarding wedding details. So Joss had volunteered to help with the ongoing communication with the wedding planning team.

Joss situated herself comfortably on the L-shaped sofa. The coffee table was piled with infant toys and baby wipes. She set them aside and put down her thick binder dedicated to the wedding. There were decisions that needed to be made, and she required the bride's attention on certain pressing matters.

"Mitsy's asleep now. It should be a couple of hours before she wakes up for her next feeding, but do you think we can make this quick? I might need a nap myself." Naomi leaned her head against the armrest.

"Sure. First things first, did you want the ceremony to be in the garden or in the banquet room? I know you love gardens, and their osmanthus garden is gorgeous, but there's always a chance of rain. Shanghai weather can be so unpredictable. Alternatively, you can utilize the garden for your bridal photos instead of the ceremony. What do you think?"

"Let's just do the ceremony indoors then, if that's easier for everybody," Naomi mumbled. Her eyes were closed.

"I mean, we can have the ceremony in the garden, it's just that I want you to be aware of some of the issues. But it's doable, if that's what you want," Joss added.

Naomi was silent for a moment. She opened her eyes and stared at the binder. She thumbed through the pages, which consisted of floral arrangement details, canapés and cocktail menus, seating charts, music selections, lists of photographers. "Wow thanks for this, Joss. For all of this, I mean it. I'm so sorry to put you through this."

"Don't sweat it. Mira's doing most of the work."

"Oh, I've been meaning to ask you," Naomi sat up now, suddenly looking energized, taking her friend's hands in hers. "Joss, as my matron-of-honor, I'd be so honored if your child would also be a part of our wedding."

Joss smiled and hugged her. "Naomi, that is so, so thoughtful, and I would love that. But I'm not sure the dates will work. The last update I received is that the Arrival Date will be sometime in October."

"Arrival Date? Is that—"

"Yes, it's the day we bring our child home!" Joss couldn't contain her excitement.

"Wow! That's big news!" Naomi clapped her hands.

"Well, nothing is set in stone yet. But the whole process has been much smoother than we anticipated. Honestly, I think the fact that Tay is Tang Zhaoyi's son helped our case tremendously. It's ironic because my in-laws are not supportive at all. But throwing their name around has helped a lot. I've heard of other cases where it took more than several years to finalize the adoption."

"Do you have any idea about the age and gender, or any other information?"

"We've put in our preferences, but it's not really up to us. And the majority of children in Chinese orphanages have some sort of health issue. We're prepared for that possibility."

"That's so brave, Joss."

Joss smiled. "Well, I think all mothers are."

A wail came from the baby monitor perched on the coffee table. "I'll check on her, you stay where you are," Joss instructed Naomi.

Naomi laid back onto the sofa. "Thanks so much, Joss."

Mitsy's eyes were only half open. Joss picked up Mitsy from her crib, rocked her in her arms and hummed a Shanghainese lullaby, the same one her mother used to sing to her, the same one Joss sang to Jamie all those years ago. Joss gently caressed Mitsy's forehead with her thumb. She gingerly lowered Mitsy back in her crib after she was sound asleep.

Joss glanced at her watch. She had purposely visited Naomi at this hour so she could catch Dante when he returned home from work. She was hoping to get feedback on other wedding decisions with both the bride and groom present. "When does Dante usually come home?" Joss asked as she sat back down on the couch.

"Eight. But to be honest, sometimes I feel like he'd rather stay late at work than deal with me and the baby." Naomi's eyes reddened.

"But I remember him looking so hands-on and happy just a month ago," Joss exclaimed, hugging her friend.

"I don't know if it's the baby or the wedding or me. Or maybe it's the stress of everything." She lowered her eyes.

When Dante had proposed last year, Naomi had truly felt like the luckiest woman. But in the months after, as they were thrown into the unromantic and sleepless throes of parenthood, there were countless doubts that surfaced in her head. They had fought about everything from Mitsy's sleep routine, to how long she should be breastfed, to future schooling options.

Naomi buried her face in her hands. "It's been tough, juggling a newborn and a new marriage. The truth is, I don't know if I'm cut out for all this, or if he was ready for this. Is it crazy that I can sometimes feel so completely alone, even when my husband is right next to me?" Naomi was crying now. The way she cried uninhibitedly was akin to a child, Joss thought, not unkindly.

"No," Joss shook her head, "that's not crazy. That's marriage." Joss had once felt this way with Tay too. She believes all couples endure such moments.

Joss reached for a tissue and blotted Naomi's eyes. "Do you love him?"

Naomi took a deep breath. "Yes. I mean, he showed me the ultimate expression of love, right? He overlooked…what had happened. He loved me, despite it all…"

"That's in the past and you both forgave each other," Joss said gently as she held her. "You know Dante is lucky to have you right? What are your hopes and expectations in your marriage?"

Naomi was silent for a minute. "What I hope for in a marriage is…is for us to bring out the best in each other. All I want is…something true, something consistent. Yes, that's the word I'm looking for, consistency…"

"Dante has been true to you. Consistently. Right?"

Naomi nodded slowly. "Yes, he has. Day in and day out."

Joss smiled and held her friend. From her vantage point, there was nobody else that suited Naomi Kita-Fan more than Dante Ouyang.

10

I DO

PAN JINSUNG KNEW WHAT HER HUSBAND WAS THINKING. THAT came with the territory after thirty plus years of marriage. Even if his mood swings had become more volatile and violent as he aged, Pan Jinsung could still predict the onslaught of a tirade before Ouyang Zhangjie opened his mouth.

The culprit that morning was the bright red envelope that had arrived in their mail. Jinsung already knew what to expect. She was at her son's place every week and had already gleaned samples of the wedding invitation. By all accounts it was elegantly designed. It was printed on a thick cardstock overlaid with intricate cherry blossom patterns. What Zhangjie didn't take to, however, was the content. It was multilingual, written in Chinese, English and Japanese. Jinsung knew that the addition of Japanese bothered her husband. She had asked her son whether it was necessary, and Dante had replied in a tone that clearly indicated: *this case is closed.* The same invitation would be sent to Japan and Taiwan where Naomi's relatives resided, and a group big enough to fill two tables would be flying in from Taipei, Tokyo and Osaka.

That information had filled Jinsung with a wide range of emotions—anxiety over the potential tension between the two families, curiosity with finally meeting Naomi's relatives, and a certain joy and pride that overwhelmed a mother when her only child's wedding was forthcoming. Those moods were soon eclipsed by more worries—there was so much to do before the big day! Jinsung and Zhangjie had finalized the list of invited family members only last week and it was already over ninety people who would be coming into Shanghai from Nanjing, Hong Kong,

London, and beyond. Even her distant cousins and their children who now resided in Shenzhen and Guangzhou were making the trip. Jinsung hadn't seen some of these relatives in years, and Dante probably didn't even remember some of them.

Dante said their friends list exceeded more than a hundred people, including former classmates residing in Europe, in the U.S., and friends made in China. Then there was the list that included colleagues. It was customary in China to invite one's boss and colleagues to the wedding. Thus, the final guest count was coming close to three hundred.

Jinsung had started a running list of tasks to be completed before the wedding. She was getting her custom qipao made at the same tailor as Naomi, and she still needed to book appointments for further fittings and alterations. The relatives traveling into Shanghai needed to be entertained and looked after, especially her uncle, who at ninety years old, was the only one still alive from her parents' generation.

Dante had reserved a block of rooms for relatives at a hotel he described as "an international resort in a central area" on Maoming Lu, where the wedding would be held. Jinsung had never been there but had thought the name of the venue sounded pleasant: *Hua Yuan Fan Dian*, Garden Hotel. It wasn't until she did a site visit that she realized it was a Japanese-run hotel, the full name being Okura Garden Hotel. The staff were all fluent in Japanese, and all signage and instructions inside the property were subtitled in Japanese.

Although Jinsung was aware that Dante had already paid the deposit for the reservation, she had asked if it was possible to move the Nanjing relatives into another hotel nearby, to avoid risking another one of Zhangjie's disapproving diatribes. Her son then took a deep breath and spoke in a firm tone. "Ma, Naomi and I selected this wedding venue together. She is getting married here in China, settling down with me here in China. However," he gave his mother an imploring but resolute look, "I want to honor her heritage at this wedding. Please Ma, do me this one favor, no more comments about this. I love everything about this woman—who she is and where she came from. *Wo qiu ni le*. I'm begging you. Not another word about this issue."

Jinsung looked away and didn't say anything for a minute. Dante had never used such desperate language with her. And that tone. It was pleading with anguish, something she rarely heard from her confident, easygoing, filial son.

Jinsung loved him more than life itself. Of course she would do this for her son, for her granddaughter Ningning.

Mira Cheung, the wedding planner, reminded the photographer to capture copious amounts of pictures of the bride in each look. Naomi Kita-Fan had three different attire and hairstyles scheduled for the day. Earlier, for the Chinese tea ceremony, she had worn a customized qipao. Her wedding dress, bought at the Tadashi Shoji boutique in Changning district, was styled in crochet lace with an open back and mounds of Chantilly lace and tulle. For the last hour of the reception, she would be donning her mother's kimono, the same one Reina Kita wore on her own wedding day. It was an intricate red kimono adorned with various auspicious and personal symbols—cranes (which mate for life), pine (representing longevity), blue magpies (a Taiwanese icon)—using the *Sashiko* embroidery technique. Naomi's hair, softly curled and side-swept, was fastened with a clip holding fresh magnolias (a symbol of Shanghai). In her hands, she held a vibrant bouquet of Phalaenopsis orchids accentuated by lavender Calla Lilies.

Mira had met the couple only six months ago through the Tangs. During one of their very first consultations, Mira had asked the handsome but nervous couple their theme of choice. Was it a Great Gatsby type of affair? That was popular in this city. Or maybe modern glam? Old Shanghai? Whimsical wonderland? Mira had an iPad chock full of gorgeous images of bespoke weddings her team had managed, but the worried couple had seemed stumped and uninspired. So Mira posed the questions: what were their biggest concerns and deepest desires for this wedding? As the couple began to speak, Mira started to get the picture. Their anxiety was exacerbated by their families, who were not familiar with each other, and in fact, lived in entirely different countries and spoke varied languages. Mira had dealt with enough couples to know that their apprehension stemmed from deep-rooted cultural tensions.

But to Mira, these were minor details. Nowadays, at least half of her clients were marrying outside of their cultural heritage or race, requesting a seamless melding of complicated wedding traditions to be honored. Mira prided herself on being a miracle worker when it came to delivering wedding solutions. Once, a Japanese-Korean who was marrying a Christian Canadian had requested a ceremony conducted jointly by a Shinto priest and a progressive protestant pastor. It took some creative maneuvering, but Mira's team pulled off the interfaith ceremony without a hitch. In another instance, a Taiwanese bridezilla and a twice-divorced Shanghainese property tycoon had seemed on the verge of calling off the nuptials when an ex-wife crashed the event. Fortunately, Mira had hired top-of-the-line security detail as soon as she knew Meng Hailin was the groom. She researched all her clients meticulously and knew when one spelled trouble.

Sometimes Mira marveled at the eccentric situations thrown at her. Although she ran weddings all throughout Asia, the most outlandish matrimonies she had conducted were all held in China. Mira found mainlanders to be more lavish, creative, experimental.

For Naomi and Dante, Mira's team had proposed a series of intercultural elements: an emcee fluent in Mandarin, Japanese and English, a reception banquet menu complete with Chinese-Japanese fusion dishes, a gargantuan floral display wall of the beloved Nanjing plum blossoms fused with Japanese cherry blossoms where guests could pose for photos with the couple. Mira would make sure every detail of the affair, from the decor and cuisine to the music and program, could complement both cultures.

Ouyang Zhangjie adjusted his blush rose boutonniere as he examined the art deco ceilings of the storied grand ballroom. The venue was fancier than he had imagined. Dante had said the ballroom's stained glass ceiling was designed in Paris and then shipped to China nearly a century ago.

Earlier, during the Chinese tea ceremony, Naomi had veered off the scripted program, and had presented Zhangjie with a card. Later, when

Naomi was changing out of her qipao and into her white wedding gown, Zhangjie had opened the envelope and read the card, laden with Chinese characters:

Dear Mr. Ouyang,

Well, here we are. I hope that today will be every bit as wonderful as you have envisioned for your son's wedding.

I know sometimes it all seems so sudden. Last year you and I were still near strangers, yet now I've given birth to your grandchild.

It's true that you and I have gone through some ups and downs, but that's the way it goes with most families, right? You and I may differ on many things, but we do have one core thing in common: we both love Dante and Mitsy very much, and that makes us family now.

I grew up without a father. He died when I was little. Growing up, I had secretly hoped my mother would re-marry, so I could have a dad like everybody else. But that never happened.

Despite the differences between us, I am appreciative that I now have a father in you, and I hope you are glad that in addition to your son, you now have a daughter too.

Sincerely,
Naomi

Zhangjie put the card back inside his suit pocket. He suddenly felt a pang of guilt at the way he had been behaving around her. It was in this moment, that Zhangjie resolved he would alter a portion of the wedding ceremony. As the music swelled in the grand ballroom and everybody took their seats, Zhangjie made his way out toward the procession line. His wife shot him a where-are-you-going look, but he just nodded at her and continued toward the back of the ballroom, behind the bridesmaids, groomsmen, flower girls, page boy and ringbearer. Naomi was standing at the end of the procession, clutching her bouquet nervously. As he approached her, he realized he was at a loss for words. He didn't know how to say "I'll walk with you" in English. So he said it in Chinese, *wo pei ni zou*, and offered his arm.

She took his arm, almost shyly, looking ever more the blushing bride. "Xie xie," she whispered.

The day started with a litany of things gone wrong. Some of the Nanjing relatives complained about the weak air conditioning in their warm hotel rooms. Zhangjie forgot his dress shoes at home so scrambled to borrow a pair from his half-sister's husband. Mitsy cried inconsolably while her mother was at her hair and makeup appointments. Huan Huan threw a tantrum because he didn't like the page boy outfit. And on top of all that, it started drizzling, despite sunny weather forecasts for this September wedding. By lunch time, Jinsung felt positively drained.

It was only by late afternoon, after the Chinese tea ceremony had begun, that Jinsung started to enjoy herself. It was quite a reunion for both Zhangjie's side of the family, as well as her own. Her cousin, Pan Yaning, who was Dante's *gan ma*, had also flown in with her British husband. All of her relatives had praised Naomi's beauty and elegance. At ten months postpartum, Naomi still hadn't returned to her pre-baby weight, although she was still thin, albeit curvier than before, amply filling out the sweetheart neckline. Ningning was still breastfeeding, and every so often Naomi ducked into a room which had been converted into a temporary nursery, adjacent to the ballroom.

All of her relatives fawned over Ningning, gushing about how cute she was, how much she looked like Dante. One of her cousins made a comment about seeing more and more foreigners marrying Chinese men. Jinsung was quick to jump in. *My daughter-in-law is half Japanese, and she is fluent in English, Japanese, and semi-fluent in Chinese. My granddaughter will be raised trilingual too.* Her relatives looked impressed. *Yes,* they nodded in unison, *it's better to raise the future generation as global citizens.*

Everybody in the room had focused on the stunning bride as Zhangjie walked down the aisle with Naomi on his arm, taking scores of photos with their smart phones. Only Jinsung had looked in the opposite direction, at her son waiting under the white arch, who beamed a toothy smile so pure and so joyful, that Jinsung wondered how she could have missed it all this time—Naomi's love made her son completely content, blissful.

After the groom's and bride's side each took separate family photos with extended relatives, Jinsung surprised everybody by asking the photographer to corral both families for one large group photograph. It wasn't on the agenda. Dante had cast a grateful look at his mother, then led his parents to stand next to him on his left, as he held his bride to his right. As he snapped away, the Taiwanese-American photographer alternated between asking the group to say "cheese," "qie zi," and "chizu," to accommodate for the three different languages spoken among the group, eliciting roaring laughter and commentary on how similar sounding the popular expression was among the various languages.

Before the dinner reception began, the emcee made an announcement: "On your table you will each find a pair of Woodgrain Onyx chopsticks in front of you. These handcrafted chopsticks from Japan are the couple's gift to each of you, to thank you for being here! Chopsticks always come in pairs. You will notice that one has Naomi's name engraved on it, and the other has Dante's. The chopsticks have a distinct pattern design that cannot be appreciated without the other, so they must always be together!"

Halfway through dinner, Reina Kita and a graceful middle-aged woman in a kimono gingerly approached Jinsung. The woman introduced herself as Ruri, Reina's sister. All of this she spewed in fluent Chinese. Then Ruri stuffed a red envelope in Jinsung's hands. Jinsung thanked her graciously and asked how she came to speak Chinese so well. Ruri mentioned she had studied at *Zhejiang Daxue* when she had lived in Hangzhou in her youth. Jinsung's eyes widened. Zhejiang University was one of the most prestigious academic institutions in the country. This woman must be very smart. She said she still taught Chinese language courses in Osaka. *You must come visit us sometime!* Ruri had exclaimed. Reina nodded enthusiastically. *And please come out to California sometime,* Reina added. Jinsung smiled and thanked them. *Yes, what a wonderful idea.*

For Joss, the day started at seven in the morning, when the makeup artist slash hair stylist punctually arrived at her hotel room. The woman and her assistant lugged two suitcases full of equipment and props, and for the next hour, Joss tried not to doze off as they fussed and primped with her hair and face.

Joss drained her espresso and then was properly energized for her matron-of-honor duties. She, along with the maid-of-honor, Frida, helped Naomi in and out of her three attire changes, posed for a million photos, and directed guests to each segment of the occasion—the Chinese tea ceremony was in the Jasmine room, the cocktail reception was in the garden, the wedding ceremony and dinner banquet would take place in the grand ballroom. *And don't forget the sushi bar and photobooth in the far left corner of the ballroom!*

All day long, Joss ran around helping with translating, with hosting guests, with assisting her own jet lagged father and sister who flew in for the wedding, with responding to the beck and call of Mira the wedding coordinator.

But Joss's most significant responsibility of the night rested in the moment she took the stage and mic, bringing down the house with her carefully crafted speech. She first recounted their college student days in Manhattan, how they had played hooky for Coney Island, how proud she had been at Naomi's student fashion showcase. She regaled the crowd with nostalgic anecdotes of their New York and Shanghai shenanigans. She praised Naomi's devotion to her daughter, and said how honored she felt to be chosen as Mitsy's godmother. Toward the end of the speech, Joss didn't even need to glance at her notecards anymore. In spite of the harsh lights shining from where she stood on stage, she focused solely on Naomi, held her gaze, and told her how privileged and blessed she felt, for having navigated one's most confusing, thrilling, senseless years—their twenties—side-by-side. And despite herself, she choked up when she spoke about how she would endlessly cherish that chapter, and forever be wistful of their memories. Sensing that she somehow sunk the atmosphere into a much-too-sentimental strata, she quickly regained composure and moved on, gushing about Dante, about the couple's first meeting on that fateful flight (*he swept her off her feet at forty thousand feet in the air!*), about her admiration for his commitment toward Naomi, about how Joss saw in him a man whom she could fully entrust her best friend's happiness with. She had hesitated to mention the Beijing riot incident in the speech. It was a sensitive topic, and she didn't want to bring down the atmosphere. But Joss knew that it was a watershed moment in their relationship. Joss wanted to touch on it lightly. She didn't give specific details, but focused instead on Dante's valor in protecting Naomi.

Then, Joss concluded her monologue. As she watched the hundreds of champagne flutes extend up into the air, she raised hers toward Naomi, and had the distinct feeling that she was saluting an era farewell.

11

WILLOW

Joss and Tay had discussed names. In her files, the orphanage listed her name as Wen Wen. The character for literature, scholarship. In a note her biological parents left, that was her given name.

Tay liked the character *liu*. Willow. In traditional Chinese poetry, the willow tree, *yang liu* was often used to symbolize "stay." "Don't leave." It was an apt name. Because they would never leave little Willow. Tang Wen Liu would never have to experience the heartache of being left again.

Joss awoke at the crack of dawn, too nervous to sleep. She checked on Willow's room. Stuffed animals and toys were neatly nestled on the shelves, newly bought clothes were folded and in the drawers. She turned the air conditioning on, then changed her mind and turned it off. She checked the railing installed on the side of the double bed, to make sure it was sturdy. Growing up, Joss remembered how her own mother had snuggled with her in bed. Joss intended to do the same with her daughter.

The ride to Lubin Foster Center took close to two hours. Without traffic it might have taken fifty minutes, but there had been an accident on the highway. Tay fidgeted all throughout the car ride like a school boy. Joss prodded him to take a quick nap, which he finally did.

When they arrived, they were ushered into the waiting room with several other families. One couple was from Nashville with two older children. Another couple was from Madrid. Joss started exchanging small talk with the Nashville family. They had been waiting for this moment for over two years.

Joss felt like she'd been "pregnant" for nineteen months. It had been that long since they had submitted their initial paperwork. The orphanage director had first mentioned October of last year as the most likely Arrival Date. Then it took two more donations to the orphanage for them to push the Tangs' paperwork to the priority pile.

Joss was still fairly calm while they waited. One by one, the other families were called into the *Tuan Yuan* room, the Reunion room. It was when it was their turn, when they were led into that sacred space, when the nanny had carried her out, that Joss felt the bursting of a well of emotion inside, tears inexplicably flowing down her face. *There you are! I've been waiting for you!* It was the most bizarre feeling. This child had come from another woman, yet there was no ambiguity around it. She was Joss's daughter. She'd always been.

The nanny sat down, put Wen Wen in her lap, and introduced herself. "I'm Fang Yu. Wen Wen, this is your *Ma Ma* and *Ba Ba*." Fang Yu was wearing a rumpled pink apron. She had chin-length hair, a wide smile, kind eyes.

Wen Wen was in a blue shirt with a big sun on it, thin cotton pants, and sandals that looked a size too small. She looked like a miserable version of the photo they had been sent. In the photo, she had been holding a pillow, smiling shyly. Now, Wen Wen's eyes were filled with confusion, terror. Her hair smelled of sweat, her skin was blotchy, her fingernails too long, her teeth a decaying yellow. She looked like she had seen a lifetime of grief.

"Wen Wen ni hao. Wo shi ni ba ba." *Hello Wen Wen, I'm your daddy.* Tay crouched down to Wen Wen's eye level now and held up a bunny stuffed animal. From her files they knew she was about fifteen months old. The files listed her other conditions: Delayed motor skills. Not walking or talking yet. Seizures. Possible brain disease.

Fang Yu gently pried Wen Wen's fingers off from her hands. Then her eyes welled a little, as she lifted Wen Wen from her lap into Joss's arms.

Wen Wen whimpered before wailing uncontrollably, unleashing a waterfall of tears while trying to wiggle out of Joss's arms. Joss understood. She and Tay were just another set in the revolving door of strangers that came and went. Joss held her while Tay tried to distract her with more toys.

"This is normal. It will take time. Maybe a week, or even a month," Fang Yu said encouragingly as she dabbed her own eyes with tissue. Joss tried to push out the defeating thoughts. *We're not connecting. Have I already crashed?*

This isn't about me, it's about her! Joss scolded herself internally. This was the only home Wen Wen had ever known since abandoned by her birth parents. It was the second devastating loss in her short life thus far.

As Joss consoled Wen Wen in a corner, Fang Yu led Tay to a desk on the other side of the room. There were more documents that required fingerprints and signatures before the adoption could be finalized.

"Here are all of Wen Wen's medical files and documents regarding her identification registration. And this document is information about her origins. She was left at the local police station on this date. Here is a police record of her being found and delivered to us at the orphanage."

While other children her age might have already accumulated a room full of things, those files and the clothes on her body were Wen Wen's only possessions.

Joss looked into Wen Wen's crying eyes and wondered if she knew that her life, along with theirs, was about to change forever.

The weeks and months after Willow's arrival were a blur of hospital visits, physical therapy, and more evaluations. Tay believed her medical records from the orphanage were not thorough enough, and insisted on having all sorts of examinations from every type of expert—nutritionists, neurologists, childhood developmental specialists, pediatric trauma experts.

It was discovered that Willow didn't have a brain disease, as the orphanage had suggested, but a mitochondrial disorder. There was no known cure. But her symptoms seemed mild, assured Dr. Kao from Shanghai East International Hospital. "She's lucky to have screened for early detection. With rigorous treatment, I'm confident she will thrive,"

Dr. Kao had said. Treatment included a ketogenic diet and a colorful group of vitamins and drugs.

For Joss, those first two weeks had been agonizing. As soon as they got home, Willow would not have anything to do with her. She screeched anytime Joss was around, quieting only near Tay. Joss had read that this reaction was not uncommon, that it was a defense mechanism stemmed from the child feeling deserted by the previous caretakers. Even though Joss knew this intellectually, the rejection still pierced.

Willow didn't reciprocate their hugs, it seemed, most of the time. Even as Joss and Tay cuddled and snuggled with her, her eyes always seemed glassy, dazed, as if she didn't know what to do with the affection. It was only on day nineteen or so when Willow didn't mind Joss's presence anymore. They were watching "My Neighbor Totoro" in the living room, when Willow suddenly leaned into Joss's lap, eventually falling asleep there.

Joss could recall every detail of that day vividly. It was the day before Mother's Day, a holiday she hadn't celebrated in nearly two decades. That morning, she woke up to three beautiful bouquets; Tay, Naomi, and Jamie had each wished her a happy first Mother's Day.

Joss would lay very still next to Willow while she napped, watching the rhythm of her breathing, the fluttering of her long lashes. *I know what it's like not to have your mother beside you*, she'd whisper to Willow. *I promise you'll never have to go through that again.*

12

RITE OF PASSAGE

WILLOW AND MITSY'S BIRTH DATES WERE ONLY TWO MONTHS APART, although the gap seemed much wider. At twenty-six months, Mitsy was running, skipping, talking a mile a minute, even if most of it was incomprehensible. Willow was petite for her age, and still largely immobile and reticent. But she delighted in Misty's presence, giggling when Mitsy ran in circles around her.

Naomi scooped up Willow in her arms now, making googly eyes at her. "You are adorable! Come to *gan ma*, come to *gan ma*," she sang in a high-pitched baby voice. Willow gave a toothy smile to her godmother.

"How's her physical therapy going?" Naomi asked, as she made peek-a-boo faces at Willow.

"She's making some strides. Not walking unassisted yet. But the therapist said her progress is remarkable. And she has a penchant for the piano, which the therapist said is beneficial for her motor skills too," Joss replied.

"I love what you did to this space! And how you still look like that with a toddler in tow is beyond me." The Tang villa living room was no longer the one Naomi remembered. Gone were the decorative Italian sculptures, the Middle Eastern rugs, the ivory leather couch Naomi had sat on countless times. In its place were colorful soft mats, bean bags, low toddler gates, pink rocking horses, princess-themed toddler cars. The lone remnant of the living room's previous life was the grand piano, still standing regally near the fireplace.

"Oh, these are just my work clothes." Joss had contemplated leaving *Shanghai Scene* once maternity leave was over. Willow's therapy and medical appointments took up the bulk of her schedule.

But Trina, the editor-in-chief, had refused to let her go. Joss was now a part-time employee instead. As much as she relished every moment with Willow, she had also missed working. She was grateful that Ah Ming was a natural with Willow.

Then Joss was regaling Naomi with the developments of the magazine. They were gaining significant advertising revenue and would be expanding to other parts of China.

Naomi was genuinely interested, but she couldn't help feel a slight sting of envy. It wasn't so long ago that Naomi herself was launching successful advertising and public relations campaigns for her clients at Jun Cleo. She had only stopped working two years ago. But with her daily diaper duties, lately she had been feeling stuck, like a chasm was growing between her nest and the world outside.

"But enough about the magazine. How are you and Dante?"

"We're...a work in progress. I think marriage is the ultimate lesson in forgiveness. The problem is sometimes I think we're failing at this. I'll get angry over the dumbest little things—that he had a crazy night out while I stayed home with Mitsy—"

"I don't think that's dumb at all," Joss placed her hand on Naomi's back. "You're right to expect him to come home earlier to help out..."

"Oh, he does. He's more hands-on than what I'd expected actually, but I think sometimes he needs a breather so he'll still stay out late." She stopped short of saying that the intimacy felt mechanical. Once upon a time, she spared no secrets with Joss. But there was a sacredness she associated with marriage now, with being his wife. She couldn't fairly blame Dante for her low libido anyway, or the fact that all she wanted to do after Mitsy went to bed was to curl up at her desk, sketching.

Naomi had resumed fashion sketching again. She had taken classes at FIT in Manhattan years ago, and recently, to brush up on her skills, she had started classes at the Raffles Design Institute on Xinyi Lu. She doesn't mention this to Joss right now. She wants to keep this part of her life to herself, for now.

"So how is Tay enjoying fatherhood?"

"Sometimes I think he's better at this than I am, actually. I don't know, some days I'm just exhausted and I wonder if we were in over our heads. But, not Tay. The other day Willow threw a huge tantrum because we wouldn't let her eat any more *qiang bing*, 'cause you know, it's too salty for her. I just about had it and was going nuts, but Tay was just a sea of calm. All he did was pick her up and sing a silly song about a *qiang bing* fairy and just like that, Willow was smiling again."

"That's great that Tay is helping a lot! He makes his own hours now, right?"

Joss nodded. Tay had resigned from Tao International Auctions several months before Willow came home, amid rising tensions with his father. He had been planning the exit and steadily building up clientele for his own art consultancy business. Currently, Wen Art Consultancy had nearly twenty employees, and with the Chinese contemporary art market gaining traction globally, he had projections for doubling the number of employees by year-end.

"Yep, although I think Tay's international travels will start to pick up soon. He has art fairs in Basel, London, Miami, Dubai coming up."

"Are the in-laws coming around?'

"I know Ruiling has been asking Ah Ming about Willow. Ah Ming said Ruiling has a stack of brand-new clothes and toys in their house. I just know it's any day now that they're going to want to meet Willow."

"Wow. So are you still angry at them?"

Joss paused. "Yes. And No. I mean regardless of how I feel about them, I don't want to deprive Willow the love of her grandparents. She's already lost the chance to know my mom, so I wouldn't want her to experience more loss. She loved seeing my dad and my sister over Christmas. They're already planning their next visit here in April for her baptism! Tay's parents, as difficult as they are, they're Willow's family—"

"We're family too! Willow will always have us, and have Mitsy as her *jie jie*." Sister.

Joss smiled. She found it hard to believe that it'd been five years since they first landed in this city, that fateful summer so many moons ago, as twenty-somethings. So much had transpired since, with this bejeweled metropolis as their backdrop. They had loved and mourned, grown careers and babies, weathered broken relationships and tied the knot. And somewhere along the way they had crossed the thirty threshold. In the past five years, they'd probably wrecked too much, drank too much, loved too much. But wasn't that the rite of passage of your twenties, of learning to adult?

And now, here they were. Mothers to daughters.

"Look!" Naomi pointed frantically. "Willow just hugged Mitsy!" She was scrambling for her iPhone now, trying to capture the moment.

It was no doubt, the first of many, many more milestones they would be celebrating together.

EPILOGUE

HOME

NAOMI SAID MITSY LIKED "ANYTHING OF THE HORSE VARIETY." MY Little Pony. Unicorns. Barnyard-themed toys. Joss had scoured the children's boutiques in the Seventh Arrondissement in Paris last week, when she and Willow had accompanied Tay on a business trip. In the end Joss had settled on an organic handsewn unicorn stuffed animal and a picture book about horse riding, illustrated by a renowned Parisian artist.

The party venue was located in Pudong, near the former Expo site. The festivities occupied the entire second floor of Takumi; it was the popular restaurant's first foray outside of Japan. Christmas decorations and birthday balloons inundated the place. The windows offered views of the restaurant's landscaped Japanese gardens, as well as Expo's China Pavilion in the distance. The party served several purposes. It was a third birthday celebration for Mitsy, and a Christmas party hosted by the Ouyangs.

Joss knew some of the people there: Sylvie Fan (Naomi's Taiwanese aunt who had started visiting Shanghai regularly ever since Mitsy's birth), Frida Du (who had flown in from Hainan Island), Roxy Gao (who looked so grown up Joss could hardly recognize her), Roxy's boyfriend Chester Wu (a local celebrity), Kouji Nishizawa (Naomi's cousin), Orca Cao (Naomi's ex-colleague), Zach Ma (Dante's colleague), Ed Yen (Dante's childhood friend), Dante's parents, and some of Dante's extended family.

Willow was chasing Mitsy around in the open area lined with foam mats besieged with toys. Both looked in need of a bath, after Mitsy thought it would be funny to smear Willow's cheeks with chocolate cake.

Joss pulled Tay over. "Look!" Tay smiled. He knew exactly what she was referring to. Willow was running, giggling, talking to the other children. Her laugh was infectious, and her eyes sparkled. Here their daughter looked like a very different child than the one they had met a year and a half ago.

The party ended when the other toddlers started getting drowsy, some throwing tantrums. Soon all the kids were wailing. *Nap time!* Naomi announced. Then all the young parents scooped up their children, strollers, diaper bags, and left. The visiting relatives went back to their respective hotels to rest before the dinner party. Naomi and Dante would be hosting a dinner at the Bund tonight for all their visitors.

Tay and Ah Ming brought Willow home. Joss followed Naomi and Dante back to their apartment in Hongqiao, helping to carry all the birthday gifts in. After Mitsy was settled in her crib for a nap, Dante left to get groceries.

"What are you guys doing for Chinese New Year? Remember when we discussed taking the girls on a trip together soon?" Joss had been hounding Naomi for a joint trip with their husbands and daughters.

"Well...maybe the year after next...we'll see..."

Joss frowned. "That's so far away! Didn't you say Mitsy did well on flights? Looks like she didn't inherit your fear of heights!" Naomi had mentioned that Mitsy enjoyed their flights to Japan and Taiwan. She had been mesmerized by the clouds, clapping whenever she saw one, like she was on an amusement park ride.

"She loves flying, but we have a busy year coming up and I won't be able to travel that far because..." Naomi paused.

Joss looked at her expectantly. Then she knew.

She was expecting!

She hugged Naomi fervently. "Why didn't you say something!"

"You're the first one to know! We didn't want to say anything until I was three months along, which is in several days."

Then Naomi went into detail about how they'd been planning to move, since their current apartment couldn't accommodate two children. Dante had been busy scouting out places with their real estate agent.

Naomi said she had something else to share. She led Joss into the master bedroom and rolled out a rack of baby clothes. Joss picked up a pink toddler tutu dress and studied it. On the back of the dress was a subtle design, a mash up of both Chinese and Japanese characters. The dress label read "Mitsue," with the E in the shape of a cherry blossom flower.

"Naomi! These are gorgeous. You designed all of these?"

She nodded, beaming. "I've started selling in some boutiques on Xinle Lu. The feedback has been positive so far! Next year, I might try to get some kiosk space in malls, maybe even expand to Japan." She told Joss how Kouji had been looking into retail opportunities in Tokyo and was considering becoming her business partner. He still worked full-time at his day job, but if this children's clothing label took off, he would quit and help Naomi market the brand in Japan.

"Here, this one is for Willow!" Naomi presented a turquoise toddler tutu dress to Joss. On the back of the dress, a subtle embroidery in emerald thread shimmered. It was *liu*, the Chinese character for Willow.

Joss held the exquisite dress to her chest. "It's just perfect."

*

They're each doing five things at once: Naomi's tending to Mitsy, urging her to finish her breakfast porridge, while jotting down notes as she conducted a video conference call with Kouji in Japan. Her fashion label had just made its debut in Tokyo, and Kouji had some brand promotion ideas. Dante was in the kitchen making coffee and simultaneously getting Mitsy's lunch box ready, checking his work e-mails and watching the morning news on the iPad.

They had developed a routine. Dante made breakfast and packed Mitsy's lunch, while Naomi got her daughter dressed, fed, and ready for preschool. Then, Dante would drop off Mitsy at school on his way to work. When Mitsy was in class, Naomi would work on the children's clothing business—do site visits to stores, call Kouji about updates, meet with the factory manager, sketch some more designs. Then at two p.m. she would make her way to the preschool to pick up Mitsy. Mitsy usually napped in the afternoons, and sometimes Naomi slept at the same time. At seven months pregnant, her energy level wasn't what it used to be, even just a month ago.

Naomi shifted in her seat on the couch and bid Kouji a friendly goodbye. She just felt the baby move and her hand instinctively went to her bump, rubbing her belly in circles, which seemed to be calming him down.

Dante was ecstatic about having a boy. Naomi didn't make known she'd secretly been praying for another girl. Motherhood entailed a learning curve. At least if she was having a daughter again, she would feel a bit more equipped. She had grown up without a father, and the relationships she had with the men in her life were largely superficial, deficient, detrimental. She knew nothing about raising a boy.

When she expressed such insecurities to Dante, he gently reminded her about last month's incident at a children's playground: Mitsy had fallen off of a play structure after a boy who looked about six years old, came full force behind her on the slide, pushing Mitsy off the edge. The boy snickered, and his grandfather either hadn't noticed or hadn't cared. Luckily, the grounds had been padded, but the episode left Mitsy's lower left thigh bruised for days. The following week, when the same boy started swatting Mitsy at the same playground, Mitsy then stomped her feet, extended both arms forcefully with her palms facing the taller kid, and repeated in a bellowing voice what her mother had trained her to say, "Zou kai! Bu yao peng wo!" *DO NOT TOUCH ME! GO AWAY!* The boy was stunned silent, surprised by her thundering outburst. He glanced at Naomi watching the whole exchange, then turned around to terrorize another kid.

Dante had smiled as Naomi described the incident. It was heartening to see his little girl growing up, defending herself, and in a way, his wife had grown too. They all had. *You taught her well. You always do*, he said, squeezing her hand reassuringly.

Naomi used to think that what mattered in love were the grand sweeping gestures, the passionate declarations, and the do-or-die affairs. But now, she appreciated the love that was manifested in the everyday, in the miniscule and mundane details. It was love when he woke up in the middle of night to check on Mitsy, to make sure she was tucked in under the covers. It was love when he spent the day googling how to make one of her favorite dishes, roasted duck breast. It was the way he changed her sheets without her knowing, without her asking. She'd wake up and realize that the pattern on the sheets was a bit different, ever so slightly. The previous one had a nautical pattern, tiny blue ships sailing in her bed. Tonight's was also maritime themed, except the striped ships now had anchors, anchored underneath the duvet, where she laid, where she had never felt more loved.

*

"Look! Look!" Mitsy squealed. "Those blue birds are back!"

Naomi joined Mitsy at the window of the master bedroom. Mitsy had her face pressed against the window, her nose smushed flat against the glass.

"Yan zi," Naomi said.

"Yan zi," Mitsy repeated, shouting proudly. *Swallows.*

"Shh," Naomi put a finger to her lips. "Wes is napping."

Mitsy nodded solemnly and echoed her mother. "Don't wake up di di." Little Brother. Her eyes followed the blue and chestnut colored swallows as they settled on the statue Psyche's head.

The view of Eros' Garden was the primary reason Naomi had fallen in love with this apartment. The Greek goddess was surrounded by vibrant blooms—creamy magnolias, canary-colored daffodils, blush begonias, indigo violets. Last month, the garden had looked as if it'd been shrouded in cotton candy clouds, as plum blossoms and cherry blossoms flourished.

"*Yan zi* mate for life," Dante whispered in Naomi's ear, approaching from behind.

Naomi laughed. "Hashtag cheesy."

Dante kissed her now. "Hashtag you-know-you-love-it."

"I do." Naomi kissed him back.

Naomi's cell phone beeped and she quickly picked it up and checked her messages. The production agency had just completed editing their brand video, to be distributed as part of the social media campaign for her Mitsue fashion label's upcoming collection. Besides Mitsy, the short reel also featured Michika, a half-Nigerian half-Japanese model who was five years old, Seraphina, a Macanese four-year-old who was a quarter Portuguese, and Fifi, a Peranakan Chinese six-year-old. Mitsy, Fifi, Seraphina and Michika were laughing, playing, jumping in matching satin floral bomber jackets and mauve-colored overalls. The video was filmed just downstairs, inside Eros' Garden.

"By the way, these came in the mail." Dante handed several letters and a postcard to her.

Naomi recognized the addresses and tore open the envelopes quickly. One letter was from Osaka, from the Japan Women's Federation Against Violence, an organization dedicated to equipping and rehabilitating victims of abuse. Another was from Lubin Foster Center, Willow's former home. Both non-profits thanked her for the donation from her fashion label. Naomi and Kouji had decided early on that a portion of proceeds from their brand would go toward benefitting these organizations.

Next, Naomi examined the postcard and its photograph of a California beach. Usually her mother sent mail from her travels outside the state. "Sounds like she wants us to visit," Naomi chuckled. "She probably misses Mitsy and Wes."

"Do you miss home?" Dante ventured.

Home. Naomi knew he meant Southern California, where her other permanent address was, where she had spent a part of her girlhood. It was a question she hadn't thought about in a long time. She had become detached to the idea of home. She carried Japan and Taiwan in her veins, Tokyo in her heart, California in her memories, Manhattan in her past, and now, Shanghai in her soul.

Home is a mental as much as it is a physical space. It's where we choose to root our existence, where we decide to build our bliss, our lives, ourselves.

For so long she had felt like a creature in flight, lost in the dark expanse, floating directionless, aimlessly always on the run. Then, she had landed in this city, she found him, she found herself. She took his hand and looked up at him tenderly.

Somehow, at this moment, exactly where she was—this felt like home.

Some people made anywhere feel like home.

ACKNOWLEDGMENTS

THIS BOOK IS A LOVE LETTER TO SHANGHAI, WHERE I LIVED AND worked for nearly a decade. Much like Naomi and Joss, I am a third-culture kid—born in San Francisco Bay Area, raised between Taiwan and California, then moved to Pennsylvania, New York, Shanghai, Taipei, with annual extended visits to Singapore and Japan. I speak, read, dream and think in two languages. Sometimes the Chinese characters dominate my mind, and I have no words in English to express myself. Sometimes it's the other way around. Where is home? It's seldom a straightforward answer. I'm fascinated with the ways we tether ourselves to places, and the journeys we take to get there, regardless of where we originated.

It was only after I had spent my first year in Shanghai, that my grandfather revealed our family had a historical footprint in this city. I still remember my grandfather showing me faded photographs of his father in Shanghai and in Tianjin, where my great-grandfather had worked as a journalist, and had once written a novel. Sadly, copies of that book which was published in Taiwan before World War Two, had been lost to the turmoil of the times.

My family is the greatest inspiration for this novel, and they have my utmost gratitude. I'm indebted to Peter Zheng, Caspar Lee, Florence Lee, Selena Lee, Jeff Sheng. Not only were they generous with emotional sustenance, but also with the physical support necessary for me to complete this book. Thank you for putting up with my neurosis, for feeding me, for the endless babysitting, for the relentless encouragement—especially to my husband, sister, mother. To my grandparents, parents and in-laws, my deepest thanks for imparting your stories and histories. It's on your faith, your values, your shoulders that I stand.

My appreciation to my first readers at Ladderbird: Beth Marshea, Annalise Errico, Paige Robinson. I'm grateful for your crucial edits and for your role in shaping the direction of this story. Beth, thank you for your vision, and for being this book's first advocate.

To the team at Balestier, and to Dr. Roh-Suan Tung, thank you for giving this book a home. To Markéta Glanzová and Rachael Koh, you have my boundless gratitude for the hard work in bringing this novel to life. To Sarah And Schooling and to Peter, thank you for a book cover that evokes exactly the mood I tried to convey. Peter, your city photographs beautifully echoes the nostalgia this novel aims to capture, thank you.

My immense respect and appreciation to the authors, friends, and creative souls that have graciously endorsed this book: Emily Ting, Jenny Lin, Grace Chon, Linda Ulleseit, Ray Hecht, Laura Rahme, Wena Poon. It's such an honor to have your support.

To my beta readers—Miory Kanashiro Kightlinger, Annie Lau Okumura, Aiko Loo, Noah Cho, Jenny Lin, Katherine Sharpe, Selena Lee—thank you for spending hours poring over my manuscripts, for your candid comments and critiques. I'm eternally grateful for your feedback.

To family and friends that provided advice, answered polls and offered support—Alice Chen, Amy Chen, Mario Lu, Edward Chen, Christine Lee, Lauren Young, Alec Chen, Grace Yang, Frederick Hsu, Wenni Hsu, Wendy Chu, Diana Tsao, Troy Okumura, Eri Masunaga Fu, Jocelyn Liu Delgado, Jennifer Chang Ko, Allison Lu Sinor, Steve Mar—thank you for rooting me on. To my former colleagues in China, many of you have shown me kindness and hospitality. My gratitude to the Expo crew, and to the teams at Chrysler, Ogilvy, Dior, Guess. To our church communities in Shanghai, Taipei, New York, California, many of you have moved me profoundly. Thank you for your prayers and grace.

Even when I had barely finished a draft, my dad already started telling relatives and friends that I was a novelist, much to my chagrin. It was always the same question on the international calls: "When will your book be published?" It is this unfaltering, incessant, continuous confidence in my work that contributed to the completion of this novel. Thank you, Dad.

To Christabelle and Gabriella: In your darling faces, I see Yeshua. You make me a better person, every day.

To Peter: Your love always inspires. Thank you for holding dear and holding me accountable to the important things in life. In your love, I live.

ABOUT THE AUTHOR

CRYSTAL Z. LEE is a Taiwanese American bilingual writer. She has called many places home, including Taipei, New York, Shanghai, and the San Francisco Bay Area. She was formerly a public relations executive who had worked with brands in the fashion, beauty, technology, and automotive industries. In China, she had worked on programs for the 2007 Special Olympics in Shanghai, the 2008 Beijing Olympics, and the 2010 Shanghai World Expo. *Love and Other Moods* is her first novel.

CPSIA information can be obtained
at www.ICGtesting.com
Printed in the USA
LVHW032006080321
680887LV00008B/1718